AGAINST THE LIGHT

AGAINST THE LIGHT

DAVE DUNCAN

47NORTH

Text copyright ©2011 Dave Duncan
All rights reserved
Printed in the United States of America

Published by 47North
P.O. Box 400818
Las Vegas, NV 89140

ISBN-13: 9781612182032
ISBN-10: 1612182038

Also by Dave Duncan:

http://www.poemhunter.com/robert-southwell/
The verses quoted on pages 342–343 are taken from "Content
and Rich," by Robert Southwell (born c. 1561, ordained 1584,
arrested and tortured 1592, hanged 1595, canonized 1970).

Principal Characters

Edgar Woodbridge, Squire of Woodbridge Manor
Agnes Woodbridge, his wife

Their Children
Rollo, a missionary, alias John Hawke
Henry
Madeline, alias Maddy, Mad, Mindy Wells
Bram, alias Brat, Bradwell Armstrong, Braxton, Hagfish

Others
Exalted Garrett Uptree, a hierarch
Osborn, Earl Uptree of Norcaster, his brother

Crown Prince Emil, heir to King Ethan of Albi
William Kipping, First Secretary to King Ethan

Smut, a dog
Corbin, a raven
Perry, a peregrine falcon

CHAPTER 1

SILAS DID NOT SLEEP AT ALL THE NIGHT BEFORE. IT WAS NEITHER care nor worry that kept him wide-eyed, staring into the dark. He had nothing to fear, for he was a diligent priest, serving the Light as well as he was able. His faith was strong; he had every confidence that his brief term of service in this world would be followed by life everlasting in the loving arms of his Heavenly Father.

No, it was joy and anticipation that roiled in Silas Fage's mind during those long hours. Justice was sweet. *Not* revenge! He must not think of it as revenge. Revenge was violence and therefore forbidden by the Teacher—excepting violence against unbelievers, of course, which this probably would be. Revenge was personal, and Fage had done nothing at all to bring about this retribution; it was all God's doing, and therefore it was divine justice, not revenge. Morning would bring punishment for an old wrong. Fage had never forgotten the crime, but he had never sought revenge. The Father had not forgotten it either, and now he was rewarding his servant's long diligence by letting him carry word of the sentence to the guilty one. Today the punishment would begin.

Morning was a long time coming. Fage must have dozed toward the end, because roosters' cries were a sudden reminder that he must rise to ring the castle bell and perform the dawn service, welcoming the Light.

Another who slept little that night was Agnes Woodbridge. As was her custom after the servants had been sent off to bed—for some were not of the true faith and hence not to be trusted—she had gone down to the hidden chapel to pray to the Mother. There, as always, she gave thanks on her knees for all the blessings she had received.

She prayed to be worthy. She prayed for Edgar, the best, kindest, most faithful husband in all the land of Albi. She prayed for her children: Bram, Maddy, Henry, and Rollo. All were dearly loved and deserving, but especially these days she prayed for Rollo. Rollo the eldest, Rollo the brilliant, Rollo the most gifted, and now Rollo in the most terrible danger. Before the awful news came two weeks ago, her devotions had taken a few minutes. Now they lasted half the night.

Yet it did not seem long before she heard familiar footsteps on the ladder and knew that Edgar had come to relieve her. She rose stiffly. He kissed her cheek, but did not speak. He had no need to. She went up to bed, and he took her place before the secret altar.

The day dawned clear and warm for spring. The orchard was a glory of pink and white blossom. Plums, apples, cherries, pears—all took their turn at this time of year, like dancers on a stage. The farmhands worked from dawn till dusk, plowing, sowing, mending fences. Larks were caroling and hares were dancing.

Maddy and Henry Woodbridge went riding. They had intended to check on the lambs in the western pasture but were turned back at a ford by a brook that normally ran small and meek but that day ran dark and swift, bloated by spring runoff. There they abandoned thoughts of duty and set off to enjoy a ride, ending with a spirited canter back to the manor house.

Maddy actually laughed during their mock race to the park gate. It was a mock race because they both cared too much for their horses to overstrain them when they were tired. The laughter sounded strange in her ears, and she realized that she had not laughed aloud since she'd heard of Rollo's arrest. At once she felt sick with guilt. She caught Henry's eye and saw his happiness vanish as he guessed what she was thinking.

Henry had always been eerily perceptive. He was almost twenty now, but he had been her stalwart big brother since Rollo left, three years ago. Like all the Woodbridges, he was tall, with jet-black hair and a surprisingly fair complexion. He trimmed his beard to a jawline fringe; an untamed Woodbridge beard would be a fearsome sight. His eyes were gray, and they fixed steadily on her now.

"What right do we have to be happy?" he said. "When our brother is in such unthinkable straits, are we monsters to laugh and enjoy life?"

He had nailed the problem exactly. "Tell me."

He smiled and shook his head. "Just that life must go on, Maddy. If someone in the family died, we would mourn, of course, but we would not live in sorrow all our lives. That is not why the Mother gave us life. Our little happiness cannot make Rollo's sorrow deeper. He would be happy to know that we are still happy. In a sense it is concern for our happiness and the happiness of millions like us that put him where he is. He knew he might have to suffer for us."

Henry filled in as preacher now at household prayers when Father was absent. She nodded, unconvinced. Laughter still felt wrong.

As they approached the front door, they saw Bram on the steps with some other boys of about his age. They were playing with a puppy.

A black puppy.

Brother and sister locked eyes again.

Henry frowned. "He's very young for that, if it's what I think it is."

"Very."

And it would be a trial for Henry, for now he would be the odd one out. Rollo had huge talent. Henry had none. Maddy herself had a little—not enough to go off and study at Gaudry, but enough to take lessons from Wisdom Edith. Now Brat? He was only eleven years old. Looking up, she saw a raven perched on the end of the gable.

"You take Dainty around to the stable while I look into this," she said. They halted beside the excitement, she slid from the saddle, and Henry took her reins.

The dog was barely weaned, its ears still trying to stand up and then flopping over. At the moment it was being offered faces to lick, which it cheerfully did, to the accompaniment of loud squeals of glee. There were seven boys there, all with dirty and ragged clothes but unusually clean faces. Other than Brat, they were children of servants. All were far too young to understand how important secrets could be.

"Where did you find that little lad?" Maddy asked. The manor had many dogs, but none of the bitches had whelped recently and none looked anything like this pup. She knelt to offer a hand. It wriggled loose and came to her at once. She rubbed its ears, and it licked her wrist.

"He found me!" Brat protested. "He follows me everywhere. Can I keep him, Mad? Oh, Maddy, can I? For my very own?"

There was not one brown or white hair on it. Its belly was still hairless, and it lacked adult teeth. And it was watching Maddy to see what she was going to say.

"Unless its real owner shows up, of course you may. What're you going to call him?"

"Smut," Brat announced confidently. "His name's Smut, 'cos he's black and he sticks to me." His followers laughed, so this must be a brand new joke. Or a revelation. "He likes you, too, Mad," he added suspiciously.

The Mother was capricious; she gave magical talents to few of her Children, but the first gift was always an animal guide. Only if that was accepted would others follow. It was the tragedy of the Church of the Light that their Teacher had denounced talent as evil and familiars as agents of darkness, which must be rejected. What was wrong with darkness? In the darkness of the Earth the Mother caused seeds to sprout. In the darkness of a womb a baby was conceived. In the darkness of the grave her Children returned to her. But the "Sons of the Sun" rejected the Mother's gifts. Only in very rare cases did followers of the Light receive talent. And they burned their dead.

Bram had clearly bonded with his familiar already, so there was nothing more to worry about.

"Welcome to Woodbridge Manor, Smut," Maddy said, and Smut leaped up to slobber on her chin. She smiled at her youngest brother—already growing stringy, the family black hair, startling blue eyes. He had no idea what had just changed in his life; likely no one would tell him for a few years yet.

She rose and went indoors. She found her father in his counting room, scowling at a ledger and fumbling with an abacus. The room was small, cramped with a desk, untidy bookshelves, and two chairs—and with Edgar Woodbridge, who was a large, solid man. No bookworm or clerk he, but a thick-limbed, weathered gentleman farmer. He owned five large farms, a game park, and half the houses in Stonebridge, and his family had lived in the same place for centuries. He looked up in annoyance, swiftly turning to alarm when Maddy closed the door.

"Brat's outside with a dog," she said. "His name is Smut—'Because he's black and he sticks to me.'"

Squire Woodbridge gaped at her for a moment like a halfwit yokel told to write a letter. "Bram? No. He's far too young! Even Rollo did not get Perry until he was thirteen."

"Corbin's up on the roof, watching."

Her father closed his eyes in prayer. When he looked up he was smiling. "We are greatly blessed." It was an uncertain smile, for a mixed blessing.

Talent was a gift from the Mother, a great gift, but these days it could be close to a curse. Probably they were both wondering if Bram the Brat was being offered as a replacement for Rollo, but neither suggested that. It was too early to give up hope.

"I must get ready for dinner," Maddy said.

Afterwards, that morning was to seem like the end of her happiness.

CHAPTER 2

HIS LORDSHIP HAD GIVEN FATHER SILAS VERY EXPLICIT instructions. He was to travel as a layman, donning his cassock just before arriving at Woodbridge Manor. Fage would have done that anyway, for clergy should not appear in public while dusty, windblown, or smelling too much of horse, but it did increase the dangers of travel. While only the very worst highwaymen would molest a servant of the Lord, many might relieve him of his horse. Angleshire was a reasonably law-abiding part of Albi, but reasonable was not good enough for a retainer of Earl Uptree of Norcaster. His Lordship assigned Fage an escort of six hussars, led by Captain Rasby. Six was both flattering and sinfully satisfying.

His Lordship had also mentioned that noon would be a likely time to catch the family together, which clearly meant, *Don't hesitate to interrupt their dinner.* With Stonebridge a mere two-hour ride away on dry roads, Rasby expected to leave Norcaster about midmorning. But Fage still had relatives there to visit. Besides, he was too eager to waste a morning biting his nails in the castle. He adjusted the captain's thinking, and they made an early start.

Stonebridge had grown since his boyhood, even since he last passed through. The government had improved the highway north from Weypool, which may well have been at His Lordship's urging, at least in part. The faster road had put this part of Angleshire within a day's ride of the capital. Even senior government ministers like His Lordship could now afford to spend time here, and the villages were prospering as a result. That especially applied to Stonebridge, where the highway crossed the Spote.

Fage the cobbler had fathered two more children since Silas had last stopped off in his birthplace, and Fage the carter, three. None of them impressed their uncle. As always, Fage impressed his siblings. Chaplain of Norcaster Castle, family priest to Lord Uptree, riding a fine horse with a six-man escort—of course, these were gifts from the Father, nothing for him to get conceited about. He must not, and need not, brag. Humble enjoyment was his reward.

The meal his eldest sister insisted on producing was not. He'd have done no worse eating at the Swan. Dining at the manor was out of the question, because that would create a debt of hospitality. But Fage had told Rasby that he and his men could eat there, and their horses, too. With a welcome farewell to Stonebridge, Fage embarked on the last lap of his journey.

Woodbridge was only a couple of miles downstream from Stonebridge, and probably marked the site of an earlier crossing. His timing was perfect. When he came in sight of its chimneys, he heard the bell ringing to summon the workers to their daily bread. There he dismounted to don his vestments: golden skullcap, sky blue cassock, and the eight-pointed sunburst pectoral. He led his escort in triumph up the driveway.

Off to his right was the park where the crime had been committed, forty-two years ago. Times had been hard in Albi in those days. The previous harvest had been a disaster, and the winter, hard. There was much hunger that year. Even rabbits and pigeons had been scarce, but thirteen-year-old Silas had set a few snares, and that day he had caught a rabbit. All skin and bone it was, but it would add flavor to the family's meager gruel.

He was just starting to skin the rabbit when a slow beat of hooves froze him to the ground. He crouched low in the grass and shrubbery, hoping to escape detection. The horse came right to him and stopped.

"So it is sly Silas who sets traps in my father's park, is it?" asked a voice from on high.

Silas rose and looked up at the unfriendly stare of Edgar Woodbridge. There was nothing to say.

Woodbridge dropped from his saddle so they were face to face. Except, of course, that the squire's son was half a head taller and allover larger. They were the same age, to the day. Fage knew this because he had often been told how the midwife attending his birth had been called away to the manor house to deliver a more important baby.

"Lost your tongue in the grass?"

"No."

"No, *what?*"

"No, Master Woodbridge." Fage could see nothing but contempt in those pale eyes—odd eyes for a boy with hair so black, with heavy eyebrows and lashes to match.

"I'll let you decide. Will you take your punishment here, or do I drag you before the sheriff?"

Edgar was quite capable of dragging Fage anywhere, even without the help of his horse. The sheriff was his father and owner of the park.

"What's the toll here?"

"Ten strokes, and another ten if you make any sound at all."

"I'll take it."

"Drop them."

So Silas Fage, the miller's son, dropped his britches, bent over a stump, and took ten hard cuts of a riding crop in stony silence. A couple of them bled.

"Well done," said the squire's son. "I wasn't serious about the second ten."

Oh, wasn't he? He'd tried hard enough to win that bet.

Woodbridge swung easily back into his saddle. Britches back in place, Silas held up the rabbit.

"Don't want that," the squire's son said. "Not after you've been pawing it."

He rode away. Silas hurled the rabbit into the undergrowth for the crows to find and limped home.

That was then and this was now.

Fine old oaks and beeches crowded around the manor house like admirers around a beautiful woman, but the building itself was not beautiful. It was a hodgepodge of a mansion, a mishmash of timber and thatch, a sprawl of many generations' additions and "improvements," whose mismatched diamond-pane windows squinted out at the sunlight at various heights and spacings. The front entrance was fairly recent, raised enough to require steps, and flattered with a heavy, studded door fit to repel any attack short of gunfire. What good would that do when scores of windows could be smashed open with a pick?

The visitors were greeted by a carillon of barking from about a dozen ill-sorted dogs, making the horses fidget and twitch their ears. Two young hussars jumped down to kick the pack away to a safer, but still noisy, distance. Fage dismounted with more dignity, gathered his cassock, and mounted the steps. The door swung open, and a liveried footman looked out at the visitor in unfeigned surprise.

The rector of Stonebridge might come calling here, but no other priests would. The Woodbridges had always been suspect heretics, followers of the Dark. No doubt Edgar conformed on the surface as his father and grandfather had done before him, because the law forced them to. By day he would support the local church and give alms generously to keep the priest quiet, but by night he indulged in the foul practices of the paganism that the Teacher had driven out of Albi almost two hundred years ago.

So whose britches were coming down this time?

"Fetch the squire," Fage told the flunky.

The boy started to ask what name and flinched at Fage's expression. "At once, Father. If you will step inside?"

Fage advanced a few paces and watched the boy's back vanish around a far corner. The entrance hall was nicely cool and dim: tiled floor, paneled walls, and some shapely furnishings. It could not compare with Norcaster Castle, but Fage had to admit it was a pleasing space. A portrait in oils of the present squire's father hung over the fireplace, younger than Fage remembered him. He could hear the murmur of many voices, smell delicious odors. A house this size would support a staff of at least one hundred, not counting laborers who ate in the fields.

Edgar Woodbridge came striding out from the dark recesses that had swallowed the footman. He was still taller than Fage, and time had thickened him, although his movements suggested more brawn than blubber. He wore his beard short, but stubble shadowed his cheeks. His doublet and britches were tailor-cut but not showy or fancy. The feather jauntily adorning his bonnet likely came from one of his own pheasants, and his calf-length boots would have cost more than a parson earned in a year. He stood like a bear, head forward and low on his shoulders. Even without the fur and padding of winter clothing, he showed no neck.

Three flunkies came after him and stopped at the corner, waiting for orders. The squire's hurried exit had caused the noise from the dining hall to fade almost to nothing. Woodbridge was still sucking his fingers as he advanced to greet the visitor.

"Father...?" Recognition came and so did the name, which was an impressive feat of memory. "Father Silas Fage! By the Light, Father, it has been a long time!"

Forty-two years. How dare this heretic swear by the Light?

Woodbridge bowed, sweeping the floor with his hat. "You are indeed welcome to this house, Father." They both knew he lied. "You will dine with us, of course."

"I think not," Fage said, pausing an instant to let the significance of that refusal sink in. He did not ask if rabbit was on the menu. Did his host even remember that meeting? How could he have forgotten? "But my men and horses..."

"Of course. How many?"

"Six."

Woodbridge did not comment on the size of Fage's retinue. He gestured and one of the footmen hurried out the front door to direct the hussars to the stable yard. Another went back in the direction of the dining hall. A well-trained staff.

Still the heretic showed no worry. Like his father before him, he was sheriff of Stonebridge. If either church or state decided to move against him, it would take the lord lieutenant of the county to deal with him, and he would send more than one priest and six armed louts.

"To what do we owe the honor of this visit? Last I heard, Father, you were assistant curate at Dog Lea."

"Ah, Edgar, that was many years ago. Now I have the honor to be chaplain of Norcaster Castle."

Woodbridge raised bushy brows to suggest that he was impressed. "Did not the Teacher write, 'Who serves well shall be well rewarded'?"

The Teacher had also written, "The evil mouth can spew good words," but Fage said merely, "And personal priest to Earl Uptree." Who was, of course, the lord lieutenant of Angleshire.

The heretic still showed no signs of apprehension, but the game had hardly begun.

"Knowing who sends you, we are doubly honored by your visit. A letter from His Lordship would have seized our full attention. As would a mere herald. What message can possibly require the services of a priest? Let us sit, while you reveal your great business." He had the gall to indicate a carved oaken bench against the wall, as if a visitor who refused hospitality were unworthy to be invited farther into the house.

Fage let his gaze flicker to the footman listening in the background and then back again to the heretic. "By all means, but my message is also to your good wife." He forestalled any argument: "Not all my news is good, I fear."

Aha! A hit. Woodbridge guessed at once who was to be the subject of the conversation, and his rugged face froze. He spun around. "Ask Mistress Woodbridge to join us in the library. If you will come this way, Father..."

The library was quite impressive, almost admirable. Norcaster Castle had nothing comparable, His Lordship not being a bookish person. The windows were large, as was the fireplace of green marble. Two comfortable chairs flanking the hearth would suffice for reading or casual conversation, and six stools around the polished walnut table for more formal meetings. Rugs on the floor and tapestries on the wall gave the room a peaceful hush. One wall was lined with several hundred books, all bound in matching red leather. How many were heretic texts? The titles on the covers would mean nothing. It would take the Church Police hours to examine each one and check it against the forbidden index. No matter—the Church had unlimited patience, unlimited manpower.

"Please be seated, Father." Woodbridge waved Fage to one of the padded seats.

He lowered himself into it gingerly. "I must admit that I am out of practice in the saddle, Edgar."

"We are none of us as young as we used to be."

If that was a plea for forgiveness, it came forty-two years too late.

His wife swept in, chin high, eyes glinting—Agnes Woodbridge, née Rowthorn. Her father had been a notorious heretic, who had cheated the public out of a spectacular execution by dying during interrogation. She was a large, brawny woman, dressed in somber gray, with a fringe of lace on her bonnet as her only ornamentation. Her husband introduced the visitor, but the name would mean nothing to her, for they had not met before. She curtsied. Fage merely spread his hand in the sign of the Light, which she would not value, of course. Woodbridge put her in the other padded chair and brought a stool to sit between them.

"Now, Father, what is the sad message you bring?"

"Oh, not all sad, Edgar! The Lord dispenses both days and nights, else life would be boring and unproductive. Some of what I must tell you will make you want to howl and rend your garments, but the rest will be like sunlight after the storm, I promise. Your son, Rollo Woodbridge." Pause, sigh. "He was charged with entering the country illegally, as I am sure you know. Then both heresy and treason were added to the charge sheet."

The woman stiffened, but Woodbridge had been forewarned.

"We heard. Both charges are absurd."

Fage nodded sadly. "He was well thought of in his youth, certainly. His Lordship made inquiries...twenty-three now, I believe?"

"Twenty-two." Agnes looked ready to tell him to cut to the chase. He would get there in his own good time, and by the scenic road.

"But responsible for his actions, no longer a boy. Well, the sad news...and His Lordship heard this only last night. Quite late last night. I came as soon as I could. The sad news is that the prisoner Rollo Woodbridge has been transferred to Swine Hall."

The woman looked blank, showing only a frown of annoyance at not understanding. Her husband grimaced.

"This would seem to indicate that the king's officers are taking the matter most seriously," Fage said sadly. "They must mean to prosecute the case with both alacrity and diligence. Most strictly."

Agnes eyed each man in turn. "And what is Swine Hall, may I ask?"

Fage left it to Edgar.

"The foulest jail in Weypool," he explained.

"The warden is Sir Ezechiel Pottenger," Fage added helpfully, "who rejoices in being known as the most expert torturer in Albi." He let her digest that, wondering what silent words made her lips move, noting how her face paint, which had been applied with such art that hitherto he had not even noticed it, now showed stark against her pallor. "He brags that he has never met a prisoner he could not break, yet has never had one die on him." *So your son will not escape as easily as your father did.*

"So Albiurn justice still includes torture, does it?" She was at a loss, bluffing, fighting for time to find a defense.

"In cases of heresy, most certainly, mistress. Treason sometimes."

"Your bad news could hardly have been worse, Father," Woodbridge said. "You have weighted our hearts with lead. Now show us the other side of the coin."

"Ah, there I bring hope. Earl Uptree is, as you well know, a member of the king's Privy Council, and therefore one of the most powerful men in the country. He is also a neighbor of yours, as your lands run together."

"We are acquainted with His Lordship." Woodbridge's tone indicated that the honor meant little.

"He probably heard the news of Rollo's capture even before you did, through his Privy Council connections. He was naturally concerned that a neighbor's son should be in such trouble. As I said, he made inquiries. As lord lieutenant of the county, he would take an interest in any native of Angleshire, and he recalled your son as a most pleasing lad at some of the harvest rallies."

His listeners appeared somewhat skeptical at that last embellishment, and Fage reined in his oratory. "You are also aware that His Lordship's brother, the Exalted Garrett Uptree, is a hierarch?"

Woodbridge's fists tightened on his lap. "We are."

"His Holiness happens to be visiting Norcaster just now, and His Lordship has discussed the case with him. His Holiness is sympathetic. So you have two of the rulers of Albi on your side, Squire! Members of the Privy Council and the Hierarchy, respectively. The state and the church, both."

Before Woodbridge could comment, his wife did. He ought to have her better trained.

"That is good news indeed, Father. Just how are they planning to help?"

"I confess that I am not certain of the details, mistress. They did not confide in me further than I have already said. I assumed that they did not wish to expose their thoughts in writing that might fall into others' hands, and they feared you might not trust some secular flunky's word. But they did send me with the message that there may be a way of staying the most serious charges against your son and—once he is convicted of the lesser crime of entering the country illegally, a verdict which can hardly be in doubt—commuting his sentence to lifetime banishment. While that may seem hard to you, it would obviously be a great deal more pleasant than the alternative."

"Obviously," Woodbridge said dryly. From the way he kept licking his lips, his mouth was probably even drier than his words. His forehead, however, sparkled pleasantly with dewdrops of sweat. "So what happens next?"

"Ah!" Fage raised a finger. "I did forget one thing. I was told to remind you that the Uptree family is very large."

"I assume that does not imply that it will march on the capital in armed insurrection to release our son from Swine Hall. So what happens now? What is the price?"

Fage tutted. "Price? Squire, Squire! You do not talk of price to such noble gentlemen. I was told to give you their solemn word that they may be able to help, and that you should come at once to discuss it with them, face to face. His Holiness has to leave at dawn to return to Weypool, so there is no time to waste."

"Both of us?" asked Agnes.

"Both of you," Fage said. "And your daughter Madeline also."

Oh, how sweet it was!

CHAPTER 3

As usual, Maddy sat between Henry and her mother at dinner, overlooking the dozens of servants and children busily filling themselves at long rows of tables and benches. The larder grew lean and the diet, monotonous in springtime; but the coastal fishing fleets could venture out now, and carters were fighting their way through the mud, so today there was fish. And there were eggs. Her father was a firm believer that good work required good board, and he saw to it that every Woodbridge employee down to the lowest scullion ate well. Rarer treats might brighten the fare at the squire's table—oysters and pigeon pie that day—but no one in his manor went hungry if he could help it.

Talk among the family was about marriage, for Maddy was sixteen and overdue to make her choice. The conversation had a strangely dreamlike quality. How could they discuss betrothal or weddings when Rollo was in prison, perhaps chained in some unthinkable dungeon? A more topical topic would have been Brat's being awarded a familiar at such an amazingly early age, but they could not discuss that where they might be overheard by the servants. So matchmaking it was.

The most likely candidate now was Guy Rowthorn, who was twenty-two and a journeyman typesetter in the king's printing office in Weypool. He was a cousin, for families that followed the old faith tended to marry among themselves, for obvious reasons. Guy had good points and bad points. He was fun and could make her laugh. He was more weedy than virile, but fortunately she had grown out of a juvenile tendency to swoon at the sight of shirtless laborers bulging with muscle and glowing with summer tans. As Henry put it, Guy would manage to do his duty in bed. On the downside, Maddy would have to move to the capital, which was an unhealthy place. She would lose her country freedom. There was less danger of persecution in the city, where people paid less heed to what their neighbors were up to, but if Guy were ever denounced as a heretic, his position in the government might lead to suspicion of spying.

Mother disapproved of Guy as a future son-in-law, because Guy had no money. Maddy's dowry would provide some comforts for them, for Father would be generous, but then she would be supporting him; and Guy, too, was very uneasy about that prospect. That was why he had never come right out and asked for her hand. Maddy thought he would do so if she dropped a hint or two. She hadn't, because if Wisdom Edith was correct about her talent, poor Guy might be unable to refuse her, and that would not be fair.

Father, sitting on Mother's far side, had other worries and paid little attention. He would have final say, of course, but he would not overrule his only daughter's choice unless she fell for some squint-eyed, crippled beggar with leprosy.

Then Watt, the chief footman, came to whisper in his ear, and Father left the table and the hall, which simply never happened during the noonday meal. The buzz of conversation took on a puzzled tone.

Then Watt returned and Mother left, too. That was enough to make everyone stare. And finally spaces were cleared near the back door for half a dozen troopers in unfamiliar livery. Too many people were gaping instead of eating. Henry moved to the squire's chair, took up the bell, and rang the five-minute warning, which set everyone back to gobbling like starving puppies. Maddy went to sit beside him.

"Whose colors?" she asked, under cover of putting an oyster to her mouth.

Wiping his lips on his sleeve, Henry muttered, "Norcaster."

Ah, the darling earl! Lord Uptree was not the best of neighbors. No matter how often Father had the fences inspected, Uptree cattle broke into Woodbridge crops. Father's herds shrank if they grazed near the boundary, and His Lordship's judgments in court often failed to ring true. Alas, no one dared argue with a personal friend of King Ethan. Uptree's morals were no better than his ethics. The odds were good that two of the boys who had been playing with Brat this morning had noble blood in them, since both were sons of unwed servants expelled from Norcaster Castle for promiscuity. Such disgraced waifs turned up at the manor quite regularly. Father never turned them away, and very few of them misbehaved in his service. If Earl Uptree was serious about immorality in his household, he should expel himself as the worst offender.

So who had come calling? Not the earl in person, for his escort would have been a hundred, not six. And why include Mother? Maddy shot an inquiring glance at the ever-perceptive Henry.

"Haven't got a clue," he said. "Unless he wants to marry you to one of his sons."

"If you make me laugh too hard, I'm liable to sneeze oysters."

"That was the idea. Or it could be news of Rollo."

Yes, it could be news of Rollo. Which might be even less welcome than marriage into the Uptree menagerie.

Mealtime was over. The children were fidgeting. Henry rang the final bell and stood up. Benches scraped on tiles as everyone rose.

"Our guests came late and are welcome to remain and finish their meal," he said, pitching his voice to reach the end of the hall. "Let us give thanks…" The grace he recited was one of Father's, so ambiguously worded that it could be addressed to the Father or the Mother, and would give offense only to zealots. Anything could give offense to zealots.

As he finished and people began to head out to their afternoon labors, Watt the page put himself between Henry and Maddy. "The squire asks you both to join him in the library at once."

Henry thanked him. Grinning, he offered Maddy his arm. As they paraded out, he hummed a few bars of a recognizable wedding anthem.

"You will get no cake," she warned.

Father was in the library with a priest, a weasel-face little man in his fifties, to whom Maddy took an instant dislike, probably mutual. Father presented, Henry bowed, Maddy curtsied. The priest gave them his blessing. There was no sign of Mother.

"Father Fage has brought disturbing news about Rollo," the squire said. "We are invited to Norcaster Castle to discuss possible relief. Henry, the brake on the coach has not been repaired yet, has it?"

"'Fraid not, Father. And this morning the smith asked to go and visit his ailing mother. I gave him leave, because I had no idea it would be needed before Mother's shopping trip."

Maddy had not heard of anything wrong with the coach, and the smith had been eating in the hall five minutes ago.

Father nodded at this confirmation. "There you are, Father. Horses it will have to be. Maddy, go and change; you are coming with us. Henry, you'll be in charge here, of course. Tell the captain to muster my usual escort—fast!"

Maddy sensed a tense atmosphere that she did not understand and didn't want to. She bobbed again to the visitor and hurried out the door. In her room she found her best riding costume being laid out by Polly, which meant that Mother was already organizing.

As Polly was unpinning Maddy's gown, she said, "The mistress thought you might want me to accompany you, miss." Polly was a farm-bred girl and an excellent rider. She was also large, buxom, and far too attractive to remain single for much longer.

"I'd be very happy to have you. It's a fine day for a ride. Now, we'll need an overnight bag, I expect, because Father won't want to return in the dark…"

As soon as Maddy was dressed for riding, she sent Polly off to tend to her own needs. Then she locked the chamber door and hunkered down beside the wardrobe, where there was a small hole at the base of the wainscot.

"Teeny!" she whispered. "Teeny?" It was a shame to disturb him by day, because mice are nocturnal, but in a moment two tiny eyes and a nose appeared. Wisdom Edith had joked that a small talent deserved a small familiar, before admitting that in fact there were no rules to explain what species a person's spirit guide would choose to inhabit. The most skilled wisdom she had ever met, she said, had been guided by a bat no larger than Teeny.

"Teeny, I am summoned to Norcaster Castle. Should I go?"

The tiny face nodded. Since Maddy's only other option was to run away and be an outlaw, that answer was logical.

"Will you come with me?"

Teeny vanished back into his hole. Did that mean no because there was nothing to worry about, or no because she would not be coming back? Maddy often thought that a small talent was worse than none at all.

∞

A parade of fifty or so people and horses could not be organized at a snap of fingers, and it was an hour before Father and the priest led the way out of the yard. Maddy followed with Mother, then their respective maids, the

Uptree troopers, and most of the Woodbridges' troopers. The rest caught up later, to breathe the dust at the tail of the procession. They clattered past the rows of servants' cottages—a small village by itself—and down to the towpath along the banks of the Spote. Dainty had done her duty that morning, so Maddy had to settle for Patch, who had an annoying tendency to shy at every leaf.

Mother and daughter dawdled until the squire's lead was wide enough that quiet conversation would be safe from the priest's big ears.

"What was all the nonsense about the coach?" Maddy asked.

"I'm not sure." Agnes Woodbridge's smile was tight-lipped. "But the brakes failed the instant Fage suggested he sit in it with us. He probably didn't want us 'plotting' where he can't eavesdrop." After a moment she added, "But there may be more to it than that. He probably doesn't ride very often, and he'd come a long way already. Father offered him a cushion for his saddle, and he showed his teeth like a pig."

"And the news about Rollo?"

Her mother's expression darkened even more. "It may be reliable, or it may be lies to trap us somehow. Fage claims that Rollo has been moved to Swine Hall, which is—"

Maddy's "Oh no!" terminated the explanation.

"So we are to be threatened with something or pressured into something. Don't trust what they say, and let your father decide."

Maddy smiled. "I'm sure he would tell me to follow your lead."

They closed up the gap and began discussing rain and the spring plowing.

During the next two hours, there were gates to pass, fords to cross, and branches to hold aside in the woods. Of necessity the riders' original grouping was rearranged. Maddy found herself for a while riding alongside an Uptree hussar, Hal Raspy, who had a stunning profile, a fine line of patter, and a smile to spin any girl's head. He skirted a fine line between disrespect and making her blush but leaned mostly toward the blushing, and sometimes even trespassed into sniggering territory. Fortunately, Mother was out of earshot just then.

She was partnered by Father briefly. He said no more than Mother had. They must wait and see what was on offer. It might be a genuine effort to help, but he put little stock in that possibility.

"Does the earl have enough influence at court to save Rollo?" she asked.

"Who can say? He's a member of the Privy Council and said to be one of the king's drinking cronies. But how much power do they have? The real clout is wielded by the Hierarchy. Rollo's trouble has very little to do with leaving and entering the country without government permission, and not much more to do with treason. A heresy charge means the Hierarchy rules. And there we may do some good." He told Maddy about the other brother they were going to see, Garrett Uptree, one of the hierarchs who ruled the Church of the Light. But Father had never met him and could not predict what his attitude might be.

Maddy also rode with Polly, after they had left the rich bottomland of the Spote River and were into gentle uplands owned by the Earl of Norcaster. Polly's father was one of the more successful of the Woodbridge tenants, and the two farmer's daughters outdid each other in disparaging commentaries. The soil was poor, the livestock unimpressive, and the management worse, in their expert opinions. His Lordship should either stay home and manage his property properly, or he should hire people who knew what they were doing.

But when Norcaster Castle itself came into view—two long, hot, and dusty hours after leaving the manor—Maddy was alongside Father Silas Fage himself, that ratty little man. Mother had taught her that making conversation with a man was easy: ask a question about crops, trade, or hunting, wait until he runs out of breath, and then ask another. Women, though, exchanged family news, and that could be dangerous for people from talented families. A priest must be even trickier. One couldn't ask about family when he wasn't allowed to have any. Turned out that Slithery Silas liked to set the topics.

"How often do you attend church, Madeline?"

"If you mean going to the Church of the Blessed in Stonebridge, Father, then the answer is almost never. I don't think I've been there since the dedication of that new west window Father endowed. But Father Snuggs comes to the manor every week and conducts worship there."

"And you attend?"

"Of course. Always." Maddy found the babbling nonsense of the sermon and prayers no worse than boring, and her talent was so small that she even enjoyed the singing, which gave Father raging headaches. Rollo had suffered even more. Now Brat might start to suffer, too, and must be taught not to complain.

"Most girls are married by your age, or at least betrothed."

"I was betrothed when I was three. My fiancé was fifteen. But he died a few years later in battle. My parents decided to wait until I could help them choose." In fact, her fiancé had been shot dead while fleeing from a mob incited by a witch-hunting priest, but the details did not matter. She decided it was her turn. "Is that where we are going? It doesn't look like a castle to me."

She was looking at a very large brick building, three stories high, which sprawled across the country like a red stain. The house and grounds between them must have displaced enough farmland to feed a fair village. No follower of the Mother would have built such a horror.

Fage smiled, which was not a pleasant sight. "After Queen Ebba fled the country and the Teacher proclaimed the Realm of Light, he issued ten decrees. Do you remember them all, Madeline?"

"Of course! The fifth one was that there must be no castles."

"It was the fourth, and it banned crenellation, but that means the same, I suppose. Norcaster Castle had mostly been blown to bits in the wars anyway, but the remains were torn down. Only the name remains. The first earl of the new realm started work on a suitable house, and his descendants have been adding to it ever since. The ornamental park is quite famous. I am surprised you have never heard of it."

"So am I, Father. This is a very exciting day for me."

"And it has not ended yet," Fage said, with another bloodcurdling smile.

CHAPTER 4

THE INTERIOR OF NORCASTER CASTLE WAS AS GRANDIOSE as the exterior. Agnes Woodbridge had visited fine houses before, but none so palatial and ostentatious. Such obscene display made her madder than ever. She was being humbled and manipulated, dragged to Norcaster without warning and virtually under duress. Worse was certain to follow. Her son was hostage for her submission, threatened with the same fiendish death that her father had suffered, and it seemed her daughter was going to be the price of his release—a release that would not mean freedom.

She was thirsty, tired, and dusty, but there were no offers of refreshments or freshening up. Oh no, great men must never be kept waiting. The visitors were rushed straight through to a vast hall furnished with mirrors, crystal chandeliers, and scattered islands of oversized furniture. The walls were hung with tapestries depicting scenes in the Teacher's life. The Woodbridges followed the priest across an acre of multicolored marble toward two men sitting at the far end under a cloud of cigar smoke.

Beyond them, a great window looked out on a small lake and manicured gardens.

What use was all this space, Agnes wondered. You couldn't heat a place this size in winter, and you couldn't dance comfortably on stone floors. It was a stage designed to magnify the mighty. Agnes had grown up in poverty. Her father had been a cobbler, and a good one. But he had also been gifted with a great talent for healing, for which he would never accept payment. It had left him little time to earn a living. He had been a saint, and for that he had been tortured to death.

Agnes caught Edgar's eye and read sympathy there, but also a warning. Edgar had several talents, although he did not come close to Rollo's awesome collection. He had mastery, and had once turned a charging bull just by speaking to it, but he refused to use that power on people because he considered it unethical. He could see in darkness like a bat, and he might have developed other talents, had he ever received the necessary training. Given a few minutes to consult Corbin, he would have gained a pretty clear idea of what was in store for them at Norcaster. The odious Silas Fage had made sure he was denied that opportunity.

Then she glanced at Maddy on her other side and was reassured. Maddy was staring around, as well she might. To anyone who knew her less well than her mother, she must seem quite unworried. Dusty, windburned, and clad in informal, inappropriate clothing, she was still a great beauty. She was tall, yet had enough poise to be graceful. Beauty, like talent, was both an asset and a danger. She sensed her mother's attention and looked around. One eye flickered in a wink that brought a lump to Agnes's throat.

Maddy was no longer a child, but she was still too young to realize how evil the world could be.

Osborn, Earl Uptree of Norcaster, rose to greet his guests. He was a heavyset, well-preserved man of around sixty, with gray in his beard. His smile was unconvincing, and the grooves in his face suggested that it was more accustomed to scowling. His clothes and jewels were as flashy as his house, with silken hose, britches, and doublet of silver and scarlet brocade; a finely ruffled shirt; and a bonnet sporting an osprey plume. He glowed with power like the sun gave light.

Fage presented the Woodbridges in turn. The earl acknowledged Edgar's deep bow with a gracious nod, Agnes's curtsy with another, and Maddy's with a leer of approval. Then he turned to Fage. "Thank you, Father."

Clearly the priest had expected to remain and gloat. However shocked at this cavalier dismissal, he recovered quickly, gestured a blessing, and departed. That was the first good moment of Agnes's day.

"Sheriff Woodbridge," the earl said, "welcome! It has been too long since you graced our halls, neighbor." Agnes was positive that Edgar had not been invited to Norcaster once in the twenty-four years of their marriage. "Brother, may I present..."

The other man was older. That paradox had been explained at length to Agnes by Father Fage on the ride. Normally the eldest son inherited a title, yes, but not if he had taken a priest's vow of celibacy. So the hierarch Uptree was a good ten years older than the earl, and his chair bore no small resemblance to a throne, being gilded and raised on a small platform.

Garrett Uptree was long and spare. His beard was snowy, and his complexion had a bookish pallor; he looked out at the world under heavy lids with a sublime, untroubled confidence. His doublet and britches were of cloth of gold, his elaborate hat was also gold, and his cloak sky blue. His clerical sunburst pectoral had sixteen rays. When told Edgar's name, he extended his right hand to let him kiss his amber sunburst ring. He held it low so that Edgar had to stoop a long way. Agnes and Maddy were merely granted a gesture of blessing.

Agnes distrusted that arrogant gaze. The Teacher had condemned all talent as evil magic. Nevertheless, there were many stories of Sons of the Sun being gifted, even if none ever admitted it. That some men's prayers were answered more often than others' was the official excuse. Magic was evil, but miracles were good, and a few of those would certainly help a man climb the clerical ladder. Several of the current hierarchs were suspected of having talent, and Garrett Uptree might be one of them.

The earl sat down, leaving the visitors standing. By this time Agnes felt ready to explode like a fusillade of canons, and wished she could portray the same unruffled and respectful calm as Edgar did. Or Maddy, for that matter.

"To business, then," Osborn said, "for time is short. I won't lie to you or try to trap you. Here are the facts. Your son went abroad without government permission three years ago, in the Year of Light 177. Three weeks ago he attempted to return under a false name and was apprehended in Clidgey Harbor. He had in his possession certain poisons and noxious potions. He was taken to Weypool and charged with various crimes. Two days ago he was moved to Swine Hall, a jail of gruesome reputation. Any questions so far?"

Edgar said, "I find it impossible to believe that my son would dabble in poisons or whatever else you mentioned. Such evidence can be planted in a man's baggage when it is inspected. I have asked for permission to visit the prisoner to confirm that he really is my son."

"He admits it," the earl said impatiently. "He has a scar on his left thigh and a brown birthmark over his right kidney. In itself, what he has done is not so serious. Twenty lashes and expulsion back to wherever he came from would normally suffice. However, he has spent three years in Xennia, and that raises issues of spying and treason, because King Clovis still maintains that his wife's sister is rightful ruler of Albi. Xennia runs a network of agents in Albi, and your son refuses to say where exactly he was headed—undoubtedly some secret hive of conspiracy— or whom he was to meet. Three days from now the Privy Council will consider his case and may authorize stricter interrogation."

He paused a moment to let the threat sink in.

"The council has held back so far, waiting for counsel from the Hierarchy. Brother?"

"The Hierarchy meets tomorrow evening," Garrett said. Even speaking softly, he had the vibrant tones of the trained orator, a voice that could inflame great congregations to paroxysms of zeal. "And the circle's position is somewhat similar to the council's. Three years ago, young Woodbridge went straight to the city of Perse and enrolled in the heretic school known as Gaudry. They speak Albiurn there. Indeed, the school exists solely to lead Albiurn youths away from the Light and indoctrinate them in the discredited heresy of the Mother. You needn't argue, Sheriff. We have spies there. Your son was under observation the whole time he was in Xennia. Guards were waiting for him at Clidgey."

The earl said, "So tomorrow the Hierarchy may decide to lay charges of heresy and take his case away from the secular government."

"I think that sums up the position," the hierarch concluded.

Edgar's turn again. "Without admitting that the facts are as you have said, my lords, I am curious to learn why you summoned us here this afternoon."

"Because," the earl said, "there are firebrands on both the council and the circle who would make an example of your son. I dare not admit this in public, but it is no secret that evidence extracted by torture is worthless. No man can resist for long. Your boy can be made to confess to either treason or heresy. Both result in public butchery."

He sighed and sharpened his tone. "My own opinion is that we have had far too much of that lately. A good government does not rule by terror. But we who think so are in a minority on the Privy Council."

"And in the Hierarchy," his brother agreed.

Edgar said nothing. Agnes knew that there were other threats that might be added. A traitor's family might be dragged down with him. So might a heretic's. Rollo's ruin might destroy them all.

"We got to talking last night," Osborn said, "my brother and I. The boy has done nothing serious so far. A sound beating and banishment should suffice. But how could we possibly talk both the council and the Hierarchy into accepting that point of view? Obviously one is not enough, it must be both. And to seem to be defending heresy and treason would call our own loyalties into question. The wolves might turn on us."

Now Agnes saw the plot.

Maddy's pallor showed that she did, too. When she spoke up unbidden, the effect was startling.

"And somewhere in their extended family, the Uptrees have an unmarried son?"

The brothers exchanged glances. Osborn smiled thinly. Garrett did not, disapproving of women venturing to speak without leave.

The earl nodded. "Several. As you have guessed, we decided that our only hope would be to ask for personal favors. In short, to stand up and mention that the accused is a distant relative of ours, and beg that his sentence be commuted to perpetual banishment. To save us embarrassment and wailing relatives, you see. There would still be some risk, but this is the sort of grace that our long services to church and state deserve. It is the only chance of saving your boy that we can see."

Maddy opened her mouth, and Agnes forestalled her. There were pit traps everywhere here.

"May we be told the young man's name?"

"Better than that, mistress, you may meet him, for obviously the marriage must be signed and sealed at once if my brother is to mention it to the hierarchs tomorrow." Osborn turned his head and called, "Sam!"

Over in the corner, a man stood up. He had been sitting in one of the oversized chairs, unseen all this time, although probably too far away to hear much of the conversation.

Agnes knew him.

Ever since Maddy had seen where the plot was leading, she had wondered if she dared hope for a reasonably *young* man. If a forced marriage would save Rollo, she would take whatever she was offered, but she prayed to the Mother not to harness her to some portly, gouty, middle-aged has-been. The Uptree family was huge. There were sisters and other brothers, grandchildren, probably uncles and aunts. Only when she recognized Sam Stroud did she realize that the Uptrees would never waste a *legitimate* son on a family with a reputation for heresy.

But she knew Sam. She could do worse.

As a child, Sam's mother had been in service at Norcaster. Expelled for gross immorality, meaning pregnancy, she had followed countless others to Woodbridge, arriving exhausted, starving, and fevered from drinking ditch water on the road. Father had hired her as a dairymaid. The last Maddy had heard of her, she was married and living in Stonebridge. Her son had been a hand at Beaconbeck, one of Father's farms. He was just two years older than Maddy.

Of course, Father's men moved around from one farm to another as they were needed for plowing, sowing, harvesting, woodcutting, whatever. Maddy had known Sam all her life. A year and a half ago, at harvest time, he had been one of the muscular bronze studs who had caught her immature adolescent eye. That and a few ill-chosen words had been his undoing. Father had fired him.

Now Father's face had gone past red and was closing in on purple. Poor Father! To be offered an aristocrat's by-blow as a suitor for his daughter was insult enough, but an illiterate plowman, one of his own dismissed employees, was unthinkable. Mother, ivory pale, was watching him anxiously, as if her greatest concern was what he might say or do to ruin them all.

Maddy remembered Sam as a half-naked youth. He was a young man now, not much taller than he had been but even broader. He was dressed as a gentleman, although his hose were wrinkled and his doublet looked uncomfortably tight across the shoulders. More than likely he had never worn such garments in his life until they had been dragged out of someone else's closet for him that very afternoon. His red-gold beard was trimmed short and hardly showed on a face already sunburned from the plowing. Even his fingernails were clean, so someone had worked him over well. He approached cautiously, eyeing Father and the earl with equal wariness.

Maddy said, "Hello, Sam. You've grown up a lot."

He had not expected her to speak first. He blinked in surprise; his hand began to rise to touch his forehead before it remembered not to. He bowed clumsily.

"The Light be on you, Miss Madeline."

"Ah, you know each other?" The earl spoke as if that were a surprise.

Sam nodded. Maddy felt sorry for him. She decided to end this politeness nonsense.

"Sam, my brother Rollo is in some trouble. As I understand matters, His Lordship is proposing that you and I get spliced, so that you, his son, will become Rollo's brother-in-law. Then family influence may get him off lightly. What do you do for a living these days?" Father should be asking such questions, but he was not capable of playing the game at the moment.

"Work in the quarries, miss. Mostly. Plow sometimes."

"So in order to maintain me in the style to which I am accustomed, you will have to be endowed with lands which will serve as my dowry. That is the plan?"

Sam nodded. With golden hair and eyes of pale sapphire blue, he was a perfect son of the Light. No one would ever suspect him of being one of the Mother's Children. He was certainly uneducated, but not stupid. He was letting Maddy lead in this unfamiliar maze.

"Have you any particular lands in mind?"

Sam looked pleadingly at the earl, who nodded encouragingly, then at Father, who just glared. "Told to ask for Beaconbeck, miss."

Beaconbeck comprised ninety-seven hides, a good third of Father's total freehold, and most of the best soil. The house was small and neglected, but that could be put to rights. It was less than an hour's walk from Woodbridge Manor itself. Maddy would be close to her family, would not have to go off and live far away in the stinking city. Thoughts of Weypool put her in mind of Guy Rowthorn. Physically, Sam was twice the man Guy was. She had no doubts about Sam Stroud doing his duty in bed.

Maddy looked around the group, and everyone was still waiting on her—the two Uptrees with cynical amusement, Father with fury barely held in check, Mother appalled, Sam sweating and totally out of his depth.

"Do you still think the way you said two years ago, Sam?"

Now they were on ground he understood. His eyes lit up. "Even more so. You still feel what you said then, Maddy?"

Father flinched. He had never heard that part of the story.

What was she waiting for? This was their only hope of saving Rollo, and she could do much worse than plowman Stroud. She might be able to make something out of Sam.

"I think you'd better ask my father for my hand before I answer that."

Sam squared his shoulders, to a sound of tearing stitches. "Squire Woodbridge...want to marry your daughter, sir. Think she want to marry me."

"Apparently so," Father said hoarsely. "You consent, Maddy?"

She nodded. Two years ago at harvest time, she had told Sam Stroud that she liked the way the sunlight made the hairs on his chest shine. She had not been quite out of earshot when one of the other boys had asked Sam if he "ever got between that one's legs," and Sam had said, "Will soon!" Father had been passing right behind them and heard. Sam had been gone down the road in minutes.

Agnes grabbed her daughter in a fierce hug. She was weeping, which was unheard of. Father shook Sam's hand. Sam was taller than he was.

The earl rose to join in the handshaking.

"You accept my son's suggestion for her dowry, Sheriff?"

Yes, Father said glumly, they could have Beaconbeck.

Now Sam knew where he was. He detached Maddy from one embrace, wrapped her in tighter one, and kissed her, longer and wetter than she'd ever been kissed.

CHAPTER 5

THE STENCH OF SWINE HALL WAS NOTORIOUS. IT polluted the streets around it and saturated people's clothes. It blended odors of feces and urine, rot and vomit, gangrene and mildew in a single terrible miasma. A prisoner released from Swine Hall, so it was said, could be identified weeks later by his smell. Few were released. Most died of disease or wounds inflicted by other inmates. No one ever escaped.

Even the necessities of life—food, water, harlots, bedding, visitations by family—were only available after the jailers had been bribed. That applied even to inmates for whom the government paid a board allowance. The starving robbed the fortunate. Female prisoners prostituted themselves, and male ones fought.

The warden, Sir Ezechiel Pottenger, had been born with no sense of smell and liked to joke that this was the best possible qualification for his job. He was a flabby man with a sallow complexion and a wispy beard of indeterminate color. He was fifty-one years old, looked about seventy, and moved in a flat-footed waddle. He loved his work, and today he was looking forward to a special treat, the start of a new interrogation. Long experience had taught him that late afternoon was the best time to begin.

Most cells in Swine Hall were dark, damp, and grossly overcrowded. This particular evildoer was confined on the top floor in one of several special cells, designed for the solitary confinement of traitors. They were spacious and very high, each with a barred skylight to let in sunshine. Or rain. Or snow. Lanterns hung well out of reach of the inmate were kept burning all night—leave heretic witches in the dark and you couldn't predict what they might get up to. Each cell had at least two spyholes, and the really dangerous prisoners were watched by two men, twenty-four hours a day.

Prisoner Woodbridge was classed as highly danger-ous, but that might be partly because he looked so hon-est and trustworthy—a well-favored kid, the sort a father dreamed might come asking for his daughter's hand and the daughter hoped would be accepted. According to his file, the heresy school in Xennia had regarded him as a star pupil. At his earlier interrogations, he had taken care to speak softly and respectfully to the high-ranking lawyers and clerics, if a stubborn refusal to supply any meaning-ful information could ever be respectful. Jet-black hair was always a suspicious sign, and two weeks' captivity had given him a hairy, wild-man look, with sunken eyes and the drawn features of a man in pain.

The warden began by inspecting him through one of the spyholes. The prisoner had straw to sleep on, a flagon of water, and a slop bucket, nothing more. He was fed once a day, and lack of a blanket wouldn't kill him at this time of year. His wrists were manacled, but in front of him, so he had limited use of his hands. His life might not be pleasant, but it was about to become much less so.

The warden had put his best men on this case, two on watch at all times. Swine Hall staff were armed with wooden nightsticks, not blades. Cudgels were handy for disciplining, and a prisoner who got hold of one couldn't kill himself with it. The only man to enter the prisoner's cell since he was put there was Tench, a dwarf who happened also to be a deaf mute and so could not be controlled by demonic commands.

Pottenger had brought Tench with him. He handed the little man a bag made of heavy black felt, and made the appropriate gestures. Dalton unlocked the door to let Tench enter the cell. Pottenger and Shipley watched through the spyholes.

The prisoner looked up warily. He had been fed at noon, so he knew he was not being brought food. He smiled at his visitor and made no resistance to having the bag pulled over his head. Tench turned and departed, his job done.

"Dalton, bring the stool. Shipley, lock us in."

The prisoner turned his face toward the footsteps but did not rise. His manacles were gold plated, and its touch had blistered his skin, a sure sign of a heretic witch.

"Just in case you're tempted to try anything, lad," Pottenger said, "there are six guards on the outer door, and they have orders to beat you unconscious if you get out of this room."

"Flattery won't get you anywhere." Woodbridge's voice was muffled by the bag and was possibly still a dangerous weapon, but not nearly so dangerous as it might be if he could see his opponents.

"I'm the warden here. You heard of me, boy?" Pottenger had been present at some of the previous interrogations, but only as a witness in the background, not one of the inquisitors.

"I've heard of you. Sir Ezechiel Pottenger. About the nastiest slime that ever oozed out of a sewer."

"That's good! I like 'em stubborn. Prisoner, I want some names and addresses from you."

"You won't get them." But the kid's head turned a fraction toward the hooks high on the wall—a vertical row of a dozen of them, half a handbreadth apart. Was it possible that he could see through the bag?

Dalton placed the stool directly below them.

"Then let's start," the warden said, "with the names of the people you hoped to poison."

"Is there nothing but crap between your ears? I told them over and over that those potions I carried were all medicinal. Or are you so stupid that you don't know the difference between medicine and poison?"

"Some of yours killed rabbits."

"Many remedies are dangerous in large doses."

"And who were you going to administer the lethal doses to?"

"I wasn't."

"You'll tell me soon enough, you know."

"Not before the pox rots your cock off." His type was brought up to speak genteel, and never like that. Bluster was a sign of fear.

Pottenger sighed. "They think it's brave to talk back like that," he told Dalton, as if the man were new at this. "And in a few days they all tell us everything we want to know. Spare yourself the pain, Woodbridge. Why risk mutilation or disablement? Say you'll talk and I'll send for a priest to write it down. I'll even take those manacles off you and give you honest iron ones while we're waiting."

"Eat shit."

The warden chuckled. "Stand up, then, and we'll get started. A piss first is a good idea."

The prisoner drank from his water bottle. He managed to rise gracefully, not the easiest move when wearing manacles, then let Dalton guide him to the bucket. When he had finished his business there, the jailer walked him over to the stool, turned him around, and told him to step up on it, with his back to the wall. He offered no resistance.

"Hands up, high as they'll go."

Still he did not fight against the inevitable. Nor did he try to cheat by bending his elbows a little, as many did. He reached up straight-armed and flipped the chain between his cuffs over the highest hook he could reach. Just two down from the top. He was tall. He was going to be taller.

But then he contemptuously kicked the stool away from under his feet, not waiting for his captors to do it. That was a piece of bravado Pottenger had never met before. Good, good! He was going to put up a fight. The easy ones were no fun.

"Now gag him."

Dalton reached up under the bag and pushed a rag in the prisoner's mouth. He removed the bag and secured the gag with a cloth binding.

"I have work to do, sonny. I'll leave you up there for an hour or two. Sure you won't change your mind first?"

The kid just shook his head, but his eyes were wide with fear. The traitors were always surprised at how much pain such a simple device could cause. Not just in the hands and wrists, but all down the arms, through the chest, and down into the belly, a fierce, biting pain. It would only get worse. Even if he had practiced back at witch school in Gaudry, that wouldn't help, because now came the realization that this time there was no magic word to make it stop. They were doing this to him deliberately, and they were going to keep doing it until he did what they said. His hands had swollen into bright red gloves already.

This one was going to do well. He was young. He was lean and sinewy, and that type endured the longest. Pottenger watched with a visceral joy, silently counting. Right on cue, he saw the tears spring to the prisoner's eyes. None of them could block that reflex.

"How long do you need, lad? Before we raise the stakes, I mean. One hour or two?"

Woodbridge could not answer and did not even try. Pottenger laughed and patted his cheek. "Hang on, sonny! You're doing fine so far."

He shuffled out, leaving Dalton on watch. He went around the corner to Shipley at his spyhole. Dalton was sitting on the stool, lighting his pipe.

"Fetch the water buckets. After that, one of you in there, one out here, every second! Get to him the moment he faints. If he dies, I'll hang you in his place and forget you, understand?"

Nothing more would happen tonight. This was just a warm-up for tomorrow. Warden Pottenger went down to the street and around the corner to the handy neighborhood brothel. When a man's got a good thing going, he might as well put it to use.

CHAPTER 6

MADELINE WOODBRIDGE WAS MARRIED TO SAMUEL STROUD by Father Silas Fage, because hierarchs like Garrett Uptree rarely officiated at commoners' rites, and never at bastards'. The earl donated the ring as his wedding gift to the happy couple. The ring was gold, and everyone watched carefully to see how Maddy would react. Fortunately, her talent was so small that gold hardly bothered her. It felt warm, but not unpleasantly so, and Wisdom Edith had taught her that a salve of crushed nettles would counter even that small reaction before it became an affliction.

The visitors were assigned rooms for the night. There was a small supper for the Woodbridges, the Strouds, and the earl. Being no relation to Sam, the countess did not attend. It did not last long, because the groom was showing unmistakable signs of impatience and declined claret and cigars after.

On her mother's advice, Maddy had drunk far too much wine and heard herself giggling childishly as her husband carried her upstairs. Any bride must have fears on her wedding night, but Maddy had an unusual one.

According to Wisdom Edith, she was blessed with the gift of inspiration, meaning that she could inspire specific emotions in other people. If properly applied, that could make for a very successful deflowering. On the other hand, were she to panic and chill her bridegroom to a snowman, then the traditional ceremony would not be anything like a success.

Sam asked if she wanted the light on or off. She told him he was in charge, so he left the light on and took his clothes off. She congratulated him on having a lot more hairs on his chest now than he had two years ago. He had more of something else than she had expected, too. But he did nice things with her breasts, and she didn't try to discourage him. He seemed to find the action satisfactory, because he pounded up and down like a blacksmith for a few minutes and then went into a sort of epileptic fit, before collapsing altogether.

She felt somewhat battered...used...more surprised than anything.

"You all right?" she asked.

"All right? God's balls, woman, you're a ride and a half!"

Whatever that meant, it must be acceptable. He promised to do it all again, but insisted on having a rest first.

❧

Edgar and Agnes sought comfort in each other's arms, as they had done for a quarter of a century.

"Did we do right, love?" she whispered in the dark.

There was a noticeable pause before he replied.

"We had no choice. With Rollo as hostage, those two can do as they will with us. I was very proud of Maddy. You'd have thought from the way she handled the situation that he was the man of her dreams."

He might have been the boy of her dreams once, Agnes thought.

"I think she was just relieved that he wasn't a total stranger," she said.

"I pray that she will be happy with such a lecher. She wasn't the only one he was after, you know."

Agnes had always suspected that the fault was not Sam's, that the girls ran after him. She did not say so, but her husband seemed to guess her thoughts, as he so often did.

"Was she leading him on that day?"

"Flirting a little, I expect. Adolescents do that—so I'm told."

"Then I was being unfair when I dismissed him and am being punished for my sin."

"Or we are being blessed with a healthy son-in-law and Rollo is safe. The Uptrees will keep their word, won't they?" She despised the plea for reassurance in her voice.

"Why would they not, after going to all this trouble? All men have some good in them, wife. Those two wouldn't have risen as high as they have if they were not men of their word."

Just from the timbre of his voice, Agnes knew that he did not believe what he was saying. Those two wouldn't have risen as high as they had if they were not utterly ruthless. There was probably worse to come.

Meanwhile, Osborn Uptree was treating Garrett to a very special cigar and some exquisite century-old brandy in his private office. Beyond the big windows, moonlight made the blossom trees glow like molten silver. Indoors, the chairs were comfortable, the lamplight soft, and the ambience precious.

"I am relieved," the hierarch said, "that you did not actually commit us to admitting our family relationship to the Woodbridge heretic. The possibility of doing so was all."

"Heaven forbid! You shame me to suggest it. I'd have had to acknowledge that Stroud ape as one of mine."

"He isn't?"

The earl laughed and blew a careful smoke ring. "I doubt it. It's possible, but I recall the slut as being much too easy to be habit-forming. I opened the door, but after me it was never locked."

Garrett blew smoke. "So what happens next? Or am I happier not knowing?"

"'Prophecy is vain and an insult to the Lord,' saith the Teacher. Do I have that right? I might ask Father Dampier's opinion. He's in the neighborhood, or will be shortly." To be exact, he was due to arrive in Stonebridge that very evening.

"Ah, the doughty Rafe Dampier! He followed up on your note, then?"

"Like a dog after a rat!" said the earl.

"An apt simile. I trust my contribution will not go unrewarded?"

That had been the plan, but clearly an amendment would be required.

"Of course. When have I ever failed to be generous?"

"Whenever you could get away with it."

The earl chuckled and raised his glass. "Death to heretics!"

Garret clinked it with his own. "Amen."

⁓

When Sir Ezechiel Pottenger returned to Swine Hall after a couple of happy hours and a few drinks, Dalton was at the spyhole and Shipley inside on the stool, puffing his pipe. Four buckets of water stood ready to revive the prisoner as soon as he fainted; lanterns swayed overhead on their chains. The heretic was right where he should be.

"Anything happen?"

"No sir. Just hangs there, lovely as a picture."

The spyholes were glazed and soundproof, so prisoners could not hear orders and guards could neither eavesdrop on interrogations nor be subverted by demonic commands.

"Then let's go in and admire our art."

Woodbridge's faced turned to the door as the warden entered. His hands were huge, and what could be seen of his face was ashen under the black stubble. There was a puddle of urine a few inches below his toes.

"Ready to talk yet?" Pottenger asked, praying that the answer was no.

The prisoner shook his head.

"Get him down, lads. We honest men have to sleep."

Dalton put the stool between the dangling feet. With an effort, Woodbridge managed to stand on it, but he couldn't free himself. Dalton steadied him while Shipley lifted the manacle chain off the hook with the end of his nightstick.

They caught him between them and more or less carried him over to the straw, where he tumbled into a heap. They went through the standard routine of blindfolding him before they removed the gag. Then Dalton held the water bottle so he could drink.

The warden examined his hands, grossly swollen with pooled blood, and the wrists burned by the gold. "Don't want these sores to fester. Shipley, go get some salt to sweeten them. How d'you feel, lad?" he asked the prisoner.

"How...," the prisoner croaked. He coughed and finally managed to say, "How do you think I feel, turd?"

"Strung up. Well, you've had the first hour. Now get yourself a good night's sleep. Hard day ahead tomorrow. We'll make an early start, but you do get twenty minutes' downtime for dinner, so you'll have that to look forward to. Sweet dreams."

CHAPTER 7

NEXT MORNING THE WOODBRIDGES RODE HOME TO THE manor with their escort. For the first part of the way they were accompanied by the Strouds, their daughter and new-hatched son-in-law.

Edgar needed time to lick his wounds. Never had he felt so humiliated, so impotent in the face of injustice. Many fine, ethical people belonged to the Church of the Light, but the Exalted Garrett Uptree wasn't one of them. Nor was Silas Fage, who had been a smarmy little poacher forty years ago and was a mean little hypocrite now. Earl Uptree would have been hanged for theft years ago had he been a commoner. The brothers were as trustworthy as thin ice on a millpond, and only a moron would believe that they were going to do anything to help Rollo.

Edgar had never claimed to be a saint, but he gave generously to the Church of the Blessed in Stonebridge and remained true to the faith of his ancestors in private. He tried to be a good husband, father, and employer. Inheriting wealth was no achievement to brag of, but Woodbridge Manor had prospered under his guidance.

Now the best part of it had been stolen from him on the pretense of ransoming his son. Mother alone knew what sort of a mess that quarry worker would make of Beaconbeck.

He would need time to accept this new relationship, a lot of time. Certainly the Stroud boy was a splendid male animal for stud purposes, but Maddy would need more than that in a man. Socially, he was several levels below her, which mattered a lot. Women who thought they could civilize a rough bridegroom into a polished husband were always disappointed. Furthermore, he was young enough to be selfish and inconsiderate. Maddy was clearly not as comfortable as she normally was on horseback, suggesting that Sam had been making ample use of his marital rights in the night.

The one faint thread of hope Edgar could perceive in the gloom was too fragile to use to try to comfort Agnes. But even if the Uptrees did break their word and let Rollo die, and even if the resulting persecution branded the rest of the Woodbridge family as traitors and heretics, so that church or state could seize their possessions and drive them out into the woods to starve, Maddy at least should survive. She was a Stroud now and would be supported by her newly wealthy husband. Part of the family holdings would endure, so Maddy would be able to help her destitute parents. If her husband let her, that was.

In his heart, Edgar had no hope at all that the Uptrees were being honest in promising to speak up for Rollo. The earl had just coerced the Woodbridges into donating a fortune to one of his many by-blows. That was all, but even that did not ring true as an explanation. That human goat had dozens of offspring and had never shown interest in any of them. If Sam was a favorite son, why had he been left hammering in a quarry all these years? There was some other game in progress. Edgar just hadn't worked it out yet was all.

Crossing from Norcaster lands to Beaconbeck was painful in countless ways. He loved every tree and field there. He was saying good-bye to the best part of lands that had been in his family for generations. Married women could not own property, so Beaconbeck now belonged to Sam the quarryman, miraculously transformed into Samuel Stroud, gentleman. Only if he died childless (and the thought was disgustingly tempting, but not to be considered) would title revert to his widow.

The farm manager was old Pete Weeley, who had been a Woodbridge hand since before Edgar was born. He and his wife were both crippled by joint pain now, and his duties were little more than settling fights and seeing the cows were brought in for milking. He and Sam must have clashed in the past, because Pete failed to offer congratulations, and Sam brusquely announced that he would be needing the house now, meaning right now. Edgar intervened to say that he had an empty cottage at the manor—which was not true and would need tactful arranging—and he would send some men and a cart down to help Weeley and his wife move. Worst of all was saying good-bye to Maddy. She suggested hopefully that she should come back to the manor to pack. Sam said brusquely that Polly could see to that, almost as if he wanted to hustle his wife into their own bedroom as soon as possible to exercise those marital rights some more.

Agnes was damp-eyed.

Maddy laughed bravely and reminded everyone that Beaconbeck was hardly the far end of the world; they could still see each other every day. Edgar agreed and suggested he must go now; he had work to do when he got home. In fact, he had noticed a raven stalking around aimlessly on the trail they must take, and that was a cue to hurry. He almost had to drag Agnes away.

Edgar forced the problem out of his mind and concentrated on business, looking around at the lambing and the spring plowing.

Not far from the manor house, their approach was noted, and a man on horseback came galloping across the pasture to intercept them. Although the Mother had not blessed the Woodbridges' middle son with occult talent, she had been generous with horsemanship. Even at a distance Henry was recognizable as one of the finest riders in the county. Moreover, his hunting dog, Bounder, was leaping along in the lead. Edgar signaled for the company to halt and rode forward alone to hear the news. That was his plan, but Agnes came with him.

"It's Bram!" Henry barked, reining in. His face was flushed, although anger was rare for him. "I was showing him how to put Charger through his paces when that accursed pup of his took off like a…like a crazy pup. Bram went after him on Charger, yelling. By the time I ran and got a horse to follow them, they'd totally vanished. And this useless mutt seems to have forgotten everything he ever knew about tracking." Bounder had flopped down on the grass to pant. His gaping jaws and lolling tongue suggested an imbecile grin.

Anxious to organize a search party, Henry glanced hopefully at his parents' escort. There stood most of the manor's horses.

A raven flew overhead, heading toward the manor. Edgar relaxed.

"I think Brat will be fine," he said. The fact that Henry had reverted to calling the family imp by his real name just showed how worried he was. "That pup is more than just a pup."

"Already?" Henry said, incredulously. "Already for him I mean? Are you sure, sir? He's just a baby!"

Edgar shivered, as if a cloud had passed over the sun or someone had walked on his grave. He wondered why. "I have it on good authority that we need not worry about Brat. Don't be surprised if he's at home when we get there."

Agnes was nodding.

Henry, who had no more talent than she did but less experience of living with a gifted man, shot her an annoyed glance, but did not argue. "Where's Maddy?"

Agnes told him, grim faced.

He did not react with rage, as Edgar expected—rage that his sister had been forced to marry beneath her station, and to a bastard at that. That would be the normal fraternal reaction among his peers.

"She had a terrific crush on Stroud two years ago," Henry said. "He's more than just beef and blue eyes. I think she'll manage him." Although that was a strange appraisal, it seemed to console his mother. Perhaps that was all it was meant to do.

"I need a bucketful of ale," Edgar announced. He waved for the escort to follow, and led the way home.

He did not call for a drink when he arrived, though. He handed his reins to a groom and headed indoors and upstairs to the bedchamber he had shared with Agnes for so long. She knew what he was planning and did not follow. Not even the love of his life must interfere when a man consulted his familiar.

The casement stood open. Edgar put a chair before it and sat down. The raven soared down and landed on the sill. It inspected him with an eye as bright as a star.

"I couldn't get away sooner," he said, aware that he was apologizing to a scavenger, a carrion eater.

Corbin nodded.

"Brat is safe?"

Nod.

Relief! "Is Rollo safe?"

Corbin glanced at the tapestry, the ewer, the door…in effect, he was shaking his head: *No.*

Despair. "Will the Uptrees play fair?"

No.

"Will Rollo be tortured?"

Yes.

"Will he die?"

Corbin shifted from foot to foot, meaning that this was a stupid question. *All men die.* But then he signaled, *No.* Or perhaps that now meant, *Probably not.* The Mother might not have decided yet.

"Will Maddy be happy?"

Another stupid question. Meaning, *Mortals are happy sometimes, unhappy other times. This is life, idiot.* Then a nod.

Edgar had his answers. They were not promises, but even an uncertain grasp on the future was more guidance than most men were given. He should be grateful. He finished with a prayer a visiting missionary had suggested once, many years ago: "I love and serve the Mother of us all; I will trust her to cherish me when I die, and will do as she commands until that day comes. Just show me what she wants of me."

Corbin turned himself around, one foot at a time. He spread his wings, flapped, launched, and vanished out the window. *Nothing.*

Edgar went downstairs to tell Agnes and Henry that Brat was safe, Rollo would probably live, and Maddy would be as happy as a mortal could reasonably expect. Meanwhile, they should enjoy life.

CHAPTER 8

THE COTTAGE BARELY DESERVED THE NAME. EVEN "HOVEL" would have flattered it. Whether it had always stood in the forest or the forest had grown up around it had long been forgotten, while sheer age had reduced it to a hollow mound of green turf. It had never had windows or a chimney. In bad weather a tattered animal hide covered the hole that served as a door, and smoke from the fire went out through whichever cracks the wind chose not to enter. Some winter soon it would collapse completely and serve as a grave for its inhabitants, if any.

For much of the year overhanging trees kept the rain at bay, and the cottage was barely visible in the shrubbery of the tiny clearing. Early in spring, though, before the trees dressed for summer, the sun shone on it. It shone for the especial benefit of a black cat asleep on a rough plank bench outside the entrance. The cat lay on its side, unmindful of a frenetic woodpecker and some mumbling doves in the neighborhood.

Then the cat raised its head and looked at the path that was the only way in through the brambles and thickets.

It was just wide enough for people walking in single file, but would be a challenge for men on horseback, almost as if the forest had planned it that way. A very young black dog came limping wearily along this very private road. It stopped some distance away to regard the cat. Then it raised its tail enough to display a small wag. The cat put its head back where it had been and resumed its nap. The dog continued into the clearing as if it had just been cleared through security.

A woman crept out from the cottage and put her fists on her hips, the better to regard the visitor. She wore a threadbare and much-patched brown wrap, wooden shoes, and a green cloth around her head to hide her skimpy white hair. The dog sat on its haunches and let its tongue hang out.

"So who are you, eh?" she said, not expecting an answer but being a type of biped that had a constant need to chatter. She hobbled over to the well, which was merely a mossy barrel, which someone had three-quarters buried in the damp ground, after knocking a few holes in the bottom and adding some sand to filter the flow. She took out the dipper and held it low for her guest. The dog drank noisily and long. He looked up hopefully, and she refilled the dipper.

She was very old. Her father's father had been able to remember hearing the Teacher speak. Even her wrinkles had wrinkles, she liked to say, and her face had caved in where teeth had once been. Her nose had always been too big, alas, and now it seemed even bigger, as if all the rest of her had shrunk. She had a hump and sore knees, and yet she could still walk a full day when she had to.

"Come a long way, eh?" When the dog had slaked his thirst, she dropped the dipper back in the barrel. "Better let me have a look at those paws, young fellow."

The dog lay down to offer a pink belly suitable for tickling. She tickled it as she examined each paw in turn. The cat came awake to stare disapprovingly at this betrayal. No, it was studying the path again. The pup rolled over to do the same, tail twitching. The forest might have planned on hindering men on horses, but it had overlooked the case of a boy on a pony. Both looked as tired as the dog.

The boy slid to the ground and led his steed across to the watering hole. "Are you Wisdom Edith?" He reached for the dipper.

"No, but this is her house. She had to go away for a few days, so I'm looking after the place for her. I'm Wisdom Frieda."

"I'm Bram; most people call me Brat." He was about eleven or twelve. He had a cherubic face and jet-black curls. And a jet-black dog.

He drank, replaced the dipper, and studied the hovel for a moment. He smiled. "Maddy told me it was more a burrow than a castle. You got a bucket, Wisdom? Charger can't reach down there."

She lifted the bucket down from its perch in the tree. It was made of leather, with a braided leather handle. Black hair, black dog, and someone called Maddy? Edith had listed Madeline Woodbridge as a likely visitor during her absence. The Children of the Mother in Albi were all atwitter about a coming missionary named Rollo Woodbridge. So Frieda's young visitor was business, whether he knew it or not, and possibly very serious business.

Brat scooped up water in the bucket, which he then held so Charger could drink. "Stupid dog! He ran away."

"Maybe he's not stupid. Maybe he wanted to lead you here."

He pinned her with the gimlet stare only a preadolescent boy could achieve. His eyes were a startling blue. "Why?"

"Well he can't tell you in words. You'll have to learn to ask him questions and understand his answers. Dogs talk with their tails, you know. Wag means happy. Curl under means sorry, don't hurt me, I'm scared, things like that."

Brat's face brightened. "And head down, butt up, means chase me! No, you can't have more yet." That was addressed to the pony. "Henry says they mustn't drink too much when they're hot. I'd better give him a rubdown," he said judiciously. "Smut, did you mean to bring me here?"

The pup seemed to know his name already. He wagged vigorously and panted.

"Are you going to lead me home again?"

The dog lay down and put its head on its paws. That settled it for Frieda—this was no ordinary mutt.

"Brat," Frieda said, "how long have you…" People didn't own their spirit guides. Often it felt as if the guides owned them. "How long have you and Smut been friends?"

"Since yesterday. He just appeared and wanted to play with me."

Worse and worse! "You must be hungry." Always a safe bet with boys. "You give Charger his rubdown while I get some food ready. I expect Maddy will come here looking for you." Or just to ask the wisdom where he'd gone. Edith had a great locating talent; she was famous for it. That might be why the Mother had ordered her to go to Weypool.

"Maddy can't. She's gone to Norcaster with Squire and Mom. Went to see some stupid lord."

Mother, preserve us! The Mother's hand was certainly visible here.

"I'll get dinner," Frieda said and disappeared into Edith's hovel.

She'd been thinking only that morning that she had far too much food in the crocks that together served as her larder. Now she suspected Famine Himself had just ridden in to relieve her of that problem. She had some slender spring onions, a great treat, and dandelion leaves she had picked fresh that morning, and a slab of salt pork the girl with the sore back had brought yesterday, and a trout from the skinny man with the tapeworm. The trout was off already, but Smut would appreciate it. So pork, cheese, bread, and a salad with raw pigeon egg dressing. King Ethan himself would dine no better.

She peeked out the doorway. Brat was rubbing down his pony with some wild oat straw he had collected. He was doing a workmanlike job, yet his courteous manners showed that he was no mere hostler's son. He had been well trained; however high his rank, a good horseman must know how to care for horses. She ducked out—the lintel was low even for her—and presented Smut with his fish.

Tail-wagging time.

Brat looked around and said, "Don't feed him!"

"Why not?" Most of the fish had gone already.

"I don't know the way home. If he's hungry, he might lead me back to where he was fed yesterday."

That was good thinking for a lad of his years, but he wasn't going anywhere until Wisdom Frieda knew the rest of the story. "Too late already."

She went back to fetch the bowls and laid claim to the bench, which was too small for two. Brat wasn't bothered. He gave his pony another drink, then told it to go eat, and happily dropped cross-legged in the long grass beside Frieda to make the larger portion vanish.

"How'm I going to get home?" he asked with his mouth full.

"Wait till somebody comes to ask Wisdom Edith where you are. They'll take you home."

He grinned at the thought, then turned solemn again. "Henry will be rutting!" He clearly meant "mad" and had no idea of the term's real meaning. Frieda enjoyed a silent laugh.

"Charger needs a rest, anyway. And so does Smut."

He nodded at that—good excuse!

In a few minutes he laid down the bowl, licked his fingers, and thanked her for the meal. Only gentle-born Albiurns went in for thanking. Frieda's greatest talent had always been to recognize the voice of the Mother. She had made a lifetime career out of delivering instructions to those whose senses were less acute. She had thought she had been sent here to tell Edith she was wanted in Weypool. Now she wondered if the main reason had been to put her here instead of Edith when Brat Woodbridge came calling.

The Church of the Light was built like a mountain with the Hierarchy at the top and deacons and lay brethren at the base. Perhaps the Church of the Mother had been structured like that in Albi once, but now it was shattered and scattered. The wise women, and a few wise men, lived solitary lives and relied on their flocks' discretion to keep their existence secret. They hid under rocks like beetles, risking arrest and death if they were discovered, although most priests were tolerant and would start with a warning. Then the wisdom would leave, and people would pine without her care. After a few years, another of the wise would move in to fill the vacancy.

There were still many old-style faithful to support them in secret, of course. There were also the tinkers, all of whom had been born in a cart and claimed their ancestors had, back to the Mother of All herself. They were Earth worshipers to the last man or woman. The priests never seemed to bother them, although landowners suspected them of stealing horses and ran them off.

Frieda had never known a guide assigned to a child as young as Brat, not even old enough to attend a bonding circle. How much did he know? Had he been serious when he called his dog stupid and claimed he had been trying to recapture it? Or had he consciously followed his guide's lead as any experienced adept would? If he hadn't yet been warned of the danger of discussing such things with strangers, then he must be warned now.

A growl jerked her out of her reverie. The pony was doing what horses do best: eating. Its saddle and other tack lay where Brat had piled it, but the grass in the clearing was much better than anything growing under the trees, so Charger should not be tempted to go anywhere. Brat, she now realized, had curled up in the sunlit grass beside his dog and gone straight to sleep also. The two of them together must have been a charming picture she had missed.

But the growl had come from Smut. He had raised his head and was making strenuous efforts to prick up both ears at the same time. His ruff was up. No approaching intruder had alerted him, though. Once he managed to gather all four legs under him, he began to creep forward, lower even than usual to the ground, stalking the pony. Frieda watched in delight, much taken by the difference in their sizes.

Charger paid no attention until something made a snapping noise at his rear. He whipped his head up in alarm. Smut feinted again, puppy teeth bared. *Snarl!* Charger tried to kick, futilely. Again the would-be timber wolf rushed in to attack. Charger snorted in annoyance and walked away. He had barely put his head down to seize another tasty mouthful of spring grass before his tormenter came at him again, growling and yelping viciously. The pony kicked up his heels a couple of times in annoyance, but nothing helped. In a few minutes Charger was being seen off smartly along the path by a raging terror of black fluff.

"Smut!" Brat wailed, sitting up. "What's he doing, Wisdom?"

"He's making sure you stay here, Master Brat."

His head whipped around on its slender neck. He stared up at her for a moment before he cautiously said, "Why?"

"You know what a guide is?"

"Sort of."

Felix came stalking out of the cottage and stretched. Then he went to Brat and rubbed against him. The boy stroked him. He did know! His face had turned white, but he still wasn't talking.

"You can trust me; I'm a wisdom. Wisdom Edith told me that Maddy came to her for lessons. The priests have another name for our guides."

"What's that?" *He* was testing *her*!

"Familiars. Felix is mine."

He broke a smile as wide and shiny as the Spote River in spate. "You're saying Smut is my *guide*? I got a guide like Squire's raven? Like Maddy's mouse?"

Frieda nodded, a lump in her throat. If he had bonded a guide as good as Smut at eleven, he was going to be a legendary adept at twenty. She wished she could be around to see.

"Rollo has a peregrine! He carries her without a glove sometimes! I remember."

A panting puppy trotted back into the clearing, looking satisfied. *So much for that brute...*

"Smut!" his ward shouted. "You know you're my *guide*?"

The pup hurtled forward and hit him like a cannonball, throwing him over on his back. Little Lost Boy squealed with glee as his guide vigorously washed his face for him.

CHAPTER 9

ROLLO SLEPT LITTLE, WHICH WAS NORMAL SINCE HIS capture. The agony in his wrists persisted. It did not compare with what he had suffered while he hung on the wall, but it was still the biggest thing in the world. He had no use of his hands, even to scratch his innumerable fleabites. A few days of this treatment and the loss would be permanent. That fear was part of the treatment, of course. What use was a man without hands?

How long could he hold out? He could not tell his captors what they wanted to know, because the questions they were asking had no answers. He had not been sent to meet someone, or directed to a safe house somewhere, as they assumed. He could volunteer other information, likely just as valuable to them as what they sought, but they would just go back to asking the same things again. Then he would have betrayed his faith and his superiors' trust and gained nothing.

The Mother had been generous with her gifts to Rollo Woodbridge, but none of his talents could help him out of his present fix. Pottenger knew all about the gift of mastery, obviously, which is why he posted extra guards outside when he entered the cell, and why the prisoner was always either blindfolded or gagged when anyone else was present. Rollo could bind one person, but not two at the same time, unless they were standing very close together. They knew that. By the time he had mastered Pottenger, a guard would have cracked his skull.

What he wanted more than anything just then was the talent they called jiggling. He had met only two people who could jiggle—a wisdom in Albi and a sister at Gaudry, in Xennia. Either of them could open locks with a glance. That would be a handy trick right now, to get the manacles off before the gold poison weakened him any further.

Unable to sleep, he leaned back against the cold stone wall and stared at the bleak horror of his cell. The floor had not been cleaned in years. Cannonballs would bounce off that ironbound door. The lack of darkness since his capture had been a surprising torment, until this new torture taught him what pain could be. He had lived three years in Gaudry, where the land itself was sacred to the Mother, a place of springs, small lakes, and hummocky little hills, all heavily wooded. Buildings there were small and inconspicuous. It was a shady place, quiet glades overhung everywhere by trees and rocks, a place where sunlight was allowed to dapple and glint and beam, made more lovely by the discipline. The Church of the Light worshiped the crude glare of emptiness, but that was shunned in Gaudry. When Rollo thought of his years there, he shamed himself by weeping. Then he lay down and turned his face to the wall, for he knew that he was watched at all times.

He had been warned what would happen. He had been told about the infamous Sir Ezechiel Pottenger. The sisters had even offered to let him sample the monster's favorite torment, the handcuffs and the hook. He had refused, frightened that it would weaken his will to serve the goddess. His imagination had fallen woefully short of reality. He had not realized that men could hate enough to do such things to their fellows.

He had known he would be captured. His purpose had been to be captured. *Oh, Holy Mother, how long must I hold out? Give me strength to endure.*

The warden was true to his promise of an early start. The sky overhead was barely blue yet, and the slowly gyrating lanterns still burned. Rollo curled up small on his straw when he heard the lock and bolts clatter. First came the deaf dwarf, of course, to put the bag over his head. Then the tread of several men.

When Pottenger spoke he was standing close, right above the prisoner. "Thought it over? Ready to talk yet?"

Rollo fought down his terror. "Go home and take your mother for a run."

The warden spat. "If that's the best you can do, then this shouldn't take too long. Hang him, boys."

He could not even stand unaided, so they treated him like a side of beef, dragging him across the cell and hanging him on his hook. They gagged him and removed the blindfold. They kicked the stool away. *Oh, Goddess!* It was worse, worse than ever. He sobbed.

"Good, good! Start singing, little bird. Soon you'll sing my song." Pottenger turned on his heel. "You know the drill. Let me know when he wants to talk, or the second time he faints." Out he went.

❧

The prelate's grotto was deeply shadowed, dark even to him, whose night vision would put an owl to shame. He stopped a few paces away from her and bowed his head. No mortal was accorded greater respect than that in Gaudry. Kneeling was only for the Mother herself, in her shrines. The air was scented with loam, water trickled, and there was birdsong nearby.

The prelate was very old, a tiny, dumpy woman, rarely seen outside this, her lair. Her name had been forgotten. Within Gaudry she was simply "the prelate." If anyone outside ever needed to mention her, she was "Prelate Gaudry." There was also an overall Arch-Prelate Xennia, and, at least in theory, there was still a Prelate Albi.

She was sitting, cross-legged, a human embodiment of her goddess. The Earth Mother was always depicted as a buxom woman with a loving smile, but when the prelate spoke, her voice was flat and joyless.

"Sit, child."

Rollo folded his long legs and settled on the sandy floor, crossing his hands in his lap. He waited patiently to hear why he had been summoned. Life in Gaudry proceeded at its own unhurried pace. He would sit there quite happily for an hour if necessary, soaking in peace through his skin.

"Dear Rollo," she whispered, "I am ashamed to speak what I must say. It is the Mother's will that in a few days you leave here, returning to Albi to perform your internship."

75

He knew that. He had been given his instructions. "I am eager and ready." He would miss the serenity he had found here more than anything.

"You are brave. You know what will happen if you are caught."

"I do not intend to be caught, Mother."

The old woman sighed. "Lad, we want you to be caught."

Incredibly, the pain he had thought intolerable kept growing steadily worse. He muttered prayers until the guard threatened to stuff his mouth with straw. After that he prayed silently. Sometimes he heard himself weeping. He could move his legs and his feet, if he did so gently, not jolting his wrists. Every other part of him burned with agony: lungs, belly, joints. He wet himself again, and fouled himself, but in Swine Hall that was normal.

When he asked for water, the guard made him beg for it. The rest of the time the man sat and smoked. Sometimes he mocked, but mostly he just smiled at the prisoner on the wall.

Rollo would get a break at noon. Pottenger had promised. He must at least wait for that. He hadn't been anywhere near a full day on the hook yet.

"We have a traitor amongst us," the prelate said. "The Mother will not name names, saying only that we must find the culprit for ourselves. So we do know that there is only one. The safe houses in Albi are betrayed when a missionary is captured and made to

*talk, but they are not being betrayed from here, and that elimin-
ates many people."*

*Right from his arrival at Perse, Rollo had excelled. He out-
shone his peers until he prayed to be given humility and a sincere
acceptance that his gifts were not of his own making. He knew
everything there was to be known about the powers the Mother
gave her Children. Nobody received all the talents, but he knew
those he had been given in abundance, and those he lacked at all
or had only in traces. He could heal as well as any. An ointment
spread by his fingers cured faster, a bandage he wrapped healed
faster, and his touch alone could often banish pain. He could see
in the dark, move more quietly than a shadow. He had no insight,
but he was surprised that the sisters who did had not unveiled
the spy. The best of them could tell a bad egg just by looking
at it.*

*He did not wish to be bait on a hook. He felt entitled to ask,
"Can you not in-see the traitor?"*

*"The traitor uses a talent given by the Mother to blind our
insight."*

*Silence then, perhaps a reproach for his interruption. "Please
forgive me and continue, ma'am."*

*"It is our arriving interns who are being caught too often," she
said. "Some are arrested when they disembark, some are followed
to a safe house. Always they are tortured into betraying everyone
and everything they know."*

Rollo shivered at the memory. Back then he had felt more
contempt than pity for those who failed to resist to the
death. He did not think that way now. He felt that Swine

Hall was falling down, that the wall was tilting and taking him with it…darkness at last…

A bucketful of cold water hit him. He gasped and jolted great spasms of pain down his arms and through into his gut. Then another bucket. He blinked blearily at the guard about to hurl another.

"I'm back!" he mumbled. "No more."

"You're sure of that, are you?" The man set the bucket down.

Very soon the other man came in to remove the empties and refill them. Which confirmed that there were spyholes, in case anyone had ever doubted.

That had been Faint Number One. He did not think Number Two could be far off. The sunshine from the skylight had reached the floor, so it must be almost noon. He could endure till then. He had lasted long enough now that another hour or so must be possible. He would decide after he had been given a break.

❧

"We send our Children by many different paths when they go back to Albi to ease the sufferings of the faithful. No matter which port we try, all seem to be equally compromised, so the treason does not happen somewhere on the journey. The traitor lurks farther upstream."

Meaning that Albi and its heretical Church of the Light had corrupted someone very high in Gaudry. That was a horrible thought.

"Four or five times a year, the council decides who is ready to go back," the prelate continued. Her voice was soft and almost

hypnotic in its sweetness. "But we do not determine when and where, so the culprit is not a member of the council. Another brother decides who shall go in which group, and roughly when. Two sisters study the gateway agents' reports and set up itineraries. Yet others prepare male and female baggage, but since both men and women are being betrayed, the traitor cannot be either of those. And so on. We have narrowed it down to one of three people."

As Rollo understood insight, it should have solved the remaining problem in a flash. An inseer should see two of those three people as shaded by the nuances of the Mother's gentle, forgiving love, and one of them stark with the pitiless absolutes of the Light.

"My insight is blocked," *the prelate whispered.* "But you have the most terrible of all her gifts. You have prescience."

Yes, he had prescience. A moment after he was arrested at the dock, Rollo had foreseen that he would be given to Sir Ezechiel Pottenger to torture. He had not known when, for his prescience had no depth. He foresaw only things that would happen to him, not other people, and never when, but they were as inevitable as death. Previsions happened rarely, which was a blessing, for otherwise he would quickly go out of his mind.

And now, dangling there on the wall in agony, he had another flash. He was going to break. He was going to talk. All this suffering was just stubbornness, for no one could resist indefinitely. As Pottenger predicted, he would tell all.

"*My prescience doesn't work very often,*" he protested. *Nor was prescience like sagacity. Sagacity distinguished between choices. Prescience was as inevitable as death, no choices allowed.*

"*I know that,*" the old lady said quietly. "*I don't expect you to pick out the poisoned chalice. But I am not without resources, and you are one of them. Everyone knows that you are our best in years. Even the missionaries already on station in Albi are eagerly waiting for Brother Rollo to come and join in the Mother's work. It is vital that you arrive safely.*"

That was chilling news, because the spy would have told the Church of the Light about him also. He could guess now how the terrible old lady might use that information.

"*You have been told many times,*" she whispered, "*that you will receive your travel instructions from Brother Nolan and no one else, that you will memorize them, and then burn the paper, telling no one. Brother Nolan writes the itinerary. Sister Eulalie uses it to send warnings to the agents who will find you a passage. Sister Anna supplies names and addresses in Albi. The traitor must be one of these three.*"

And this was where the sublime Rollo came into play, of course. Sly, cunning, old lady!

"*I sent for the one I suspect most, and pointed out that you are special. You, above all, must arrive safely, and yet the Albiurn officers will be especially eager to catch you. That person understood and agreed to arrange another itinerary for you, one that no one else would know about.*"

"*And did you spin the same web for the other two?*"

"*You are impertinent, child, but I will make allowances under the circumstances. The directions you were given yesterday are now canceled. Because they will never come into effect, they cannot* have given you any foreboding. I now give you new directions, which I have not opened. Only you and one other can know what is in this package. You may or may not foresee the ending, but prescience is not evidence enough. I know I may be sending you a terrible death, but you had almost certainly been betrayed already. We must both do our duty."

Dry-mouthed, he nodded. "I understand, ma'am."

"Here it is, then. I warn you, this was prepared by the one I think is the spy." She offered an envelope, barely visible in the gloom.

He took it. It felt like ice, or acid, or a child screaming in the night. It was a dagger in the heart.

"Prescience?" the prelate asked.

"Yes, ma'am. I will be arrested on the dock." Even knowing that, he must go through with it.

She sighed. "Then I guessed right. But I will not test the other two unless I hear that you have arrived safely. And I will find a way to delay all other departures until then."

Or until he was dead or as good as. Given a greatly superior pupil, as he was reputed to be, she had a strange way of using him in the deadly game of opposing churches. But if by sacrificing him she could ensure the safety of dozens of others in future, then it was clearly his duty to cooperate. He would, and he would be caught. Merciful Mother!

She said, "We shall put incriminating evidence in your baggage. Ignore any instructions that concern safe houses or contacts within Albi. If possible, do not even read them. If you are allowed ashore, head for Weypool. Anyone following you will arrest you before you have a chance to vanish into the great city. If you decide that you have escaped detection, your peregrine will guide you to *a safe house. But if your prescience says you will be captured, then it will be so."*

Then, appallingly, she chuckled.

"I would not do this if there were not a back door, my son."

CHAPTER 10

ROLLO WAS SLUMPED ON THE FLOOR AND SOAKING WET again. He must have fainted for a second time. They would not have unhooked him unless they had been scared he was going to die on them. One guard was holding a water bottle to his mouth, while another supported him. He was blindfolded, but his blindsight could just detect Pottenger standing behind them, scowling.

"You're stupid, boy," he said. "You are going to talk. Keep this up much longer and your hands will die."

Rollo gave him the foulest language he had ever heard uttered, although the warden must know much worse. It made him laugh.

"So there's still some spirit there. Good, good! It's early yet, but we'll count this as lunch break."

Rollo could not imagine eating anything. His lips were bitten ragged, and hours of being gagged had made his jaw ache. Yet when a mug of warm broth was put to his mouth, he swallowed and went on swallowing until it was gone.

"Got to keep your strength up," the warden said, puffing happily on his pipe. "Want some more?"

Either answer could be refused, so he said nothing.
"Time's up then. Hoist him, lads."

⸰⸰⸰

*"We never try to rescue anyone," the prelate said. "There are so
few of us and so many of them. We have always known we might
get one out, but after that the guards would be quadrupled, and
we would lose more people trying than we saved."*

*"I understand, ma'am." He had been told that on his first
day there.*

*"But I am not just putting you in harm's way, I am sending
you marching in through harm's front door. You are special, and
they know that you are special. So we are going to rescue you."*

"Is that wise, ma'am?"

*Again she ignored his impertinence. "I warn you that a rescue
will need organizing and must succeed at the first attempt. King
Ethan's officers do not report to us where they are taking you, so we
must first find you and then plan your breakout. I cannot promise
that you will not be tortured before we get to you."*

*So far his prescience had given him no details, just that he
would be arrested, nothing beyond that. Either the Mother had
not decided, or she would not tell him. Or there was nothing there
to foresee.*

*They sat in silence for a while. He savored the peace that he
was about to lose, probably forever. Very few missionaries ever
returned to Gaudry.*

*"And one other thing," the prelate whispered. "You carry with
you my curse on Ezechiel Pottenger. Do not loose it while you are
in their clutches, or they may slay you out of hand. The Mother
go with you, Rollo Woodbridge."*

Rollo fainted and was revived, fainted and was revived… he lost count. There was nothing in the world except pain.

"I don't give up, stupid," Pottenger said. "We stay here until you talk, all day and all night and all tomorrow. But I won't let you die. There is no easy way out."

As before, Rollo was gagged but not blindfolded. That small blessing puzzled him, but it might just be so that they could be sure he was still conscious.

Dalton and Shipley were back on duty. He had been hanging up here a whole day. The patch of sunlight had reached the far wall: rosy evening sunlight and the shadows of the bars. There was another shadow, too. Rollo stared at it stupidly. Gulls and crows and pigeons landed on the roof sometimes and peered in. But this bird was perched on a bar. Different sort of feet. That meant something, if he could think. It spread its wings, pointed, curved like a sickle.

Perry! It was time. Perry had come to tell him so.

Pottenger was sprawled back on the stool, working his way through a bottle of wine. The two guards were leaning against different walls, bored.

It was time to talk. The sense of relief was overwhelming; it brought tears to his eyes. He made the loudest noises he could manage and shook his head.

Pottenger smiled. He stood up, placed his bottle on the stool, and came close. "Ready to give up?"

"*Mmm…*" Vigorous nodding.

The warden reached up to untie the knot holding Rollo's gag. "Don't try anything, witch, or I'll have Dalton break your balls with his nightstick." He pulled the slimy rag out of Rollo's mouth and dropped it on the floor. "Now tell me a secret."

Rollo gasped and croaked. Pottenger fetched a water bottle and let him drink. "I'm waiting."

"Get me down."

"You can come down just as soon as I know you mean it. Let me hear something I don't know."

"I will curse you…if you don't…don't let me down."

Pottenger loosed a scornful guffaw, although one of the guards spread his hand in the warding sign of the Light.

"You'd better do better than that, sonny."

"You were…meant…to catch me," Rollo said, mumbling the words through scabbed lips.

"Oh, were we? Tell me something I can believe. Tell me the safe house you were going to."

"Don't know any…houses. My guide would take me."

"What guide?"

"Up there."

Pottenger looked up at the skylight and frowned.

"Tha's a peregrine, sir," Shipley said. "Never seen one in a city before. Or this late in the day. Must be lost?"

"So it's a peregrine. Boy, you still haven't told me anything I don't know. You're going to stay there until you do." He turned away to recover the gag.

Rollo struggled against panic. The pain must stop! He could bear no more. "There was…spy in Gaudry…gave himself away. Was…only one who knew I…come Clidgey in that caravan."

"Pig shit."

"And I'm going to be rescued, turd."

The warden studied him for a moment with narrowed eyes. "Oh, are you? Get him down."

They sat Rollo on the stool, and Pottenger brought the wine bottle. "Dalton, fetch the priests waiting downstairs so they can write down what he says. Warn the guards up here and down at the gate to be on the lookout for trouble. Shipley, keep watch outside in case this trash tries something."

Both jailers departed, locking the door. After giving the prisoner a few gulps of wine, the warden took a key from his belt and unlocked the manacles. He had to pry them out of the swollen flesh, and they took skin with them. Rollo thought he would faint again, but Pottenger slapped his face a few times and tipped more wine into his mouth, some of which he managed to swallow.

Perry had gone. Where was rescue? Rollo was at the end of his strength. They must come soon, or he would be too weak to help. Even now, he doubted he could walk unaided. And he had betrayed them after all, for now the guards were alerted. He had ruined everything.

The bolt on the door clicked. The lock rattled, as if someone unfamiliar with it was having trouble finding the right key. The warden heard, too, and turned to frown at the noise.

Rollo summoned the last of his strength. "Ezechiel!"

The warden looked right at him.

"Dream, Ezechiel. Dream of what you like best."

Pottenger straightened up and stood like a statue, staring into space with a vague smile on his ugly face. Proper mastery needed more work than that, and it would not hold a man like Pottenger for more than a few moments.

It did give the intruder time to open the door. To Rollo's amazement, two women burst in.

The one in front was large, elderly, and armed with a sword. She seemed familiar. The other was younger, slighter, and carried a jailer's staff and a bulky leather bag. They both wore nondescript ankle-length gowns, ragged and filthy, with matching scarves on their heads. He had seen many just like them around Swine Hall when was he was brought in, inmates or visitors. They gasped in horror at the sight of him.

"Can you walk?" the elder demanded. "Oh, Mother, your hands!"

"Up!" said the younger, going to his other side. They gripped his elbows and lifted him. Choking back screams at the pain in his shoulders, he stumbled along between them, half walking, half carried.

At the door, he said, "Wait!" He turned to look back at the warden, who was already starting to frown as he awoke from his trance. "Ezechiel Pottenger, I lay the curse of Prelate Gaudry upon you!"

Rollo just had time to hear Pottenger's first scream before he was hustled out into the corridor and the door was shut. He swayed as the younger of his rescuers let go of his arm while she locked the door. Then she gripped him again, and the trio staggered along to where Shipley stood before a glassed peephole, lost in his personal dream world. The younger woman returned his nightstick and his keys.

She said, "You will stay like that until someone else speaks to you. Then you will wake up. Do you understand?"

"Yes, ma'am."

The rescuers hurried Rollo along in the same direction as before. When they reached the stairs, lights and voices warned that men were already on their way up. Hope died then. He was trapped and the rescue had failed. But the women pushed open the door of a cell and dragged him inside. It was unoccupied and furnished with nothing but a cot. He made it that far, collapsed on it, and passed out.

CHAPTER 11

WHEN RAFE DAMPIER WAS FOURTEEN, THE LIGHT SHOWED him the road, the pathway of his life, and gave him two gifts to guide him. The first was a new voice. His childhood treble had been so unpleasantly squeaky that he had been mocked by his friends and rejected by the church choir. His manhood voice was one of resonance and astonishing power.

Soon after that came his mother's martyrdom. She pined with an unknown malady. The doctors tried poultices and herbs. The local priest prayed up a storm. Still she sank, weaker day by day. Then Rafe's father, ignorant divot, called in a so-called wisdom, a follower of the old ways. That repugnant, dirty old man spouted blasphemous appeals to his heretical Earth Mother and burned smelly things in a brazier. Appalled, Rafe ran from the house and took refuge in the village church, weeping and beseeching the Heavenly Father to spare his mother.

Hours later, as he trailed homeward, hungry and exhausted, he met his father in the street, leading a group of grieving neighbors to the church to pray. As that was the custom after a death, Rafe knew instantly that she had been gathered to the Father in Heaven.

"Fool!" he bellowed. "Heretic! You forsook the Light, now see what you have wrought."

When his father tried to reprimand him, Rafe shouted him down, quoting scripture to show that invoking devils was blasphemy against the Father and would be punished. He was very loud, and Troutwalk was a small place. Soon most of the population had gathered around to listen. Hemmed in, Dampier senior could do nothing but stand and fume under his son's tirade. And finally, Rafe, sweating and shaking in his passion, reached a climax and thunderously cursed him. His father dropped dead.

All the witnesses agreed that there had been a flash of light and a clap of thunder out of a clear sky. They fell on their faces and gave thanks for the miracle. Rafe Dampier's career was revealed for all to see. He saw that his mother had indeed given her life to lead him to righteousness, and ever afterward he kept the anniversary of her death holy, with prayer and fasting.

His father, heretic and backslider, was buried under a ditch, as the Teacher commanded in Verse 542 of the *Illuminations*. Rafe's mother's funeral was attended by half the county. Rafe was allowed to preach. Her pyre was barely cold before he was on his way to the seminary at Royal Rock, to be enrolled as the youngest novice in its history.

At seventeen he was granted the honor of speaking the welcome to the alumni at the opening of the summer convocation, which happened that year to be attended by no less than four of the ten hierarchs. Traditionally the most senior guest provided the theme, and Rafe was given Verse 66:

"If the teachers teach not and the leaders lead not, then the people shall scatter." Traditionally, the student so martyred stammered out three or four sentences and sat down. Rafe delivered an extempore, closely reasoned, two-hour sermon. Every hierarch present congratulated him afterward.

After an exhaustive interrogation on his beliefs, his theology was declared sound in every detail, and he was ordained by special decree, more than ten years below the minimum age for a priest. He rapidly became known for his inspirational preaching and his miracles. The Church quietly asked him to limit those to one every two years or so—it was important to maintain their rarity value, and too many might give rise to rumors that he had accepted a gift of demonic powers.

Now in his mid-thirties, Father Dampier was chief investigator for the Congregation of Conformity. That meant he was in charge of stamping out heresy, which usually involved stamping out heretics. The most common, of course, were the so-called wisdoms, but they bothered him much less than they had when he was younger. They were small-scale pests. Every village and back alley seemed to have one, but most were fakes, just crazed old women who gabbled nonsense and knew nothing. As his mother had learned, they did more harm than good. If Dampier and his men showed interest, then neighbors tended to hide them or warn them, but a lightly veiled threat to the local priest was usually enough to clean them out. They weren't worth more effort than that.

The constant seepage of missionaries in from Xennia was troubling, but the civil government had the means of dealing with those. When the Teacher had appointed Amos I as the first king of Albi, the last queen regnant, Ebba V, had fled the country. It amused the present King Clovis of Xennia to claim that his wife was descended from her, which meant that his sister-in-law must be rightful queen of Albi. That was nonsense, but convenient nonsense for both sides. The Albiurns could brand the missionaries coming from Gaudry as traitors as well as heretics. King Ethan's officials and security officers were constantly tracking them down, like terriers after rats, and all the Church need do was watch and make sure they were suitably dealt with. For his part, King Clovis could use the festering ill will to justify the upkeep of his oversized army.

Father Dampier's main targets were the native hypocrites, the secret heretics. Even after two hundred years, many still lurked in the shadows like fungus in an attic. They were the ones who sheltered the missionaries, supporting them with money and introductions, spinning webs of corruption across the face of Albi. Quite often they were wealthy, influential families whose pretense of uprightness concealed their underlying depravity. Either their servants and neighbors were deceived, or pretended to be, and so the evil spread like a stain: *Illuminations*, Verse 483.

The Congregation was helped in its work by complaints from the faithful. Although some whistle-blowers were motivated by spite or jealousy, many reported priests not doing enough to root out heresy in their parishes. Dampier saw to it that all such correspondence was carefully followed up and stern action taken when needed. Only in the most serious cases did he need to intervene personally. But one day a thick package arrived with a covering note from

Hierarch Uptree. The report His Holiness forwarded had been written by Earl Uptree of Norcaster, his brother, so its truth could not be questioned.

His Lordship drew the Congregation's attention to a scandalous situation in his county, an egregious breach of the laws on conformity. The man he accused was actually sheriff of the village of Stonebridge, as his father and grandfather had been before him. This sinner had either perjured himself when he took office or had somehow evaded the oath of faith and loyalty. Lord Uptree provided no less than seven affidavits describing demonic rites performed in a secret chapel, together with strong hints of missionaries being sheltered there in the past.

The culprit's very name condemned him: Woodbridge! A dangerous missionary heretic by that name had been apprehended entering the country only a few days earlier. Father Dampier requisitioned the best horse in the temple stables and raced up the north road to Norcaster. Lord Uptree graciously made him welcome and promised to cooperate in any way he could. As they sat on his terrace that very evening, puffing on excellent cigars, Dampier delicately pointed out that the case might require extreme measures.

"Violence?" His Lordship muttered with a frown. "I should have to report any rowdy behavior to the lord lieutenant of the county."

"Who is?"

"Me."

Father Dampier had learned to recognize such deliberate nonsense as what was called humor. He smiled appropriately. "Then you foresee no repercussions?"

"A lot of noisy outrage," Uptree said patiently. "I shall denounce villainous intruders disturbing our peaceable and law-abiding community. But since I shan't know who they were, I won't be able to do much about them, will I?"

"Blessed are the believers." Verse 78.

"There is one thing, though. My esteemed and exalted brother is coming to stay with me for a few days. An outburst of fervor while he is in the county could be embarrassing. Can we set a date about a week from now?"

Of course they could. Missionary Woodbridge was safely in jail and due to be put to the question very shortly. With the shoot cut off, it would be time to chop down the trunk and dig out the roots.

ⓒ⁓

The week passed slowly for Father Dampier. On the afternoon that Madeline Woodbridge married Samuel Stroud, he was back in Stonebridge in time to attend the sunset service. He sat at the rear of the church and disapproved of everything. The building was old and unimpressive, a typical stone barn thrown up after the groves burned, almost two hundred years ago. Father Snuggs was also old and unimpressive. Dampier made a mental note to have him replaced, if what was about to hit his parish didn't make him die of shock first. It was good to have someone expendable to blame if the need arose for a scapegoat.

After the service, Dampier introduced himself to Father Snuggs, agreed that the west window was very fine, accepted a night's lodging almost before it was offered, and announced that he would like to take the sunset service tomorrow, leaving no doubt that he would do so and Father Snuggs would announce it in the morning.

Soon after dawn, Hierarch Uptree and his escort rode anonymously through Stonebridge on their way back south. The time had come! Dampier spent the day on horseback, reconnoitering the countryside, especially the trail to Woodbridge Manor, which he had no trouble locating from the earl's description. It was farther from the church than he would have liked, for enthusiasm tended to flag when a march dragged on too long. No matter—the true believer took any difficulty as an incentive to try harder. The Heavenly Father would provide.

News of the famous preacher's presence spread through Stonebridge like a strong wind, and his reputation went with it. Most of the inhabitants decided it might be safer to show piety and attend the sunset service for once.

Even some strangers were noted wandering about the village: large, burly men. They were, of course, Dampier's assistants, stern and fervent in the rule of righteousness, handy with a cudgel.

Long before sunset the church was filled to capacity with every age from adolescence to senescence. The weather had been astonishingly warm for the time of year and by late afternoon was turning oppressively muggy. The heat in the church was oppressive, and no doubt that created the strange currents of excitement that many were to report later.

Dampier never planned a sermon in detail. He rarely even chose his text in advance, for he could trust the Lord to guide him. He sang along with the hymns; the choir was better than average among hayseed parishes he had known. When his time came, he mounted the steps to the pulpit filled with gratitude that he should be chosen to do the Father's work. As he paused to look over the congregation and allow them to look over him, he heard a rumble of distant thunder.

That was mildly worrisome. He must not become so carried away by his own preaching that he did not keep track of the weather. Nothing could dampen a parade so literally as a cloudburst. On the other hand, the thunder was clearly a sign to him to preach on one of his favorite texts, Verse 253: "He makes the sun to brighten your path by day, and at night he sends the lightning."

He waited for silence and then began to speak.

CHAPTER 12

Around sunset, Henry Woodbridge walked out the front door to where his father stood on the steps, puffing a long-stemmed clay pipe and contemplating the sky.

"Father?"

The squire did not turn. He used his pipe to point. "See those clouds over there? Sheet lightning! It's early in the year for thunder."

"Yes, sir."

The hint of reproof in his tone won him a sideways smile. "Troubled?"

"Yes."

"There's a raven perched on the roof."

"Ravens can fly."

"Spill it, Son. 'Pleasures shared are doubled, troubles shared are halved,' your grandsire used to say. He really was a windy old bore."

"Rollo's in jail, probably in Weypool. Brat's disappeared. Maddy's in Beaconbeck, being humped by a quarryman."

His father sighed. "If girls didn't enjoy being humped almost as much as boys enjoy humping, there wouldn't be so many of us around. Stroud's an ignorant laborer, I admit, but he's built like every maiden's dream. The first few weeks of that marriage ought to be berries and cream. It'll be when the music fades that there may be trouble. I think Maddy will be able to handle him, though." He sucked on the pipe. "Your mother's going to organize a proper wedding feast for them."

"There was a stranger riding around this morning, and I saw him again in the afternoon. Good horse."

Puff... "I noticed. A snooping priest if ever I saw one."

"Summoned by Earl Uptree?"

"You want to go and visit Guy Rowthorn? Break the news about Maddy?"

"I'd rather we all went." Henry let it spill out: "Father, Rollo's in fearful danger, possibly dead already. But they may have made him say anything, true or false. The truth would be dangerous enough. I'm scared that the Mother has moved Brat and Maddy to safety."

His father studied him. "And left us here? This isn't the first time you've shown hints of prescience. If the Mother is sending you warnings, you must heed them. Go!"

"Damn it, I'm not a coward!"

"Never thought you were, Son. I know what you're reluctant to put into words, but I'm scared, too. It's unthinkable, and yet it's entirely possible. In fact, it's the only logical explanation I can think of for what His pukey Lordship is up to—dragooning your sister into marrying one of his by-blows and choosing the prettiest to make her noble sacrifice more palatable. Now you're being warned off?"

"And you're not?"

"There's a raven on the roof."

"What is Corbin telling you?"

His father went back to studying the clouds. After a moment he said, "He isn't. This is not the first time he's refused to come to me, though."

"Father!"

The old man was as stubborn as granite. He thumped a heavy hand down on Henry's shoulder. "I've asked your mother, and she won't leave unless I do, and I'm staying. I refuse to be scared away. The Woodbridges have been here for three hundred years. There's Woodbridges here tonight, and there will be Woodbridges here tomorrow."

"Three of us, then," Henry said.

"No, you should go."

"Three of us!"

The squire sent the staff off to bed a little earlier than usual, warning that the night looked likely to be noisy, so it would be a good idea to get some sleep in before the storm arrived. Father and son went around the barns and other buildings to check that all was safe and secure.

Then they went into the library. Edgar pushed with the sole of his shoe on one of the tiles behind the door. It slid an inch or so in under the wainscot. The gap created was just wide enough for him to insert his fingers and raise a square of four tiles fixed to a trapdoor. Henry followed him down the ladder but paused halfway to lower the trap and pull the trick tile back into place. No sign of the hidden cellar then remained above it.

Bailiffs sent to search the house were not likely to notice that two fireplaces vented through a single chimney pot and its partner topped an air shaft from a cellar. A cross draft was available through a gap behind the lowest row of books in one of the library cases, but even that could be closed off if there was ever cause to hide from a hunt.

The chapel was narrow, spanned above by massive beams to support the tiled floor, but surprisingly long. At the ladder end stood a couch, chairs, a table, and other comforts.

The simple altar at the far end bore a sprig of blossom and an oatcake that evening. Agnes was already kneeling there. Son and husband went to join her. Henry was very aware that he was the last one of their brood left, and the only one who had not been gifted with talent. His father's courage made him feel like a nervous ninny. But even if his fears were confirmed and the snooping priest had been sent to organize a lynch party, the mob would have to be content with trashing the house.

Edgar's great-grandfather had built the secret chapel so he could hide visiting missionaries from church or state authorities. Many such a visitor had stayed in it over the years and had led bonding circles there for the local faithful, but the manor house had never been searched. No family members had ever had to hide in it, either, but that was what they planned to do that night. No matter who came looking, the Woodbridges would not be found down there.

Father Dampier had never met a harder audience. Even a few experimental cries of agreement from his planted helpers failed to meet with support. The poison must run deep in this community, and he had underestimated Father Snuggs's incompetence. He must not only be replaced but also investigated for secret heretical tendencies.

Just when Father Dampier began to fear that he had met the first failure of his career, he was saved by the rising storm. As he thundered from the pulpit, the Father began thundering back from his heavens. The church was very dim, but each lightning flash seemed brighter than the one before, each cannonade louder.

Every quotation from the *Illuminations* was greeted with a divine, "Hear! Hear!" The Lord's approval was unmistakable and the threat, irresistible. The helpers' enthusiasm began to be picked up by a few of the natives, and then, of course, with breathtaking suddenness, the whole flock took wing.

"Will you risk the Lord's judgment on your village?"

"No! No!"

"Will you drive out the heretics?"

"Yes!"

Streaming sweat in the heat, Father Dampier descended from the pulpit to lead his army forth. Torches, drums, and trumpets he had arranged, but it was the Lord who provided the greatest support. Dampier led the parade out of the village to the rousing strains of "His Will Be Done, His Rule Imposed." Behind them and above them the inky heavens flashed and roared, but still the rain held off. He always felt a great personal exhilaration at times like these, but never had he known the Lord to give him such visible support.

When he stood aside to view the column, he had to admit that it was not as large as he had hoped, but the young men had stayed with him, and he could count on them to follow through. Not many people could resist a torchlight procession, especially a torchlight procession with a holy purpose. He knew that many of them were coming along in the hope of witnessing a lynching, and others just had the scent of loot in their nostrils, for the heretic Woodbridge was the richest man in the area. Those facts were regrettable, but the Lord's will must be done. "Suffer not devil worshipers to live," Verse 512.

They had sung all the battle hymns that most people knew and were back to "His Will Be Done" for the third time when the manor house came into view. The approach of the Army of Light had been heard, of course, and Dampier had no quarrel with that. He had no wish to hang innocent—if deluded—servants, although some of them must be heretics also. Those could be reeducated and saved. He wanted the faithless, recusant sheriff. Candlelight began to glimmer in windows as inhabitants became aware of the horde assembling on the driveway before the front door.

One of his helpers had "just happened" to bring along a hailing horn. Dampier found a handy bench and climbed on it, so everyone could see. Three helpers with torches stood close to illuminate him. He raised the horn to his lips.

"Woodbridge!" he boomed. *"Woodbridge, come forth!"*

The army roared its agreement.

"Come out, Woodbridge, or we will come in and get you!"

This time the accord was even louder.

And suddenly Dampier knew the Lord's will. The Lord approved the heretics' death, but forbade looting. So be it. Dampier threw down the megaphone and raised both arms as if to hurl his forces forward. He called for a miracle.

He had the impression of three distinct strokes in very quick succession. Flame blazed along branches and gables. Incandescent trails of purple fire were written on his eyes for hours to come, and the noise was stunning. Thatch and ancient timbers exploded like gunpowder. Most people were hurled to the ground, and many remained half-deaf for days.

Dampier fell off his bench. It was several minutes before he could even sit up and realize that he was in danger of bursting into flame himself. He scrambled and staggered back to safety, following his flock. Only then could he turn to stare at what he had done—with the Lord's help, of course. The whole manor house was ablaze. Flames were pouring out of holes in the roof; people in burning nightclothes were leaping from windows. Some of the trees were on fire, too. In moments the remains of the roof collapsed in an avalanche of red-hot coals. Sparks were pouring high into the sky. All around him people were weeping and praying.

Amen.

CHAPTER 13

"BROTHER? BROTHER ROLLO!"

Rollo forced open crusted eyes. The night had clouded over; the sky above the grille was dark. His blindsight did not need light, though. He knew the woman leaning over him. She was tall and also gaunt, which was understandable in one who lived on charity and dandelion leaves. She looked younger than he remembered, probably because his years in Gaudry had taught him what truly ancient people looked like.

"Wisdom Edith!" She had been the first to recognize his ability when his talents began to show. She had taught him much. And she had always been good at finding lost things or missing people, so he should not be surprised that she had been conscripted to find and identify him.

"Drink," she said, offering a flask in his general direction. She could not see in the dark as he did.

Someone else raised his shoulders. He tried to move his hands and was reminded that he was wearing red-hot manacles. All the agony and terror came rushing back so fast that he almost cried out. He took a few sips and chinned the flask away because it contained wine and he was going to need his wits.

He was still in Swine Hall. The nightmare was not over. Act Three was now. He managed to struggle into a sitting posture. He was on the bunk in the empty cell, and he knew vaguely that he had been there for several hours. The two women must have been sitting on the floor, for there was no other furniture. The door was still ajar, praise the Mother.

"This is Sister Nell."

"Nell," he whispered. "Nell, Edith, you have no idea how happy I was to see you two. The most welcome sight of my life. What's been happening?"

"It was quite exciting at first," Edith said, not lowering her voice. "A lot of running and shouting. Whatever you did to the warden, he never stopped raving. They could get no sense out of him at all. They finally gagged him and led him away in irons. The jailer at the spyhole had no memory of his dream trance, of course, so he insisted the cell door had never been opened. He was swearing fearful oaths that you just suddenly vanished and Pottenger started screaming. The other guard had gone downstairs to fetch the priests, so he knew nothing either. Both of them were taken away to be locked up."

"Fortunately, not in this cell," said the other woman. Nell was much younger than Edith. She carried what Rollo first thought was a mouse on her shoulder, until he realized it was a bat.

"And nobody looked in here?"

"Of course they did, but we can both distract, so we stood in front of you to hide you and nobody noticed any of us."

Edith chuckled nervously. "The priests exorcized your cell with a lot of chanting and stinky perfume."

The women were trying not to show how worried they were about his condition, so he made an effort to sit up straighter and speak more clearly. For his rescuers' sakes he must play the hero, however little he felt like one.

"Must have been stinky if you smelled it in Swine Hall. What happens now?"

"Now that it's quiet we have to get you out of here," Edith said. "Can you walk?"

Good question. He tried to swing his feet down, but that was surprisingly difficult without using his hands.

"Can we hold your arms?" Nell asked.

"Touch anything except my hands and shoulders. The rest of me is fine."

They gripped his legs and turned him so he could put his feet on the floor. They steadied him by holding his arms, which were not as fine as he had hoped, but he could stand that pain after what he had been through.

Nell had produced a sword and sword belt.

"Not yet," he said. He was drained. Pottenger had broken him, and healing would take weeks or months. He had nothing left. He doubted he could even stand up, let alone walk, and the sight of jailers closing in on him would make him burst into tears. "What happens now?"

"I remember your distraction talent," Edith said. "You used to shout, 'Boo!' right in front of me and frighten me half to death. Nell and I have enough of it to get by. The three of us can walk down the ramp and out the front door. If that's locked, use your mastery to make someone open it for us."

Oh, Mother! That won't work! Was that the best they had?

He flogged his crippled brain to work. "You're not whispering?"

"This is the traitors' wing. There's no one else up here."

He thought about that, thought about what he had seen of Swine Hall the day they brought him in.

Traitors were not the normal run of rapists, debtors, highwaymen, and pickpockets that made up the prison's regular clientele. Traitors were Privy Council business, and dangerous, in that they might know secrets that should not be spread around. Worse, the Children of the Mother had bizarre and frightening powers. So traitors must be kept apart.

The traitors' floor had been a late addition. The original Swine Hall jail had been four stories high, with access to the cells from a ramp that spiraled up along the sides of a central well. The main jail had been packed with prisoners when he arrived and still would be. He had seen sconces for lamps, so it would be illuminated and patrolled at night. There might not be very many guards, but every one of them could watch the other three sides of the well and see anyone coming down.

The ramp was wide enough for two prisoners and their escorts to pass. It ended at a door, which Pottenger had told him was guarded by six men at all times. Beyond the door, a narrow staircase led up to the traitors' block.

"How did you get in?" he asked.

"We said we'd come to visit some man we invented," Nell said. "The sergeant on the door demanded three stars. He settled for two and just let us in. The place was swarming with visitors, so no one noticed us."

Edith took up the story. "When we got to the top, though, I knew you were somewhere higher yet, but the big door was shut and there were a lot of guards standing around. They were chatting up the women, mostly, or taking bribes. Just what those sort of men do. So we were stuck there for a while. But then a man inside demanded to be let out, and the guards all lined up while he told them that there might be a rescue attempt. While they were listening to him, we just walked right by them and they didn't notice us."

How could they possibly have found the courage to do that? The man they had seen had been Dalton, of course, sent by Pottenger. So Rollo's shameful confession had aided his escape after all. Or else it had trapped his two would-be rescuers in the same hell he was in.

"Distraction got us in, and distraction can get us out," Edith said.

Not necessarily! Distraction was tricky. A pickpocket working a crowd escaped the witnesses' notice by sheer ordinariness and by not doing anything unusual. Some such lowlife might have no true talent at all, although they would never rise far in their profession without it. At its best, distraction could induce virtual invisibility, but only if it could be highly concentrated. The number of victims to be distracted, the skill of the distractor, and the magnitude of the action to be concealed: all these mattered. For inmates to walk out of a prison unnoticed by professional jailers already on the lookout for an escape attempt would require distraction on an epic scale. There were no visitors milling around at night to provide cover, no exotic dancers to hold the victim's attention. Guards on lower floors would

see the strangers approaching until they came near enough
to be deceived and would see them again after they had
gone by. Swine Hall's finest might not be the cream of any
crop, but they could not be stupid enough to overlook that.
Someone would certainly sound the alarm.

But Rollo could think of nothing else to suggest,

"How do we get down to the ramp?" he asked.

"Down the stairs," Edith said, but he saw worry on
Nell's face.

He looked to her for her answer, then remembered
they couldn't see him. "But the door?"

"Hope it won't be locked," she said. "This block is empty,
no inmates."

"Not a lock. Bars." He had seen them leaning against
the wall as he was brought in, two great balks of timber
that could be dropped into brackets. The government
must know about jiggling, although it was a very rare gift;
must know that an adept who had such a talent could move
trifles like the tumblers in locks but not lift heavy weights.

But if there were no traitors in custody, would the acting warden waste manpower guarding the door? As far as
the authorities knew, the prisoner Woodbridge had simply
vanished. The stable was empty; the horse had flown. *Oh,
Mother, please let them have left it unguarded!*

"Bars then," Nell said. "If is barred, we have to hope it's
also guarded, because we'll have to call through the grille
for the guard to unbar it."

That might work for one man. When he came to the
grille, Rollo could use mastery on him, or Nell could; Rollo
had seen her mastery work on Shipley. But the government knew about mastery, too. When the port officers had

arrested him, the first thing they had done was gag him. Anytime he wasn't securely locked up, he had been gagged or blindfolded, and at no time had they left him with less than two guards. Even when he had been hanging on the hook in agony, there had been at least two watching him. So there would be either six guards or none at all.

If the door were open and unguarded, thank the Mother. Barred and guarded by just one man, probably doable. Unbarred and guarded by two or more men, very slim chance—the problem would be that they would see the door open before they saw who was opening it, and no one could make a door disappear. There were too many unknowns. Suppose the door had a lock as well as bars and the key was on the warden's belt, far away?

Whatever had possessed these two women to attempt this? There were times when loyalty became suicidal, and the least he could do was try to help, instead of sitting there like a corpse.

Rollo struggled to his feet, swayed for a minute or two, and then steadied. He tried a few steps. He was shaky, but he could do it. He wondered if this performance was being watched through spyholes. It would make a great comedy if armed guards were waiting at the foot of the stairs to perform the finale of returning him to his previous cell.

Nell produced the sword and sword belt again. He tried to raise his arms and couldn't.

"Put it on me," he said. "I see very well in the dark. How did you ever manage to smuggle a sword in?"

"By walking with a very stiff back," Edith said. "Thank the Mother that nobody ordered me to sit down anywhere." As long as Rollo could remember, Edith had lived alone in a sod hut in the forest near Stonebridge. Even the big city would seem alien to her, a nerve-racking strain. How had she ever found the courage to set foot in this hell of a prison?

While Nell was adjusting the sword, he admired her delicate features and creamy-smooth complexion, knowing she couldn't see him doing so. Young women were rare in Gaudry, because more boys than girls chose the wandering, dangerous life of a missionary. When he felt stronger, he might start taking an interest in Sister Nell. Priests of the Light were sworn to celibacy, but the Children of the Mother considered that a perversion, a denial of life. How in the world could he be thinking about that in this situation?

"Can you really see in the dark?" Nell said, perhaps sensing his attention.

"You have a dimple in your chin. And now you're blushing."

"If you're feeling that good, you can fend for yourself." She unfurled a cloth. "Cloak to hide your hands." She clipped it around his neck.

Clever! Coming or going, a sword made him an officer, not a fugitive or even a jailer. The sword hilt showed from the front, the scabbard lifted the cloth at the back. His hands couldn't draw it, of course, far less use it. He had never worn a sword in his life except for show. She put a floppy hat on him, pulling it down to shadow his face and tucking his hair in as much as his hair would ever do what it was told.

He had never realized how utterly helpless a man was without hands. He couldn't feed himself or attend to the most intimate functions without help. And was he strong enough for the rest of this escape? His legs were trembling already.

"How far am I going to have to walk?"

"Down to the main gate and around a corner. Can you manage?"

"Just watch me." He saw relief flash into the older woman's face. He was tempted to add, *But don't let them take me alive.* He would rather die than go back to the hook.

"Wouldn't want to have to carry you, lad." She had forgotten that he was Brother Rollo now, but better that she forget to use his title in private than that she use it by accident in public. "Ready to go?"

"No," he said. "Wait here a moment." He struggled to open the heavy door with an elbow, but he had no strength even in his shoulders. Edith did it for him.

Very much aware of his pounding heart, he peered out and saw only a dark and empty corridor. Forgetting about his sword, he promptly jammed in the gap, banging his left hand against the wall. He almost screamed. A scream or two might not draw much attention in Swine Hall, but better not to find out. He set out to explore the traitors' block, a corridor with six cells along one side. He had been kept in perpetual light and under twenty-four-hour watch, but he could see no signs of other cells receiving such attention. Tiptoeing along to the far end and back, he saw no chink of light and found no one—not at the corridor spyholes, nor in the side branches between each pair of cells that let watch be kept on the inmates from another direction. No signs of life. Nell and Edith had told him that, but now he knew he could walk without staggering too badly. He returned to the women.

"Ready," he said.

"Go," Nell said. The bat spread its wings and circled up to vanish between the skylight bars.

"Your familiar, I assume?" he said.

"Not mine, no."

He went first, to display the sword, and because any other arrangement would seem wrong in Albi. In Xennia, women normally went first. Edith came next with Nell at the rear. He took the steep stairs very slowly, unsteady on his feet and unable to grip the hand rope strung along the wall. Merely moving was taking all his attention, and he would need a lot more to distract the jailers. If he stumbled, he would roll down the stairs, and that would be the end of everything.

There was light coming though the grille. And voices! After the sweetness of hope, despair was bitterer than alum. Rollo was going back to the hook, and he could not even draw his sword to kill himself.

"Let me try," Nell whispered very softly in his ear. "I can inspire."

So that was why Rollo had found himself thinking about sex a few minutes ago—Nell had tried to perk him up a bit. She slipped past him and tried a very gentle push on the massive timber door, but it did not move.

She put her face close to the grille and whistled softly. Pause. She whistled again. A man's face appeared on the other side.

"What...? Burning shit! Hey, Bill, come'n see this!"

Nell whispered something to him. Rollo couldn't hear the words, and yet even he felt a thrill, so she must have great power. A second face appeared beside the first, and she switched from inspiration to mastery.

"YOU WILL OBEY MY ORDERS. YOU WILL NOT RAISE THE ALARM. OPEN THIS DOOR."

The faces vanished. There were thumping noises, but no shouts from anyone else. There must be only two of them.

"That was magnificent!" Rollo whispered.

"Do not count chickens."

The door swung open. Lamplight that would be barely visible by day seemed dazzlingly bright after the darkness upstairs. Freedom eased a handbreadth closer.

There were two scraggy men-at-arms out there. Not the special traitors' guard, just the regular jail night watch. They looked at Nell in bewilderment, not understanding what was happening or why they had done what they did. But there were other guards at other levels, and they must soon notice the strangers.

"YOU WILL OBEY THIS MAN."

Feeling very far from masterly, Rollo took over. He made them jump to attention and salute him, for the benefit of the watchers. They closed and barred the door. He ordered them to forget that it had been opened at all or that they had seen anyone come out, and they were not to notice him and his companions leaving. They saluted again, then turned to lean on the parapet and stare vacantly into the well. No doubt that was how they passed the night.

Rollo strolled down the gentle slope to the first corner, wishing he could raise an arm high enough to wipe his forehead. His clothes were stuck to his skin; he would not have believed he had so much sweat left in him. They were not out of the jungle yet—far from it. Eight or ten men-at-arms were patrolling the ramp, all of them in pairs. They could all see that a man and two women were coming down from the top floor. They must wonder who they were at this time of night, for visitors were allowed only during daylight.

The large cells had barred fronts, so the inmates were visible at all times, packed in like fish in barrels. Two or three of the toughest or richest had cots, and the rest slept on the floor. Smaller cells were hidden behind timber doors, although those were fitted with grilles, all of which were dark. The only sounds were snoring and the babbling of the insane.

Terror roiled in Rollo's gut as he approached the next patrol. Two men again, one leaning against the balustrade and the other against the wall. They had seen the fugitives approaching and were going to make them pass between them. That was a clear sign that they were suspicious. If only one of them was mastered, the other would have time to attack, or just raise the alarm.

"No distraction!" Rollo said. "Mastery. Nell, take the one on your side. I'll take the other. Make him salute, whatever you do."

It worked again, and the Children of the Mother continued their progress, leaving two hapless guards doomed to stand at attention for a whole hour as punishment for their sloppy behavior. It wouldn't teach them a lesson, because they weren't going to remember the incident at all. It alerted their fellows, though, and the next pair saluted smartly. Rollo paused to congratulate them and wipe their memories.

Three men guarded the main gate, but two were close enough together to be mastered, and Nell dealt with the third, who opened the gate for the fugitives. Rain was falling as Rollo Woodbridge stepped out into freedom.

CHAPTER 14

HE COULD RELAX A LITTLE THEN, FOR THE ROAD WAS EMPTY and black as a mine. Edith and Nell, blinded by the dark, each laid a hand on his shoulder to direct him in the right direction and then be guided by him. Their touch hurt like fire, but he did not say so. The road was muddy, foul, and slippery, but even Weypool air seemed fresh after the reek in Swine Hall. He was staggering with weakness and reaction, afraid of losing his footing, afraid much more of being recaptured. He had cursed Pottenger, and for that he would be burned at the stake. *Oh, Mother, how much farther?* They reached a corner. He jumped as a voice spoke out of the alley darkness.

"The bats are out tonight."

Edith said, "The hunting is good."

There were two men there, and a sedan chair. Oh, thank the Mother!

They helped him into the chair, whose seat and floor had been draped with rags so his jail foulness would not contaminate them. The curtains were closed, the chair raised. Less than five minutes after leaving Swine Hall, he was on his way to safety. Every minute he stayed at liberty made recapture less likely. He could tell from the jostling that the bearers were setting a fast pace, but he was certainly not going to complain about that.

He gave thanks, praying more earnestly than he had ever done in his life. The Mother had rescued him from the notorious jail and put hope back in his life. Given a few days to recover his strength and let his hands heal, he could begin to live again. It would be too dangerous to visit his family just yet, but even that might be arranged in a year or so. He caught himself smiling at the thought of a missionary Woodbridge hiding from the king's men down in the secret chapel. He thought of Henry, Maddy, and Bram. How old would Brat be now? Did he still remember his big brother?

The chair slowed, turned corners, was set down…a door creaked. Lifted again, moved a few paces, set down again…another creak. And then light beyond the curtains. They were pulled back, and strong hands reached in to help him out.

He was, improbably, in a carpenter's workshop. The flicker of a single lantern in the darkness showed workbenches, tool chests, and a pole lathe. The two wise women stood back in the shadows, looking both happy and haggard. The pair of burly, grinning youngsters must have been Rollo's bearers, and the older man with a face like a bulldog was clearly in charge. The family resemblance was so strong that they could only be father and sons, and in that case they must be the legendary Molesworths. The father pulled off his cap and bowed.

"We are greatly honored to meet you, Brother."

"Not as honored as I am to meet you, Master—" An almost imperceptible stiffening in the man's face was a warning not to speak his real name, a reminder that from now on Rollo must dwell in the underworld of the persecuted and hunted. Even the two wisdoms might not know who their helpers were. Rollo himself would not, except that Prelate Gaudry had shared with him many secrets that were normally kept even from graduates about to embark on their mission. Rollo was special. "And grateful, too, of course. My blessings on you."

He looked to the sons, and they both dropped on their knees to receive his blessing, which was also disconcerting. "You, too, have my blessings. I cannot make the proper gesture at the moment, but I'm sure the Mother will forgive me. And please rise! Never kneel to me. I am forever in your debt. Um, you must be the elder?"

Their grins flashed back to tell him he had guessed wrong. So the larger was the younger, Kip, the stonemason. Rob was a carpenter like his dad.

The father, Charles Molesworth, turned up the wick on another lantern, which he handed to Wisdom Nell. "You please go ahead, Sisters. We'll bring our guest to join you shortly. You can start filling the bathtub for him. Boys, get that chair back up on the horses, wipe its feet, take down the drapes, and get rid of the rags inside it. And brush that damned sawdust off your knees. How'd you ever explain that, huh?"

Had the chair been brought in for repairs, and thus been available for the rescue, or had it been needed for the rescue and therefore made to seem that it was in for repairs? The planning that had gone into Rollo's escape was as daunting as the risk involved. He must learn how to live with one eye in the back of his head at all times. He stepped out of the way as the brothers fetched sawhorses to support the chair.

"Brother...who? What name?" asked Charles, lighting another lantern.

The aliases assigned to Rollo in Gaudry had been compromised by the traitor. He had another in reserve, known only to him and the prelate. "John Hawke."

"Aye. Well, Squire Hawke, you'll not take offense, but we needs get rid of those rags you're wearing. King's men use dogs sometimes. And any old lady could follow your scent now, if you'll pardon my saying it."

"You amaze me. If you could give me a new skin, like a snake, I would accept it willingly. I'll need help, because I have no use of my hands yet."

Molesworth raised his lantern and led the way into the darkness beyond the chair. "We'll give you hot water and soap in a minute. Could you stand for a bucket or two of cold water to get the worst off?"

"Gladly. I feel like a walking dung heap."

The carpenter set his lantern on a bench and began undressing his guest. Acutely embarrassed, Rollo stared at a doorframe and several window sashes clamped for gluing. He could see no sign of the two women or guess where they had gone. Clearly the long room had started life as a coach house, for it had doors at both ends and ample space for a carriage. The horses' mangers were still there, but the partitions between the stalls had been removed to clear the shop area. There was even a gutter along the middle of the floor, leading out to a road or yard beyond the door. Clanking and gushing noises from somewhere behind him told him he had overlooked a pump.

When he had stripped Rollo naked, Charles stepped aside. Kip appeared carrying a large bucket, heavy enough to make even his bulk tilt sideways.

"Ready, Squire?"

Rollo braced himself, remembering not to clench his fists. "Ready."

Kip tipped.

Oh, Mother, that was cold!

"More?"

"Keep going. Got a sanding block you could use on me?"

After four bucketfuls, he still felt filthy, but he was shivering so violently that they took pity on him. Charles wrapped a cloak around him. It was light stuff, which would not warm him but did hide his nudity.

"We'd best put your shoes on you again, Squire," Charles said. "Nails and splinters here, and rough where we're going."

Then they led him to the secret exit. The shop was cluttered along both sides with benches, timber, or work in progress, one piece being a half-finished oak desk. A flagstone in the knee space below it had been tilted up to reveal a small, rectangular hole, which Rollo regarded with dismay. Two days ago he could have slid his lithe form through that as easily as threading a needle, but not now.

Rob and Kip lifted the desk forward, out of the way. Kip reached into the hole and began to haul out a ladder. When it reached a length of about ten feet, it came free and he leaned it against the wall.

"Made a sling," Rob announced, producing a small plank, to which were attached ropes, like a child's swing. "You manage to hold on with your elbows, like?"

Rollo could not trust his shoulders. "No. You'd better tie me."

The carpenter laid the plank by the hole. Rollo stepped on it, and the stonemason trussed ropes around him so he couldn't fall off.

"Now, if the kid can take the strain..."

"Kid?" the younger brother snorted. "Look out for his side, Squire. He's hammered his thumbs so often he can't hold a nail anymore."

They raised Rollo with little visible effort, threaded the board into the hole at the third attempt, and then lowered him into darkness. He bumped against the sides of the shaft a few times before reaching bottom. The air was cool, with a curious musty, sweet smell, but breathable. The walls were rough rock, and he could guess that he was in the famous Weypool catacombs.

"Look out for ladder, sir," Charles called anxiously.

"Just a moment." Rollo managed to slide his shoes off the plank and shuffle a few steps, pulling the sling with him, until he was out of harm's way. Then the ladder was slid back in place. Charles came down with a lantern and untied him.

The tunnel was narrow and low for tall men, carved out of bedrock. Niches in the walls, two or even three high, extended as far as even Rollo could see, and he knew what lay on those shelves. In the old days, the Albiurns had buried their dead and the large and ancient city of Weypool had spread far and deep underground. The Teacher had ordered the catacombs sealed off, but obviously that edict had not stood the test of time.

The remains lying in the niches were mostly shapeless tatters of long-rotted shrouds lying on bones like dry brown sticks, with only skulls recognizable under the dust of centuries. Here and there he saw a lead coffin, or fragments of a wooden one, and once in a while a much more recent burial had been crammed in on top of the rightful owner. By and large, though, the dead of centuries slept undisturbed, and Rollo had no sense of ancestral disapproval at his intrusion.

He followed the carpenter, being careful not to jostle his damaged shoulders against the walls. The tunnel frequently crossed others, but Charles knew exactly where he was going: past rock-carved stairs that rose to blank roofs or descended into darkness and deeper layers, along newer, low-roofed tunnels hacked through the rock to connect each cemetery to another. The roof and sides were mainly dry, and the floor usually was, but where it was muddy, it showed signs of much traffic. Before the Church of the Light had sealed them, the catacombs had offered silent repose for the dead; now they were secret roads for the living.

Rollo wondered briefly how the two wisdoms had found their way through this maze, and then he remembered Edith's legendary ability to find anything. That would include her way back to wherever he was being taken.

What looked like a blank rock wall turned out to be a well-disguised wooden one containing a circular door, which opened into a brewer's cellar. From that side, it appeared to be the end of a barrel. Charles led the way

through two more cellars and then opened another disguised door into more catacombs. By then Rollo was
thoroughly disoriented, but he was sure he must be streets
away from the carpenters' shop.

"Did you make any of this?" Rollo asked, his voice
swallowed by the darkness, for the rough stone did not
return echoes.

"Just a few doors and ladders. Most of it's a thousand
years old. The deeper levels are newer, the ones that
were still being dug when the Children lost the Gods'
War."

"There's an old tradition in my parents' house that
the secret chapel there was built by a man named Mole."

"Same in my family, sir. My great-grandfather or
such got his start doing a special job for the Squire of
Woodbridge. That was the first. The squire set him up
building hides for others 'mong the faithful. We were
Molesworths even then, though."

"But in Gaudry, too, you're known as the Moles.
Everyone assumes it's just a code word. You are greatly
honored there." The Molesworth family had built scores
or even hundreds of secret hiding places for the Mother's
missionaries, across the length and width of Albi. They
were usually referred to as "mole holes."

Rollo worried that there would be another ladder
wherever he was going, and he would have to be hauled
up like freight, but when light appeared ahead, it showed
the passage ending at a staircase. The trapdoor at the top
was of ample size and stood open. All he need do was walk
up. He emerged in an untidy cellar, and another stair took
him up to a very ordinary domestic kitchen, the sort that

would serve a family of five or six with a similar number of servants and a couple of apprentices.

The room was hot, because the fire in the brick range was roaring. Nell and Edith were busily tipping pots and kettle of water into a steaming oaken tub. The Molesworths had been bad enough; Rollo was not going to let those two wash him like a baby.

"Ready for you, Brother," Nell said cheerily, and laughed at his expression.

Charles was a humorless man. "I think you have done a noble work tonight, Sisters. The brother does not need your services further."

Edith smiled and started to bid everyone good night, but Nell spoke up.

"I won't sleep until I know the answer to one question. What did you do to Warden Pottenger, Brother?"

"I just passed on Prelate Gaudry's curse."

"Well, then, what did the prelate do to him?"

"She filled his ears with the screams of his victims. He is effectively deaf, for he can hear nothing over the constant screaming, night and day. And he never learned how to read or write."

His audience now included Kip, and all four looked impressed.

"No more than that monster deserved," Nell said.

The men nodded in agreement. Edith seemed less sure.

Rob emerged from the trapdoor and closed it. Rollo had no doubt that the other end of the tunnel was now safely disguised under the desk and probably some fragments of furniture.

"Off you go, ladies," Charles said. "And you, lads. I'll assist Squire Hawke."

"I can do that, sir," Kip said bravely.

His father bristled. "No you won't. Be off with you! I know what I'm doing here. I washed your backside often enough."

Exhausted though he was, even Rollo had to smile at the stonemason's blush. Once they were alone, he happily let the old carpenter bathe him, dry him, and help him upstairs to bed.

CHAPTER 15

WISDOM FRIEDA WAS BORN THE FIFTH CHILD IN A PROSPEROUS family descended in a junior line from a baron who had joined the Teacher's Legion of Light early, and had thus come out on the winning side in the Gods' War. Her parents were conforming churchgoers, although never fanatical about their faith. Her mother had suffered from an ill-defined debility, probably as a way of escaping further pregnancies, and in her housebound boredom had taught even her daughters to read and write.

The dreams began when Frieda was about thirteen. Even then she knew enough not to mention them to anyone, but they grew clearer and more demanding as the months passed. One night she dreamed of a black kitten. Next morning she found a black kitten at the front door. She petted it. It walked a few steps and turned around to look at her with bright yellow eyes.

"You want me to follow you?"

The kitten purred briefly and resumed its walk. Frieda picked it up and set off down the driveway. She never went back.

Ever since then, more decades ago than she could bear to think of, she had been the Mother's messenger to the wise folk. She knew most of them, and they knew her. If she dreamed of one she didn't know, there would always be clues in the scenery to guide her, and Felix would know the way. He had grown up in Frieda's first year on the road, but he had never grown old. He was her cat; he was a thousand cats. She could leave him, travel a month, and meet him again when she faced a puzzling fork in the road, or when she reached her destination.

So now she had been sent a child, Bram Woodbridge, known as Brat, although in her presence he behaved like a cherub, anything but a brat. Among his peers he would be more inclined to lead than follow, she suspected, but that was expected of a squire's son. To be granted a familiar while so young was certainly a mark of the Mother's especial interest. So what was Frieda expected to do with this lad?

The Mother would direct her.

At sunset she spoke one of her favorite evening prayers.

He looked at her expectantly. "Aren't we going to sing?"

"My voice isn't as good as it used to be. Why don't you sing?"

So he did. Quite unselfconsciously, he sang three verses of a dance song that was a slightly disguised hymn of thanks to the Mother, a glorious soprano voice in perfect key soaring to the treetops. Which answered the question of whether he had been introduced to the secret faith. Most of the time he was such a perfect little gentleman, solemn and polite, that it was hard to remember how young he was. He must have been treated as an adult all his life.

Frieda made him as comfortable as she could in a corner of the cottage, pleading that her old bones deserved the bed. He thought for a moment. She wondered if he would quote a guest's right of hospitality, but then he just smiled and agreed it would be fun to sleep on the floor with Smut, because his mother didn't allow dogs on beds.

"They often have fleas," he explained solemnly. "But Smut doesn't."

"I'm sure he's much too grand a dog to have fleas."

Smut wagged his tail at the compliment.

Frieda sat on the bench outside for a while, plucking petals from a sprig of blossom. Steeped, they would make a pleasing perfume as a gift for a lady. Young men often dropped by their local wisdom to ask for advice they were too shy to seek from anyone else, and a small gift to help promote their wooing usually brought payment in the form of a pile of firewood or the odd illegal rabbit. To add a hint that the scent or potion had some magical erotic power would be unethical, strictly speaking, but would often make it work better.

The stars began coming out. She was about to retire when she heard a rumble of thunder. So? Of her own experience, she knew this cottage had stood for half a century in fair weather and foul. It could survive one more storm. She confirmed that her guests were sleeping peacefully in each other's arms and paws, and made herself as comfortable as possible on the low platform that served as a bed. Thunder would not penetrate the massive turf walls.

There were dreams and there were visions.

She stood by the side of a trail winding through an orchard. The blossoms had mostly fallen, littering the grass with giant white flakes, and the ground was wet. Small puddles shone in the ruts. A pony and trap were approaching. The pony was black, and the trap was a simple two-wheeled cart with a driver's bench in front and a passenger seat in back. The solitary passenger was a woman in a tall hat; there was no driver. Even a vision was a dream, after all.

When the cart came level with Frieda, it halted. Not a word was said. Frieda handed up a shiny broadsword, hilt first. The lady accepted the gift, but it was too long to lie on the seat beside her, so she set the point near her feet and propped the hilt against the backrest of the driver's bench. That would have been a very unsafe arrangement anywhere except in a dream. She gestured, and the trap moved on.

Frieda watched her go, and in the impossible manner of dreams could still see her from the front, instead of the back. The woman was no longer alone, although she seemed unaware of her new companion, a full-sized, black-maned lion with its back paws on the passenger seat and the front ones on the driver's bench. Towering over her, the great beast was staring straight ahead, ignoring the scenery going past.

Later Frieda was sitting in a snug little kitchen-parlor with her feet in a warm bath and a cup of dandelion wine in her hand. She was talking to the woman who lived there, Wisdom Ora, an old friend, probably even older than she was. Ora was weeping.

A flash and a roar startled Frieda awake. Dazed, she sat up and struggled to remember where she was in real life and where she had been in the dream world. A lightning bolt must have struck very close. The wind had blown down the drape over the door, and rain was pummeling the forest outside. There was no sound from the floor. Either Brat was still fast asleep or he had fled into the trees in terror. Unable to imagine that solemn little lad doing anything so stupid, she lay down and told herself to go back to sleep.

The instructions had been clear, so she need not expect any more visions that night. She was to turn Brat over to the woman in the tall hat, and then go on to visit with Ora. Ora lived in Pertwee, about two days' journey away.

"Wisdom! Wisdom!"

A man was shouting outside the cottage, although it was barely first light yet. Frieda struggled awake and gathered her wits, which had been roaming in the distant past.

"Wisdom! They're going to come and get you!"

Frieda's bare feet hit the sandy floor; she staggered and almost fell. Brat was a blur in the corner, still asleep as far as she could tell, although Smut had his head up. She pulled her blanket around her and ducked out to see.

"Wisdom…you're not Wisdom Edith!" He was a hulking young man, well-meaning but very loud.

"Wisdom Edith had to go away for a few days. I'm Wisdom Frieda." She spoke quietly and soothingly, hoping to calm him. "What's wrong that you come a-calling in the middle of the night?"

"The village went mad, Wisdom. Last night…visiting priest…Father Damn Something."

Her heart sank. No, it dropped out of the world. "Father Rafe Dampier?"

"That's it. He preached in the church. And he got the people all riled up, see? That and the storm. And he roused them against the sheriff, Wisdom! Squire Woodbridge wouldn't hurt anyone—he sent men with a cart to get my little Ann to Wisdom Edith when she was too sick to walk. He used to give money to folk down on their luck."

Frieda made hushing noises and wished she had some reasonable way to edge this yelling maniac farmhand away from her door without making him suspect she was doing it. This news was definitely not something Brat must overhear.

"They all went marching...well, not all. Most of the women went home, and I wasn't there, nor my brother. They marched all the way to the manor..."

Oh, Mother! Please, please, not another lynching!

"And he called down the lightning!"

"He did *what?*" Frieda caught herself shouting also.

"He called on the Light to strike, and the Father smote the manor with thunderbolts. The whole house went up like gunpowder, they say. In seconds it was all a great bonfire. The thatch, the trees..."

"But the squire? And his family?"

The big man sniffled as if close to tears. "Gone. And servants. The rafters collapsed, and the walls fell. By the time the rain came, there was nothing left. And some of them were talking 'bout coming to get Wisdom Edith and 'making a clean sweep.' That's what they were calling it, Wisdom, not me. You'd best go. Most had sobered up by the time they came home in the rain, but a few are crazy still."

"Thank you!" She took his great hands in hers. "You did very well to come to warn Edith. Of course I'll take your advice and go away until the troublemakers return to their senses. The Mother's blessing on you."

She watched him stride off down the path, batting branches aside. More deaths on Rafe Dampier's bloody, bloody record! Sadly she turned to the door, and the ashen-faced little boy standing there, who had obviously heard it all.

ॐ

The entire world had been well washed by the storm. The footing was a choice of mud or wet grass. The branches and underbrush were soaking, and had soaked the three travelers. By the time the sun peeked over the skyline, they were well away from the wisdom's cottage, following a trail that Smut had chosen, leading with his nose to the ground and his tail wagging. His tail had not wagged while Frieda first comforted Brat. Had *tried* to comfort Brat, for how do you explain to an eleven-year-old that his whole family has been burned alive by a hate-filled, mad priest? How do you explain that the god his parents had worshiped in secret had not protected them from the god they insisted was a fraud? How do you explain a mere man telling lightning where and when to strike? Or why a benevolent divinity leaves a child without parents, brothers, sister? Or allows such evil to flourish at all? In a lifetime of comforting, Frieda had never met a more difficult case than this.

"There's Rollo," Brat had whispered. "He's been away somewhere, but he's expected back soon. If I can find Rollo, he'll look after me."

Rollo had been in jail, the last Frieda had heard. She'd even wondered if that was why Edith had been ordered to Weypool—to help locate and identify him. But the odds were that Rollo was either already dead or about to die in some horrible public barbarity. No Rollo. Another problem to explain.

Brat's shoulders slumped. "You'll look after me, then?"

"You wouldn't enjoy sharing my life, Brat. I have no home of my own. I walk from place to place as the Mother tells me. You need a home and friends and a couple of good meals a day to let you grow big and strong. I'm taking you to meet a lady who can look after you much better than I could."

"What's her name?" he asked suspiciously.

"I don't know. The Mother speaks to me in dreams, and last night she told me to take you to this lady. Even after what happened last night, we must trust the Mother."

"Where does she live?"

"I don't know that either. All I know is that she will be riding in a pony cart and wearing a tall hat. And we'll meet her on a trail with a lot of blossoms on the ground."

That was probable, for rain had beaten all the blossom off the branches, and hail had crushed the spring flowers. Traces of hailstones lingered where drifts had formed.

Brat said nothing.

"The Mother saved you, you know, Brat. She sent Smut, and Smut led you to the wisdom's cottage, so the bad men missed you. But, speaking of names, it might be a good idea if you stopped being Bram, or even Brat, Woodbridge for a while. Some people might want to know how you escaped. Let's choose another name, and you can use that until you know it's safe to be Brat again." Hard to imagine a teenager wanting to be called that.

He shrugged. "All right."

"How about Bradwell? Your friends can shorten it to Brad." She flailed for a moment, trying to find a surname that would appeal to him. "How about Armstrong? That's a very manly sort of name. Bradwell Armstrong?"

He nodded, not caring. "Who was that priest?"

"Father Rafe Dampier."

"I will kill him."

"That's not a good thing to promise, Brad. The Mother doesn't approve of killing."

"I don't care. I swear by my mortal soul that when I grow up I will kill Rafe Dampier."

A cold shiver ran down Frieda's bent old back. Truth was, every rule had exceptions. She could not imagine anyone she herself would rather kill than that murdering, sanctimonious zealot. Where had the boy picked up that terrible oath, even if he had gotten it wrong?

The young need dreams.

"Perhaps that's why the Mother saved you, Brad."

For the first time that day, a hint of a smile crossed his face.

Strangely, they saw nobody in the field or pastures. Frieda's feet grew sore, and she was hungry. Brat never complained. He was too numbed by sorrow to notice physical discomfort.

Where the trail cut through an orchard, Smut sat down and let his tongue dangle. That seemed to be his version of a smile.

"Can you hear anything?" Frieda asked.

"What sort of something?"

"A pony and trap. My ears are not good anymore."

"Yes," he said.

A pony and trap came into sight around a bend. The pony was not as dark as the one in the dream, and it was being driven by a gangly youth wearing the drab garb of a servant. The passenger behind him was clearly a lady, for she had a fur collar on her cloak, and her tall hat was trimmed with lace and brilliant feathers. She was probably in her forties, but well preserved. She said something, and the boy reined in alongside the bystanders.

She frowned at Frieda and even more at Brat, as if he were a surprise.

"I am Wisdom Frieda, may it please you, ma'am."

The lady pursed her lips. "I believe we have met before."

"So do I, ma'am."

"And you gave me a present."

She might have seen anything in her dream. A broadsword was possible, but not a full-grown lion. She would not have come here for that.

"This time, my lady, I commend to you young Master Bradwell Armstrong. He has just lost his parents in very tragic circumstances. I was directed to bring him here to meet you."

The lady's eyebrows expressed disbelief.

Brat bowed. A child should leave the talking to the adults in such a situation, but either instinct or quick wits told him to speak up. "I have no home of my own left to return to, ma'am. I am not yet strong enough to do a man's work, but I will willingly undertake whatever tasks your steward might set me, in return for bed and board. I can read and write and sum. I am honest and truthful."

That was quite a speech for his age, and he spoke like gentry, not peasant.

"Is that your dog?"

"Yes, ma'am."

"Then put it here and climb in."

Brat bowed to Frieda. "Thank you, Wisdom. I shall never forget your kindness." Then he lifted his puppy into the trap and followed.

The lady rapped out directions. The trap surged forward and vanished around a bend. Frieda had been hoping to be offered a ride, but there had barely been room enough for the boy, so that was not possible. She might be lucky and meet with a tinker cart going in the right direction. Otherwise, she would be sleeping under a bush tonight. Pertwee was a long way off.

But the driver found a place wide enough to turn, and the trap came rattling back. Until it went past her, Frieda saw it from the front again, as she had in her dream. It still contained one woman and two boys, all of them staring straight ahead.

No lion. Not yet.

CHAPTER 16

HAVING A THUNDERSTORM PASS OVERHEAD IN THE MIDDLE of the night had never been one of Maddy's favorite things, but it did have certain advantages when one was married to, and packed into bed with, a sexual glutton like Sam Stroud. Her first reaction to the indescribably stupid and undignified procedure required for procreation had been disappointment, but experience had already changed her attitude. She was married to him, could not be unmarried, and was determined to make the best of it. Since sleep was quite impossible, she cooperated, and then blatantly inspired him to keep on trying. It was a slow-moving storm, and one quality Samuel Stroud did not lack was stamina.

Consequently, she was still abed long after dawn. Sam had gone off to oversee the milking and set out the workers' day. She had several hours' sleep to make up and felt she had earned them.

A knock on the door.

"Go away!"

Another knock and Polly peered in. As Maddy's personal maid, she had followed her from the manor house to

Beaconbeck and been assigned a cot in the female servants' attic. "Ma'am?"

Looking up angrily, Maddy saw that Polly's face was pale as flax.

She sat up. "What's wrong?"

"The manor house, ma'am..." She was still talking as Maddy leaped from the bed to find the previous day's discarded clothes, still talking as they ran down the narrow stairs. Sam was standing at the door with two horses. He looked pale, too, under his tan.

The sodden ground made for heavy going, but they pushed the horses hard.

She could smell the ruins before she saw them. Any wildfire quenched by rain had a sour, acrid odor. All that was left of the manor house was black: heaps of charcoal, blackened wood, blackened trees, even the one surviving chimney stack was blackened, standing as a stark grave marker. Some of the outbuildings had gone, not all. Most of the horses had escaped or been rescued, for they were still milling nervously in the paddock, spooked by that fearful stench of destruction.

Maddy reined in and stared in horror. This was the landscape of her childhood—fields, pastures, orchards—and now, in the middle of it, this obscene black wound where its heart had been.

Sam had halted at her side. "God in heaven!" he muttered. "I never expected this, Maddy."

They rode closer. Men were exploring the ruins, but carefully, because a few small fires had survived the drenching and still smoked. A square hole marked the site of the cellar, now a pond of black water with remains of kegs standing as islands and smaller debris floating. Another, more elongated hollow showed where the library wing had been—half-charred books, remains of bookcases, another pond.

Just outside the devastation, near the front door steps, Father Snuggs from Stonebridge was standing guard over a line of baskets. Maddy guessed that those were for human remains, although few of them were the long handbaskets used to carry corpses. The rest likely just held bones. A blackened man was bringing another to join the collection and receive the priest's blessing.

She saw Watt, the chief footman, walking in her direction and rode forward to meet him. He had been weeping, but tears could not wash the soot from his face or beard.

"Oh, my lady..."

"How many escaped?"

"About half, ma'am. Seventeen of us got out. We think nineteen didn't. Some broke bones jumping out windows. Three or four are badly burned."

"And my family?"

He shook his head, avoiding her eye. "No...some doubts about the boy. Morning time yesterday, Master Henry had people out looking for him. He gone off on his pony, but search was called later." He didn't need to add, *So he must have been found.*

She glanced over at the paddock and saw Brat's pony right away. He must have been found. More likely he'd ridden in of his own accord, wondering what all the fuss was about. He wasn't...*hadn't* been called Brat for nothing. If the pony had returned alone, Father would have roused half the county to look for his son. No, Brat had come home and perished with the rest.

Dazed, Maddy dismounted, handed her reins to Sam, and walked across to Father Snuggs. He had a dozen baskets in his mortuary now. Seeing her approach, he advanced to meet her. So she wouldn't see their contents, likely.

She accepted his blessings, his mumbled consolation. Snuggs knew very well which god the Woodbridges had worshiped, but they had conformed in public, and they had been good people, generous and law-abiding. He had settled for what he could get. And he looked genuinely crushed by the disaster, his snowy face more lined than ever. His blue cassock was stained by soot, and even his golden skullcap had black marks on it.

"What happened?" she demanded.

"A thunderstorm. Thunderbolts."

"There was a parade?" So Polly had said.

The old man nodded warily. "We had a guest preacher at the sunset service last night. Father Rafe Dampier. A great honor for a small parish. You may have heard of him?"

Yes, she had heard of him. She had also heard about the sort of parades he organized.

"Did they bring ropes with them, by any chance, these paraders?"

The old man studied her for a long moment, as if willing her to withdraw the question. She held his gaze defiantly.

At last he nodded. "I fear they did, Madeline. There were strangers in the church last night, and they were the ringleaders. A few village men joined in—not many."

Of course Snuggs would blame the frenzy on the outsiders, taking what comfort he could from that. Dampier would claim that the locals had awakened to their sin, and so on. She would get a better account from someone else later.

"Is there any doubt that lightning started the fire? Our Heavenly Father got in ahead of them?"

"Be careful, Madeline," he said softly. "Father Dampier will undoubtedly claim that the Light answered his appeal and wreaked justice upon a nest of heretics."

She nodded, too choked to speak. With a crazed mob closing in on the manor house, her parents would have taken refuge in the chapel, and Henry also. Brat had not known of the secret sanctuary before, but in the emergency they would have taken him down with them. When the house collapsed on the library, the beams under the tiled floor would have burned away. By then the Woodbridges would have suffocated. That black pond was their grave.

She wondered if she should suggest a search for bodies there and decided not to. Followers of the Light cremated their dead, but the Children of the Earth buried theirs— when they were allowed to. Let them rest where they were. Meanwhile, where was the husband she had now acquired to partner the rest of her life? She could not see him. She needed a shoulder to weep on, and his was the only one left to her.

Father Snuggs blessed her again and returned to his temporary mortuary. Maddy wandered over to the ruins.

She had a morbid craving to look more closely at the chapel pond, but was reluctant to draw attention to it. Would any of the servants wonder why they had never known of a second cellar in the manor house?

"Mistress Stroud!"

It took her a moment to remember who Mistress Stroud was. She turned to see the unwelcome figure of Father Silas Fage approaching, blue cassock swirling around his ankles. She should curtsy to a priest. She didn't. He noticed the omission and gave her a blessing anyway. She wished she could throw it back in his face. Even he had soot on his hands.

"The ways of the Lord are often mysterious," he said sadly. "We must trust in his goodness."

Maddy shrugged. She did not deny that a god could perform miracles. But she also believed that certain people were gifted with powers that others lacked. Rafe Dampier had blasted people before, then blamed his sins on his god. A god made the perfect scapegoat for any crime one fancied.

"You must give thanks to the Father for preserving your life, child. Only your marriage to Samuel has saved you from the same terrible death so many suffered here." Fage sighed.

"Were you part of the lynch...I mean, were you one of the marchers?" That was as close as she dared come to asking if he was a murderer.

His weaselly nose twitched. "Marchers? Last night, you mean? No. I was at Norcaster Castle, attentive to my duties. News of the disaster was brought to His Lordship this morning." He gestured to a small group of horsemen at the far side of the ruins. Sam was among them. "He is lord lieutenant of Angleshire, remember. He will have to report this tragedy to the Privy Council."

Of which the noble earl was himself a member. He was supposed to be attending a meeting tomorrow, at which he would plead for the life of his "relative" Rollo Woodbridge. Or would he? Could a cow fly?

When she did not speak, Fage pressed ahead, rubbing in more salt. "His Lordship will no doubt order special prayers in all the county's churches. He may even remit next year's taxes on the manor, to aid in rebuilding."

Why should he tell Maddy that? Oh. Yes, of course. As the full extent of the plot came into focus, Maddy felt a strong desire to vomit all over Father Fage just to wipe that sly gleam from his eye. What had the Woodbridges ever done to him that he should be so happy at their terrible deaths?

"Is this a proper time to discuss taxes, Father?"

"Perhaps not. I will leave you to your prayers, then." He spun around and stalked away. The strain of not laughing aloud must be getting to him.

Maddy thought momentarily of revenge and dismissed the thought as evil, also unjustified. Fage was a nonentity, a mere toady. The real mass murderer was Osborn, Earl Uptree of Norcaster.

Shunning the chapel area, she studied the trees instead, wondering which might survive and which must be cut down as unsafe. They were old friends, for she had climbed every one of them when she was a child. Nineteen people at a stroke. Rafe Dampier had outdone himself.

A thump of hooves announced the approach of the arch villain himself. Unlike everyone else she had seen there that morning, Earl Uptree bore no speck of soot. Not one beard hair was out of place. He sparkled in clothes and jewels that must have cost a fortune. His horse certainly had.

He reined in and looked down expectantly. To neglect to curtsy to an earl would be an excuse for him to have her whipped. She bobbed.

"This is indeed a sad day for us all, mistress. Your parents were widely respected."

"Your Lordship is kind to say so."

"I will send some men over to assist with the cleanup. I promised your husband I'd put Ken Kennard in charge. He's a competent and experienced steward to run things until…in the meantime."

Until when?

"Your Lordship is very kind. I hope the sad news will be conveyed to my brother?"

"Ah," said Osborn, Lord Uptree. "Your brother…"

"A relative of yours, my lord."

"Possibly, although your husband's mother told various stories about that."

They were both fencing with words, but then their eyes met and saw truth: she was a heretic and he was a murderer.

"Your brother is accused of heresy, Mistress Stroud. This tragedy makes a difference. You must see that."

Meaning that Uptree's god had so blatantly executed the rest of the family in the same way that heretics died that now the noble lord couldn't possibly acknowledge any family relationship to the prisoner in Swine Hall. How scandalous that would be! No, Rollo Woodbridge would just have to suffer the same fate as his parents and brothers, but tied to a post in a public square to give the people a good show.

And if Maddy cared to make a fuss about it, then she could be included.

The first time she had met Uptree, two days ago, she had seen him as radiating power, and he had not lost any of that aura since. He had probably not foreseen Dampier's so-called miracle, for even that murderous priest had never gone as far as this before, but the marchers had brought ropes with them. Uptree had planned the murders. Would they have hanged Brat, too, or merely disinherited him?

Maddy curtsied properly. "I understand, my lord." Yes, she did.

The earl smiled approvingly. "You must mourn, of course. That is only natural, but soon you must get on with your life and strive to be a good wife to Sam. May the Light shine on you."

He wheeled his splendid horse and trotted away. Maddy stared after his retreating back. She toyed with the image of a knife hilt in the middle of it. Uptree, not Fage, was the proper target for revenge. He paused for a moment to exchange a word with Sam, who was heading her way, still leading Dainty.

But Sam had been in on the plot, too, or some of it. Two days ago he had been hidden in the hall of Norcaster Castle, just waiting to be pulled out of the hat when they needed a young bachelor, wedding ready. Uptree had sent for a quarryman he had ignored all his life and offered him a fine young wife with a fabulous dowry. Why?

Yes, Sam had been forewarned. When he first saw the ruins of the manor house that morning, he had said, "I never expected this." Maddy had thought he meant he had not expected it from what he had been told when the news reached Beaconbeck that morning. But he might have meant that he had not expected it from what Lord Uptree had told him two days ago.

The villains parted, and Sam arrived with her horse.

"His Lordship suggests I take you home, wife. Nothing we can do here."

No? It was a revealing remark under the circumstances. Sam knew who was in charge. Seeing that her husband was not about to dismount and assist, Maddy mounted unaided. They moved off at a walk.

"I would have thought," she said, then paused until she caught Sam's eye, "that there would have been a lot you could do here."

Suspicion flashed. "What do you mean?"

"It's all yours now, isn't it?"

"Not yet. I mean, His Lordship..." He floundered, turning red. Sam was not stupid, but he wasn't a good liar either.

"His Lordship just told you, did he not, that my brother Rollo is certain to be executed, so I am the only surviving heir? But a married woman cannot own property, so the entire manor is now yours, and will be inherited by our children."

"It does look that way." Sam Stroud stared fixedly at his horse's ears, trying not to smirk. He thought he was rich beyond his dreams.

"Not to me, it doesn't."

Smirk became glare. "What do you mean?"

"I mean that if you and I also die suddenly, it will all belong to Uptree. All this rich land bordering his own? No doubt he's been coveting it for years. You think he's doing this for you? There isn't enough real estate in Albi to treat all his bastards this way, so what's so special about you?"

Apart, of course, from a square jaw and muscled arms and golden chest hairs, guaranteed to turn a maiden's head like a windmill.

Sam had turned pale. "That's a terrible thing to suggest!"

"You think you can run the whole estate the way my father did? Not a hope, Sam Stroud. You're smart, but you're ignorant and you have no time to learn. I'm sure Master Ken Kennard is a very competent steward. He's going to manage the entire manor for you whether you like it or not. Don't doubt that all the profits will flow north to Norcaster, but if you keep your mouth shut and don't complain, you may live for a few years yet."

Long enough for the title deeds to become muddled enough to show that the manor belonged to Norcaster and that S. Stroud was only a tenant.

Unable to argue, Sam blustered, "Shut your mouth before I take a switch to your pretty little ass. If you behave yourself and start producing sons for me, you won't get beaten too often."

Not a hope. Maddy had three brothers, two parents, and a fraudulent marriage to avenge. One of the skills Wisdom Edith had taught her was how a woman could block unwanted conception. Let Sam try as hard as he liked—Maddy enjoyed that nonsense, too—she was not going to drop any noisy babies for Sam Stroud.

They would just get in the way of her campaign against Earl Uptree.

CHAPTER 17

MARY WHATMAN HAD BEEN REARED AS A STRICT FOLLOWER
of the Light. Her husband, Sir Mark Whatman, had been
equally staunch in the faith. He had also been a wit, a
horseman of renown, a handsome young giant, and owner
of Rose Hall, the finest home in the county.

Alas! Sir Mark, so virile and vivacious, fell ill of a fever
just two years after their marriage. Orthodox doctors
could do nothing to ease his suffering. When she could
no longer bear to watch his pitiful decline, Lady Whatman
spoke a quick prayer for forgiveness and sent for the local
wise woman. But the wisdom had cured so many people of
that same sickness that the Church Police had taken her
away for questioning and probably trial. The next closest
wisdom, who lived just across the county line in Angleshire,
had prudently taken an extended vacation elsewhere. Sir
Mark died.

Lady Whatman was left with Rose Hall, a one-year-old
son, and a burning grudge against the Church of the Light,
which she blamed for her widowhood. She converted to
the Children of the Earth and, like converts everywhere,

became more zealous than anyone raised in the faith of their fathers. She managed the Rose Hall estates well, using her considerable income to support her new beliefs. With remarkable cunning, she had evaded the notice of the Church.

Her son, also named Mark, grew up the image of his father, except that at sixteen he acquired a familiar, an owl. Soon he developed a talent for healing. When he turned seventeen, his mother sent him off to Xennia to study in Gaudry.

He returned at twenty-one as a qualified missionary. He taught and he healed, but he was too generous with his healing talent. He was betrayed and taken into custody. Eventually he was sentenced to death and burned at the stake for heresy, but his interrogation had damaged him so much that the executioners had to burn him on a chair. He had refused to talk, not even giving his true name, so there was no retaliation against his mother.

Lady Whitmore's hatred of the Church of the Light blazed even hotter. Only the Mother knew what she might have done had she not been sent persistent dreams of her son—and sometimes his father as well—counseling patience. Winter passed, and she contained her rage.

The following spring, she had a remarkably vivid dream of riding in her pony and trap, being driven by Josh. One could always tell dreams because they were so ridiculous. Josh driving was ridiculous, because Josh had been taken on as junior dung shoveler and was too stupid to do even that well.

There were blossoms on the ground.

A ragged woman, recognizable as a wisdom by her green head scarf, stood at the verge, signaling that the trap was to stop, which it did. Characters in dreams usually had familiar faces, but Lady Whatman had never seen that wise woman before. The woman said something incomprehensible, so it must be her features that mattered, not her name.

Then Sir Mark Whatman the younger came strolling out of the trees wearing plate armor. That was more dreaming, because no one had worn armor for over a century. He carried a shining broadsword in his hand, but he was smiling. He was young and beautiful again, not the ruined cripple they had burned. At his side walked a large black dog. Mark sprang up on the driving bench—both sword and Josh had disappeared—and his dog leaped into the trap beside Lady Whatman.

Jolted awake by a deafening crash of thunder, she sat up and heard the unmistakable sound of hail beating on the windowpanes. That would knock all the blossoms off the trees. The time for revenge had come. Not a dream but a vision! She was to be sent a knight in shining armor.

Next morning she ordered her trap brought around and appalled Derek, her chief hostler, by requiring that it be driven by Josh. The idiot managed to knock over an ornamental urn on the way to the front door and scrape the cart's paintwork going out the gate. Frightened to make the mare go faster, he let her amble at a snail's pace, yet still managed to find all the potholes. Lady Whatman sat on the seat and fumed. Perhaps she had been mistaken about Josh. He might have been included in the vision merely as a sort of title page: *A Dream, a Work of Fiction.*

Where was she expected to go? Most of the orchards she knew were on the Angleshire side of the county boundary, so she directed Josh in that direction. He wasn't likely to meet any traffic on that road, which was another blessing. Her instincts had been right, though, for after twenty minutes or so she saw the woman in the green head scarf. Her heart began to beat painfully fast.

But there was no knight in shining armor. In reality, the woman had a child with her, Bradwell Armstrong—a fake name if ever there was one. And a black puppy. Puppies, of course, grow up. So do children. Lady Whatman had no wish to clutter up her house with prattling children to brighten her misery and leaven her hatred, but when the boy spoke, it was clear that he was gentry and intelligent. She ordered him aboard. She had already decided that Josh had to go. The new lad could always take on Josh's shoveling duties if she had put too much faith in her vision.

Now what? She might as well go home. That meant having Josh turn the rig around. Could he possibly manage that without rolling it into a ditch? When she told him what she wanted, though, and he had halted, Bradwell jumped down, took the mare's cheek strap, and led her around in a half circle. Mission accomplished. The boy scrambled aboard again, and off they went.

Lady Whatman noted two curious things: the dog had remained in the trap and just watched, not jumped down to get in the way, and when Bradwell returned he did not grin as if he had done something praiseworthy. He remained as glum as ever. The bereavement story might be genuine.

After a few moments, she said, "It might be a good idea if I say you are my nephew."

"Yes, ma'am." He nodded seriously.

"Bradwell Armstrong? Then my sister is newly dead of a fever..."

She spun a yarn, and he just nodded. She had him say it back, and he had the names memorized. She was very curious now to know what the real story was, but she was confident she'd find out in due course. A furlong or so from her gate stood some laborers' cottages she owned. Josh came from there.

"Bradwell, could you drive this trap?"

Just a hint of hesitation, then, "Yes, ma'am." Likely he had seen it done but never done it.

"Josh, stop at your father's door."

Josh halted several yards past it, but his mother came scurrying out, wiping her hands on her apron, flour on her face. Half a minute was enough to dispose of the insufferable Josh and enough money to silence any complaints. Now there could be no gossip around the servants' quarters that her ladyship had found her nephew in a ditch.

Another half minute saw Bradwell on the bench and the trap moving at a spanking pace along the trail, veering around the worst of the potholes. Almost despite herself, Lady Whatman was becoming intrigued by this anonymous orphan and his curiously self-possessed pet. Mark's owl had often given the impression of being driven by a human intelligence, and so did this dog. Owls often did that; puppies didn't. But surely Bradwell was far too young to have a familiar?

When they came rattling up the driveway, he showed his first traces of normal boyish behavior. He said, *"Wow!"*

"This is my home, Rose Hall."

"It's very grand, ma'am. Beautiful!"

"I had better be Aunt Mary to you."

"Sorry. Forgot." He halted at the front door steps, put on the brake, and jumped down to help her disembark.

"We shall have to find you a room. I have lots to choose from."

Eyes wide, he stared up at the facade. "Does anyone sleep in that turret?"

The turret, the stables, the maze, the swimming hole—he politely praised them all. He was presented to the servants as Bradwell Armstrong and was gracious. But there was no sparkle. He was still a solemn little tyke, a boy with a broken heart.

The news arrived on the butcher's cart. It was brought up from the kitchen to the mistress, and she knew then that she did have her knight in shining armor after all. Bradwell's grievance against the tyrannical Church was even greater than her own. Fortunately, he was not present when she heard. She told him later about the terrible fire at Woodbridge Manor, over Angleshire way. She did not mention miracles. He broke down then. It was very nearly twenty years since she had hugged Mark for the last time, for she was not a demonstrative woman. Even when he left for Xennia, she had merely let him kiss her cheek. But that evening she hugged the Woodbridge boy, and he sobbed in her arms. She would tolerate even that if it brought her closer to her vengeance.

The next day they talked about ponies, and he described one he had owned "once." Skewbald—"That means brown and white"—with front hooves white and back hooves black. About twelve hands.

Lady Whatman instructed Derek, her hostler, to keep an eye on horse sales in the area, and especially to look out for skewbald ponies. Two weeks later Charger turned up at a sale in Norcaster and was duly acquired for Master Armstrong. Master Armstrong began to smile again.

In a few weeks he started playing with the servants' and the plowmen's sons. Lady Whatman noticed that he liked to lead and even the older ones let him do so, but that might just be because he was milady's nephew.

CHAPTER 18

THE MOLESWORTH HOUSEHOLD WAS COMPRISED OF CHARLES himself, his two sons, a couple of apprentices, and three female servants. All were devout worshipers of the Mother. After the Molesworths themselves, the most important resident was Mistress Baird, the housekeeper, a woman of gimlet eye and formidable size. She answered the door to all callers. As she had excellent insight, no government spy was ever going to slip by her. Her talent deserved much credit for keeping the Molesworths safe in the Mother's service for so long.

Charles was a widower, and his sons were unmarried. All three traveled a lot, building secret hiding places all over Albi. The sons grumbled that they never found time for courting, but Charles confided to Rollo that Rob was recovering from a failed romance and Kip had a close friend in the next street.

The house was crowded. Rollo was honored with the guest room, while Kip had moved in with Rob so the two wisdoms could have his. On the day after Rollo's rescue, Wisdom Edith left to return to Stonebridge, promising to pass the good news to his family. Wisdom Nell insisted on moving into the servants' attic so that Kip could have his room back.

That first day Rollo stayed in bed, being nursed by Charles, for he could not eat, drink, dress, or even relieve himself without assistance. Most of the time he slept, but fitfully, because of the pain in his hands and wrists. Even the greatest of healers could not heal himself.

By the end of the second day, he was well enough to lead the evening prayers. Next morning, he insisted that Charles go back to work. The carpenter's absence was not only costing him money but might also attract attention. His workshop was only a few blocks from Swine Hall, and saner heads in the government should have realized by then that their prize prisoner might have been smuggled out under their noses, not carried off by demons. Any unusual activity in the vicinity might be investigated.

So every day from then on the men went off to work, the servants cleaned and cooked, and Rollo was alone with Wisdom Nell. They sat in the parlor and talked by the hour. The parlor was a small room, more snug than fancy, set up for three large men to gather around the fire on a winter evening, puffing on their pipes and discussing the day's work or plans for another refuge somewhere. In springtime the grate was empty and the windows stood open, looking out on a quiet yard. It was typical of the careful planning the Molesworths put into their lives that no other windows overlooked theirs.

Nell was a very attractive young woman, with dark eyes and hair; her teeth shone like stars when she smiled. She brought Rollo up to date on a lot of Albiurn news that he would need to know in his mission. She took over the task of feeding him and all but the most intimate personal matters. She was excellent company. Rollo was curious to know why she was still there, now the rescue had been completed, but he was happy that she was.

He wondered about her personal life. Where did she live? Was she married? Betrothed? He did not know how to ask such questions, and she volunteered only that her father was a clerk in the service of Baron Bancarrow, who belonged to the Church of the Light but was sympathetic to the Children's cause. Nell had grown up in a cultured household. She could play the spinet and quote poetry. She had acquired a guide at fourteen.

"I haven't met your familiar," Rollo said.

She smiled. "You may regret asking. Striker, come out and meet Brother Rollo."

The front of her dress writhed of its own accord, and a triangular, scaly head appeared over the top of her bodice. Eyes like glass beads regarded Rollo.

"Um, pleased to meet you, Striker. Sorry I can't shake hands just yet."

Two grins exploded into laughter—his first laugh since leaving Xennia.

"Striker's bite wouldn't kill an adult," she said. "But it would hurt a lot."

Yes, any would-be rapist must be distracted when bitten in the face by an adder. The snake slithered back out of sight.

"So you have gifts for mastery and inspiration," he said. "For which I was supremely grateful the other night." It was bad manners to inquire openly about an adept's talents, but he had a feeling that Nell was waiting to tell him.

"And distraction," she said, "but that's just a special form of inspiration. And some insight. Not up to Mistress Baird's, but I can tell the bad eggs more often than not." After a moment she added, "And the good ones. Rumor has it that you got the complete set."

"No. Insight is the one I regret most. Any rogue in Albi could sell me a mule and have me think it was a horse. And I can't jiggle, or I wouldn't have worn those manacles so long." His bandaged wrists were itching fiercely.

"I thought jiggling was a myth."

"No, I've seen it done. Just moving small things, though. No one can make himself float through the air."

"We make a good fit, though, you and I."

Rollo changed the subject.

So the days passed happily, but in the nights he was alone, and it was then that doubts emerged like ghosts from graves. Physically he was going to heal—his hands would not hurt so much if they had died—but would he ever regain his nerve? Pottenger had broken his spirit. The horse had thrown him; could he find the will to remount? The first time he had to take refuge in a mole hole and hear the tramp of boots as the Church Police searched the house for him, would he endure, or would he just crumble with terror?

 e&

On his third evening there, just as the household was gathering in the parlor for prayers, the doorbell rang. Mistress Baird ran downstairs to answer it, while Kip peered out a spyhole.

"Trull," he said, and everyone relaxed.

Everyone then trooped out, leaving Rollo alone. He waited, oddly nervous, hearing the visitor being greeted and relieved of his cloak. Trull declined refreshment, insisting he could not stay long. When he was ushered into the parlor, Rollo bowed.

Jake Trull was fifty years old but looked older. His face had sagged into folds, his waist into a paunch. His clothes were so nondescript that he could pass as a prosperous artisan or a down-at-the-heels minor nobleman, except for a small fruit bat clinging to his doublet; no doubt it was normally concealed by his cloak. Rollo had met that bat before. Trull seemed tired. He approached Rollo with both hands outstretched to grip his, winced when he saw Rollo's hands, and gently embraced him instead.

In as much as the Children of Earth had any organization at all left in Albi, Jake Trull was the prelate. He had run the mission for twenty years. Dozens of times he had escaped from the government's agents by a hairsbreadth, often hiding for days at a stretch in one or other of the Molesworths' secret refuges, while the enemy tapped and measured, seeking him out. The price on his head had now reached two thousand suns.

"Brutes," he said. "You know you're not supposed to bow to me. Where were you sitting?"

They sat down simultaneously and smiled across the fireplace at each other. Rollo saw a man who had worn himself out in the service of his goddess, a man who had lived most of his life under the threat of the stake or worse. A man who had survived by being cunning, secretive, and distrusting, although he might have been none of these things before he accepted his calling. Rollo was appalled.

"How are you feeling, lad?"

"My shoulders are much better. Can't move my hands yet."

"It'll come, two or three weeks. You must stay here until you can sit a horse."

"Yes, sir." Rollo tried to keep his face and voice inscrutable, but he knew that Trull was gifted with almost every talent known and could probably read him like a poster.

"John Hawke, I hear."

"Yes, sir."

"Good one. Well, you're safe enough here. The Privy Council hasn't announced your escape yet, but it didn't make much of your arrest in the first place. Besides, it doesn't know what happened, so how can it explain? My sources close to the Hierarchy report that the holies are spitting fire. They may force King Ethan to dismiss First Secretary Kipping."

"That'll teach them to meddle with me," Rollo said, smiling. He realized that Trull wasn't saying everything he might, that he was testing him, deciding how much to tell him. They were talking around things, not talking them over.

The older man chuckled. "I think you scared them. The rescue and the curse on Pottenger, these are new tactics for us. They'll wait and see where you surface and what we do next. They have spies everywhere, you know."

"Yes, sir."

"When will you be ready to take over my job?" Trull's eyes were masked.

"I don't know who started that stupid rumor, but I have absolutely no ambition to succeed you."

"It came from someone with prescience."

"Not me, sir."

Trull said, "No, not you," but his smile said more than his words.

It had been common knowledge for years that Rollo Woodbridge would succeed Jake Trull as Prelate Albi. Rollo had given up protesting that he would do anything in the world to avoid such a fate, because no one ever believed him. Prelate Gaudry had given him special instruction for his future responsibilities. Even the Albiurn government had heard the story.

"I'm told you have no insight."

"No, sir. Not a trace."

"That's a shame. Insight has saved my hide more times than I dare count. You'll need a companion with insight when you start traveling. How are you getting along with Wisdom Nell?"

Not too subtle, that.

"Fine." That was too cold. "Very attractive young lady."

"A bit of a wildcat at times."

"She's been quite domesticated around me."

"Give her time." Trull rose and fetched a stool so he could sit close to Rollo. "Let's get those bandages off you..." He scowled at the festering burns on Rollo's wrists and then closed his hands around them. "I can speed things along for you."

"They feel better already."

"That's just your imagination; they'll need a few weeks yet. Remember, lad, this is one of the very few times and places you will be safe. Make the most of it. From now on there will be a dragon behind every tree. Relax, get your strength back, and take comfort from the fact that you won the first round. That monster Pottenger will ruin no more fine men—thank the Mother and thank you. I'll be back in Weypool in a couple of weeks; I'll drop in and see you again then. Soon as you're fit, we'll start you on your travels."

Rollo might lack insight, but he had enough common perception to know that Trull was holding something back. If he thought Rollo was not yet strong enough to hear it, then Rollo was happy to wait.

"I've wanted to meet you for many years, sir."

The shrewd old eyes regarded him from deep in their nests of wrinkles. "And I've been eagerly waiting to meet you. My insight tells me you're as good as they said you were. Now, I realize that you can't clasp with those hands yet, but you could let other people hold them if they're careful. I'll bring the others in and we can have a brief bonding circle."

"That would be wonderful," Rollo said. Trull's touch had already soothed some of his pain, but a bonding could start to heal his damaged soul.

After the service, the prelate slipped away to his lonely vagabond life.

Rollo wanted nothing more than a good night's sleep and thought that might even be possible, since Trull had reduced his pain load. But it wasn't Charles who followed him across the passage to his room. It was Nell. She shut the door behind them, and then snuffed out the lantern she was carrying.

"I have a favor to ask," she said.

She was smiling in a way he did not think she would be if she had remembered that he had blindsight. She came over to him and started helping him remove his doublet.

"Sister Nell, after your efforts to rescue me from Swine Hall, I can refuse you nothing."

"Good!" She clasped his head in both hands and kissed him. There was nothing sisterly about that kiss.

He kept his lips clenched tight and turned his head away. "Wait!"

"Why?" She began to unlace his shirt.

"I don't approve of sex outside marriage."

"Who mentioned that? You just said you could refuse me nothing. Now can I have that kiss? A real kiss!"

He distrusted her intentions, but this time he accepted the kiss. All he could manage to return her embrace was a gentle hug with his forearms, so weak that she would hardly feel it. But there was nothing wrong with his kissing muscles, and there he gave as good as he got. It would have been discourteous not to. He felt his resolve melting like butter and realized that she was inspiring him. He countered.

She stopped and frowned at him. "You're blocking me."

"Let's talk about this."

"Why? It is unthinkable to discuss such matters. Gentlefolk *never* talk about it! But they all do it."

"It is unethical to inspire someone without good reason."

"Since we can both inspire, this should be a scorcher."
She removed his shirt and stroked cool fingers down his
back.

Oh, Mother! It had been years...and he did owe her his
life. His moral dilemma was suddenly solved by a flash of
prescience. Yes! His conscience agreed that sex *before* matri-
mony was not quite so improper. And she had his britches
down to his knees, so he couldn't deny his desire anymore.

"Where's the snake?"

"I left Striker downstairs. Besides, he wouldn't bite you."
She sensed that he was not un-inspiring her anymore. "Now
either scream for help or shut up."

"Go ahead. Do whatever you want. All I can do is lie
here and leave the heavy work to you." For the first week
or so.

From then on Nell was both his nurse and lover. As she
said, they were an obvious team. Trull had planned it that
way. The Moles knew right away and had obviously been
expecting it to happen.

Three days later, Charles came home early, with a face
that proclaimed disaster. He took Rollo into the parlor
without even Nell present and told him of the "miracle"
at Woodbridge. So there would be no homecoming, no
reunion. The news Trull had held back was now general
knowledge in the capital.

Father, mother, a sister, and two brothers.

When the time came for prayers that evening, Rollo spoke about revenge.

"I laid a curse on Warden Pottenger, and already I regret that. At the time it seemed necessary, for without that distraction I could not have escaped, and my rescuers would have been captured also. Pottenger had tortured me for two days. Being human, I find that very hard to forgive, no matter how strongly he believed in his cause. But I sentenced Pottenger to a lifetime of torment. I am worse than he is. I must live with the memory and the guilt.

"Ends cannot justify means. Only means can justify ends. Always the problem with revenge is that it drags the avengers down to their victims' level, or lower. To hanker after revenge is a form of hatred, which eats the soul like a canker. An eye never seems enough for an eye, so you take an eye and a nose; then your enemy claims an eye, a nose, and lots of teeth. So it goes, until you have both sunk to the worst atrocities you can imagine.

"Today I was told my whole family had been slain by a thunderbolt. According to the Church of the Light, their god answered the prayers of Rafe Dampier and thus showed how holy and correct he is.

"We know better, you and I. We know that the Mother gives talents to those she chooses, and they use her gifts as they see fit, just as Kip there uses his strength or Mistress Baird her insight. Rafe Dampier has been striking people dead for years, starting with his own father when he was only a boy. I do not blame the God of Light for my family's death, nor do I blame the Mother. I accuse Rafe Dampier of murder.

"But I will not seek him out to punish him. I pray that if I ever find him at my mercy, I will be strong enough to grant that mercy. Above all, I pray that someday the Kingdom of Albi will return to the rule of law, where people are held responsible for their own actions and cannot blame them on their god. Then, I hope, Rafe Dampier will answer for his crime—not to me, but to a court of justice that can judge him in cold blood.

"Now, I hope you will join me in a bonding circle. It will be special for two reasons: it will be the first I have conducted since I was ordained a missionary, and it is mostly for myself. Even a bonding cannot wipe away my sorrow, for that will need years, but I know it will dull the saw edge of my loss."

CHAPTER 19

MONTHS PASSED BEFORE MADDY COULD LAUNCH HER campaign for revenge on the Uptree brothers, and the summer was a time of sorrow and loneliness. Her friends must believe her dead in the Dampier "miracle," and she did not advise them otherwise. In any case, few would dare associate with her, now that her family had been officially branded as heretics, and most would spurn her when they learned of her marriage to a laborer of ignoble birth. She had no means of transportation, for Beaconbeck's stable contained only carthorses. Wisdom Edith lived beyond easy walking distance.

For a mere farmer's wife to dream of revenge against two such powerful men might seem absurd, but Maddy had talent, and she knew how she would have to use it. Years ago, her mother had taken her to consult a wise man, Brother Alfred, who looked like a shrunken gnome left over from some ancient folktale but had a talent for detecting talents. Maddy, he had decided, had only two. Most important, she could inspire, meaning she could invoke any emotion she wanted in other people, although very few people at a time and only at very close range. The main advantage of that, Alfred had said, was that it made her rape-proof. She could quench a man's unwelcome aggression instantly and make him devoutly ashamed of himself. As her mother had pointed out on the way home, it could also be used the other way, to encourage a lover.

She could also distract people so they would not notice her. Handy, the little man had chuckled, if she wanted to collect other people's silver plate. The two talents often went together, in that most adepts who could inspire could also distract, although people with distraction could not necessarily inspire.

Maddy practiced her talent on her husband. She learned how to rouse Sam to superhuman exertions, but also how to neuter him for days on end. It was unfair, of course, but so was murder, and he had let himself be used in the Uptree plot. Lord Uptree's steward, Ken Kennard, was a cold-blooded man in his fifties with snaky eyes, so she tried a wile or two on him, too. One glance and a sigh were enough to dilate his pupils and puff out his chest. A faint shrug deflated him again.

She could also rouse men's rage, their second favorite emotion. One day, on a whim, she set Sam and Kennard at loggerheads. She said nothing. They were not fighting over her. They hardly seemed to be fighting over anything, but soon they were waving fists and screaming at each other. When Sam was ready to punch out all Kennard's teeth and Kennard was threatening to have Sam flogged, Maddy calmed them down with a few soothing words.

Thus she sharpened the weapon the Mother had given her while the summer dragged on. She was not idle.

She honestly tried to educate Sam. As she had foreseen, Kennard had taken over management of Beaconbeck as if Sam did not exist. Since Sam had already made himself unpopular by lording it over his old workmates, the hands were content to do whatever Kennard told them and ignore their official master.

First, she told him, he must learn to read and write and sum. Once he could do those things, he would be taken seriously. He did try, but his heart wasn't in it. In Sam Stroud's world, problems were solved with knuckles, not knowledge. He was a competent plowman and quarryman, no more.

Kennard was also managing all the other lands that had made up the Woodbridge estate. Maddy was never officially informed that she had inherited the rest, which would mean that they now belonged to her husband. It was equally possible that Rollo had inherited and then been convicted of treason. A traitor's property was forfeit to the crown, and a privy councilor like Earl Uptree would have been johnny-on-the-spot to claim first dibs. One way or another, His Lordship had gotten what he wanted, and the Woodbridge line was now considered extinct.

Not quite, and sooner or later the last of the Woodbridges would strike. She would avenge her parents, even though her methods would have appalled them.

꿍

Every fall, Earl Uptree hosted a hundred guests at a grand hunting party. His normal staff could not cope, so he had to borrow servants from friends and round up some of the more presentable hands from his many outlying properties. Kennard picked out a few for him, and Maddy was one of them. Her duties would be to dust and polish and make beds, so she would have no reason to mingle with the visitors. No official reason, that is, but she had her own plans.

Sam was also selected, to his disgust, but let his wife talk him into cooperating, to his surprise. He looked very handsome in livery, the calves in his white stockings being much admired. All he had to do was follow orders: move that table, carry this tray, take the baggage upstairs. He could handle that.

Maddy's uniform was a black dress extending from neck to ankles and wrists, with a frilly bonnet that left only her face visible. For three days she was trained, assigned duties, and taught the geography of Norcaster Castle. She slept in a grossly overcrowded attic with a dozen other women.

And she kept her ears open. Earl This, Baron That, and even, so it was whispered, First Secretary Kipping, might attend. There had been talk of Crown Prince Emil coming, but now his name had been scratched and the royal suite reassigned. Maddy did not feel ready for privy councilors or royalty yet. What she needed and must find was some middle-aged nobleman who hung around the fringes of Weypool society. She was relieved to hear that Hierarch Garret Uptree would not be attending; she suspected that the senior clergy of the Light might be gifted by the Mother, although they would call their talents by another name.

She also stayed out of Earl Uptree's way. He knew her and would not want her around. She knew she could arouse some younger man to kill him in a frenzy of mindless rage, but that would be hard to arrange and not a satisfactory vengeance anyway. Something lingering and shameful was required. Men like the earl could not be toppled from below, so when she attacked, it must be from higher ground. The only way women could acquire power in Albi was by working through powerful men.

On the morning of the day the guests were due to arrive, she came face to face with Father Silas Fage, the castle chaplain. They rounded the same corner in opposite directions, and she had no time to apply her distraction talent. Despite her all-enveloping uniform, he recognized her at once and showed some bad teeth in a smile.

"Madeline! Madeline...um, what was the name of that handsome young swineherd you married?"

"Stroud, Father."

"Stroud, yes. Madeline Stroud. No children on the way yet? Is he not doing his duty by you?"

Fage was not on her death list. She considered him lower than dog shit. But he might serve for target practice.

"It is certainly not for want of trying, Father. He is a wonderfully strong lover—three, four times every night." *Swallow that, you nasty celibate.*

Evidently the jibe did not taste good, for his face soured. "Doing one's duty to multiply is not the same as rank lechery, Madeline. Try spending more time in prayer and less in rut." He blessed, she curtsied, and they parted. For now.

By evening the castle was full to bursting and the staff run off its collective feet. All except Maddy. Camouflaged by her distraction talent, she wandered where she liked and eavesdropped on whom she pleased, and no one noticed a chambermaid mixing with the high and mighty.

On the third evening, she observed the Reverend Silas Fage in conversation with His Lordship and a jewel-encrusted matron whose name she did not know or want to know. They were standing beside a pillar on the edge of the dance floor, which was crowded, although the orchestra was not currently playing. Guests milled around at will, sipping wine and shredding reputations. Spurring her distraction ability to a gallop, Maddy walked up behind the earl.

She didn't catch what His Lordship had said. It didn't matter.

"Oh, I wouldn't say that," Fage remarked.

"Wouldn't you? And just what would you say?"

"I'd say he was a sinner who must be brought to the Light in repentance."

"And I think he is a disgusting pervert and you are probably another for defending him."

"My son, you should not speak to a man in holy orders like that!"

The matron looked alarmed as their voices rose.

"Don't you 'son' me, you parasite. I have had about enough of your canting, holier-than-thou hypocrisy. Don't think I don't know about the choirboys you abuse in the bell tower."

"Liars!" Fage screamed, turning heads all around. "They are all filthy little degenerates. There are never any witnesses, and you are a damnable fool for believing their lies."

He kept shouting, drowning out the earl's tirade, until both were yelling at the tops of their voices, faces turning purple. The matron fled. The great hall fell silent to listen.

Then Earl Uptree hurled the contents of his wineglass in the priest's face, momentarily silencing him, and looked around for assistance. The closest footman, by the Mother's grace, happened to be Samuel Stroud, holding a tray of glasses. Sam had not noticed Maddy, and the earl was beyond recognizing Sam.

"Get this priestly turd out of here! Throw him in the fucking moat!"

Sam said, "Yes, my lord," very contentedly. He dropped the tray with a clang and a crash. The priest turned to flee, but he was out of his element when it came to brawling. Sam grabbed him as he might seize a wayward child and stalked off across the hall with Fage draped over his shoulder like a towel.

The earl looked across the sea of horrified faces and yelled, "And nobody let that buggering little hypocrite back in!"

Very satisfactory. Maddy slipped away.

❧

Almost too satisfactory, she decided as she climbed the servants' stairs. She might have provoked a split between the Uptree brothers, even between church and state. The priest might be defrocked and the earl evicted from the Privy Council. But such extremes were unlikely, for Uptree had not insulted a gentleman. If anyone did question, he would just claim that he had been drunk, which was a perfectly acceptable excuse among the gentry. Fage would be banished to some remote parish. Whatever the origin of his spite against the Woodbridge family, it was a shame that he would never know who had won in the end.

More alarming from Maddy's point of view was the possibility that she might have broken up the party. Prudish guests might show their disapproval by going home, and a leak could easily become a flood. As yet she had made no progress in her search for the patron she needed to escape from Angleshire. It was time to seek help.

The attic dormitory was deserted, clothes and bedding heaped everywhere. She had noticed a few mouse holes in corners, and any mouse hole where she wouldn't be overheard would do.

She lay down close to one and whispered, "Teeny?"

Whiskers and two shiny eyes appeared. This could not be the same mouse she had known back home at the manor house, or the one she consulted sometimes at Beaconbeck. But it would be the same Teeny.

"You told me this would be good place to find a patron who will take me back to Weypool with him and gain me access to high society."

Nod.

"Then please find me find one!"

The mouse scampered out of the hole and wriggled in under her collar. She felt him settling in under her breasts. He tickled.

Right. Back to the battlefield…

After that it was easy. A lively galliard was underway in the hall. Few guests were dancing, though. Most were standing on the sidelines, chuckling over that scandalous quarrel between their host and his chaplain. As soon as the news reached Weypool, it would be the talk of the town.

Maddy hesitated. Teeny tickled her right breast, so she turned that way and began wending her way between the clumps of gossiping gentry. Left tickle. She turned that way. Another tickle came as she was passing a group of three: a young man and two middle-aged women. None looked promising. The women were fat, grossly overdressed, over jeweled, and over painted, all lace and pearls and coiffures a mile high. The man was flabby and almost as bedecked as his companions. They were laughing uproariously at whatever he had just said, and he wore a vacuous, smug smile.

Maddy withdrew to the sidelines to wait until the human currents rearranged the groupings. Then she tried again. Again Teeny directed her to that same young man, so there was no doubt. She had no idea who he was, and to ask anyone she would have to relax her distraction defense, which would be a risk. She contented herself with watching him for the rest of the evening, which wasn't difficult. No one else was wearing that shade of purple, and he was usually surrounded by peals of laughter. He never danced; he associated mainly with persons older than himself. She was intrigued, for he did not fit any of her categories. Other young men were either flaunting mating plumage and stalking the younger women, or were the windburned and bored types, anxious to go to bed and rest up for an early start and another day of slaughtering animals. Purple's face had rarely seen the sun, as if he did not know one end of a horse from the other. Older men were either already half stupefied with wine or clustered heads down, talking money and politics. Purple drank sparingly and seemed to be a constant source of amusement to his current listeners, so he could not be discussing either money or politics. Unlike most men there, he was clean-shaven, and he wore his auburn hair down to his shoulders.

When the band departed and footmen with lanterns were escorting guests to their rooms, Maddy followed her quarry as he went to his. She lingered at the end of the corridor for about twenty minutes before he emerged, then trailed after him, down one flight to the floor where the most important guests were billeted. He tapped on a door before going in. The guests' rooms were labeled, so Maddy now knew that her grace the Duchess of Dorsi was currently entertaining the Honorable Tristan Rastel, and vice versa.

CHAPTER 20

NEXT MORNING MADDY PUT A FEW DISCREET, AS SHE thought, inquiries to members of the permanent staff regarding the young man who had worn purple at the ball. The replies varied from rolled eyes to urgent warnings to stay away from that one. At best he lived by his wits; at worst he was deep into prostitution and the white slave trade. He was not the sort of aging, decadent man-about-town she had envisaged as her first patron-to-be, but Teeny said he was the best available, and what was the use of having a spirit guide if you didn't trust it?

How reliable was a mouse's judgment?

There was no easy way for an insignificant chambermaid to arrange a private meeting with the Honorable Tristan, and the guests would start leaving the next day. Maddy resigned herself to spending several hours keeping watch on his door from near the top of the stairs, armed with a silver tray bearing a cup of hot chocolate, soon very cold chocolate. When guests or other servants came along in ones or twos, she simply distracted them so they detoured around her without registering that she was there at all. If a larger group appeared—a group she judged too large for her slim talent to manage—she pretended to be delivering her burden, then returned to her post when they had gone by.

Her plan was simple. When the Honorable Tristan emerged, she would try to collide with him and spill the chocolate over herself—not him, because she did not want to enrage a man who obviously took much pride in his clothes. She would gratefully accept his help if offered and let him take her back into his room to wipe off the worst of the mess. And then, or sooner if he did not offer to help, she would inspire him to frenzied lust and make his day. After his epochal performance, they could discuss a long-term arrangement. She would, in effect, offer to be his kept woman, retaining the option of climbing higher on the social ladder later.

What would her mother think of what she proposed to do? Maddy refused to think about that. Her father, she thought, might grudgingly approve. She could not ask their opinions because they were both dead, which was the whole point.

The hunters had left before dawn. The rest of the guests emerged from their rooms in ones or twos much later, many of them bleary-eyed and eager for restorative fluids from bottles. Maddy had not observed the Honorable Tristan drinking enough to give him a hangover. After a couple of hours, she began to wonder if he had spent the entire night with the duchess, not returning to his own bed at all. That was not how such affairs should be conducted, she thought, but her experience was based entirely on secondhand information.

Before she gave up, but not long before, the Honorable Tristan's door swung open. Maddy sprang into motion. Ideally, she would reach him just as he emerged, so the collision would not seem too contrived. She hurried along the corridor, slowing as she reached the doorway and the strip of sunshine on the floor. She glanced in as she passed, and saw an undisturbed bed. So he had not slept there? Then who had just opened the door?

"I hope," said a voice behind her, "that you weren't planning to tip that all over me."

Maddy spun around in horror. The Honorable Tristan deftly relieved her of the tray before any accidents could be accomplished. He freed one hand to gesture at the open door.

"'Step into my parlor,' said the fly to the spider."

At a loss for words, Maddy went in. The Honorable Tristan followed her and closed the door. He laid the tray on the dressing table and then advanced until he was close enough to look down on her. He was taller than she had realized. He brought a scent of violets. Today he was clad in garments of buttercup yellow silk, exquisitely cut, and there wasn't a hair of his shiny auburn mane out of place.

"What's your name?"

She had an answer ready. "Mindy Wells, sir."

"Oh, you poor thing! But I do admire your distraction talent. It's the best I've never seen."

"Oh, sir, please explain that oxymoron."

"You were following me around last night with the doting gaze of the fawn for the doe. It was as much as I could do not to notice you. I mean, not let you notice me noticing you." He smiled. His face was soft, pale, almost effeminate. He had fleshy, voluptuous lips, but his teeth were perfect and his smile charmed. "And you've been waiting out there for hours. No matter, we're together at last. What happens next, Mindy?"

There could only be one answer.

"This." She kissed him, inspiring for all she was worth.

He was very good at kissing, too.

"That's splendid!" he muttered at the first break, but after that neither said a word. Kissing, fondling, stripping each other, they sent clothes flying until they could tumble naked onto the coverlet and made frantic love in the sunshine, not even closing the bed curtains. What *would* her mother have said? Where Sam was all hard muscle, Tristan was soft. He was smooth where Sam was hairy, and gentler by far. And he was skilled. He held back until he had coaxed her to a climax, and she did not have to fake her moans of joy. She could not be certain that his were genuine, but they certainly implied approval.

They lay there a while in damp embrace, with heavy breathing and the slow thump of their hearts.

"I detect that you have a distraction talent, also," she murmured.

"It shields me from admiring mobs."

"But…but if your talent lets you detect mine, why did I not see you come out of your room this morning? You must have other gifts."

"I have one called insight, but I do not need it to know that you are more than a servant wench out to earn a little blackmail. Your vowels are deliberately rusticated, but your vocabulary is hyperbolized."

"You worship the Mother?" She had thought that city dwellers were all followers of the Light.

"I have an agreement with the gods," the Honorable Tristan muttered, nibbling her ear. "If they don't bother me, I won't bother them."

She sniggered and deliberately tried inspiration again.

"Stop, please," he said, squeezing her breast. "I have promised a certain lady that I will boost her self-esteem right after lunch, and if you wear me out first, I shall be mortified in more ways than one. But I will willingly submit to your uplifting skills after that. Say midafternoon or—"

Knuckles tapped the door. "Chambermaid."

Before Maddy could say a word, Tristan rolled on top of her and kissed her. His hair fell over her face. Cooperating, she wrapped her arms and legs around him.

The door opened, gasped in horror, and slammed shut.

Tristan and Maddy disentangled. He rolled free.

"Nicely done," she said.

"A reputation for depravity requires constant vigilance."

To her astonishment, Maddy was feeling genuinely aroused by this bizarre character. He might have inspirational talent also and be playing with her. "You are quite sure you don't fancy a rematch?"

"If I didn't have that business appointment after lunch, I would cheerfully lie here and fornicate with you until we both died of exhaustion. From midafternoon until breakfast I shall be a willing slave to your rampaging lust. And your occult talent won't even be required. Your splendid young body is incentive enough."

Sam Stroud couldn't have managed a statement like that in a thousand years. She was starting to realize what she had missed.

"You are too kind, Your Honor."

"I mean it, although normally it is folly to speak the truth in sexual matters. Quickly, then, tell me what you are really after."

"I want to find a rich patron to introduce me to Weypool society."

"Then I am the best man to come, er, to. That is my specialty. Even my discussion after lunch today will primarily concern that lady's need for a confidential secretary. Male, of course, but I need her exact specifications on age, build, and more private topics best raised in bed. I have several candidates in mind for her, and I can already think of half a dozen for you."

Holy Mother! This was a glimpse of a world Maddy had never guessed existed. "And your, um, fee for this service?"

Tristan slid off the bed and began dressing. "You have just provided a generous retainer. We shall discuss details in my coach tomorrow. You can accompany me then?"

"I am at your service, sir."

"Back here midafternoon for that, please."

Tristan dressed, brushed his hair, and departed. Maddy locked the door and began gathering her clothes.

The next day she folded her wedding ring in a piece of paper and fastened it with a pin. She wrote Sam's name on it and gave it to a senior footman to be delivered, distracting him just enough that he would not be sure who had given it to him. She left Norcaster Castle in the same dowdy blue dress she had worn when she arrived, but also in the belief that she was heading for a whole new life.

Many guests were leaving at the same time. Not knowing which coach belonged to the Honorable Tristan Rastel, she waited on the sidelines, masked by her distraction talent. When he appeared, he was accompanied by porters bringing three huge trunks of luggage. The carriage that pulled up for him was as grand as any, although it lacked armorial bearings on the door.

Tristan embarked, leaving the flunkies to load his baggage on the roof. Unnoticed, Maddy walked over and followed him aboard. Heart racing, she sat on the bench opposite.

"Greetings, my dear," he said. "You slept well?"

"In what was left of the night, I did. Thank you."

"No, the thanks are due to you!" He yawned. "These house parties are quite exhausting. Ah, here he comes."

A young man wearing inconspicuous livery scrambled in and sat beside Tristan. A footman closed the door. The coach began to move.

"Mindy, meet Roddy Pryde, my valet. Roddy, Mindy Wells, a new client."

They nodded to each other, but Maddy felt an instinctive distrust. Although he sported thin, sandy sideburns, he was hardly more than a boy. His eyes were shifty and his smile as genuine as a stuffed mermaid.

"How did you make out with the baron?" Tristan inquired.

"Putty in my hands," the boy said.

"How disappointing for you."

"I didn't mean it that way! We're down to arguing terms."

"What did he offer? Oh, don't mind Mindy. She's one of the team now. Aren't you, my dear?"

From what Maddy recalled about insight, lie detection was one of its strengths, so she told the truth. "If you play fair with me, I'll play fair with you."

"You are absolutely untroubled by dishonesty or immorality of any kind?"

She took a moment to think about that. "I have my own standards, but I don't care about yours. Or Roddy's. I'm not in this to be moral or honest."

The coach was rocking now, rattling down the long castle drive.

"Excellent! A girl after my own heart and other vital organs. Now, the baron?"

Roddy shrugged. "Room and board. Ten silvers a month, plus three for dress allowance. All right so far, I thought, but he wants me to be secretary or librarian or something. I said nephew and my days are my own. Nights are his."

"More than fair. Will he go for it?"

"I'll give him a few days to brood on what he's missing."

"That's my boy!" Tristan patted his knee approvingly. Roddy smirked triumphantly.

"What else did you pick up?"

Roddy shrugged. "A few nice bits of plate. And this. Of course, it will have to be reset." He produced what looked to Maddy like a diamond ring.

Tristan hardly glanced at it. "No. It's paste. Shop it right away and don't expect more than two moons for it. That's an order, Roddy! You promise?"

"Yes, Tristan."

A man with such insight could probably trust even an obvious gutter rat like Roddy. And Tristan, Maddy decided with a shiver, might be ruthless toward anyone who double-crossed him.

"Now, my dear. Your real name, station, and purpose?"

"Mindy Wells will suffice. I have done no wrong, but I have been greatly wronged. I want to climb in society until I have powerful friends. My life's ambition is to destroy a pair of prominent persons. No matter how long it takes or whatever the cost."

Roddy looked disbelieving; Tristan accepted what she said. "I do not wish to know who those persons are. Not now, maybe later. You are no peasant, but to prosper in Weypool you will need coaching in dress, speech, manners, dancing, and so on. Not in bed. There you are supremely qualified, but you want to be a trophy, not a hidden treasure. If you are a quick study, we should be able to launch your career at the start of the social season next fall."

And how was she to pay for the lessons? She did not ask. Eventually the rocking of the coach lulled her to an uneasy doze, only to jolt her awake again on the rough patches. Tristan did not sleep, greeting her return each time with a quiet smile. He had his arm around Roddy, who was fast asleep with his head on Tristan's shoulder. Had Maddy been more experienced, she would have known to sit beside Tristan, not across from him.

⌒◯

The sheer size of Weypool amazed her. For an hour the carriage would crawl along fetid alleys, speed up to rumble past grand mansions in park-like grounds, and then slink back into slums again. The postilion took a shortcut through the Royal Park, quite permissible to anyone who could afford a coach. The royal palace itself was a marble marvel, with fountains, statues, and a thousand staring windows. Coronet Temple, with its soaring, gilded towers, was even grander and still being enlarged.

The Honorable Tristan's home was short of palatial but well above slum, one in a continuous row of houses four stories high, opening right off the street. By that time the daylight was fading. Tristan handed her down and offered his arm to lead her up the steps to the door, which swung open as they approached. Firstly Maddy was introduced to two young ladies and two young men, who were other Tristan protégés; and after them to a bewildering number of servants all lined up to greet their employer's return. Porters ran down to help Roddy and the postilion with the trunks.

Tristan led her upstairs personally to show her the room that would be hers. It was small but decorated in exquisite taste—as she would now expect of him. The furniture was finely enameled, the draperies bright silk. The bed, she was happy to note, was only wide enough for one.

Tristan's own chamber was considerably larger and his bed was huge, but Maddy did not see it then. That night Roddy had the honor.

CHAPTER 21

By summer, Lady Whatman had accepted that Smut, her pretend nephew's dog—no longer a puppy—was without question a spirit guide. That meant that Bradwell Armstrong was destined to develop talent and become an adept. When Mark had reached that stage, she had been advised to consult Wisdom Alfred, who had a gift for analyzing gifted youngsters. He had correctly determined that Mark was destined to be a healer, and had later arranged for his escape from Albi and admission to Gaudry, in Xennia.

Alfred had been an old man even then. She made inquiries through her many contacts among the Children, but was unable to learn where he was, or even if he still lived. The one person who would know for certain was Jake Trull, the prelate. He was an old friend but even harder to find, because he lived a wandering life, often just a few days ahead of the Church Police. Fortunately, Rose Hall was one of his favorite stopping places. In due course he was bound to turn up there again. Early in the fall Lady Whatman received notice that an unnamed teaching brother would probably arrive within ten days or so. She passed the word around among the neighborhood faithful and made plans for services, but only for the small groups that could attend without attracting unwanted attention. The Moles had installed several of their holes in Rose Hall, but the Church Police were becoming ever more skilled at locating those. If they suspected that Trull himself might be present, they would tear the house apart to find him, so it was a stressful time.

One evening a family of tinkers came by with their donkey cart and asked leave to set up their tent in the orchard. Permission was granted, but Lady Whatman's steward posted guards all night to make sure that nothing was stolen. As promised, the tinkers left at dawn. They had taken nothing and left nothing—except Jake Trull.

Long before that, Lady Whatman had whisked him upstairs to a room that had a securely hidden annex, and seen that he was provided with wash water and anything else he required. He was looking less chubby and much older, she thought, but the hunted life he led would age anyone.

Later, as Trull was eating a fine supper in her private withdrawing room, the two of them made plans for prayer meetings over the next four or five days, starting with a bonding circle for trusted members of her own household that very night.

Then she said, "I have a proposal to make, Brother. With your permission I will outline it now, so that you have time to consider it during your stay with us."

"Your ideas are always worth considering."

"The Mother has seen fit to make me guardian of a young lad named Bradwell Armstrong. He is a sharp, seemly lad, and several months ago, he acquired a familiar. He has just turned twelve."

Trull's face registered surprise, but he did not ask if she were sure.

"Young as Brad is," she continued, "I would like Wisdom Alfred to meet with him. Is he still around?"

"He is, but the Church Police have come very close to him several times. He is laying low. Frankly, he is too old for the migratory life. I sympathize."

"The problem I foresee is that Brad's family are county gentry." She had unconsciously implied that they were still alive, because such minor deceptions became second nature to the persecuted. "They are not nobility, but they brought him up to be polite, well-spoken, and so on. I know from experience with my own son that children learn more from their peers than they do from their parents, and Brad has no companions of his own background. Already he is starting to talk and act like the servants' children."

"Some of the finest Children I know are servants' children." Trull smiled to take the reproof out of the words. "But I understand. You fear you will betray his parents' trust. And your suggestion?"

"Back in Mark's time, I ran a small school for the sons of minor gentry. When he grew up, those friends were very helpful to him in his mission. It was none of them who betrayed him. I am thinking along the same lines this time."

Trull nodded, chewing while he considered. Candlelight and shadow made his face hard to read. "The Church requires schools to be supervised by priests."

"Only schools that have more than ten pupils. If I stick to six or seven, there should be no problem. I can reasonably claim that Rose Hall is far too large for my needs."

The prelate eyed her thoughtfully. "So far I have no objections, but I suspect you haven't finished."

"That is the basic plan," she said, ruefully aware that she could no more smuggle an idea past Prelate Trull than she could find a stable without flies. "I also wonder about hiring some aging wisdoms as teachers. Alfred, for example. He might even find some promising talent in prospective pupils."

Trull chuckled. "I'll be seeing him shortly. I'll ask him how he feels about retiring to a home of feather beds and gourmet cooking. I think it's an excellent idea, and I trust you to make a great success of it. Will I get to meet your young prodigy this time?"

Lady Whatman hesitated, then said, "Probably better not. He is of the true faith, and wise beyond his years, but to trust him with such a secret at his age would be unfair. Maybe next time you come by you could conduct his first bonding."

He nodded, and the talk turned to other matters.

So Jake Trull never met Bradwell Armstrong. During his visitation to Rose Hall, he several times mentioned a skilled healer and missionary who had recently joined the circuit, but he always referred to him by his nom de guerre, John Hawke.

A few weeks later, old Wisdom Alfred arrived and was introduced as Master Alfred Turpin, who would be principal of the proposed Rose Hall Academy for Sons of Gentry. He was bent and toothless, but his eyes still had a twinkle, and his humor was as a sharp as ever. He did not recall Lady Whatman, for he had appraised hundreds of youngsters in his time, and it had been many years since she had brought her son to him, but he knew her tragic story and much admired her work for the cause.

He chose an office one floor up, and it was furnished for him with a fine table covered in green leather, some bookshelves, and a few chairs. A handsome chestnut tree stood just outside the window. Very close to the window, in fact.

Next morning he sent for the Armstrong prodigy. The boy arrived promptly, forewarned by Lady Whatman. No matter what she might have told him, he was understandably tense at the prospect of being tested for illegal magic by a complete stranger. At his heels trotted a very large, woolly black dog.

Alfred was prepared for the sort of interview he had conducted hundreds, if not thousands, of times. The young people he had vetted had varied from nobility to churls, with appropriate speech and manners. Physically they had ranged from angelic little girls to hulking male giants. He thought he could no longer be surprised by anything. He usually surprised them, though, and especially during the last few years as he had aged. To any youth now he must seem like a shriveled relic, a sun-dried ancient of no account.

"You must be Bradwell. Come in and sit down, please." Alfred kept his eyes on the dog, which was staring at him with its ruff up. As guides, dogs were very communicative, but they had to learn not to give away their feelings too obviously to other people. Very slowly, its tail began to wag, and the hair on the back of its neck sank. It made no attempt to come and sniff him, which proved that it was no ordinary dog.

A squirrel jumped from branch to windowsill to bookshelf to desk. It chattered angrily down at the dog. The dog growled, tail wagging furiously. The boy grinned and flopped onto a chair, relaxed.

"This is Nutty," Alfred explained.

"And this is Smut. Come and lie down by me, mutt."

"Right, what do you know about talent?"

Brad's guards went up again. "Very little, sir." He was lying, but that was wise of him.

"Move your chair closer. You know what these are?" Alfred reached into his bag of useful gadgets and produced two ivory cubes.

Brad accepted them and looked suspiciously at the old man, as if wondering how senile he was. "Dice, sir."

"Roll me two sixes."

That startled him. "You mean first go, sir?"

"Yes. Don't worry about how. Just do it."

The boy rolled and stared in astonishment at what he had done. So did Alfred. Not long turned twelve, and he could *jiggle*? Very few adult adepts could do that. Alfred himself could, and always began with this test so he could then cut the candidate down to size by demonstrating his own talent. By the time they got to him, they usually thought they were young gods. This time he was the humbled one.

It could have been a fluke.

"Now two threes."

Right again. Then a one and a four, which was harder. Right again! The youngster's worry had became an enormous grin. Visions of vast gambling profits?

"That is enough to get you burned at the stake," Alfred said with deliberate cruelty.

Shock.

"It's called jiggling, and it's a very rare talent."

Alfred brought out a black cloth. "Drape this over your head so you can't see." He rolled the dice. "Point at the dice and tell me what I threw."

Brad thought for a moment, then pointed in very nearly the correct direction. "That one's a five and that's a three."

"Half right. Let's try that again."

His blindsight wasn't as good as his jiggling, *but he was only twelve.*

"You see well in the dark, I assume." Alfred had blindsight, too, and could see the grin under the cloth.

"Auntie calls me 'Bat.'"

Alfred took him through the tests. He couldn't do everything, of course. Nobody could. But Brad was the youngest candidate he had ever tested, and easily the best since Rollo Woodbridge, close to ten years ago. It would be dangerous to tell him how rare he was, although he must already know. He wasn't stupid. He could see that he was flying through two-thirds of the tests without touching the sides.

He even looked a little like Rollo Woodbridge, with the black hair and brilliant blue eyes, but that young man could not be discussed nowadays. Months ago the government had announced that he had been arrested, but then it had fallen strangely silent. He was rumored to have died in jail. But perhaps not, because Jake Trull, when asked, just smiled and changed the subject.

At the end, Alfred leaned back to regard an understandably smug youngster.

"You are extremely gifted. That means you must be extremely careful! If you start showing off to your friends or even perform a wonder by accident, word may get back to the Church Police. Then not only will you suffer, but also Lady Whatman and all of Rose Hall."

The boy nodded solemnly.

Alfred thought for a moment. "Despite your youth, I think…" Alfred paused. "Have you ever heard of Gaudry?"

The reaction startled him. Brad's face went white. The dog leaped to its feet and barked furiously at Alfred.

"There are Church spies in Gaudry!" the boy said.

That possibility had been discussed among the faculty, and Lady Whatman had raised the question in conversation. Only she could have put that idea in the boy's head. Which didn't explain why his dog agreed.

"I think spies may have gotten in at times, Bradwell, but no spy could survive there for long, any more than a wisdom of the Children could hope to escape detection healing people in Weypool's Coronet Temple. You don't have to go, if you don't want to." He was young yet. He would change his mind in a year or two.

CHAPTER 22

As summer mellowed into fall, a visitor came to Rose
Hall. Strictly speaking there were two of them, but one was
either a guide or a defender, depending on who was clas-
sifying. In Sister Nell's experience, she was quite capable
of looking after herself. Any man who molested her would
find himself in much trouble very soon, and she could
probably deal with two or even three of such scum. If she
ran into a larger gang than that, she could outrun them,
for she was very well mounted. Perversely, she was in more
danger from the upright than the highwaymen, for the
Church did not approve of a woman traveling alone, and
discouraged women from traveling at all. On the other
hand, she did not know the way, and her serpent familiar
was not at its best in cross-country guidance.

Young Dick Malory was an earnest, cheerful companion, who had developed a soul-destroying crush on Mistress
Hawke the moment he set eyes on her, but was doing his
utmost not to show it. He did not realize that no one hid
anything from a woman with insight. His silent longing
was both flattering and saddening, but he had been more

than happy to stuff a cumbersome flintlock pistol in his belt and become her escort.

The Malory family were true to the Mother and kept Moor Manor, their home, as a safe house for her missionaries. Rollo was there now, preaching, healing, keeping the faith. Nell served as his harbinger, scouting out his next destination with her insight and seeing everything was made ready for him. It was a worthy task, and she enjoyed the itinerant life, her only complaint being that it took her away from Rollo so much. When he arrived at a place, it was almost time for her to move on to scout the next. Their hours together were very precious to them. Love always brought pain as well as joy, and her love for Rollo was a thousand times stronger than young Dick Malory's puppy pangs.

Dorsia was a prosperous county, with rich soil and level fields ripening to gold. The farmhands were out from dawn to dusk: brown, near-naked men scything hay, women and children gathering it into sheaves, horses pulling wagons piled mountain-high. The villages were small and many, but the houses were neat, with whitewashed walls and red tile roofs. Nell had seen no finer land on her travels and probably never would. Yet when Rose Hall came into view she said, "Oh, Mother bless!" She was probably seeing it at its best, for it truly seemed to glow in the low evening light.

"A grand place, is it not?" Dick said. "Been in the Whatman family since eggs were square."

"And yet their line has died out?"

"Aye. Thank the barbarians. They toasted the last Sir Mark because he cured too many people of the ills their god had sent them to teach them humility."

"The Church has healers, too, you know. Not many, and they do a lot of noisy praying."

"And accept donations, I'm hearing." He pouted with youthful scorn, a young man who had never wanted for food on his table.

It had been a long day, and Nell was happy to rein in at the ancient doors of Rose Hall. Dick was off his horse in a flash to hold her stirrup and take her hand as she dismounted. She was careful not to give his hand even a hint of a squeeze, but she had to smile as she thanked him, although that could only increase his yearning.

She was expected, and the lady of the house waited to greet her. Mary Whatman was gaunt, rather than slim, somewhere in her late forties or early fifties, with a flinty face accustomed to getting its own way. Even when it smiled a welcome, its eyes stayed hard and alert. Her clothes were high quality but understated.

The two women spoke greetings, and Nell struggled to continue the conversation. How to compliment a woman on a home she had inherited from a now-dead husband? How to praise her reputation for furthering the cause when that reputation might cost her everything if it came to the ears of the Church?

"I am eager to hear how your school progresses," she said instead.

"It prospers," the lady answered, belatedly adding, "thank you. Six pupils now, and four teachers."

"A worthy service to the Mother."

"Worthier than most," Lady Whatman said. "Far too many of her Children lie around like doormats waiting for a miracle. It is long past time that we stood up for our rights under the ancient laws."

It took two to start a fight. "I suggest you discuss that with Brother Hawke when he gets here. Now, where shall we start?"

"I'll show you to your rooms. Our principal is most eager to meet you—Brother Alfred. You have met him before?"

"Indeed I have, and Nutty also."

After Nell and Dick had been shown to their respective rooms and been given a chance to freshen up after their journey, and even then only after Dick Malory had been tactfully entrusted to a couple of students even younger than himself for a tour of the house and grounds, Nell found herself closeted with her hostess and the legendary Brother Alfred. They inquired after John Hawke's health and welfare, but he and Nell said very little of substance in the presence of Lady Whatman. There were many layers of secrecy among the Children of the Earth.

The following day, Nell inspected the cunning mole holes in Rose Hall and met every inhabitant: teachers, students, and servants, both indoor and outdoor. She saw students being lectured on the ethics of distraction and others on the basic accounting a gentleman should know. Later the boys put on a display of horsemanship in her honor.

Most important, by evening, she was able to assure Lady Whatman that there was not one spy or potential traitor in Rose Hall. It was safe for John Hawke to come and stay. Later she repeated this to Alfred, as the two of them conversed by candlelight in his study. The room was warm after the fine day, the wine excellent.

"Only two people make me uneasy," she said. "One is Lady Whatman herself. She is a zealot, and zealots can hurt friends as well as foes in the name of their cause, whatever it is." Nell was repelled by the ravening bitterness in the woman, however understandable it was after the loss of both husband and son. Mary Whatman was dangerous, capable of evil, and a living testament to the dangers of vengeance that Rollo described in his preaching.

The old man sighed agreement. "Well, the poor lass has her reasons. I don't let her preach her revenge to the boys, though, and six won't make a revolution."

Six adepts might make a start on one.

"I am amused that your school encourages the pupils to keep pets."

"Of course! They must learn responsibility!" Alfred chuckled. "We could hardly forbid them their guides, could we?"

"They all have talent?"

"Yes, at the moment. We're going to add some that don't for the sake of those like poor Alan, who feels shamed because he has so little. Brad has wagonloads. He amazed me when I met him, three, four months ago, and he gets stronger all the time."

Nell said, "Yes," and took a sip of wine. She knew Alfred was holding something back, although nothing dangerous. "Brad is the other one who bothers me. He isn't her nephew, I'm sure. He's so gracious and polite and *intense*. His pretend aunt has been preaching revenge to him, because he has even more hatred bottled up inside him than she does."

"He has causes of his own, and needs no sermons from her. But he's young yet. They're a fine bunch of lads, and in time the others will blunt his edge."

Or he would sharpen theirs. "Who's the leader?"

Alfred refilled the glasses, perhaps seeking a way to disguise an unpalatable truth. "Leo, because he's the oldest. Ask me next year and I'll be telling you Brad. He's easily the youngest, but they neither bully him nor baby him. Of course, it helps that he's supposed to be her nephew, but he is the champ."

"He reminds me of someone. My husband, maybe. I must be sensing all that talent."

"Could be," Alfred said with a smile. "I'm really looking forward to meeting John Hawke."

"Four or five days to go. I can report that Rose Hall is safe, and he'll soon be done at…at his present location." More secrets.

❧

Soon after first light, Dick Malory and Sister Nell rode out the gates and retraced their hoofprints to Moor Manor. They decided the weather might be going to change, and clouds were gathering by afternoon. Whatever was coming, they thought they would arrive before it.

Or maybe not. Brother Hawke was up in his room, Mistress Malory told Nell. He had asked for some quiet time alone. The message seemed innocent enough, but even at secondhand, Nell sensed something bad in it. That was not like him. She hurried up the stairs.

Rollo was slumped at the table, his face in his hands. He jumped up when she entered and hugged her tight. She struggled free before he broke her ribs and looked into eyes full of horror. Something was very wrong.

"Trouble shared is trouble halved," she said.

"They caught Trull," he whispered. "Or maybe killed him, I'm not sure."

"How do you know? Who says so?"

His attempt at a smile was a horrible grimace. "No one. I just suddenly knew that I was now Prelate Albi."

"You mean the Mother spoke to you?"

"Something like that. Like prescience, but now, not in the future. About two hours ago I simply knew. Oh, my darling, I didn't want this!"

Nor did she. Now the man she loved was next up. The appointment was a death sentence. The price would be on his head as soon as the Church Police or the Privy Council learned who had succeeded Trull. As his wife and companion, she would be caught with him, but she mourned for his sake, knowing how his conscience would drive him. Personal risk would not stop him.

"I'm sure Jake didn't want it either," she said. "He is such a wonderful man. But he knows everything and everyone, all the people and places. They will make him talk. Can we rescue him?"

"No. They'll put an army around him. I remember Prelate Gaudry telling me that we could only ever make one rescue, and I was to be the one. We must go back to

Weypool and make sure everyone gets warned as soon as possible."

So next day Rollo and Nell rode back south to the capital, and Dick Malory returned to Rose Hall alone to say that John Hawke would not be coming after all.

CHAPTER 23

THE HONORABLE TRISTAN RASTEL WAS THE MOST extraordinary person Maddy had ever met. There was some doubt that he was truly entitled to the title of Honorable with a capital letter, and without the capital it would be an outright falsehood. He was a pimp, thief, fence, and probably blackmailer, but also amazingly witty, charming, and cultured, a professional houseguest invited to parties to amuse everyone else. He was also a legendary sexual athlete and pervert, although he was always gentle, never unkind. He was universally known simply as "the Hon."

His household usually included four or five clients, both male and female, meaning commercial lovers currently without full-time benefactors. They came and went all the time. Maddy was propositioned twice on her first full day there, and when she complained to Tristan he encouraged her to accept all such offers.

"That is your profession now, my dear, and the better you are at it, the sooner you will achieve your goals. To accomplish what you told me you wanted, you will need to be at the very least the mistress of a privy councilor. What do you think of Roddy?"

"That small-time, thieving pervert? He revolts me."

"Then he is a challenge for you. You won't get far if you stick to the easy ones. Go and make his day."

Maddy obeyed and soon wished she hadn't. If she made Roddy's day, he ruined hers with a lesson in what humiliation could be. She was more than happy to see him leave the next morning, even if he did go off in a carriage with armorial bearings on its door. He showed up again at irregular intervals thereafter and had brief meetings with Tristan, probably delivering the Hon's commission.

It did not take Maddy long to work out in general how Tristan's business worked, although the details were recorded only in his head. He would provide her with the training and social contacts she needed, then expect to be reimbursed in money or favors. He was very successful, employing eighteen or twenty household servants, owning a coach and stable, and spending thousands on his own wardrobe. It was rumored that he could supply anything for the right price, from a murder to an earldom. She doubted he employed murderers, although she could imagine him arranging an introduction to persons in that line of work.

One sunny afternoon, a couple of weeks after Maddy joined the team, the Honorable Tristan took her to the home of a certain Lord Bulpin. His Lordship, as she had been told, was elderly and infirm and not the man he had been. He still had ambitions, though, and it would now be Maddy's job to satisfy them. She had been carefully coached by both Tristan and Jacquetta Sweeting, His Lordship's current server, who had just been hired as live-in mistress by a senior rural clergyman.

"You're not nervous, are you?" the Hon inquired innocently as the coach rattled through ever-grander streets.

Nervous? No, but she did feel nauseated.

"This will be a pushover for you," he said. "Your inspiration is even stronger than Jacquetta's, and you are years younger."

Maddy nodded miserably. She no longer dared wonder what her parents would say. She appalled even herself. But she had made her decision, and she did not doubt that Tristan would toss her out in the gutter if she balked now.

"Your lessons do not come cheap, my dear." That was the closest he had ever come to a threat. She spent hours every day being coached in the finer social skills.

She managed a smile. "I'll fix the old fart for you. I'll blow his mind."

Tristan laughed, which was rare. "Or something. Don't overdo it. The goose may stop laying golden eggs after a heart attack."

His Lordship looked even older than his official age, but he was charmed by Maddy and grew impatient for Tristan to leave. So Tristan did leave, and Maddy did what was expected of her. Lord Bulpin was so pleased that when the coach returned to take her home, he gave her two silver moons extra, "Just for you, my darling." Suspecting a trap, she turned it all in to Tristan. From then on, she had a weekly date at Bulpin House and no doubts at all about her profession.

By spring she had two more regulars and seemed to be working night and day. Tristan praised her progress but confirmed his intention of waiting until fall to launch her on the social circuit. The current season wound down as the nobility returned to their country estates. Maddy was impatient. She was ready, she was sure of it. Months of indoor living and fatty food had swelled her bust and hips to fashionable curves and given her complexion the basic pallor needed for a society beauty. With her hair bleached and her eyebrows plucked, she could probably smile at Earl Uptree of Norcaster and he wouldn't have a clue who she was.

But summer was not all lost. It was a slack time in Weypool, when even the wealthy districts stank in the heat, but Tristan spent much of his time at house parties in country homes. Most of those were situated in cooler climes, in the hills or along the shores, and he took Maddy to some. She swirled around in skimpy summer dresses and absurd coiffures. The women knew what she was at a glance and ignored her, but male eyes followed her everywhere. Tristan's orders were strict: she was his ward, and any expressions of interest must be referred to him. For some reason the country house johns were usually younger men than those in the city, which added some sincerity to her expressions of passion. She had no way of knowing how much her procurer charged for her services, but one of her partners hinted that she was now priced in gold suns. That amazed her. She had never realized how far lust could rot men's brains, but the news confirmed that she had chosen the best road to meeting men of power. Only power could bring her the revenge she sought.

She sometimes wondered how Sam was managing without her, but she had no regrets.

$$\infty$$

Summer faded into fall.

One morning, on the silken sheets of his bed, the Honorable Tristan rolled over to face her and ask the question she had been waiting a long time to hear. No one else conducted so much business while naked as he did.

"Earl Uptree," she replied. "And his brother, the hierarch."

"Holy Light defend us! You aim your musket high, lady."

"They murdered my family and stole our land."

"I never doubted you had a strong motive, my dear. But those two will not be easy. You can't turn the Church against the statesman or the king against the priest, which would be the normal strategy. But I do not doubt your abilities. I am sure you will succeed in the end. You remember Sir Sheldon Causey?"

"He was at the beach party. About thirty. Loud, athletic."

"Yes. You'll find him a pleasure to work with. You caught his eye, but I refused him access to you. He is an aspiring courtier, whose ambitions exceed his income. He can't afford your prices." Tristan kissed her breast admiringly.

"And?"

"And he asked my advice. We came up with a four-party arrangement. What he needs is a useful monopoly—exclusive rights to import molasses or export, um, acorns or something. Those can be very profitable. Monopoly licenses are granted by the king. On the advice of the Privy Council, of course. His Majesty does not even visit the privy except on the advice of the Privy Council."

She stroked his thigh to reward him. "And?"

"There are two privy councilors who are currently... in need, shall I say? Susceptible to the wiles of a seductive fifteen-year-old."

"I'm seventeen."

"You just turned fifteen. You must stay no more than sixteen for the next ten years. The arrangement is that you will be Sir Sheldon's niece. You move in and brighten his lonely life; he starts taking you to parties."

"What sort of parties?" Maddy asked suspiciously. A girl had to keep up her standards. "Tea parties?"

"How could you even suspect me of such perversion? Balls! Salons! Recitals! High society." Kiss. "The sort of places one meets privy councilors." Nuzzle...

"And Sir Sheldon trades his niece off for a monopoly on the import of molasses?"

"Or pickled fewmets..."

His fixation on her breasts was impeding his ability to talk. She dispassioned him.

"Don't worry about those details," he said, looking up with annoyance.

"Which details do I worry about?"

"Timing. Sheldon promised not to keep you for more than three months. If he hasn't succeeded in placing you by then, he never will. We'll have to try another plan. Be expensive to keep, so he is encouraged to trade you on. I specified a mistress of robes, a personal coiffeuse, seamstress, perfumer, and two maids."

"And your share?"

Tristan sighed. "Nothing as crass as money, my dear. I will rely on your future generosity. Perhaps a few crumbs from the table when you carve up Osborn and Garrett? Now, please, will you let me finish what I was starting?"

As Maddy had said, Sir Sheldon Causey was thirty-ish, loud, and athletic. He could not be blamed for the first, but he was everything else to a fault—frenetically active, dolled up like a town fair, talkative, tactless, tasteless, ebullient, exuberant, extravagant, and constantly harried by creditors. He gave the impression he had been born drunk and had never sobered up, although his capacity to drink everyone else under the table was legendary. On Maddy's first night in his house, he downed two bottles of wine, carried her upstairs, and performed flawlessly four times before dawn. Life as Sir Sheldon's niece was never going to be dull.

Maddy had arrived with two trunks full of gowns. She interviewed the staff her new uncle had supplied for her and fired half of them on the spot. In the next three days, she hired substitutes at much higher wages and ordered another six gowns. That was the end of the honeymoon. The dressmaker politely asked for a cash advance. Maddy flew into a rage at this insult. The woman was adamant. Sir Sheldon's credit was lower than zero.

There was no doubt in Maddy's mind that it was a business to do pleasure with her. She was engaged in a commercial transaction, and this would not do—no lady could be seen twice in the same dress! An immediate return to the Honorable Tristan was required. She stormed down-stairs to beard her uncle in his withdrawing room, where he happened to be negotiating with his bankers.

The room was small and the bankers numbered four, two of whom looked as if they had been recruited at the docks and brought along as bodyguards. All five men stood up as she entered, leaving a severe shortage of space for bowing and curtsying. There was plenty of space for an injured virgin's outrage, though. Maddy launched into a scene intended to reduce Sheldon's credit even further.

The senior banker was a portly, white-haired, somberly clad person of great dignity. The moment she paused to draw breath, he quietly asked to be presented. The sweat-beaded Sheldon grasped at this respite like a torture victim and did the honors. The banker bowed low over Maddy's hand and kissed it.

"And what brings you to Weypool, Miss Wells?"

Even Maddy couldn't quite blush to order, but she could give the impression that she was mortified. "My dear uncle promised to introduce me at court, at the debutantes' coming-out ball!"

"Did he, indeed?" The banker eyed Sheldon thought-fully for a moment, then turned back to Maddy. "Then I wish you every success. We have concluded our business with your uncle and will leave you with our best wishes and complete confidence in your triumphant coming-out, Miss Wells. Sir Sheldon, I will send over the papers for your signature before noon. Will you be requiring a cash advance at that time?"

A curiously subdued Sheldon showed his visitors out and then exploded. He came roaring back to the counting room, swung Maddy up head-high, and spun around with her until she was giddy. "Magnificent! Perfect! Couldn't have done that better if we'd rehearsed it for months. You were stupendous, Mindy my love, my sweeting, my teeny turtledove."

When he set her down, she patted her coiffure with her hands and decided it was canted well to the left, in urgent need of repair.

"All part of the service," she murmured. She was, of course, a potentially lucrative resource now. Even a hard-headed banker could recognize a tangible asset when he saw one.

CHAPTER 24

BRAD ARMSTRONG REACHED HIS THIRTEENTH BIRTHDAY IN the fall. It was an important milestone because he could stop thinking of himself as a child. His voice had dropped two octaves. He was growing taller—like a mushroom, the housekeeper said every time she had to issue him new clothes—and also growing manly signs that only he knew about. He was going to mature early, which meant that he would be able to avenge his family all the sooner. He was taller than Frank, the latest newbie, who was fifteen.

He was still the youngest boy, er, student in Rose Hall, but not by much. Gilbert and Ben had gone home to help with the harvest and might not come back. Mick had set off to Gaudry, in Xennia, and ought to be there by now. There had been no news, which was starting to be worrisome.

Students were allowed to choose a treat for their birthdays, and it was traditional to ask for some sort of contest. The trick was to think of something where the winner could not be foreseen. A race or test of strength wouldn't do, not when Leo was nineteen hands tall and muscled like a farrier. Everyone knew that Brad himself would win any test of talent, but talent mustn't be talked about, because some guys had more gifts than others and a couple had none at all. It would only take one of the ungifted to go tattling to the nearest priest, and Rose Hall would be swarming with Church vermin. So devising a reasonably fair contest was itself a challenge, and Old Alfie or Aunt Mary would veto any really dangerous ones.

Treasure hunts were done to death, although Ben, whose birthday was in the summer, had come up with a cute variation. He had persuaded Aunt Mary to throw a double handful of coins into the millpond to see who could collect the most. Brad could have won that one with his eyes shut, but he had deliberately lost.

He had been thinking about his contest for months. His carefully written request asked for a race from Rose Hall to Water Meadow Farm and back. The twist was that this would involve going either over or around Hog Hill, which was very rough terrain. To go around would take hours but could be done along an established path. To go over the top, not once but twice, would test even Leo the Lion. It would be a test of judgment as much as strength, Brad explained. It would also be a test of familiars, although he did not say that.

A few days ahead of his birthday, Aunt Mary announced the contest at dinner. It was, she said, a clever idea. Brad got a lot of scowls, but he knew that most of them were fakes and the guys approved. Tearing up and down a mountain was better than sitting in a classroom any day.

"However," Aunt Mary added, and attention switched back to her, "we have made two changes. First, there will be a cart at Water Meadow Farm, so anyone who feels tired may come home that way."

Scorn! Any dud who sank that low would be horse dung evermore.

"Secondly, some of you have advantages, so we are going to handicap the race. Each of you will be issued a backpack, which you must carry all the way. Some will be filled with straw and some with rocks."

Leo wailed and covered his face in despair, and everyone else laughed. Then they all looked at Brad and laughed again. Aunt Mary had a small mouth, full of small teeth, but Brad had often thought she would inflict a very nasty bite. Now he was sure of it.

There was frost on the grass, and breath smoked when the six of them assembled at the front door on the morning of the big day. Having all dressed lightly, they jumped up and down or jogged on the spot to keep warm. Auntie never appeared at such an hour, but Old Alfie was there, looking like a frost gnome, wrapped up in a fur cloak with little more than his nose visible.

Servants brought out the handicap packs. Each one was labeled and had been weighed, Alfie explained. They would be weighed again at Water Meadow Farm and back at Rose Hall. Tampering with the packs would be cheating.

Leo made a big show of lifting his as if it weighed tons, and it did look nasty. Frank threw his in the air and caught it, to show it weighed nothing. Brad was horrified at the weight of his. Then water bottles were handed out, and everyone wished them good luck. They all started with a sprint, to get warmed up, but they had a long day ahead and soon slowed to a jog. Soon they came to the trail that followed the river around Hog Hill. Alan, Frank, and Brad all turned off that way. The other three jeered that they were sissies and real men went over the top.

They slowed to a fast walk, but Brad soon let the other two draw ahead, because he had a secret plan. There was a small stream just ahead, running down from Hog Hill, and he was pretty sure it would make an easier trail than a bull-headed straight up and down. By going over the shoulder of the hill, he could compromise between the two routes. Smut happily trotted ahead of him, sniffing at everything, playing at being a real dog. And when they came to where the road forded the little brook, Smut headed off the way Brad was planning to go without even a backward glance, so it really must be the best way!

At first he had to cross a stubbled field, then a pasture. He was warm by the time the ground grew steep and the shrubbery closed in...brambles, big trees, ferns, mossy rocks, nasty trip-you-up roots. Soon he was sweating, and the stream had disappeared. At times all he could see of the sky was a sprinkle of tiny speckles overhead, and he wasn't at all sure which way he was supposed to be going.

"Smut! I'm relying on you to lead me to Water Meadow Farm."

Smut wagged his tail and went back to guiding. At least, Brad hoped that guiding was what his guide was doing. He was going to look like a real sheep if he got lost on his own contest and had to be rescued. He would be rescued, of course. There was plenty of talent around Rose Hall, and he could send Smut for help.

The day went on a long time. Like a week. He took a rest. Then another. His water bottle was almost empty. The backpack dug into his back and weighed more than a full-grown carthorse. He wished he'd told Alan about his secret plan and brought him along. This would be more fun with two.

Then he began to see daylight between the trees, and he was definitely going downhill. That was better. He hoped he didn't come down to the river path and see Alan and Frank ahead of him. That would be *hum-il-i-a-ting*. The sky wasn't blue, just gray, and when he really escaped from the trees, he could see that the day had clouded over and was threatening rain. The wind blew cold on his sweaty skin.

He couldn't see Water Meadow Farm. He wasn't at all sure where he was now. It would be even more shameful if he'd doubled around and come down on the Rose Hall side again! He'd never live that down. He'd have to fall off of a rock and break a leg and wait to be rescued. "Smut! Smut?" Stupid animal! Where…

Smut was standing fifty yards away, looking back at him, while beyond him, in the distance, was Water Meadow Farm. Somehow Brad must have crossed over the route that Leo and the other two had taken. He'd veered too far left and taken a longer way instead of a shorter. Idiot! He set off at a weary plod.

When he caught up with his dog, he told him exactly what sort of a useless mutt he was. A cat would make a better guide. Smut just wagged his tail.

Worse and worse! When Brad reached the farmyard, he found the Rose Hall cart waiting, with George on the bench. He had a water barrel and a basket of apples and hoops of blood sausage. He had a steelyard to weigh the packs. But he also had Frank, sitting in the box with a cruel, cruel grin all over his stupid face.

"I suppose I'm the last?" Brad said, handing his water bottle to George to be filled.

Frank nodded. "Climb in. Return half's been called off, because of the weather." He gestured to where the sky was as black as a postilion's boot.

Brad drank while he thought about that.

"Where are they all?"

"They all went back in the other cart. Except Leo. He was first to get here."

"Said he was on the men's team and was going to finish," George said. "But that was a long time ago. Climb in, Master Brad."

Brad said, "No. I can't beat Leo, but I'm on the men's team, too." He grabbed a hoop of sausage and turned on his heel.

"Brad, no!" Frank shouted. "Principal's orders. Everyone has to go back."

Brad kept going. It was his contest, and he was going to finish the course if it took him till midnight. George brought the cart after him, saying Brad was going to get him into trouble, too. Frank shouted much the same. Brad climbed a stile into a pasture where the cart couldn't follow and kept on going. Smut trotted ahead of him, nose to the ground.

⤫

He knew he was being stubborn and perhaps foolish, but giving up would be worse. By the time he reached the rocks and trees, the cart had gone without him and he had no choice but to continue. That felt better. Except that the rain was starting. And the hill this side was much steeper than he had expected, or had encountered before. In some places he had to clamber, using his hands to hold on. Moss made the rocks slippery and treacherous. Wet moss was worse.

Whenever he scrambled up a particularly nasty patch, he found Smut ahead of him. Stupid mutt didn't know real dogs couldn't climb cliffs. The sky had turned black, and there was almost no light at all under the trees. Luckily blindsight was one of his talents, and one that Alfred rated him highly on. Smut steered with his nose.

Brad took a rest in a dry place under a fir tree. He ate the last of his sausage, sharing with Smut. He drank a lot, and tried to tip enough into the palm of his hand for Smut to drink from, but that didn't work well. Then he crawled out of his little shelter and dragged himself to his feet. He ached from his feet to his shoulders. He didn't mind much, because he had brought it on himself; nobody else was doing this to him, and a man had to finish what he started. Except now he couldn't remember which way he'd been going.

"Smut, show me the way home, please?"

Smut sat down and looked like he was waiting for a punch line.

"Home, Smut!" A black tail wagged, sweeping the mast on the forest floor.

"Idiot dog! You are s'posed to be my spirit guide. Well, guide me back to Rose Hall."

With what looked suspiciously like a shrug, Smut rose and set off uphill, but soon the grade turned and they were going down. Thunder banged like cannons, but the lightning couldn't penetrate the forest. Brad liked thunderstorms. He ought to fear them, he supposed, after what had happened to his family, but he didn't. That thunderbolt had been caused by Father Rafe Dampier, and one day Brad would kill him for it. The slope grew steeper. Smut paused and peered over an edge, tail wagging. This contest had been a stupid, stupid idea! In the silence between the thunderclaps, Brad could hear rain on the high leaves, but now he could also hear a trickle of water. Must be a spring down there. Smut wasn't leading him home. Smut was thirsty and looking for a drink.

But water ran downhill, so if Brad followed the stream, they would eventually reach the river, and the road, and then they wouldn't be lost anymore. Sure enough, Smut found a way down, with Brad scrambling after him. Water was trickling out of the rock face and tinkling into a pool, so they could both drink standing up. There was no visible stream leading away, but there was some very mossy ground and a hint of a gully. In a few yards he found water moving underfoot. Feeling rather clever, Brad followed the stream and Smut followed him. Except that Smut did not follow him when he fell down the cliff.

The pool wasn't deep enough to break his fall completely. The cliff was high enough to break his leg. He dragged himself out of the water and lay on a patch of ferns and fought against a very childish impulse to weep. The pain wasn't too bad as long as he kept still, but any movement was red-hot iron.

Whine? Smut came and nuzzled him, tail and ears down, meaning *I'm sorry,* either sympathy or apology.

It took all of Brad's now shaky manhood to manage to sit up. He rubbed Smut's ears. "Now will you go and fetch help, please?"

Smut whined more and lay down. What was the matter with him? The last time he'd behaved as maddeningly as this had been the day he led Brad, or Brat as he was then, to Wisdom Edith's cottage and Wisdom Frieda.

Panic! "Is there trouble at Rose Hall? Am I here for my own protection? Because if anything happens to Rose Hall..." If the Church Police had raided Rose Hall, nobody would come looking for Bradwell Armstrong, and he would starve to death on Hog Hill. Didn't sound like the sort of protection a familiar should supply.

Or he might freeze to death. He must have found one of the few places in the forest where he could be rained on, and he was already soaked. His teeth were chattering. He needed dry clothes and a fire, but he had no flint and steel, no tinderbox.

Boom! said the sky.

Fine. Just aim your next thunderbolt at that dead bush, will you?

Direct the lightning? Like Rafe Dampier?

Brad broke a fingernail tearing his backpack open. Inside he found two bricks and a lot of straw stuffing, kept dry by the leather. He pulled out some straw and made a wisp of it.

"Burn!" he said. Didn't feel quite right. He tried again: "Burn!" Was that a hint of smoke? *"Burn!"* That worked. He watched in delight as smoke curled up, with just a hint of flame. He had not known he could do that! Old Alfie had never tested him for that. He had never heard anyone suggest that he try it—perhaps such a talent was too dangerous to trust to juvenile adepts. Or it was too rare. The discovery was so exciting that he burned his fingers, which made him wrench his leg and cry out at the pain. But that didn't last. He used the bricks to make a hearth, the straw as kindling, and as much of the dead bush as he could reach as fuel. He told it to burn and it burned.

Smut leaped to his feet, barking furiously, his tail a blur of joy.

"Now what, dumb dog?"

His guide turned and plunged away into the darkness. What he meant was: *Now you've got it, dumb boy, I can go and get help.*

Brad did not freeze, although he did catch a chill, which Sister Maud later cured for him. Rescuers led by Smut and Barney, Alan's owl, found a very cold, very sorrowful boy a couple of hours later. He had used up all the fuel he could reach, so the fire had died, and in the rainy dark no one noticed the ashes. He told no one about the fire, and Smut never talked.

Officially Brad had sprained his ankle, so that the remarkable speed with which his leg healed did not alarm the servants and others who were not Children of the Mother. The other guys ribbed him mercilessly, of course, but he did not take offense. It had all been worth it, because he had gained a very valuable weapon. He was not just a man now; he was a dangerous one.

CHAPTER 25

IN VIEW OF HIS FAILING HEALTH, THE HIERARCHS HAD forbidden King Ethan to attend unessential ceremonies, especially those they disapproved of on principle. So Crown Prince Emil presided at the royal debutantes' ball, and was much more interested in the latest crop of beauties than his ailing father would have been. Maddy found the procedure offensive—scores of the noblest and richest men in the kingdom parading their daughters like cattle at a show. Waiting for bids, in effect. Disgusting! The performance was so absurd and everyone took it so seriously that she had great difficulty keeping a straight face. A mere baronet like Sheldon was relegated to the end of the line, and even the crown prince was looking jaded as lovely maiden after lovely maiden curtsied before the throne, offering glimpses down cleavage for his approval.

The priests who ran Albi knew all about the Mother's gifts, so the ritual allowed no debutante close enough to exercise inspirational talent on the prince. Besides, Maddy was no maiden and with her unknown background had no hope of ever becoming a royal mistress. Emil was not impressive. Without his robes and jewels he would have seemed plain and probably stupid.

But after all that nonsense came fine wines, great food, and dancing till dawn. Also suitors, or at least gentlemen who wished to dance with her. The elderly restricted their offers to the slow dances, which required nothing more strenuous than a walk and enough sobriety to remember which smile belonged to one's partner through all the circling, advancing, retreating, and promenading. The young stalwarts crowded forward to vie for the fast dancing, with leaping and lifting and whirling about, the showier the better. Maddy had been well coached, and she could leap, pirouette, and ad-lib with the best of them.

So began the social season, and for months hardly a night passed without an event somewhere: balls, plays, masques, banquets, concerts. By the time she fell into her own bed, the servants were eating their midday meal. When winter closed in, she rarely saw daylight. Most days she rose, bathed, and went straight into a ball gown.

There were suitors. Many had inquired, but all had failed Sheldon's vetting. A very few were allowed to come calling in the afternoons, thus seriously cutting into Maddy's sleeping time. The conversation was always banal chatter about the weather and the latest scandal, with overtones offensively close to haggling over price.

But no arguments followed the visitors' departures. Sheldon was in no hurry to lose his paramount sex partner, because he was now so hopelessly indebted that no imaginable compensation for the loss of her services could clear him. He was doomed to die a lingering death in debtors' prison, so the later that started the better.

Maddy had met no one she fancied as her next patron. Unlike the other predators in the market, she was not seeking a life of pampered luxury. Even the handsomest, richest young stud would not satisfy her if he did not also have influence. Her objective was two Uptree heads on spikes, and on that she was never going to yield. So far she had not explained this to her temporary uncle.

Meanwhile they wined, dined, and danced, and the band played on. The wheels would certainly fall off before spring.

⁓

One major event took place in daylight. The heretic and traitor, Jake Trull, who had been arrested in the summer and subsequently convicted of treason, was to be publicly executed in Amos I Square.

"It's the day after the charity concert," Sheldon announced in the carriage one evening as they drove off to a ball. "We shall have to go straight there, or we shall never get through the crowds."

Maddy said, "I am not going."

"But everyone who is anyone will be there. I have engaged one seat and the standing room behind it at a third-floor window."

"This someone is not anyone. You enjoy steak. Did you ever go to a slaughterhouse to watch them eviscerate a steer's carcass and quarter it?"

"That is a revolting suggestion!"

"If it is revolting when done to a dead animal, why is it fun to watch it being done to a living man?"

He did not answer the question. "Anyone who doesn't go will be suspected of treasonous sympathies."

"No one will notice whether we're there or not. What did you pay for the places?"

"Five suns."

Mother preserve! Most families lived for a year on a fraction of that. The man had grease for brains. "Wait until the day before and sell them for ten."

He sold them for fifteen.

About a week later, Maddy was shaken awake not long after Sheldon had left her bed. Through the fog, she learned that Sir Sheldon…downstairs entertaining visitor…an unexpected caller…they were waiting. Her maids dressed her in a rush, and for once she let them do as they liked without a chirp of complaint or instruction. It felt about noon. Ball last night, masque tonight…in record time she was deposited at the door of the withdrawing room, which was then rapped on and opened. Maddy forced a smile and went in.

The two men rose, and she had no idea who the other one was. He was around forty and nothing much to look at physically, with narrow shoulders and a skimpy, pointy beard. Nor was he much to look at otherwise, being quite drably, almost humbly dressed in brown, although there was a small jeweled order pinned on his jerkin. The men bowed to her. She curtsied to him and took her favorite seat for interviewing prospective patrons.

"Tea?" Sheldon muttered. "We were just having some tea and, um, biscuits, while we, um…" He was far from his usual dapper self, with eyes red as blood, jerkin cross-laced, stockings wrinkled, and cap askew. "Tea…?"

"Allow me," said the other man, reaching for the teapot before Sheldon could drop it or knock it over.

"Very kind of you…um…" Sheldon had mumbled the introductions so badly that Maddy had no idea who this beetle of a man was. She had danced a slow dance with him somewhere a few weeks ago, she thought. She had certainly seen him around, but his name…

The visitor delivered the tea and retreated to a chair by the window. He sat with his feet and knees together, very prim. Then he glanced at Sheldon and said, "I wish to speak with Miss Wells alone."

Maddy came more awake with a start. That was a serious breach of manners and protocol. Sheldon would never…

But Sheldon said, "Ah, um, yes, of course, your…um." He scurried out and closed the door.

The man in brown smiled across at her.

She smiled back, implying that, of course, she had known that he could put Sheldon in his place like that.

"I apologize for the inappropriate hour, Maddy," he said. "And for not making an appointment. Pressure of business, you know."

"Your visit is a surprise, but a very welcome one, um, sir. I am greatly honored." It was difficult to speak appropriately when she did not know if he was "my lord" or "Sir Somebody," or "Your Grace." "Your Excellency," if he were an ambassador, although he spoke Albiurn without an accent.

"I have been trying to catch a few moments with you for days now, and this was the only time I could get away. I know how hectic your own schedule is. How on earth do you keep it up, Maddy, night after night?"

That time it got through. He was watching her with sharp little eyes, like a bird's. He reminded her of a sparrow. Or a hawk in sparrow's clothing?

"Er, it is 'Mindy,' my lord." Yet she was certain he had not made a mistake.

He shook his head. "Madeline Woodbridge, now Madeline Stroud, but always known to her friends and family as Maddy."

Nothing woke a girl up in the morning faster than sheer terror. She had avoided the Trull execution, and now they thought she was a traitor, too? He saw her shock. He laid down his teacup.

"I beg your pardon! I did not intend to frighten you. I mean you no harm—quite the reverse. And I have no fancy title, just plain Master Kipping."

"Of course I remember you, Master Kipping, although I forget where it was I had the honor of dancing with you."

"I don't. I have thought of that dance a lot. My wife is an invalid, you see. I do entertain, although on a modest scale by your standards. My niece—a genuine niece, my brother's daughter—has been acting as my hostess, but she is expecting her first child and will have to forego the duty. So I have been wondering...I live very comfortably, but not ostentatiously. Over by the Royal Park."

Maddy nodded, thoroughly bewildered. A banker? A rich commoner landlord, as Father had been? Had he any idea how much Sheldon wanted for her? Who was he, this sparrow who had sent Sheldon off with a flea in his ear?

"What are you after, Maddy? I do love that name! What is it you seek? Suppose one suitor could bring you lands, a castle, and a title. And another offered you two Uptree hides on the floor. Which would you take?"

Aware that her hands had started trembling in her lap, she said, "You would not ask such a strange question if you did not already know the answer, sir."

He smiled almost mischievously. "Well, I cannot go quite as far as hides on the floor or heads on the wall yet, but I do intend to trim those brothers' claws in the near future. You must have seen my lord Osborn at various functions around town. Has he seen you?"

Maddy shook her head, although it was spinning. "I don't think so. We have not come face to face. I dye my hair now. He was a witness at my wedding."

"Alleged wedding. From what I have been able to discover, that nonsense was in breach of both civil and church law. So how would you like to be hostess at my table when I entertain the Earl of Norcaster one evening, hmm?"

Nothing she had learned from Sheldon or the Honorable Tristan had prepared Maddy for this conversation. The man might be totally insane...or...*oh, Mother!* He might be First Secretary William Kipping, the king's chief minister. No wonder Sheldon had fled.

With a gulp she said, "Am I correct in thinking you are a member of the Privy Council, sir?"

His eyes twinkled. "Some people would tell you I *am* the Privy Council, Maddy. The king would make me an earl in fifteen minutes if I wanted, but I prefer to keep my head down, where it is less likely to be cut off. I am not rich in money, but I do have influence."

Not mere influence, but power! More power than anyone in the land except the king and the Hierarchy, she had heard. She pursed her lips to make sure her jaw was not hanging open.

"Your suggestion is most appealing, sir. I am sure you have the details worked out?"

He nodded. "I am asking you to be my social hostess. My housekeeper is aging, and you may wish to take over her job, but that decision lies in the future. Your life will become a lot less hectic than it is now, almost dull. You sparkle in society, yet everything I have heard about you indicates that you have a lot more brains than your present occupation requires."

Maddy nodded graciously to acknowledge the compliment. The difference between this suitor and all his predecessors was as day to night. So far he had not praised her complexion or raved about her bosom. He was negotiating a business contract, and she approved.

"I suspect that you were raised in the old faith, Maddy. I shall expect you to be discreet in such matters. His Majesty would not tolerate open heresy among his advisors or their households."

She passed it off with a smile. "I doubt he expects them to escort ladies of my reputation to divine service, either, First Secretary? I can tolerate Church ceremonial if I must." Unlike Rollo. But she must not think of Rollo when she was planning to sleep with the man who must have signed his remand to Swine Hall. She must remember instead their parents, also foully murdered. "I cannot raise much enthusiasm for a church led by such men as Rafe Dampier and Garrett Uptree."

Kipping sighed. "I cannot defend either of them. The Teacher's revolution toppled the old faith only because it had grown so corrupt, you know. Now the replacement he created is showing signs of the same sickness. I personally believe that most of the Children of the Mother are just as honorable and devout as those of us who worship the Light. I do not argue this subject with His Majesty, you understand. But as long as you are discreet, you will be safer in my house than almost anywhere. You are loyal to your king?"

"Of course. And so were—"

"So not a traitor. You have never visited Xennia, or studied at Gaudry?"

"No, sir."

"Not a spy. You practice witchcraft?"

"Certainly not." If one counted arousing men's lust, then almost any woman was guilty. "But surely your political enemies will accuse you of harboring a spy-traitor-witch in your house?"

For an instant the veneer of amiability cracked, and she caught a glimpse of the ruthless statesman beneath it. "Could they produce evidence?"

"No, sir. Only that I am a harlot, but that is public knowledge."

"Well, then." He smiled happily.

His spies must already have learned everything there was to be known about her or he would not be here, and he must know that she was Rollo Woodbridge's sister. He must also know what had happened to Rollo, but now was definitely not the time to ask him. She would be putting a lot of trust in him, but women in her profession were always vulnerable, and he could certainly protect her from almost anyone else—as long as he wished to.

There must be more to his plans than he was saying. He would always have pages he did not show.

For the first time he hesitated. "Have you any questions?"

"You have not mentioned the one thing most men regard as the only topic worth discussing. I will sleep in your bed?"

He nodded without meeting her eye. "I told you, my wife is an invalid. In fact, she is dying. Although I have always been faithful to her and still love her, a man needs a woman for more than conversation, which is all my darling can now offer me. She knows what I am up to this afternoon. She not only approves, she suggested it."

He spread his hands as if trying to grasp something, and she realized that it was the first time he had gestured at all. "Let me be frank. A gentleman may keep a mistress and no one will think the less of him. In some circles it is almost compulsory. But marriage—"

"—to a whore is out of the question. I understood that when I embarked upon my career, Master Kipping."

He was relieved that she had said it, not him.

"No further questions, sir. Except: when do I wake up and find it was all a dream? If you will pardon my timidity, Master First Secretary, it does seem too good to be true."

Some men would have taken offense, but he approved, or wanted her to think he approved. "I believe you and I can offer each other a lot. Earl Uptree is being difficult, and there we can be allies. He arranged your wedding, which was a farce, and the title deeds by which he claimed your family's lands would have any lesser man hanged for forgery. You can help me bring him to heel. We can dance on his grave together."

Of course he wanted to use her as a political lever. That was obvious. But she had been used as a sex toy for a long time now, and revenge was her chosen reward.

And one day she would learn what had happened to Rollo. Had he died under torture, like her grandfather? Was he still in jail, possibly now insane? Had he been shipped back to Xennia?

"Sir, I am too amazed by your offer to think of a polite way of saying it. Yes! Yes! Yes!"

"One 'yes' is enough. I am overjoyed to hear it. Now, we must dispose of your supposed husband, or Norcaster will try to blackmail us with him. What's he good at?"

"Sam's a good plowman," she said warily.

Kipping's eyes twinkled again as he caught the double meaning. "Then I'll find him a grossly overpaid job on one of the royal estates, far away. Plus a royal pardon for committing bigamy when he pretended to marry you. When he accepts that, you will no longer be married."

"He was married before?"

"That will be the implication. How much does Sir Sheldon owe the moneylenders?"

"I wish I had a star for every sun. About ten thousand suns, I'd guess."

"No, it's at least fifteen. How can any man have bungled his affairs so badly?" Kipping sprang up and strode to the door, whipping it open and stepping aside as Sheldon staggered in sideways, having been leaning on his ear.

Kipping's manner cooled abruptly. "Did you hear it all?"

"Not much, sir."

"Your pretend niece has accepted a position in my household. I can offer you a hundred suns toward your—"

"Not nearly—"

"I know that. But I can also have you appointed warden of Kynaston Castle at a salary of ten suns a year." Before Sheldon could open his mouth, Kipping continued. "As long as you remain an officer of the crown, you will be beyond your debtors' reach. They cannot impound your property or garnish your income. Kynaston is remote, but it has good hunting, and those strong-limbed mountain women are epicurean."

"I have to live there?"

"An annual visit there should suffice to fulfill your duties."

Sheldon stood motionless for a few moments while last night's wine percolated through his brain. Then he smiled and bowed. "Your Honor is most generous."

Kipping returned the bow. Then he turned to Maddy, who had risen. He took her hands in his and decorously pecked her cheek. She wondered what the Honorable Tristan would say when he heard the news.

CHAPTER 26

THE KIPPING RESIDENCE WAS A ROOMY BUT UNPRETENTIOUS house in the Royal Park. Maddy needed six trunks and two carriages to move herself, her wardrobe, and a mere three personal maids there. As if her appointment were a state secret, the transfer took place under cover of darkness. Master Kipping was a secretive person.

He employed a large staff, including several footmen and stable hands with bull shoulders and prizefighter knuckles. All, from the housekeeper down to the chambermaids, were icily polite when introduced to the master's new hostess, but she knew that in their eyes she was a common harlot. She had been a harlot in Tristan's and Sheldon's houses, too, but such men were expected to indulge in debauchery, and she had also been seen as a valuable asset for the master's advancement. Master Kipping's employees were deeply shocked that His Majesty's first secretary should stoop so low. There could be no secret about her duties, for her room was next to his and they had a connecting door.

The new whore was therefore apprehensive when Kipping took her to meet his wife, Mistress Irene. She was bedridden, a large woman with white hair and a face ravaged by pain. She was charming. She took Maddy's hands and offered a cheek to be kissed.

"Sit down, my dear. How gorgeous you are! No wonder William raved about you. Go away, William. We girls need to talk. Pull your chair closer, dear. Are they making you comfortable?"

Maddy made polite responses, waiting for the mask to slip and reveal the hatred and resentment beneath. She waited in vain, and gradually Irene put her at ease.

"...works so hard...carries the kingdom on his shoulders...people who should be helping working against him... never able to give him children...can't give him anything now, just a burden...want you to be kind to him."

Maddy knew her purpose was more than mere therapeutic adultery. She was also a pawn in the game against the Uptree faction, and a supreme tactician like Kipping might have yet other uses in mind for her. She came from a notorious family of heretics smitten by the abominable sky god. The Children were known to have strange powers of healing. Was she supposed to heal this crippled woman? If she explained, quite truthfully, that her gifts were limited and did not include healing, would she be hurled out into the street?

"...get very bored here...you are country stock?...you must ride...pick out a palfrey, and Steven will provide a couple of the grooms to escort you...Royal Park...gentlefolk may ride all over the Royal Park..."

And if Lord Uptree had stolen the Woodbridge estates, should they now belong to Maddy? The only other possible survivor was Rollo, although she had no hope that he was still alive. One day she would ask Master Kipping what had happened to him, but not yet. Let the tiny candle flame of hope burn on...

A nurse appeared with a tray.

Irene sighed. "More food! I swear that all I do is eat and sleep, more eating than sleeping. The rest of the time I get so bored I could scream. So if you ever find the hours heavy, dear, come and talk with me. Do you like poetry? I adore hearing poetry well read..."

Maddy withdrew, almost convinced that Mistress Kipping was genuine.

She ate a solitary supper: Master Kipping was working later than usual. She retired, leaving the connecting door ajar. Eventually Master Kipping tapped on it. She invited him to enter. He peered in, wearing a nightcap and a voluminous nightgown.

"Everything all right?" he asked. "Anything you need? I don't want to disturb you if you're tired after your journey..."

"There is something I need quite badly," Maddy said. "In fact, I am worried by its absence."

"Tell me."

"I need a man between my legs, thumping away like a blacksmith. Come here at once and take off that ridiculous nightgown."

He laughed and obeyed, and she made him feel young again.

The next few days saw a routine develop, and the most important part of it was the evening supper. Kipping worked long hours, and his first duty when he came home was to visit with Irene. That done, he would settle in his study for wine, a snack, and a chat with Maddy. She soon realized that this quiet confab was at least as valuable to him as the sexual part of her duties. How could he relax while talking with a wife who was dying? So Maddy made sure she was available, attentive, and discreet.

The Steven Irene had mentioned turned out to be Steven Veal, officially Master Kipping's almoner, although that title seemed to be a joke. He was a large, graying man, massive muscle now turning to flab, whose resemblance to a porter or dockworker was increased by a scar on his forehead and a cauliflower ear, but he spoke like a gentleman and missed nothing. He seemed to have authority over everyone, even the housekeeper and chief hostler, and Maddy decided that he must be chief of security.

When she rode in the park, he sent husky young grooms along to escort her; no doubt they would defend her if necessary, but they would also report everything she did back to him. She paid no calls, wrote no notes. After the hectic social life of the last half year, near solitude was restful—provided it did not go on too long. She knew that she was on probation.

One evening Kipping handed her a sheaf of high-quality, crackling papers, all densely inscribed with complicated prose.

"Here," he announced, "we have the downfall of the Uptrees. The rape of your family property was only one of their crimes, but it will figure largely in their trial. These are statements of claim, which I should like you to read carefully. If they meet with your satisfaction, I shall witness your signature on them."

"I doubt if I shall understand one word in eight."

"I shall be happy to explain anything you ask. There is no hurry on these, because it would be best if we did not proceed too soon. The sailing will be smoother later, I think." He smiled blandly.

She knew what he meant: when there was another king on the throne. Ethan was a personal friend of Osborn, and a devout follower of Garrett, but he was old and failing.

∽

"Two days from now," Kipping announced a week or two later, "I am invited to a reception at Norcaster House. That's Earl Uptree's Weypool residence. It will be a small affair, no more than a dozen couples, likely less." He smiled. "But star-studded even without counting your glittering presence."

She felt sudden panic. "He may recognize me!"

Kipping smiled. "I want him to recognize you! I want him to choke on his caviar and spill claret all over his bodice. He and his brother cheated you out of your inheritance, so you are a threat to them. At the moment he could deny knowing you. Recognition establishes his guilt, step one on our path to revenge. There will be witnesses present he cannot impeach: the crown prince for one. But aside from that, there will be talk, a light supper, and more talk. I do not anticipate dancing."

About a hundred possible gowns blurred through Maddy's head. "How should I dress?"

"Don't be shy. I want you to show up the frumps." He chuckled. "But you will not be the only young woman present. The Duke of Thaneshire will bring his delightful young grandniece. She is genuinely his grandniece, but that doesn't stop the gossip. Crown Prince Emil usually brings his cousin, Princess Emily. She's not many years older than you."

She had a face like a horse, though. Maddy had seen the royal couple several times at a distance and been unimpressed. Emil had a sickly grin and a silly laugh. Emily would be fourth in line to the throne if the Teacher had not forbidden female monarchs. She'd have been heir apparent under the old ways.

"And Lord Uptree is to recognize me?"

"Definitely. His Lordship is plotting an action against one of the crown's most important ministers. It would drag up a youthful indiscretion and blow it out of all proportion, causing damage to the government and me personally. I do not intend to haul him down yet, because his brother would rouse the Hierarchy against me. Their day will come, I promise you! Meanwhile, you are a threat-in-being." Kipping raised his glass. "Down with Uptrees!"

Maddy drank to that.

∾

The only commoner invited, First Secretary William Kipping, managed to arrive later than everybody else, which was a feat in itself. On this, her first visit to Norcaster

House, Maddy saw its opulence as overdone and old-fashioned. It was even gaudier than Norcaster Castle, and she was saddened to recall how impressed she had been by that ugly pile on her wedding day. She had been an innocent country girl then. Now she had seen the insides of most of the grand houses in Weypool and was anything but innocent.

With Maddy on his arm, Master Kipping was led through to a sizable salon, glittering with candles and remarkably warm for midwinter, where the earl and countess rose to receive the last of their guests. The countess was a wasted, dry rag of a woman, who looked thoroughly cowed by her massive, domineering husband. Osborn had grown even larger in the last two years, his beard grayer, his jowls more petulant. His expression at the sight of Miss Mindy Wells conveyed withering contempt, thinly painted over with a wash of masculine lechery. When a middle-aged man with a bedridden wife was seen squiring a beautiful girl half his age, in Albiurn society the implications were obvious.

There is a smile that says how-nice-to-meet-you, and there is another that says we-have-met-before. As Maddy rose from her curtsy, she gave her host the second at full strength. He reacted with a momentary puzzled frown, then shocked recognition, and finally disgust. He had seen her before as Sir Sheldon Causey's trollop, but only at a distance. Now he glanced at Kipping, unable to believe that he knew who his companion really was. Then back to Maddy.

"Miss Wells? Not Mrs., er...?"

"Stroud?"

"Yes. Mistress Stroud, of course. I am surprised to see you so far from home."

"I am surprised you forgot the name of one so close to you, my lord."

The earl frowned at such insolence. His scraggy countess was already glaring, although she could not possibly understand the real reason for her husband's distaste. Were Master Kipping a political ally of her husband, she could make allowances for minor moral lapses, but an opponent's depravity must be censured in the strongest terms.

"That marriage," Kipping said, "was totally invalid."

Uptree's contempt froze. "She had been married before?"

"No, although the groom had. I mean the procedures. Quite, um, *culpable*."

The threat rang out like a silver tray hitting a marble floor: coercion, forgery, grand larceny, who could guess what else? Uptree rocked back on his heels. Clearly Master Kipping had just scored an important point. That alone would make Maddy's evening.

After that it became quite boring for a while. The crown prince and his cousin were there; also the Exalted Nathaniel Wybrow, a fat, pompous man whose face indicated years of dissipation. The fifth man was a diplomat just appointed ambassador to some remote place Maddy had never heard of. He was so diplomatic he hardly spoke at all, and his wife even less. They both smiled a lot.

Nine in all, they sat around the room, sipped wine, and chatted. Crown Prince Emil talked far too much and said nothing of value, confirming Maddy's opinion that he was a halfwit. But when he began repeating some scandal that she had heard for the first time weeks earlier, the hierarch took offense. "I hardly think that is a suitable topic for conversation in such company."

"Oh...um...quite, Excellency." Turning scarlet, His Highness deflated.

Like a jousting knight, Princess Emily charged into the embarrassed silence. If Emil was a halfwit, his cousin was a wit and a half, who had easily been holding her own in both humor and astringent comment. She had green eyes, red hair, and was robed that evening in audacious gold and bronze colors that only royalty could possibly get away with. Her horsey appearance came mainly from her nose and teeth, but she was also tall, large-boned, and loud.

"Quite right, Your Excellency! By all means, let us elevate the discourse. Why don't we play the question game? Ask one."

Wybrow's fleshy mouth narrowly avoided a sneer. "'What is the purpose of life?'"

"Excellent!" Her Highness boomed. "Profound! Your Ladyship?"

The countess, whose gown bared too much flesh for a human prune, had been chosen because she was sitting to Wybrow's left. She flustered angrily, like a wet hen. "A woman's purpose is to serve her husband."

Green eyes rolled, then looked to the next victim, the ambassador.

"A man's is to serve God, king, and country. In that order."

Maddy was next. "Reproduction," she said.

Several people gasped. His Excellency puffed up like a bullfrog. "That is a disgusting obscenity!"

"Only if by 'life' you just mean 'people,'" she said sweetly. "Birds and insects and fish reproduce. If they didn't, there wouldn't be any more of them. What else do they do, except produce, rear, and defend young?"

The crown prince brayed a laugh. "Well said! We can't have chickens without eggs, what?"

"I think Miss Wells wins the point, Your Exaltation," Emily said. "Emil? What do you say is the purpose of life?"

"Mine doesn't have any at the moment," her cousin said, freezing the conversation completely. The king's health was known to be causing concern.

❧

The light supper would have fed a rural family for a week. Several of the male guests became loud and flushed, but not Kipping, for he was sparing in his drinking. Eventually the men called for tobacco, and the ladies returned to the withdrawing room. Before they had all settled in chairs around the fireplace, Princess Emily summoned Maddy with an imperious toss of her head, even more horselike. Maddy obediently followed her out of earshot of the others.

For once she spoke quietly.

"Loved the way you squelched Wybrow, but what caused that little contretemps when you arrived?"

With anyone else, Maddy would have said, "What contretemps?" but lying to royalty was a serious matter.

"My family's lands used to adjoin the earl's estate at Norcaster. They are now part of the earl's estate at Norcaster."

"Ah. And are the title deeds a trifle smudged? Or bloodstained?"

"Both."

"Then I hope," said the princess, "that Master Kipping makes him pee blood in his britches. Come." She strode back to join the others.

$$\sim\!\!\infty$$

That was Maddy's coming out in her second career, but few people had witnessed it. The following night Kipping squired her to a masque, and they had the best seats in the hall. Several hundred of the *best* people saw them together, and the news was certain to roll over high society like a thunderstorm.

Next morning a huge bunch of flowers arrived for Maddy from the Honorable Tristan Rastel. At that time of year they had to be artificial flowers, but her letter of thanks was genuine.

CHAPTER 27

EVERY WINTER TURNS TO SPRING AT LAST. SWALLOWS return. Stark twigs sprout blossoms and buds. In their own time, boys become men.

Lady Whatman's Rose Hall school had served its purpose, guiding her adopted nephew into growing up as a young gentleman. Some of her wards had gone to Gaudry and would doubtless return in time as missionaries to nurture the cult of the Mother in Albi. Those with lesser gifts had gone home, either to be wisdoms or merely persons with talent. Only two remained, Brad Armstrong and his best friend, Alan Sizer. Alan's mother had died when he was young, and his father was currently in jail, charged with harboring a missionary, a crime that could bring the death penalty. Alan had nowhere to go. Now that looked like a problem.

One bright morning, Lady Whatman called a meeting of the faculty, the six aging wisdoms who had taken refuge with her in their declining years and made her school a success. Three wise men and three wise women gathered in her withdrawing room. Brother Alfred was still principal and had helped her decode the warning letter, but his health was failing and she intended to break the news herself.

Last to arrive were the remaining students, Brad and Alan. Clearly flattered at being included, they moved quietly around the room to take the two empty stools at the back. They were young men now, their talents well developed. Alan had the gift of sagacity, but a single talent, no matter how strong, was not enough to get him admitted to Gaudry. Brad was enormously gifted and should be in Gaudry already, despite his youth, but he flatly refused to go.

"You have all heard of Father Rafe Dampier," Mary said. She sensed the whole group come to attention and saw hatred flash in Brad's eyes. "He has recently been admitted to the Hierarchy, so he is now the Exalted Rafe Dampier. We have our own opinions on how well he deserves that title. He continues to lead the Congregation of Conformity, meaning the persecution branch of the Church. We have just received worrying news concerning Dampier. He appears to be preparing a major drive against our faith, and we have reason to believe he has his eye on this area."

The old folk pulled faces at the thought of trouble. The youngsters at the back exchanged glances that she distrusted. No one else could predict what those two might get up to, but Brad had prescience and might know already.

"Rose Hall may even be his target." The letter had come from John Hawke himself, now Prelate Albi since the barbaric execution of Jake Trull. He had sounded sure of his information, as if he had sources high up in the Church of the Light. "A week from now will mark the anniversary of the massacre at Woodbridge Manor."

Nobody looked at Brad. No one ever mentioned his connection to Woodbridge Manor, but Lady Whatman would be most surprised if she were the only other person present who knew of it.

"I mention that," Lady Whatman continued, "because if Dampier suspects how Rose Hall has been serving our cause, he may treat it the same way he did Woodbridge." That was unlikely. Even for Dampier, that so-called miracle had been an exceptional event, but his thugs could do ample damage by traditional means. "Please keep that in mind. You must decide whether to remain here and hope the storm misses us, or leave and take refuge elsewhere for a while. We have mole holes, as you know, but they won't hold eight of you, and Dampier's men are very skilled at finding the holes now."

Again Brad and Alan exchanged glances, and possibly even nods.

"Master Sizer," Lady Whatman said, "you can see your own future better than anyone else here. What do you choose to do?"

Alan stood up and instinctively adopted the student's pose, feet apart and hands behind his back. His gift of sagacity let him make the wiser decision when he must choose between alternatives. Everyone with talent had an animal guide that served much the same purpose, but his response would be a clue as to what Brad might do.

"My lady, I haven't had a chance to think about it yet. All I know at the moment is that I must stay with Brad. The thought of parting from him sickens me." He glanced down at his friend and whispered something that was no doubt an insult, because Brad sneaked a punch at him, down low where he did not expect Lady Whatman to see it. They were very *young* young men.

She said, "Then let us hear from Brad. I believe he may be in more danger than any of you." Gold was poison to anyone as gifted as he. The touch of it might char his skin or send him into convulsions. Dampier's hounds would have no trouble identifying him as talented if they were willing to risk killing him in the process.

So Alan sat down and Brad rose, but he rested his hands on the back of the chair in front of him and leaned forward, deliberately informal. Some boys mature much faster than others. Alan, although three years the senior, was fair and slight and seemed the younger. Since Leo left, Brad was the tallest person in Rose Hall, other than a couple of the gardeners; a stranger would take him for seventeen or eighteen.

"Brother Alfred tells me I have prescience, Aunt, but if I do it's very patchy, not reliable. I nearly froze to death on Hog Hill, remember."

"But you didn't," Alfred muttered.

"I don't foresee any...I mean..." He paused and blinked. Every eye on the room was on him. "I don't anticipate any disaster, anyway. In fact, things look quite encouraging." He flashed a grin that stripped away the veneer of maturity. Had he had a real prevision or just realized the advantages of saying that he had?

Although Lady Whatman had no divine gift of foresight, she now foresaw trouble.

She foresaw even more of it a few days later, when local news arrived that the Exalted Rafe Dampier was coming to Stonebridge to lead a service to commemorate the second anniversary of the miracle—or massacre—at Woodbridge Manor. By then four of the wisdoms had gone off to find temporary shelter elsewhere. Only the oldest, Maud and Alfred, remained.

She sent for her nephew. Brad turned up in riding clothes, accompanied as always by Smut and Alan Sizer. All three seemed very cheerful.

Brad accepted the seat she indicated and stretched out his pipe-stem legs. "What can I do to serve you, dear Aunt?" He would listen, but that did not mean he would obey. Those days were gone.

"I need to know your intentions. Dampier is due to appear in Stonebridge in three days. If you are going to leave here, you ought to do so now."

"He can't do to you what he did to Woodbridge Manor. It's too far to march."

"No, but he could do his gloating at Stonebridge, then move to Roburgh and lead a march on us from there."

Brad looked to Alan. "What'll you do?"

"Go with you."

"Where to?"

"Wherever you go."

Brad looked back to Mary and sighed. "He's a lot of help. I think we'll saddle up, if we may borrow our usual mounts for a few days? And just disappear. Then no one can be forced to say where we've gone."

She was quite sure this had been his plan all along. He saw himself as a man now, and every mirror confirmed that, but he was still a child inside, with no practice at making decisions and no experience to base them on. His powers were frightening. He ought to be in Gaudry, learning how to use them properly and ethically. Alfred had told her that Brad could probably stop a stranger, ask for all his money, and walk away with it, leaving the legal owner uncertain where it had gone. She had raised the boy; the knight wore no shining armor, but he was armed and dangerous now, also rash and cocksure.

She said, "Alan knows who you are?"

Brad frowned. "I haven't told him. Have you?"

"I haven't told anyone; I don't think even Brother Alfred knows."

"So who are you?" Alan demanded, justifiably annoyed at being bypassed.

"I'm Bram Woodbridge. My family died in the massacre. I thought everyone had guessed."

Alan lost color, so he couldn't have known. That was extraordinary. His lips moved but no words emerged.

"And," Brad said, "that day I swore vengeance on Rafe Dampier."

"I'm with you."

"Not so fast!" Mary snapped. "I swore also, remember. We agreed together to avenge the deaths of your family and mine. But now, Bram Woodbridge, you are breaking the partnership, riding out alone on your own mission, and forgetting the debt you owe to me."

Fast as a pouncing cat, Brad was on his knees beside her chair. He took her hand in both of his. "Dear Aunt! I have not forgotten one word of what we swore, although I was very young then. I know what I owe you for taking me in and nurturing me so generously. But my enemy has moved within my reach and does not know of my existence. I would be an idiot not to take advantage of this opportunity. How could I hunt him down in Weypool?"

"What does your prescience tell you?"

He hesitated, watching her with a foxy expression she had never seen on him before. "It doesn't say that I will kill him."

"What does it say?"

"It says that I will see something very good happen in Stonebridge, three days from now."

After a brief silence, Alan said, "Like to see that, too."

"Me too. And then, Aunt, I promise you that Alan and I will come back, and we can plan how to avenge your son and Jake Trull and all the others so monstrously treated by the sky worshipers."

He had always been gracious, and now he could twist her like string, in a way that Mark never had.

"Then go with the Mother's blessing and my prayers."

The knights errant rode out the next morning, Alan on Swallow and Brad on Bramble because he had long outgrown Charger. Smut led the way, tail wagging. Alan's guide, Barney, preferred to fly by night.

Brad took a deep breath of fresh spring air. "Welcome to manhood."

"*You* are welcoming *me*? I happen to be three years older than you, boy."

"You don't look it."

"I have hairs on my chest."

"Visible only in bright sunlight."

And so it went. Life was good, and this did feel like the start of manhood.

"You really planning to kill Dampier? Can you? Deliberately kill?" Alan said.

A good question. Killing somebody would not be easy. "Just watch me."

"If you had a razor at his throat, could you cut?"

"Probably not. I hate mess. But I do have means."

Brad had shown Alan his fire-starting talent on the day he went up Hog Hill to practice and see what his range was. Nobody else knew about it. Brother Alfred had never even mentioned such a gift, let alone tested him for it.

They followed the road where Brad had met Lady Whatman, which he knew well now, although he had never been sure of the exact spot where he had waited with Wisdom Frieda. Soon they crossed over the county line into Angleshire, planning to visit Wisdom Edith, but they found the path through the trees so overgrown that there was obviously nobody home. Rafe Dampier had scared the Mother cult away from this part of the county.

From there it was only a short ride to Woodbridge Farm, which had once been the manor house. The adventurers rode past without stopping, not wanting to attract attention. The barns, paddocks, and workers' cottages were still there and in use, but the house had not been rebuilt. Its site was a wasteland of weeds and thistles that Brad hardly recognized. Many of the surrounding trees had been cut down, probably because the fire had killed them and they had been unsafe. The most distinctive landmark was a set of stone steps surrounded by long grass. Once those steps had led up to the front door. He could remember sitting there with his friends. His eyes blurred with tears.

Killing Rafe Dampier would be more than a duty; it would be a pleasure.

Soon after that they came to a fork in the trail. Brad wanted to go left, along the riverbank. Alan veered right, and they both reined in.

"This way," Alan said.

"Stonebridge is this way."

"Not a good choice. You could be recognized."

Alan was the expert on choices. Smut had gone right, too, and was looking back with his tail down.

"Right it is, then," Brad said and turned Bramble. Prescience was weird. It told him something very good was going to happen soon, and Brother Alfred would tell him to trust that feeling. Nothing he could do could change what he foresaw, the wisdom said. If he prophesied his own death, it would track him down him no matter where he went or what he did. That meant that his prescience had even foreseen that he would let Alan turn him aside from the road he had intended to follow a moment ago. He found that idea worrying, because it denied him any free will. But Alan seemed to have that, because his sagacity let him choose whenever he had a choice. It never told him what would happen if he chose the other path, though. Prescience was always right, and sagacity could never be proved wrong.

They still had two days to scout out the land before Dampier was due in Stonebridge. Dampier had two more days to live.

Two days was enough for them to tire of aimless freedom. Few people ever traveled far from the village of their birth, so there were no inns except along the king's highway, and caution suggested that those should be avoided when so many Sons of the Sun would be coming to hear Hierarch Dampier preach.

Instead the would-be assassins ate and slept at isolated farmhouses, chosen by an unbeatable combination of Alan's sagacity and Brad's insight. Their hosts would always turn out to be secret worshipers of the Mother, so when the visitors dropped a few hints to identify themselves as her Children also, they were awarded a warm welcome. Their offers to pay for board and shelter were always refused, but Brad left money anyway. Lady Whatman had given him plenty of silver.

On the big day they moved in closer to Stonebridge, and chatty locals confirmed that the Exalted Rafe would be preaching in the church that evening. Brad became conscious of a dry mouth and a tightness in his gut. He noticed that Alan was talking much less than usual.

As the sun sank westward, Alan said, "Shouldn't we be making some plans, or is that beneath our dignity?"

"There isn't much to plan. We wait until sunset, when we know the service begins. Then we ride into the village, you hold the horses, ready for a fast getaway, I walk over to the church, go in, kill him, and leave in the confusion."

"You make it sound so easy I wonder why we don't do this more often."

"Maybe we will in future. You'll probably hear the noise, but either Smut or Barney will tell you when to bring the horses. Then we ride like the wind."

"Where to?"

Embarrassed pause. "I haven't got that far," Brad admitted. "I would entertain suggestions."

"You would entertain suicidal maniacs. I never ride like the wind at night. You break your neck or your horse's legs. There won't be a moon until much later. I think we ride slow so as not to attract attention."

"And we go where?"

"Anywhere there's a comfortable ditch to sleep in. I will choose one sagaciously." After a moment Alan added, "With nettles for you, without for me."

It wasn't much of a plan, but it was the best they could find.

They hid themselves behind a barn at the Woodbridge end of the village because that was downwind and they could listen to the church bells. Brad wished he'd been the one to think of that. Nobody came to see what they were up to, and if any dogs noticed them, Smut told them to keep quiet. Bradwell Armstrong must be more than a little nervous if his mind was throwing up such idiotic ideas.

The bells stopped. The sun set. Brad took yet another pee. He knew the Church's evensong rite, because a curate or deacon from Roburgh would come to Rose Hall on holy days and Lady Whatman insisted that everyone who could attend do so. Brad had been excused for the last year, because the hymns made him turn green and throw up. He would have enough worries tonight without that.

So he knew that there would be a hymn, some announcements and prayers, a second hymn, then the sermon. That was when he must strike.

"Isn't it about time you went?" Alan asked.

"It isn't far. But better early than too late, I s'pose."

"Mother be with you."

Prescience must be trusted. Brad squared his shoulders and headed off to assassinate. Stonebridge seemed strangely small, perhaps because he had grown so much. He still fell over his own feet sometimes, not having gotten his coordination worked out. He saw an owl swoop overhead and guessed that Alan had sent Barney to look after him. Smut would be around somewhere in the shadows.

After he turned ten, he had been allowed to ride Charger as far as Stonebridge, and had done so often. The street was dark enough now that no one would recognize him, and even in daylight few would know the tall man that little Bram had so suddenly become. Nothing had changed in the village. He caught a faint hint of singing from the church, but not loud enough to bother him yet.

He ought to be shivering with terror at what he was about to do and what would happen to him if he got caught. He wasn't. His bladder was clenched, but the sensation was almost pleasurable. He could foresee triumph very close ahead now. The singing had stopped. What he hadn't foreseen was the crowd blocking the church door. Evidently Exalted Dampier's reputation had filled the interior to capacity, and at least fifty people were packed close outside, trying to hear what the saint was saying.

No matter how strong a man's gift of distraction might be, he couldn't hope to muscle through a mob like that and remain unnoticed. *Excuse me, I have a murder to commit...Excuse me, I...* The fringes were too far back from the doorway; he needed to be closer to his target for his incendiary talent to work.

For a few minutes he stood in a dark corner and chewed a nail. If Dampier was going to burn to death, then he could guess why and who had to arrange it. There had to be a way.

Whimper?

Brad looked down. "Smut?"

Whimper again, from farther away. Did the church have another door on the north side? If so, it should be just as besieged as the main door, or simply locked, more likely. Brad strode around to see, aware of Smut trotting ahead of him. The churchyard there was heavily wooded and dark, which didn't bother either of them, and there was no crowd. No door. But there were windows, set too high for him to see inside. A small pane at the top of one light was broken, and he could hear a man declaiming. There was a tree stump not far off. He scrambled up and managed to balance unsteadily on the uneven surface.

The interior of the church was only dimly lit, but the brightest lamp hung over the pulpit, where a man in cloth of gold was spewing bile, waving his hands. He didn't look especially dangerous. Sometimes his voice was loud enough to make out the words.

"...there be rot in the walls, the house cannot stand..."

Brad's viewpoint was close to the east end of the church, where the great golden sunburst hung above a dais. The choir sat on either side of that area, and the pulpit stood high on the edge of it, offset to the north, so it did not obstruct the congregation's view of the holy sunburst. The body of the church was packed with people, many having to sit on the floor, shoulder to shoulder, with every eye on the preacher up in the pulpit.

"...heretics the cancer of the body politic," the Exalted Rafe Dampier roared. "They eat it away from within, weakening the only true faith..." He did have a splendid, compelling, resonant voice.

Brad was frozen. There he was, the enemy, the monster who had murdered the Woodbridges, all of them except one small boy who had been saved by his dog. This was how Brad had dreamed of catching him: vulnerable, unaware, and thundering hatred. The Mother had given him fire talent just for this. But would the window block his magic? Would that golden pectoral Dampier wore? More and more these days Brad was realizing that Lady Whatman had been right; he should have gone to Xennia, to Gaudry, to be properly taught.

"...vermin! The Teacher warned us that pestilence grows in the stench of gutters and heresy is excrement of the mind..."

Alan had been right to question whether Brad ever could kill a man in cold blood. How could be roast a human being? How could he interrupt that magnificent, inspirational tirade, repulsive as its actual words might be? It was music. The effect was overwhelming. The crowd was moaning in pain or ecstasy.

"Burn them! Root and branch, the evil must be cut out. Smite them, O Lord, seek out the evildoers and burn them with your holy flame!"

That did it. *Right! This branch didn't burn that night.* Giving Dampier a taste of his own medicine, Brad set his golden clothes on fire. It was as easy as wishing.

Oh, beautiful!

The priest screamed like a horse as the flames lapped up from his belly to his beard. He toppled back and rolled down the stairs to the dais, where he writhed and thrashed, trying to extinguish the blaze by rolling. Two men from the choir rushed forward to smother it by wrapping their cloaks around him, but those just added more fuel. Eventually Dampier either fainted or died, for he fell still, his whole body engulfed in fire and smoke, the cloth burning away to show charred flesh below. The entire church was in an uproar, with the congregation jamming into the doorway.

A sharp tug on his cloak almost made Brad cry out. Smut had his teeth in it, pulling, telling him it was time to leave. The night was loud with the tumult of the mob leaving the church. Brad jumped down and ran through the dark to the road, where men, women, and children were fighting their way out of the building and fleeing from the horror. They parted for a horseman coming the other way, leading a spare.

Brad swung into the saddle. He and Alan turned their mounts and rode off. Soon the wailing and shouting faded into the night.

"Well done," Alan said. "I don't know if I could have done it."

And now Brad almost wished he hadn't. He wasn't sure he would be able to sleep ever again without dreaming of that screaming, tortured *thing* thrashing on the church floor. "He smelled like roast pork."

"You're making that up."

Yes he was. "You wanna go back and sniff?"

"Glad you did it. It's stupid of us to take all their shit and not fight back."

"Yes it is."

They had slowed to a walk. The horses were nervous, so Brad dismounted and led Bramble. Swallow followed. After a while they heard an owl hoot off to their left.

"That's Barney," Alan said.

"And there's a track through the woods. Maybe going to lead us somewhere dry to sleep." Brad turned off. Alan dismounted and led Swallow after him.

Things had changed. Brad Armstrong was a killer now. If they ever caught him, he would certainly go to the stake. And he must never revert to his own name. The priest's death in the same area while celebrating his own miracle left no doubt that a Woodbridge or Woodbridge supporter was behind it. One man's miracle was another man's demonism. Brad wondered if it was even safe to return to Rose Hall. Old Alfie would certainly guess who had torched Rafe Dampier. He would disapprove.

"I know someone who'll scream with joy when he hears the news," Alan said.

"Who's that?"

"My dad. He'd burn the lot of them if he could. He rants about revolution and bringing back the old ways. Alfie would call him a fanatic."

Alan was lucky to have a dad, except he'd probably never see him again. Which led to an interesting question.

"You know where he is?"

"The letter said he'd been taken to Umberly Castle, outside Weypool. Course that was a month ago, and the man who wrote me was just a clerk and might have been wrong."

Stealing a man out of a government jail would be harder than bushwhacking one in a church. But Alan had helped him on his quest. Tit deserved tat.

"Why don't we go and rescue him?"

Silence. Then, almost inaudibly: "You serious?"

"Of course. Glad to help." Brad was a killer now, so he had nothing to lose. It would be a good excuse not to go back to Rose Hall until things cooled off a bit. "The sooner the better, in case they move him." Or kill him.

"You mean just head that way tomorrow, not go back to Rose Hall?"

Obvious. "Old Dearie can't stop us if she doesn't know what we're doing."

CHAPTER 28

THE DAY WAS HOT, THE ROAD LONG AND DUSTY. AT NOON they stopped for lunch to rest the horses and eat their rations. Sprawled in the shade of a beech tree, Nell toyed dreamily with the thought of unlacing Rollo's britches and of the nice events that might follow. Unfortunately, they were still visible to the good folk gathering hay on the far side of the road. To suggest moving farther into the trees would ruin the mood. Save it up for tonight.

Even after two years, she loved him insanely. She knew many marriages cooled off after the first mad passion, but theirs had not. How could it, when he was in constant danger? Any day he might be seized and dragged away to suffer the same awful fate as Jake Trull. She would never see him again. Trull had remained silent under torture, but supposing they captured her as well and then tortured her to make Rollo talk? She had to stay with him because he lacked insight and needed hers. Twice she had detected spies in houses he was planning to visit, but someday their luck would run out. He took risks, preaching to large congregations, lingering too long in one place to complete a healing.

"I think you're crazy," she said.

A pause suggested Rollo had been asleep, or close to it. "You're the crazy one. You married me. Look where it's got you."

"It's got me heading straight into an area that you know Monster Dampier and his trolls are presently terrorizing in the name of God. They are certain to be at Stonebridge, and our destination is the closest Children's safe house there is. Don't tell me he hasn't got Rose Hall in his sights."

"I do tell you." Rollo sat up. "My prescience does not foresee danger. It tells me that Brother Alfred is dying and I will be there. I should be there. No one has done more for the Mother's cause in the last half century than that old man, maybe not even Jake Trull."

"You're sure he's not dying in jail?"

"Certain. Stop lying there looking so lascivious or you'll have those haymakers scything their neighbors' ankles. Let's be moving on and see if Lady Whatman has a swimming hole we can muddy up. Vixen, come here!"

Vixen came. Rollo's mastery even worked on horses.

Lady Whatman was less than pleased when she came hurrying downstairs to greet the unexpected visitors. She hid her displeasure behind a practiced smile, but Nell sensed at once that something important was bothering her. Lady Whatman was troubled, possibly frightened, but at the same time exultant—a strange mixture. Rollo was a perceptive person, but too ready to trust people, so he likely noticed nothing wrong in her manner. The lady made conventional remarks about being honored to meet the revered prelate. Hitherto they had corresponded only by coded letter.

"You knew that awful Dampier man was coming to this area," she said crossly. "You told me so yourself. Are you not taking an unreasonable risk, Brother?"

"I don't think so."

"Oh well. We do have holes, but we shall be very cramped to put you both up as well if the boys return and then trouble comes calling."

"I only came to visit with Brother Alfred. If we may impose on you for a night's lodging, we can leave in the morning. The old man is ailing, I heard."

"News must travel fast. He was taken ill just two days ago. Seriously so, I fear, but he will be happy to see you. He has been very agitated since he heard the news. Indeed, he mentioned your name."

Together, Nell and Rollo said, "What news?"

Lady Whatman glanced around and frowned. The entry hall was large, and the footman hovering discreetly in case she wished to issue instructions was too far off to hear words. He was not too distant to see reactions, though, if the lady had something startling to share. She led the way out to the terrace and to a marble gazebo, safely removed from any eavesdropping. She did not sit or invite her guests to do so. She was letting down her guard, showing more agitation.

"Last night the Exalted Rafe Dampier was preaching in Stonebridge, celebrating the anniversary of his most successful butchery."

"He is certainly a hard man to like," Rollo said.

"Not anymore. He drew a full house, of course, because everybody would be scared of attracting suspicion by staying away. He had hardly begun to preach when he burst into flames. Right in the pulpit. The word is that he is still alive, but so terribly burned that he cannot survive."

"That's terrible!" Rollo bent his head and murmured, "Holy Mother, forgive them. Have you any idea who did this, my lady?"

"None at all."

To Nell the lie rang as false as a cracked bell. Even Rollo noticed and looked hard at her.

She flushed. "No one has been arrested, so far as I know."

"And the congregation just sat there and watched the preacher burn?"

"There was a panic, of course. Some people were trampled, I believe."

"Mother, save us! This will set the land ablaze. No, do not smile, my lady. I foresee disaster. But who committed this crime? The record keepers at Gaudry know of only three instances of incendiary talent, and one of them was Rafe Dampier himself. Assuming he did not commit suicide, we must have a fourth on our hands."

Lady Whatman's face had shut up as tight as a tomb.

Rollo could force her to speak, of course, but Nell had never seen him use mastery on people since the night of his escape from Swine Hall. He regarded it as a form of violence, and unethical. Even now he rejected it.

"You said, my lady, 'If the boys return.' What boys?"

"When we received your warning of the Dampier visit, we naturally took precautions. Most of the instructors went elsewhere for a while, only Alfred and Maud remaining. All our students except two have already graduated and departed. The two who remain in residence rode off to explore the countryside, as boys will."

Even yet Rollo did not force Lady Whatman to release the information she was obviously keeping from him.

"Their names, my lady?" he asked softly.

"My nephew, Brad Armstrong, and Alan Sizer."

"Sizer? Any relation to Richard Sizer?"

"You know him?" the lady said with pretend innocence. "A man of strong views. Alan's his son."

"Very wrong views, in my opinion." Rollo glanced at Nell. Sizer was one of the leaders of the partisans who called themselves the Underground and preached armed resistance to the Church's repression. "And is the younger Sizer greatly gifted?"

"Oh, no. The truly talented have all gone on to Gaudry."

Nell remembered the other boy, though. He had made her uneasy when she visited Rose Hall a year ago. He had the same core of bitter hatred as Lady Whatman herself, and Alfred had testified that he had "wagonloads" of talent. She had told Rollo that, because major talents were important.

Rollo said, "You would classify your nephew as not truly gifted?"

"Brother Alfred wants him to go to Gaudry," Lady Whatman said. "But he is still very young, not even fourteen yet."

"I am appalled by your news, my lady. This murder will result in a massive witch hunt that will endanger us all. Rose Hall may not escape attention this time, so I suggest you take a vacation yourself. Now let us go and speak with Brother Alfred. Then Mistress Hawke and I will head straight back to Weypool."

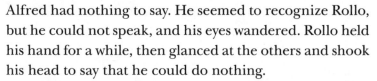

Alfred had nothing to say. He seemed to recognize Rollo, but he could not speak, and his eyes wandered. Rollo held his hand for a while, then glanced at the others and shook his head to say that he could do nothing.

"You're not in pain, are you?" No reply. "I was hoping to receive your blessing."

The colorless old lips seemed to smile at that. Rollo blessed him instead. A little later he gently closed the old man's eyes and told him to go in peace.

CHAPTER 29

BRAD WAS AS FILTHY AS A CHURL, HIS CLOTHES WERE stained and torn, and he longed for a decent meal. Alan was in no better shape but just as stubbornly refused to suggest they turn back. They admitted to feeling abandoned and vulnerable without their familiars. Neither Smut nor Barney had been seen for days, which was worrisome.

Weypool was a very big city, big enough to hide many castles. They had to ask directions several times before they even discovered that Umberly wasn't a place, just a family name. It was around noon, three days after the torching of Father Dampier, that they came in sight of their destination, a gloomy, turreted pile a couple of miles east of the capital. A suburb had grown up around it.

They stopped in a small square to water their horses at the trough and drink at the pump. Glorious odors were wafting out of a baker's shop nearby. Brad hitched his reins to the post and strode inside, ducking under the low lintel.

The interior was cramped and dim. Voices were arguing from beyond a draped doorway, and the only person present in the tiny store was the baker's apprentice, a surly-looking youth as tall as Brad himself. All that mattered was that he stood behind a table covered with loaves and other gorgeous stuff. The hot meat pies were oozing gravy and would be hard to transport, so Brad pointed to the row of cold ones.

"What's in those?"

"Jellied pork."

"How much for two?"

"Eight stars." The youth had summed him up as a stranger and wanted to haggle.

"YOU'LL SELL THEM TO ME FOR TWO." Which was still too much. Brad laid the coins on the table. "What's the big building?"

"Umberly Castle."

"Who lives there?"

Surly eyed him with open suspicion. "'S the traitors' prison."

"Only traitors?"

"Why don' you go an' ask them?"

Brad was tempted to order him to strip naked and bathe in the horse trough for an hour, but the argument behind the drape was growing louder. Any moment whoever was losing might give up and come storming out into the store.

"FORGET ME AND FORGET TALKING WITH ME." Brad walked out with his pies, handed one up to Alan, sprang into Bramble's saddle, and led the way along the dirty, rutted street. The pies were mostly gristle, but a hungry man could eat anything.

"Learn much?" Alan asked.

"It's a prison for traitors. Not criminals. Let's ride up there and ask to visit with your father."

"And what if they throw us in a cell?"

"Why should they? If they do, then we break out after dark. I can use mastery on guards, remember. I can open locks." That was his secret weapon, because jiggling was so rare that the warders wouldn't be expecting it. Even Brother Alfred had been surprised to find him with it, and Old Alfie knew more than anyone about the Mother's gifts.

"What does your prescience say?"

"Nothing." Either the Mother had not decided, or she wasn't telling. "Your sagacity?"

"It says to do it," Alan admitted unhappily. "But I'm scared shitless."

❦

A castle surrounded by houses wouldn't last long in a siege, but no castle would stand up to modern cannon anyway. It might look impressive, but would it even be much good as a jail? Castles were built to keep people out, not in. The rescue squad dismounted at the main gate, which was flanked by a guardhouse on either side. The gate itself stood open, revealing a dark and forbidding tunnel beyond. Sentries armed with long-barreled muskets stood like statues, ignoring the visitors, but an officer came strutting out of the right-hand guardhouse, very flashy in the king's livery. He looked over the newcomers with a sneer and chose Brad, which was flattering.

"Who're you and what'ja want?"

Brad played stupid, which was suddenly starting to feel easy. "I'm Cedric, his cousin."

"I'm Alan Sizer, and I came to see my father. Was told he was here."

"Maybe he is, maybe he ain't. You'll have to come and ask the warden. The lads'll look after your horses. Follow me."

The "lads" were gigantic trolls-at-arms, seven or eight of whom had now surrounded the visitors. Exchanging worried glances, the would-be rescuers handed over their reins and followed the captain into the tunnel.

The attack was so sudden that Brad had no chance to react. The butt of a pike between his legs and a hard punch between the shoulder blades sent him pitching forward. Knees landed on his back, crushing all the air out of him. A foul cloth was stuffed in his mouth and another pulled tight over his eyes. Cold manacles clicked around his wrists.

After the ox got up off his back, he was left lying there for a few minutes to reflect on how unspeakably, unthinkably *stupid* he had been to walk into the rats' nest without any proper plan or preparation at all. Then a boot nudged his ribs, not gently.

"Get up, both of you," the captain said.

Brad struggled to put himself upright—not the easiest maneuver with hands cuffed behind him and what felt like a dozen broken ribs. Blindsight worked best at very short range. At a distance, it required prizing hints out of dense fog. He made out some of the faces around him, and they weren't even grinning at how easily the two kids had been suckered. There was no concession for cuteness in the real world. A hand of steel closed around his upper arm, almost *all the way* around, just to humiliate him further. He was jerked forward and forced to walk.

He could detect the captain leading the way and Alan behind him, and the echoing footsteps told him the whole squad was still on escort duty. It should be very slightly flattering that the two of them were being taken so seriously. It wasn't. It was terrifying. Just three days ago, he had killed a priest, a famous priest, or had wounded him fatally. Dampier might still be lingering in his death throes, but even the best healers couldn't block a fatal injury, only speed up natural healing.

The echoes stopped, but there were still cobblestones underfoot. A change in the feel of the air told him that he had left the tunnel and must be in the central courtyard of the castle. Then he was jerked to a stop and turned to his right. A hinge or pivot squealed, metal on metal. He was urged forward two paces and halted. Blindsight said he was in a cage, a small cage.

"There's a cot one pace in front of you," said a voice, not the captain's. "Turn around, back up, and you can sit down. Someone will be along to question you in an hour or two. Meanwhile, you're being watched all the time, and you're not allowed to speak. Is that clear?"

Brad tried to say, "Sir, we only came here to visit my uncle," but managed only a muffled mumble.

"Shut up. If you say one word, the guards will throw a bucket of water at you. Then you and your bedding will be wet and stay wet. The second time, it'll be a bucket of piss. I'll let you guess what's in the third one. Your decision."

The gate clanged shut and a lock clicked. It sounded like a big lock, not finicky, easy to manipulate. Footsteps retreating. Brad found the cot and sat down. Another gate clanged some distance away, which told him where Alan had been taken. What a balls-up!

A man coughed a few feet to his left. On the other side, one cleared his throat. He was being warned not to speak, but it was no comfort that there were witnesses to his shame. He wondered if the prisoners were kept blindfolded all the time or just sometimes. Or just some of them. His gag felt and tasted like a dirty washrag in his mouth, held there by a cord tied painfully tight. He jiggled it to loosen the knot a bit.

He explored with blindsight. The cage was tiny, about six feet square, maybe. The walls and top were made of steel bars. The cobbled floor must be the original yard. A strong man might shift or overturn one cell, so they would be welded together to make immovable blocks of them. A vague something overhead puzzled him, but he eventually resolved it into a solid roof a few feet above the cage. So the animals wouldn't get rained on.

He peered inside the lock. Yes, he could open that. But boots were going by at irregular intervals, sometimes slow, sometimes fast.

What a fuckup! Poor Auntie. Many times she'd told him of her vision of a knight in shining armor. She'd built her hopes, her school, her dreams on him. For years she'd put herself in danger—for him. Now he'd thrown it all away. Not to mention what he'd done to Alan. Yet Alan's sagacity had told him to follow Brad's lead. Of course, what was good for Alan might not be good for Brad, and sagacity only judged chances, gave no guarantees. He tried pre-science and still found his future a blank. Too uncertain to call? Even uncertainty was better than most of the futures he could imagine for himself.

It was a long, long time before he heard voices in the distance. It sounded as if they were talking to Alan, but he couldn't hear Alan replying.

Footsteps, then a new voice in front of him.

"I'm the warden. You just call me 'sir.' Come here so we can take that gag off of you."

Brad stood up, took two steps to the bars, and waited for hands to reach in.

Then everything happened at once.

What came through the bars was the tip of a red-hot poker to press against his forehead. Without the gag he would have emptied his lungs in a scream of pain. Instead he just leaped back, caught his calves against the cot, fell on it, and cracked his head hard against the bars behind him.

They roared with laughter, about six of them.

"Looks like you got a live one there, sir!"

"Did you see that frog jump?"

They had touched him with gold. He was marked as an agent of darkness. They wouldn't take any risks with talent like his; a few days from now he'd be run through a quick trial and burned at the stake. He was a dead man.

Unless he did something quicker than they could.

He opened his handcuffs, ripped off the gag and blindfold, and leaped to the bars. The warden was a thin, dry-looking man in silks, with four fusiliers at his back.

"You will obey me. You will protect me. So will you and you and you and you."

The men's eyes went glassy with shock as the power hit them. They mumbled and slobbered.

"WARDEN, BRING ME ANOTHER FOUR FUSILIERS. THE
REST OF YOU, RELEASE ALL THE PRISONERS. KILL ANYONE
WHO TRIES TO STOP YOU. MOVE!"

As his slaves ran to obey, Brad surveyed his surroundings. The cages extended along both sides of the castle
courtyard, about two dozen of them in all, and most of
them seemed to be occupied, at least along the far side,
which he could see. A cover of stout timbers and thatch
had been added to protect the inmates from the weather,
but they would be kept under observation all the time,
both from men in the yard itself and others at windows
overlooking the yard. The battlements of the castle would
face out, not in, so those weren't available.

The inmates were leaping to their feet as they watched
the unbelievable happening. Some of them were women,
caged like animals, on public display.

The warden arrived with four troubled-looking fusiliers,
and Brad enslaved them, also. By then he had unlocked the
gate to his cage. Firing began as the rest of the garrison
woke up to the emergency. Unarmed prisoners were joining
in the battle, swarming the guards as they tried to reload.

A musket ball screamed off the bars beside Brad's ear.
He located the puff of smoke at an upstairs window, and
the marksman frantically swabbing his musket, preparing
to reload. Brad tried to incinerate him. He would probably
have been outside Brad's range, had he not been wearing
a powder horn on his belt. He exploded like a cannon.
The report echoed off the walls, and the fire set the room
ablaze. Good idea. Brad turned his attention to the thatch
roofs above the cages and set them on fire also: *there* and

there and *there.* Flames shot up. Smoke billowed over the battlefield. Wounded were screaming.

Brad found the warden in the smoke. "ORGANIZE THE ESCAPE! GET THE PRISONERS OUT OF THE CASTLE."

Alan appeared with a fair-haired man who must be his father and grabbed Brad's arm. "Let's go!"

Go where? Brad let himself be dragged away. They ran for the gateway. They had to wait a moment while the warden and his troop of rebels stormed the guardhouses to kill the loyalists. Then Brad and the Sizers led the stampede of inmates, jumping over bodies, heading to freedom. Outside the archway he was greeted by familiar barking from an excited Smut.

Behind them, Umberly Castle was ablaze.

Townsfolk came running to find the cause of the smoke, but no one tried to stop the breakout, and some spectators cheered. About a score of fugitives vanished into the maze of streets. Brad just followed Smut, who obviously knew where to find safety. The Sizers followed Brad, but when Smut reared up to scratch at an inconspicuous door, Master Sizer said, "Well, Mother bless us!" as if he knew it.

It flew open, a woman said, "Quick, then!" and all four stumbled down a step into her kitchen. The door shut, leaving them in near darkness.

"Master Sizer, what a pleasure!"

"Widow Netley, upon my soul, a sight for sore eyes. May I present, my son Alan, and, um…"

"Brad Armstrong," Brad said, bowing. Hard to bow gracefully when you are panting. And trembling. Ever since the gold burned him, he had been driven by sheer fury. The sudden plunge into safety had him shaking like an aspen leaf.

Widow Netley was very short, but wide and deep. Her clothes indicated a woman of humble means, neither rich nor poor, and her home was livable for one person, clean and tidy. No other rooms opened off the kitchen, but a ladder led up to a sleeping loft and a trapdoor down to a cellar.

Although her hair was gray, the eyes deep-set in her plump face were dark and shrewd. She had noticed Brad's forehead.

"Nasty burn you got there, young sir. Mayhap a body might do something about that?"

The black cat crouching on the table was looking down at Smut, whose nose was very close to its front paws. Purring and wagging explained the situation.

"Very kind of you, Sister. It felt like a hot poker—but I don't think it was."

"Likely not." She laid a pudgy hand on his forehead.

The pain faded. He stopped shivering.

Wisdom Netley announced that she was going to feed her guests and that was that. Nobody protested very hard. She also said that the king could send the army and navy and all his tax collectors and they wouldn't be able to recapture anyone now. If trouble did come a-knocking at her door, there was a safe way out through her cellar.

The end of her kitchen farthest from the street was also the bathroom, but she did not offer to fill the oaken tub for them. She did provide kettles of hot water and kept her back firmly turned as the three men stripped to the waist and did the best they could to clean up.

Richard Sizer was a smallish man, with hair as flaxen his son's but a trace of red in a scanty beard. Brad already knew, from tales he had heard of Alan's childhood, that Sizer was a merchant and probably a wealthy one. He wouldn't be wealthy now, of course. His appearance was not appealing, for his features were too small—small mouth and small, quick eyes—and he had a slight stoop. He spoke quickly, eagerly. Shrewd certainly, perhaps grasping. Do not buy horses here. Alan had a similar face but was a frank and honest sort. Perhaps commerce squeezed those qualities out of a man.

Alan told how he and Brad had come to Umberly Castle for the express purpose of rescuing his father. It was a short tale and completely unconvincing.

"I've heard of gifts like yours, Master Armstrong," the older Sizer said, "but I've never seen them demonstrated. You are incredibly talented. The only person I know of who can start fires like that is Rafe Dampier, the hierarch."

"Ach, and he won't be doing that to honest folk anymore," the wisdom announced, ferociously beating eggs in the background. "You not heard? He went back to Stonebridge, where he murdered all those innocent folks two years ago. Gloating, I'd call it. And his god struck him down right in the pulpit. Burst into flames. Dozens trampled to death fighting their way out of the church."

Alan and Brad looked at each other in horror.

Sizer was beaming. "No, I hadn't heard that. How wonderful! Had you heard of that, Alan?"

Alan squirmed, looked at Brad, and then muttered, "We were there."

Brad did not try to deny it. "Is he dead, Sister?"

"Last I heard he wasn't, but they were praying for his release and saying it couldn't be long."

"I'm sorry to hear about the other people being hurt."

"Don't be!" Sizer snapped. "Sometimes great good trails small evils. I daresay some of those soldiers killed today were decent enough men, kind to their children, but they chose a dangerous life."

Why did he have to mention them? Brad would never know how many people he had killed already—unless he was put on trial, of course. They would tell him then. He feared more deaths must follow if he were to stay alive. What must Old Alfie be thinking now?

"We must get word back to Lady Whatman," Sizer said. "You say you gave them your real name, Alan, and it won't take the Privy Council long to find out where you came from. Her ladyship will have to flee, as will anyone else in Rose Hall who can't stand interrogation. Wisdom, can you arrange for a message to be sent?"

Widow Netley was intent on her cooking. "Soon as you're fed, I'll take you around to the Fielders. They got more resources than I have. Sit down and eat this, Master Armstrong. *Now!*" she roared as Brad tarried to lace up his shirt.

So without his doublet, he took a stool at the little table and gazed in awe at a trencher loaded with the hugest omelets he had ever seen, oozing hunks of ham and onion and melting cheese. He almost drowned in saliva.

"This all for me?"

"It'll get you started."

He reached for his belt knife, but it was gone—removed in the castle, of course—so he was forced to load omelet onto a slice of bread with his fingers, burning both them and his mouth. It was glorious. He was still eating omelet when Sizer took the other stool to tackle a much smaller portion. Brad had moved on to bread and a tangier cheese by the time Alan pulled up a beer keg with a cushion on top. There was excellent small beer to drink.

Becoming aware of a calculating stare, Brad said, "What are you looking at?"

"You remind me of someone," Sizer said. He glanced up inquiringly.

"Yes, I noticed that, too," Wisdom Netley said with a smile. "It's the dark hair and light eyes."

Before Brad could ask who was so like him, the trader began a trader's spiel, somehow using his little hagfish mouth to eat and jabber at the same time.

"The Mother has sent you, Squire Armstrong. You are her gift to us, her suffering Children, in these terrible times. Too long we have endured persecution and suppression. Now you have reached manhood and come into your powers, just as we are readying our plans for the revolution. We call ourselves the Underground, and we will throw off these evil yokes that the Light has laid upon us for so long.

"They dare to call us heretics, but our ancestors worshiped Mother Earth in peace for thousands of years before one man started having visions and claiming he was right and everyone else was wrong. They should have locked him up and gagged the poor fool. Now we must lead Albi back to the true faith."

"But—"

"Lady Whatman is a fine lady, and she has done great work for the cause, but I admit I hoped for more when we sent Alan to Rose Hall. I urged her to train warriors, not more missionaries. When Jake Trull was butchered, I wrote suggesting she bring all the pupils up to Weypool to watch and see what they were to fight against. She refused. It would have been educational for you."

But was not a fit topic for dinnertime conversation.

"It was especially enlightening for those of us who could recall other martyrdoms in the past. The first disemboweling I saw was Eric Mallet's, and the crowd jeered and mocked him as they always did. But when Mark Whatman was burned—although he had never told them his true name and they had to burn him as John Doe—when he was burned at the stake, tied to a chair because his torturers had crippled him—the spectators were much quieter. And for Jake Trull most of them were silent! The nation is tired of this savagery and bloodlust. You heard them cheering your escape from the prison not an hour ago."

Alan was attending to his meal, carefully showing neither approval nor disapproval of his father's rant. At Rose Hall, Brother Alfred taught that the Children of the Earth had been crushed by a bloody civil war long ago and could not hope to do better in a second one, because they were greatly outnumbered now. To meet violence with violence would just provoke more repression. That was not an easy creed for even a boy to follow, and harder still when he had reached manhood *and come into his powers!* A juicy phrase, that.

"But we are so few," Brad said, trying to be realistic and aware that even small beer could be potent in large amounts. He had certainly drunk large amounts. "What can we possibly do?"

"Oh, we have plans," Sizer said darkly. "I cannot reveal them to outsiders, you understand. You must be enrolled in the Underground and take the oath of loyalty, and so on. Of course, admission will be a mere formality in your case, Squire. You have already claimed a place in Albiurn history. Today you struck the greatest blow against tyranny since Queen Ebba was driven from her realm. Indeed, you can claim the two greatest, for you exposed Dampier as a murderer. Even on his own terms, he was rejected by his own supposed god in his own pulpit. Magnificent! You are undoubtedly destined to be our leader, Squire, although likely not for a year or two yet."

"What does Prelate Albi say about your plans?"

"John Hawke? That ninny? He creeps around the country, from rat hole to rat hole, curing runny noses and preaching patience. Well, we all find peace with the Mother at last, but what of this world, eh? They'll catch him soon enough and do to him what they did to Jake Trull and Mark Whatman and Eric Mallet and all the hundreds of others. It's thanks to John Hawke that I'm here now; he's the reason I was arrested and the reason Alan and I can never go home and the reason all my wealth and possessions will be confiscated by the government. I put Hawke and his pretty wife up for a few nights, less than two months ago, so that's how close on his trail the Church Police are, or it's maybe the Privy Council; but whichever it is, Hawke is going to be netted pretty soon, so don't worry about him

anymore. I admit that Lady Whatman has done much for
the cause, although I could never persuade her that we have
submitted to tyranny far too long and outright resistance
is long overdue. Now her ladyship is in the same position I
am, because Rose Hall is not all that far from Stonebridge,
and the authorities will be asking our neighbors exactly
which school Alan Sizer attends, the youth who brazenly
turned up at Umberly Castle with a witch in tow. So Lady
Whatman is now a fugitive, or about to become one, and
you dare not go back to Rose Hall, either of you, because
the government will seize it and sell it off to the highest
bidder, who will undoubtedly just happen to be a member
of the Privy Council or the Great Council or the Hierarchy.
May I pour you more beer, Squire Armstrong?"

Brad shook his head, but the next time he glanced at
his beaker it was full again. His head was much more than
full; it was bursting. In his stupidity, he had ruined Lady
Whatman, driven her out of her home, cost her everything.
She had taken in a homeless, friendless boy and raised
him as his own family. In return, he had borrowed a horse
and gone riding off on his own private revenge without a
thought as to what might happen after. If he had told her
or Alfred about his power to burn, they would have guessed
what he had in mind and stopped him. Oh no. This witless,
arrogant, upstart young oaf had gone charging off on his
own and ruined everything.

"I should be very honored to introduce you to some
of the leaders of the Underground, Squire Armstrong,"
Sizer said.

Alan was trying to hide a grin. No doubt he had watched
his father greasing suckers many times and was amused

to watch him working on Brad. But what choice did Brad have? He had a few stars and moons left in his purse, but no horse, no home to go to, no friends he could trust to hide a man on the run; he was wanted for treason, heresy, and mass murder.

"The honor will be entirely mine, Master Sizer."

CHAPTER 30

As they rode through the gate to Moor Manor, Nell spotted a peregrine on the rooftop eating lunch. Today's special was probably starling, to judge by the number of rackety starlings mobbing her, which she was ignoring.

"Is Perry telling us this is a good place to eat, do you think?"

Rollo laughed. "It's certainly a noisy one. I hope we don't attract quite so much attention."

His plan to head straight back to Weypool from Rose Hall had gone awry, as Nell had expected. With tired horses, they had not gone far the first evening, heading away from Stonebridge rather than toward the capital. Then had come the usual pleas to heal Mistress This and Master That, which Rollo never refused, although this time he did decline to hold prayer meetings. Two days later, they were not much closer to their destination.

No one could have posed for a portrait of the Earth Mother better than Mistress Malory, the lady of Moor Manor. She was buxom and white-haired, but still vigorous after outliving two husbands and rearing seven sons.

Although Nell and Rollo had sent no warning of their arrival, she greeted them with joy and fulsome hugs.

"Of course you are welcome, my dears, always, always! Old age is boring, did I ever mention? No one to talk with except servants. No one to nag. Come along, your usual room is always ready. I just wish some of the family were here to meet you." She bustled up the stairs, chattering news about sons, daughters-in-law, and grandchildren. At the top she turned. "And Dick is off courting." Her twinkle, almost a wink, was directed at Nell, who smiled back.

"I am sorry to miss him, but I shan't miss all the heavy breathing."

Rollo joined in the game. "Wait! Is there something I should know?"

"The danger has passed," Mistress Malory said over her shoulder as she rolled along the corridor. "This one's father sees a useful addition to the family haying and harvesting team. Dick knows what he's buying, but he hasn't yet realized what he's selling."

⁤⁤⁤

⁣⁣⁣⁣⁣⁣

Over an intimate supper in the mistress's parlor—not raw starling—the three of them discussed the disaster at Stonebridge. Faithful Child of the Mother as she was, Mistress Malory approved of the death of Rafe Dampier but mourned the rest of the fallen. The death toll was up to twenty-three, with about thirty injured.

"Who did it, Brother Rollo? Who *could* have done it?"

Rollo seemed sickened every time he was reminded of the disaster. "I don't know, mistress. I wonder if the pulpit wasn't salted with gunpowder, lit by a slow fuse. You must pack gunpowder in a cannon or shell to make it explode. Loose gunpowder just flares."

The old lady's face brightened. "But then it needn't have been one of us. Anyone at all could have done it!"

"Yes, but will anyone believe that?"

Before the meal was over, the litany of local ailments began. "Her eldest has fits...rheumatics troubling him something terrible...can't keep a thing down..."

Studiously avoiding Nell's smirk, Rollo agreed that he would visit these unfortunates before he left in the morning.

⁂

Lacking Dick or another son to act as guide, Mistress Malory sent them off with a footman named Percy, who had no grasp of the concept of shortest route and managed to get lost twice. Nell recognized some landmarks going by three times. A mere seven house calls used up so much of the day and left Rollo so weary that there was no point in starting out for Weypool. Evening found them back in the same parlor, sharing a similar supper.

This meal did not end as peacefully as the previous day's, though. Moor Manor had been built long ago to last forever, and its walls were massive. Nevertheless, a wild hammering of the front door knocker was audible even in the parlor. Hostess and guests started to full alertness.

"Trouble!" Mistress Malory said. "Maybe. Drink your wine up, quick!"

Rollo swallowed his at a gulp and hastened to the tall bookcase near the fireplace. He had to pull hard, because the books made it heavy, but it swung out smoothly, on hinges cunningly hidden by Rob Molesworth's superb craftsmanship. Beyond it, a narrow passage stretched a dozen feet to a blank wall. A straw pallet lay on the floor and a covered commode stood at the far end.

By then Mistress Malory had gathered up the tablecloth with food, dishes, three empty goblets, a wine bottle, and all. As she was handing the bundle to Nell, the parlor door flew open and Dick Malory burst in, dusty and windblown.

His eyes widened at the sight of the visitors. "Was afraid of this. Armed men, at least a dozen. They're only minutes behind me."

"Then we still have time," his mother said. "Down to the river, my dears. There's a boat."

Rollo said, "No. Too risky. They may have the boathouse staked out. Dick, please go and turn our horses out in the paddock and clean up the stalls they're in. We'll trust the Moles to see us through. Go warn the kitchen staff, ma'am." He eased Nell ahead of him through into the darkness and pulled the shelf-door shut behind them. He shot the bolts to make it firm. In airless pitch darkness, Nell embraced him, together with the tablecloth bundle. The contents jangled. "Oh, darling, what can we do?"

"You wash and I'll dry."

"*Idiot!*"

"Put that load down quietly and let's make ourselves comfortable. We may be here for some time." He stepped over the bundle and kissed her.

Nell had never been so frightened in her life, not even when she followed old Sister Edith into Swine Hall to rescue Rollo. This was her worst nightmare. For two years, ever since she had met John Hawke and fallen instantly in love, she had dreaded the day the Church Police would catch up with him. She had always believed that it was inevitable. She had been right. This was the end of everything good.

The Moor Manor hole was a Molesworth masterpiece. One side was an original stone wall; the other had been added by Kip, stealing space from whatever room lay beyond it. He had used much thinner stones than the original builders had employed, but a tap on any ashlar wall sounded much the same. Only detailed measurements of the entire house would detect the missing space, and that would take days. In the meantime, the two fugitives would be trapped in an area no larger than two coffins laid end to end.

Rollo pulled her down beside him, side by side, knees up.

"We can whisper," he said. "We won't be overheard. If we sit like this, my legs will break. Let's try back to back."

They readjusted, leaned against each other, held hands. Not truly comfortable, but better.

Rollo whispered a prayer. "Holy Mother, do not forsake us in our troubles. Help us to bear them and to understand that what we cannot understand may still serve your purpose for all your Children. Amen."

Silence. There was something odd about that prayer...

"You have a very bony back, Master Hawke."

"You'd rather I was fat?"

"I'd rather you were a long way away from here. Who did it?"

"You're the one with insight," he said. "Who do you think?"

"The first one, the epileptic girl's mother. Her mood turned mean when you said you couldn't do anything for her child."

"Makes sense. There's been time for her to tell the local priest and for him to summon the nasties. She knew Percy." After a while he added, "She can certainly use the money."

It had always been inevitable. Jake Trull had lasted a long time, but the witch-hunters had grown more skilled now, and the price on Prelate Hawke's head seemed like vast wealth to simple folk.

"Making love might be a good way of passing the time," he said.

"How can you even think of that at a time like this?"

"Always easy when you're around."

"Try me later. Only one mattress. Have to take turns sleeping."

Silence. Her eyes filled the darkness with strange lights. That prayer…he hadn't asked the Mother for safe delivery from this trap.

"Darling?"

"I'm still here."

"What does your prescience say?"

"I've told you before, it has no depth. Near and far look the same."

"So you will get caught?"

"Someday, yes."

"How can you stand it? Why doesn't it drive you mad?"

"Maybe it has. I'm—"

Clonk! Clonk! Clonk!

"Oh, Mother!" Nell said. That was the noise of some-one knocking on wood, hollow wood. Someone had taken books out of the bookcase and was rapping on the back of it. They had been found.

"Betrayed!" Rollo whispered very softly. "They came straight to it."

It came again: *Clonk! Clonk!* Showing the boss?

More silence. Nell's heart was racing faster than she would have thought possible. She wondered if she would vomit. Then she jumped at a new sound.

Scritch-scratch…scritch-scratch…

"A bow drill," Rollo whispered. "Keep quiet now."

Nell released his hands, squirming around to kneel behind him and stare over his shoulder at the door of their refuge. She hugged him tight.

In a moment the remaining wisp of wood gave way with a tearing noise. The drill was withdrawn and a tiny ray of light shone through. Another minute crawled by; then a cane was poked in, extended for a couple of feet, and pulled out again.

If the hunters had known exactly where to come, they might also know that Moor Manor had only one hole. They had found their quarry.

The light was blocked again.

"Master Hawke, we know that you and Mistress Hawke are in there. I am Walter Carey, senior clerk to Master William Kipping, the king's first secretary. Master Kipping has authorized me to give you his solemn oath that if you and your lady now surrender voluntarily and give your

parole that you will not try to escape and will not use super-
natural powers while in custody, you will not be tortured or
ill-treated. If you are put on trial, it will be in open court
according to the laws and ancient customs of the realm.
If you are not put on trial within six months, you will be
released and free to go. These guarantees apply to both of
you. I have good reason to believe that the Church Police
are on their way. I will wait out here for your decision.
But if the police arrive before you emerge, I will tell them
where you are."

Pause.

"It's a trap," Nell said. "He's lying!"

"Does your insight tell you that?"

"No," she admitted. "He's too far away and the bookcase
blocks him."

"I don't think we have any choice, then. It's time to take
a walk. Coming?"

CHAPTER 31

THE TEACHER HAD NEVER SPECIFIED THAT THERE MUST BE ten and only ten hierarchs, but he had appointed nine. After he was gathered to the Light, the nine had elected a tenth, and there had been ten ever since, each year electing one of their number to serve as supreme hierarch. In the Year of Light 182, the honor rested upon the capable shoulders of Garrett Uptree. He was enjoying his life in the Temple Palace, the luxury and adulation, and even the way the juniors referred to him as "the Chief" behind his back, because he knew from his own years as an acolyte that he was meant to overhear them and they would have some less attractive name for him to use among themselves.

He even enjoyed the responsibility of chairing a general assembly of the Hierarchy and summoning one whenever it was warranted. It was up to him to decide when it was warranted, but obviously it was now, so he did.

The Coronet Temple comprised a circle of ten buildings around a wide piazza, which at major festivals, such as Midsummer, would be filled to suffocation with throngs of the faithful. The Basilica itself stood on the east side, and the Temple Palace on the west. Other, lesser edifices were spaced around the circle, joined by a high colonnade to uphold the image of a giant crown. The Meeting Hall was on the north, an undistinguished building, mostly taken up by apartments assigned to the other hierarchs. Few of them lived there full time, but those who lived far away found them convenient when visiting the capital. Those who resided in Weypool might sometimes prefer to sleep there, for reasons that were nobody else's business.

Spring drizzle had not yet yielded to summer heat, so His Holiness decided to walk to the assembly. A flunky at his back held an umbrella over him, and his heavily armed guards clanked along behind. He could have had himself carried in a sedan chair; his choice was dictated more by a desire for some exercise to clear his head than any false humility. He could have gone in public, across the plaza, but that would have required everyone he passed to kneel on the wet paving. He chose instead to go by the private path along the top of the colonnade, where he could see out through the latticed sides without being observed by others.

Two hundred years in the making, the great complex was very nearly complete. Only the new seminary in the southeast was still under construction, and all indications were that it would be completed by next year, so next year's supreme could preside over a special ceremony of dedication. Exalted Uptree rather fancied himself in that picture. Some supremes had managed to hold on to power for nine or ten terms, so why not he?

Sentries saluted when he entered the foyer of the Meeting Hall. Leaving his escort there, he went on into the robing room, where two priests were waiting to remove his outer cloak and replace it with his formal vestments. They assured him that the others were assembled and the rest of the building had been cleared. Only when the guards had left did His Holiness take up the Teacher's staff and enter the hall, his golden train rustling along in his wake.

The hall was larger than it need be, and far grander than the Teacher would have approved. The walls were decorated with a gilded ivory fretwork that must have cost a fortune. Mosaics on both floor and ceiling displaying scenes from the Teacher's life. Garrett's personal favorite was the one showing his famous denunciation of decadence among the Mother's clergy of his day, because he enjoyed the irony of that episode being illustrated in gold and precious stones. Certainly a priesthood should be well rewarded for its labors, but rewards could be overdone. Fortunately, almost no one ever came in here except the hierarchs themselves. When they were in session, the door was bolted, and one of their own acted as recording secretary.

He settled on the throne and gestured for the others to rise from their knees and be seated.

While the deputy supreme led the opening prayer, Uptree looked over the gathering with disapproval close to contempt. All the members were present except the ancient Wyatt Ostler, who hadn't shown up for months. The Teacher had decreed no way to dispose of hierarchs who had grown senile, infirm, or excessively corrupt, and examples of all of those were present. A couple of the younger ones were hardworking and staunch in the faith, but two of the others should be given stern warnings and at least three ejected outright.

Some supremes summoned assemblies on trivial excuses and were then forced to fill up time with speeches of welcome and other nonsense. Not this one. After the final amen, Uptree went straight to business with the traditional opening, Verse 514.

"'The Light has given thee this day; use it to good purpose.' Four items urgently require your attention, Your Excellencies. First, we must welcome, and formalize the election of, the Exalted Abel Eastwell to our number. Secondly, you should consider the appalling murder of the Exalted Rafe Dampier, which created the vacancy that Exalted Eastwell will so competently fill. Thirdly, we are all aware that the government's prison of Umberly Castle was destroyed by fire a few days later, and several accused traitors and heretics staged a breakout. Clearly, the Privy Council must discipline its officers and tighten security."

Heads nodded at that notion.

"And finally, Your Excellencies, I wish you to start considering..." He was annoyed to realize that he—even he!—had dropped his voice as if the next words should not be spoken, so he pronounced them loudly, "...the succession."

No one nodded. Indeed, no one met anyone's eye. For ordinary folk to discuss the succession was treason, and even the hierarchs should tread carefully. Since the Teacher had appointed Amos as first king of Albi, the Hierarchy had meddled with the succession only twice, and the second effort had led to a confrontation with the nobles of the king's Great Council, accusations of treason, and finally a humiliating compromise.

This program was accepted without debate. It mentioned none of the three items on Garrett's personal agenda.

New hierarchs were nominated by the supreme, subject to confirmation by the full Hierarchy. That was automatic, so Eastwell was duly approved. The new boy—and he was still very young, barely forty, but keen, clever, and loyal—then knelt before the supreme to take his oath of office and be welcomed by a smatter of applause.

Pushing on, Garrett called for a report from the Commission on the Powers of Darkness. Each hierarch was responsible for both a diocesan district and one or more administrative portfolios. Regrettably, the Darkness file was held by the Exalted Nathaniel Wybrow, a notorious degenerate, who drank his breakfast and seemed to believe that celibacy meant one at a time and fasting was a means of eating more at a sitting.

Stumbling over every long word, the old soak read out a report that had clearly been written for him by someone else. He denounced Dampier's incineration as a monstrous, barbaric innovation without mentioning that Dampier himself had set the precedent two years earlier. Garrett was only too familiar with that incident, because he had helped his greedy brother organize it. Wybrow also spoke of the mass escape from Umberly, denouncing the lax security in the king's prisons. It was, he noted, only two years since a dangerous suspect had been winkled out of Swine Hall and its warden reduced to imbecility. This escalating torrent of terror must be nipped in the bud.

Their Excellencies might even consider, he suggested, expanding the Church's own prisons and directing that any suspected traitor be automatically handed over to it as a possible heretic. This was about the stupidest suggestion Garret could imagine. Spectators at Umberly had cheered the escapees. No one was likely to mention that, though.

In conclusion, Exalted Wybrow blamed the outbreak of dark magic on the civil government for allowing an ongoing flood of trained witches to enter the country from Xennia, and on the Congregation of Conformity for not rooting out indigenous heretics. He sat down, looking as if he had done a good day's work.

"I note," Garrett said, "that His Excellency combined the Stonebridge and Umberly events into a single topic. I will allow this modification of the agenda, as the two incidents are obviously related."

Several hands were up. Usually members were called in order of seniority, but he ignored that tradition and gave the nod to Abel Eastwell, who was scarlet with fury. The fledgling leaped to his feet and let rip, apparently unaware of the custom that hierarchs did not criticize one another's performance or competence. Garrett had warned him of that rule, admittedly while hinting that it was probably an outmoded tradition.

One of the hallmarks of a good underling was an ability to pick up hints. Another was a willingness to do his superior's dirty work for him, and Eastwell had that almost to a fault. He was tall and spare, with a mean little toothy mouth and a stare that made people uncomfortable, although it was hard to say exactly what was wrong with his eyes. They might be too close together, or perhaps the lids did not fit properly around the iris. He had a loud, strident voice.

"Your Holiness, I am shocked, indeed appalled, to hear the exalted hierarch suggest that these atrocities are entirely the fault of other people, never his, although he is responsible to the Church for suppressing the Powers of Darkness. He supposes the arrival in Albi of a teaming coven of witches but presents no evidence for it. He entirely failed to mention the two youths who were observed at Stonebridge just minutes after Rafe Dampier was smitten, and who fit the description of the two admitted to Umberly Castle shortly before it burst into flames, one of whom was positively identified as an agent of Darkness by—"

The hall exploded in outrage at this news. Garrett let the storm roar for a while. Wybrow's travesty of a report had, of course, been written by the priests on his staff, who probably found him even more disgusting than Garrett did. They had been happy to keep the supreme hierarch abreast of the evidence coming in, and he had passed it along to his new hatchet man. Eastwell now chopped and hacked enthusiastically. A couple of the most ancient members tried to object to the assassination but were shouted down and soon subsided, realizing that they were outnumbered.

After twenty minutes or so, the Exalted Nathaniel Wybrow resigned for reasons of ill health and left the hall. Satisfied by achieving his first objective, Garrett called the meeting to order. He suggested that the Powers of Darkness portfolio be awarded to Exalted Abel Eastwell, a decision greeted with applause. Eastwell promised to track down the missing Weypool merchant, Richard Sizer, whose self-identified son had entered Umberly in the company of a proven witch just before the breakout.

Garrett said, "I shall also write to our ailing Father Wybrow, assuring him of our prayers. A testimonial dinner might be out of order in his case, but I do think his long service to the Light deserves a pension, so that he may live out his retirement in comfort. Would one of Your Excellencies care to move a stipend of, say, one hundred suns a month?"

This obscenely generous proposal raised gasps of indignation, because Wybrow had been feathering his nest with swansdown for decades. Frowns turned into smiles as the implications sank in, and the motion was carried unanimously. With that precedent in hand and a few threats, Garrett should be able to oust at least two more of the drooling corpses. By election time he would have seeded the Hierarchy with four of his own nominees and guaranteed himself another term, which had been his second objective. Things were going well.

"The final item on the agenda, Your Excellencies, is the succession. As I have the honor to hold the political portfolio, I ask your permission to present a report personally."

No one dared object, of course.

"It is no great secret that His Majesty's health is causing concern, although several of the Church's most honored healers are praying for him daily. King Ethan has been a staunch supporter of the Church all his life, and will be sorely missed when he is called to the Light, long may that sad day be postponed."

Amen…

"His son, Crown Prince Emil…" Garrett paused and sighed. Several honorable clerics permitted themselves understanding smiles.

"I can testify that His Highness plays the spinet well. His grasp of political affairs is, um, tenuous. Should we, the Hierarchy, decline to ratify his succession, as the *Illuminations* permit, then the next in line would be his cousin, Prince Amos. He is a firm son of the Light, strong in the faith."

In fact, the man was the sort of raving, rabid zealot Garrett despised. Faith was praiseworthy but should be seasoned with intelligence.

He threw the matter open to debate.

A couple of speakers warned that any interference with the normal laws of inheritance would provoke resistance from the nobles of the Great Council, all of whom were landowners and expected to leave their wealth to their eldest sons. Others mentioned, as tactfully as they could, that a malleable idiot would be better than a pigheaded fanatic, provided the right people were doing the malleation.

Then Hierarch Ledbury made the motion that Garrett had supplied to him prior to the meeting: *WHEREAS* Illuminations *7:12 decrees that senior officers of the civil government shall be sworn in by a member of the Hierarchy, BE IT RESOLVED that the said member may refuse to swear in candidates he deems unsuitable.*

The motion carried unanimously. And, although his name had never been mentioned, that decision marked the end of the road for Master William Kipping, who had been growing increasingly dangerous lately, prying into affairs that did not concern him. Thus Supreme Hierarch Garrett Uptree achieved the third and final item on his personal wish list.

He adjourned the meeting and invited his revered colleagues to partake of refreshments in his palace.

CHAPTER 32

ON THEIR FIRST TWO NIGHTS IN WEYPOOL, BRAD AND Alan were billeted with a family named Gower. They spent the days sightseeing because Alan knew his way around the great city and was happy to show it off to his comrade-in-arms. Everywhere was teeming with people and horses, loud with sounds of horses and wagons and voices. It made Brad's head spin.

They wandered through the great markets, gazed in scorn at the ancient walls of the old town and the Queens' Palace, now used as law courts. They admired the impressive buildings of the new town and saw the high wall that enclosed the Royal Park and the modern Kings' Palace, but nothing of the palace itself. The main gate was heavily guarded against intruders such as vagrant youths; it stood open, but only empty parkland was visible beyond it. Of course, they went to the Coronet Temple, the grandest sight of all. They walked through one of the thousand arches of the arcade into the circular plaza, which seemed almost empty, although there might be several hundred people wandering around in it. Alan pointed out the Supremes'

Palace on the west, and the great Basilica on the east, and managed to name a few of the other buildings in the circle, sounding less and less sure of himself as he went along.

"Wanna see inside the Basilica? It's free."

"No. I'd go into convulsions."

"Yeah, me too."

Brad doubted very much that Alan had enough talent to react like that, but they weren't kids anymore and didn't insult each other by saying such things.

On the third evening, Master Sizer reappeared and took them to stay at a house owned by a family called Elphick. There he led Brad, but not Alan, to an upstairs room to meet a group of eight men seated around a big table, all puffing on pipes or cigars. They seemed to vary in age from twenties to seventies, and their clothes from artisans' to gentlemen's. The air was thick enough to walk on, and light from the overhead lamps shone only feebly through the murk to illuminate the books and papers littering the table.

Sizer said, "This is Master Brad, Lion," and departed.

"Pray be seated, Master Brad," boomed the big man at the far end, gesturing to a gap at the end of the table, where an empty stool awaited. "I go by the name of Lion."

In the real world downstairs, he was Master Elphick. He wore his thick, tawny hair down to his shoulders and his beard cut square across. "We are greatly honored to meet you. Gentlemen, I give you a toast: to Master Brad, who in spite of his youth has struck the greatest blow for freedom and the Mother since the end of the Gods' War."

The men all chorused his name and drank, although they didn't stand up to do so. The man on Brad's left put a goblet in front of him, and the one on the right filled it with dark red wine. Brad always drank his wine well watered, but there was no water in sight. He took a small sip. He resented the stool when the others had chairs.

"Likewise," the big man said, gesturing with his cigar, "Leopard, Bear, Eagle, Shark, Owl, Wolf, Lynx. If you agree to join our group, you will choose a code name for yourself. And I am happy to inform you that your aunt has arrived in Weypool and is safe."

A comment seemed wanted. Brad said, "I didn't know she wasn't safe."

Lion shook his big head sadly. "It didn't take the Church Police long to track young Sizer to Rose Hall. She fled not an hour before they arrived. There is a warrant out for your arrest also."

Hardly surprising. Brad nodded. He got the hint that he was welcome to leave if he wanted to but would soon be dog food out there if he did. He didn't like this menagerie of fire-breathing old men. The smoke made his eyes sting.

"You *do* want to help us, don't you?"

"Help you do what, sir?"

"Fight back against tyranny and oppression, of course."

He sounded like Aunt Mary. Brother Alfred insisted that violence would just provoke worse oppression, and the Church of the Light was a lot stronger in Albi than the Children of the Earth were, so why provoke fights you can't win? On the other hand, there was the dog food problem. He did need protection.

"Of course, sir."

Smiles all round. Lion leaned forward. "It is true that you can throw fire?"

"Not quite. I can make things burst into flames...usually," he added with a sudden pang of caution.

"Not always, though?"

Brad shook his head. His fire gift had never failed him yet, but he hadn't tried it very often, so he wasn't quite lying.

"And you can see in the dark?"

Alan had been blabbing! In Rose Hall it had been dorky to brag about one's talents, and here it would be plain fucking dumb. Brad waited for the next question.

Frowns all round.

Leopard said, "And you can open locks?"

Brad turned his gaze on him and said nothing. Staring someone down was easy when you were seething mad. He didn't need his insight to know that they saw him as no more than a useful tool that had fallen into their hands.

"You say you'll help the cause," Lion said. "Just how will you do that?"

"Give me something to do and I'll do it, sir. Except I won't kill any more innocent people."

"The people in the Stonebridge church weren't innocent. They were Sons of the Sun, and guilty as all the rest of them. They had gone there to flatter the murderer Dampier. The men who died at Umberly served the forces of oppression."

"Then I guess what I mean is I won't kill anyone."

"The other side kill us, and in the vilest ways they can think of."

"I want to think I'm better than them, sir."

Lion's stare was cold as winter. "Very well, Bradwell, we'll find you a noncombatant role to play. You may go."

Brad rose from his stool and went out. He took the goblet of wine with him.

He had to share a very lumpy bed with Alan that night. He was shaken awake before dawn, and a voice said, "You're Armstrong? Got a job for you. Get dressed and come downstairs."

As the owner of the voice was going out the door, Alan said, "Me too?"

"No, just him."

When Brad arrived in the kitchen, the speaker was filling leather water bottles at the pump. He was dressed as a laborer and didn't look much older or taller than Brad but was twice as wide. He paused to offer a hand.

"Mule."

"Brad."

They shook. His hand was big and rough as a farrier's rasp.

"Have a drink. We've got dusty work to do. We can pick up some fresh bread on the way."

In a few moments, they were walking the alleyways of the old town in the gloom of first light, each of them draped with two canteens and gnawing at half a delicious warm loaf.

Brad *wasn't* going to ask.

Mule explained anyway. "Know anything about the catacombs?"

"No."

So Mule began yammering about the old ways and the Mother's way of burying instead of the cremation today's Church of the Light required. Weypool was honeycombed with the ancient cemeteries, he said. The local rock was ideal for tunneling, being a type called tuff, which was soft to dig but hardened on exposure to air. The Teacher had ordered all the catacombs sealed off, but now the Underground had gone back and opened up many of them. They had dug new tunnels to connect the old systems, and that was what Brad Armstrong was going to be doing that day. Probably, Brad guessed, for several days to come. He was being pressured, but hard work wouldn't hurt him.

Mule puzzled him. Despite his calluses and gobbling Weypool accent, he spoke more like a gentleman than a laborer. Of course, no one would wear good clothes to dig tunnels.

He had a key to open the gate to a cramped yard containing a wagon and a lot of timber. He had another key to open a small shed at the back, which was full of barrels. He rolled one barrel aside to reveal a tunnel heading down into the hillside. He produced two lamps and a tinderbox. Then he began to strip, although the morning air was on the cold side of comfort.

"You won't need much clothing in there," he said. "And it'd get filthy. Keep your shoes on and anything you're too shy to take off." He kept his shorts on, so Brad did the same, although his badly needed a wash.

Then Mule led the way into the tunnel. This was starting to feel like a real adventure. A few days of digging might not be a bad thing if it grew muscles like Mule's.

The air soon grew warmer. It wasn't long before they were passing niches containing old burials: yellow skulls, bones like dry sticks, fragments of shrouds and hair. Creepy but not frightening. The living were a lot more dangerous than the dead.

Then came another tunnel, lower, narrower, and less well finished than the real catacombs. After that, another cemetery. Right, left...

Maybe it was a little scary, because even a man who could see in the dark might get lost down there and never find his way back out. Or be abandoned, maybe. They must have walked almost a mile before Mule stopped and raised his lantern. The way was blocked by a wheelbarrow, a heap of dirt, and a shovel.

"This is the dump, where we put the spoil." Spoil obviously being what they'd dug out, mostly sandy stuff and lumps. "You pack it into the graves and as high as you can in the passage, see? It takes up more space here than it did before, and we don't want to fill up any more catacombs than we have to. Got it?"

"Got it." The day had stopped looking interesting. "You dig and I pack?"

"That's it. I'll be back every half hour or so. Now you have to make room for the barrow."

Which meant that Brad had to squeeze flat against the wall so Brad-Mule-barrow could be rearranged as barrow-Mule-Brad. Mule disappeared off along the passage, wheeling his lantern, making shadows dance, until he vanished around a corner. Brad set his lantern and his canteens in a niche, spat on his hands, and set to work disposing of the heap of dirt.

He had almost done so when he heard Mule returning. Then he had to climb into one of the grave niches and lift his feet out of the way to let the barrow go past, and Mule tipped out another heap on top of the first.

All he said was, "You'll have to go faster." Then he left.

Right. Faster it was, but faster was hard to keep up. He hadn't finished before the next barrow load arrived.

"Better. Keep it up."

He couldn't keep it up, of course. The handle of the shovel was gritty and tore his hands. The dust got in his eyes and mouth. His muscles weren't Mule's muscles. But he kept on, going slower and slower, getting dirtier and dirtier. The pile of spoil grew larger, and now he had to heave it higher, into the top layer of niches.

Mule said, "Mm. I'm going to wall you up in here if we go on like this. Why don't you take a turn mining?"

He took Brad back with him to what he called the mine face, at the end of a tunnel sloping downward—which meant that Mule had been wheeling the loaded barrows uphill. There were two picks and several shovels there. He demonstrated how it was done, watched from a safe distance while Brad tried it, and then left him there. Mining was slightly more interesting than what he had been doing, but he had produced less than a barrowful of spoil before Mule came back, almost invisible because he was the same color as the walls.

He laughed and thumped Brad's shoulder with his armored hand. "You're doing great, lad! I didn't expect you to keep going this long. Take a break now."

"I'm fine!"

"You're damned nearly out on your feet. I don't want to kill you. You'll be useless for days if you overdo it. Go back up to the cemetery and take the first right turn. You'll be out of my road there. Don't go too far, because we use that corridor to piss in, but the first ten feet or so is safe. Lie down and nap for an hour. That's an order!"

∽

About noon, probably, a man in coveralls came to see how they were getting on. He brought dinners of sausage and cheese, and filled water bottles. He measured the new tunnel to make sure it was going straight and was wide enough to take something not mentioned. Brad got no chance to speak to him. Mule addressed him as Lizard.

The day did end at last, although Brad suspected a few times that he might end first. He dragged himself along behind Mule until they reached the shed. Someone— probably Lizard, because very few people knew about this project—had left a tub full of water and two grubby towels.

"Clean up," Mule said, rolling the barrel back over the mouth of the tunnel. "Can't go walking the streets looking like that. You first."

So Brad cleaned up, but he could do little about his shoes and shorts or the raw patches on his hands. Mule had brought spare shorts. Brad had none. The few spare clothes he'd taken from Rose Hall had been lost at Umberly.

The walk back to the Elphick house seemed a lot longer than it had in the morning. When he arrived, he found that Alan had been moved elsewhere. He would miss Alan almost as much as he missed Smut, whom he hadn't seen he left Widow Netley's. He wondered whether Smut disapproved of the Underground or just thought that a prisoner didn't need guiding, because Brad was starting to feel very much like a prisoner.

Things got even worse when he was given a meal. He was ravenous and didn't mind that he was fed in the kitchen, because he knew he wasn't presentable enough for company. The cook must have had her orders, too, because she went away and left him alone. He might have found that amusing if he hadn't been so beat. It stopped being in the least funny when Lady Whatman marched in, sat down opposite him, and began to nag as if she wouldn't draw breath for a month.

"You are being very stupid!"

"Mother bless you, Aunt."

"And you. Why aren't you helping your friends when they are helping you? You expect to be fed and..."

"Clothed?"

"Looked after, and yet you are not doing what you could to help the cause." He held up a bloody hand. She flinched but barely drew breath. "You are no laborer. There are dozens of things you could do to help that no one else could."

It was hard to eat and fight off a wildcat at the same time. He spoke with his mouth full. "I said I would do anything except kill people. How many murders do they want?"

Even that failed to slow her. "I don't believe it. I do believe that Master, um, Lion, is a very fine..." *Gabble, gabble, Mother Goose.*

Brad concentrated on eating and let her rage. Insight told him she was frightened at being wanted by the law, furious at being dependent on others, and despising herself because she had been bullied into haranguing him. Eventually he rose, wiped his mouth on his sleeve, and bade her good night.

"I have not finished, Bradwell!"

"But I have finished listening, Aunt. Mother bless you."

The next day Mule brought a companion, who called himself Horse and was clearly a laborer, built like his namesake and about as smart. But the work did go better with Mule digging, Horse packing, and Brad pushing the barrow. He could manage only half a load up the slope, but he got to rest while Mule loaded what he had dug while Brad was away, and between them they managed to keep Horse busy.

On the evening of the sixth day, as Brad was eating his pay in the kitchen, he reflected that he must be stronger than he had been. His muscles didn't look any bigger, but he was pushing an almost-full barrow up the slope now. Then in walked Bear. He was probably the youngest of the menagerie Brad had met the first night. He was a slender, swarthy man with a hooked nose, a dense black beard, and meadows of black hair on the backs of his hands. He sat opposite and smiled.

Insight said that there was a trace of genuine amusement behind that smile, so Brad encouraged it by smiling back, but he kept on chewing.

"Lion handled you very badly that night, friend."

Shrug. Any idiot knew that.

"So let's start again, please?"

Nod. Chew.

"Lion told you what he wanted. What do you want?"

That was more like it, and insight said that Bear was anxious to negotiate.

"First, I need some money to buy clothes. I can't even wash these because I haven't any others."

Anger. "I didn't know that. I'll see to it. Beyond that?"

"I'd really like not to have done the things I did." Rafe Dampier, yes, but nobody else.

"Can't work miracles. You gotta pray for those."

"I want to go to Gaudry and learn how not to make mistakes."

"We can arrange that."

"I'd be safe there? Xennia won't turn me over to Albi?"

"So far as I know, it never has. I'll ask."

Insight told him that Bear hadn't lied yet. Of course, anything he promised might be overruled by Lion, but he was definitely trying. Brad stopped eating and licked his fingers. He held out a hand. "Brad Armstrong. I wasn't always, but I expect that's the name on the warrant."

Bear accepted the clasp. "I'm Matt Hewson, but you're only the third person in the Underground who knows that." He was good. They should have used him the first time. His youth helped, of course.

"And the price, Matt?"

"We need your help on a very important job."

"Just one?"

Hesitation. "I think so."

"Tell me about it."

Matt said, "We plan to break into a warehouse and steal something we're not allowed to buy. There are three sentries on the gate, none inside. Without your help we'll have to kill them. You can use your, er, powers on them so they won't give the alarm and won't remember us afterwards."

Brad nodded. Saving lives was good. Three might be tricky to handle, but he could use distraction, too. Grand larceny seemed an almost trivial crime now. "That's all?"

"No. Second, we need you to open the locks on the gates and the doors of the warehouse itself, about half a dozen locks in all. The sentries don't have keys. And third, we need you to go inside first and open the shutters to let the moonlight in. Close up after us when we leave. That's all."

What treasure would be guarded by three sentries outside, none inside, six locks, and stored in darkness? Only one that Brad could think of, and word that the Underground was trying to get hold of it would send both Hierarchy and Privy Council into screaming frenzies. Had Matt been told to tell him all this, or did they just think he was too stupid to work it out after what he had been doing all week? Or was this the reason the cook, with even more than her usual surliness, had put down his supper on the far side of the table that evening? He had gone around to sit by it instead of taking his usual stool and pulling the platter across to him, but the change had put him beside the window, which was slightly open. Someone could be outside, listening. Someone with a gun. Brad had escaped from Umberly; he could escape from anywhere. They would take no chances on him. If he didn't accept this second offer, he was likely to have a sudden lead headache.

His prescience hadn't been very helpful lately. He checked it again, but there was still nothing there. About as much use as a lame mule.

"That's all? Sounds like small beer after what I've been doing. I do that for you and you get me to Gaudry?"

Matt relaxed with a rush, almost visibly. "That's all."

"I'll need a guide when I get over there, not just my fare."

"No problem. You're in?"

"Deal!" Brad offered his callused hand to shake Matt's hairy one.

Matt was grinning wildly. He had just made himself an Underground hero by signing up the sorcerer. "Let's go and tell Lion. You'll need a code name."

"Hagfish," Brad said. That was about as low as he could imagine.

CHAPTER 33

AFTER THE NEW RECRUIT HAD BEEN TOASTED WITH RED wine and some breaths of cigar smoke, he found himself walking the dark streets with his new friend Matt-Bear. He had been given a day off from digging so he could acquire new clothes, and it so happened that Matt was in the rag trade. There were no streetlights, but the moon was a few days short of the full, bright enough for anyone to see the way and look out for danger. Brad didn't need it.

"My father was a teacher," Matt said. "I was the youngest of six kids, but we got by until he came under suspicion for unorthodox beliefs and was blacklisted as a heretic. Then no one would hire him, not even to dig ditches. Soon he and Mother were reduced to selling off their clothes to put bread on our table. He saw an opportunity and went on to build a business. When he died, Mother carried it on. She's old now, and I'm the only one left at home."

Then the unspoken question was why Brad had joined the Underground.

"Alan Sizer's my best friend, and his father was arrested and shut up in Umberly. I went with him when he went to visit him, but they bound us, blindfolded and gagged us, and shut us up in the cages they had there. Then they tested me with gold. It burns me. 'Fraid I lost my temper."

Matt laughed aloud. "And destroyed the castle? That'll teach them not to mess with you." He paused at an ominously dark alley. "There is a shortcut…"

"Put your hand on my shoulder and walk where I do." Brad strode confidently into the blackness, detouring around the worst heaps and puddles. "Left or right ahead?"

"Right. Just before we reach the next corner, there's a door on the left."

There were two doors. One had a sign above it that read, *Hewson and Sons, Drapers*, but of course the alley was as black as the inside of a cat. Brad halted.

Matt fumbled. "I've got my key somewhere…"

He was testing again.

"I'll do it." Brad jiggled the lock open. "What I like about you, Bear, is you're so frigging subtle."

⸺⟣⟢⸺

The store was full of secondhand clothing and its usual stale-sweat odor. A very steep stair led up to a two-room home, where Brad was surprised to be introduced as "my friend Braxton" to the Widow Hewson, who had just unpinned her wispy white hair before going to bed. She had a well-worn look, as befitted a dealer in used clothing, and a scarcity of teeth caused by bearing six children made her speech hard to understand; but her welcome was genuine. She at once began planning a meal for the guest. The newly minted Braxton protested that he had just eaten and wanted nothing more than a place to sleep. That could not be upstairs, for her room doubled as the living room and Matt's as the kitchen. Both were tiny. But down in the shop there were pillows and cushions and quilts galore, ample to make a bed for a workingman. Brad could sleep on bare rock these days.

Next morning he was told to help himself from the stock, but then Matt insisted on thrusting far more garments on him than he would have taken on his own. He worried that a family so close to poverty should have to support him when "Lion" Elphick was so obviously rich. Matt just chuckled and told him not to worry about that. Understanding came later, when the store opened and Brad realized that the frail-seeming Widow Hewson was a tiger at haggling. She was buying for stars and selling for moons. Pupils at Rose Hall were taught how a gentleman should keep an eye on his finances, so Brad could judge that the Hewsons' overhead must be very close to zero, and the widow must have hundreds of suns squirreled away somewhere.

Over the next few hours, he learned more fragments of the family history and decided he approved of Matt's mother. Officially, she knew nothing of her son's work for the Underground, but in fact she probably knew much more of what he was up to than he realized.

A day off from digging was enjoyable, yet Brad felt guilty that Matt and his mother were both working non-stop, either in the store or upstairs, cleaning, cooking, mending garments—all duties they shared. Brad found the bargaining fascinating. The starting price was whatever the customers looked good for, and the final one as high as they would go. Despite the Hewsons' skill, his insight detected several false "final" offers. His chance came when Matt was busy with one customer and another was interested in a royal blue, fur-trimmed cloak.

"How much is this?"

Pretending to glance to make sure that Matt wasn't listening, Brad whispered, "I could let you have it for ten moons."

"What? You are out of your mind, sonny. I'll give you three." And so it began, but the man dearly wanted that cloak.

Eventually they settled on seven moons, six stars. Not presuming to touch the cash box, Brad nudged Matt and handed him the ten-moon coin. "Seven and a half," he said.

Matt glanced at the garment in question, shot Brad an astonished look, and made change. From then on the new boy was on staff and could feel that he was earning his board. When Matt asked him that night if he wanted to go back to the Elphick house and resume his digging job, Brad laughed in his face and said he liked live people better than dead ones.

Next day around midmorning, though, who should turn up but Bear's boss, Lizard. He caught Brad's eye and gestured for him to come outside to the alley. Seen in daylight, Lizard was a short, wiry man with a long nose and a perpetual air of suspicion. He tended to come very close and speak in whispers. His breath was straight sewer gas.

"Hagfish? Why in fire did you choose a name like that?"

"Because I'm slimy and hard to hold on to."

Surprisingly, Lizard laughed, showing horrible teeth.

"You come to tell me the holiday's over, I suppose?"

"No. But I do have a job for you. Won't take more'n an hour. No digging."

"Let me tell Bear."

The hour began with a ten-minute walk along streets that soon began to seem familiar from Brad's sightseeing with Alan, and eventually led to a wide avenue with statues, which he certainly remembered. Lizard veered into a short, dead-end alley that led to three steps down to a door. Steps down showed an old building, Alan had said, one that had been built before the city streets were paved. Above the door hung a sign showing a blue, tusked animal, something between a bear and a walrus.

Lizard walked in without using a key. The gloom-shrouded room inside stank of pipe smoke and beer; the tiled floor was uneven and very dirty. A table and two benches extended along each side; three men were hunched over beakers of, presumably, beer. All of them seemed locked in silent personal misery.

The door had jingled a bell, and a wizened old woman appeared in the doorway opposite to answer it. She nodded when she saw Lizard and stepped aside to let him pass. The rear room was smaller, with a single chair, two barrels on stands, a table bearing pottery mugs, and a basin of water for washing them. The gray rag was either an old shroud or the dishtowel or both. The stench of yeast was even stronger there. A staircase went up, a ladder led down through a trap in the floor, and that was where Lizard went. Brad followed.

The cellar was very dark and full of the sort of dusty junk one expected in an old cellar. A dozen or so wooden poles leaning in a corner looked new, as did a dozen or so barrels, but the place smelled more of catacomb than beer. A ramp led up to a back door, currently barred. Brad could see how the beer got into the cellar, but he wondered how they got it up to the tavern. If the old woman brewed it in the rear room, as he had assumed, then why did she have so much of it stored down here? Or did she trade barrels on the side?

Lizard opened a sliding wall panel and began striking flint and steel. Brad did not offer to fire the tinder for him. When Lizard had lit a lamp, it revealed, unsurprisingly, a tunnel—a recent excavation, not a catacomb. No cloaks and daggers, though, but dirty coveralls on hooks and lanterns on a shelf. Either they were going to visit a different catacomb system, or Lizard knew another way in.

They donned coveralls over their clothes. Lizard produced a roll of paper and held it under the lantern.

"Lookee here. This is the cemetery we've been aiming for. Mule's broken through, and we think he should be about here. He's testing the air, but it seems to be clean. Isn't always. When it is, that can mean the catacombs are being used for something by somebody. The maps are very old and not too trustworthy. Sometime the tunnels are partially walled off, sometimes they've collapsed, sometimes they've been extended since the map was made. Want you to scout this out for us."

Brad tried a flip of his prescience coin and still sensed nothing, neither good nor bad.

"Two questions. Why me, and what am I looking for?"

"You because you don't need a light, so if someone else is down there, they won't see you coming or even smell lantern fumes later. And because you can squeeze through a smaller hole than the rest of us can."

"Can I change my name from Hagfish to Whale?"

Lizard had no sense of humor. "We want to know what's along at this end."

"Give me the map," Brad said, realizing that he was looking forward to being the first visitor in two hundred years.

"You can read it in the dark?"

"If I try hard enough."

Lizard led the way. Coveralls were hot wear in the stuffy tunnels, but there wasn't far to go. In no time they were in a real catacomb, passing cemetery niches, then a place that stank of latrine, and a few steps after that they came to a crossing Brad knew only too well. To his left was the raw tunnel he had helped extend, straight ahead was the dumping place, and to his right was the passage that Mule had brought them in by. All those long walks through the town and then underground had been mere camouflage to deceive Brad. Or had they been intended to deceive Mule himself? More and more the Underground, with its code words and trickery, seemed like the sort of secret-club game that ten-year-olds played.

At the end of the tunnel, they found Mule sitting on the ground, waiting for them with his lantern turned down very low. He rose up, a naked, dirt-colored giant streaked with pale sweat runs. At the base of the mine face was a hole, dark and ominous.

He smiled at Brad. "Been promoted, I see. Air's all right. I tested it." He reached for his lantern. "Want to see?"

"No, I trust you," Brad said. He'd have detected a lie. "Just let me take another glance at that plan." Maps could be oriented any way, so he assumed this one had north at the top. It was a sketch, not an ancient original, and showed a very stretched letter E, three east-west tunnels joined at their west ends by a north-south crossbar.

Lizard thought the new excavation should have encountered the topmost of the three very close to the junction. "I want you to look here, mostly," he said, and pointed again to the east end of the south tunnel. "But check the original entrance, here, and remember that there may be more of it than this shows, so don't get lost."

"I won't. That hole looks pretty deep…"

"Put a foot in this." Mule produced a rope with a noose at the end.

Brad sat on the edge of the hole, while Mule backed off a few paces and then wrapped the extra rope around himself. Brad slid through, feet first, and Mule walked forward, lowering him to the floor.

The air was cooler than he had expected, smelling more fetid than musty. The bones were just like others he had seen. He turned to his left and explored the topmost tunnel, which Lizard had said was the original way in. He didn't get far before he came to a cave-in, where the way was blocked by a landslide. The gap in the roof led up higher than he could see, and that probably explained the fresh air.

He returned to the hole in the roof with its faint glimmer of light. "Caved in, back that way," he said and continued on westward. The corner was farther away than he had expected, so Mule's breakthrough had not been quite where Lizard had expected. Why was he more pleased than worried to learn that the Underground could make mistakes?

The crossbar tunnel was obviously old but had no burial niches. The middle tunnel was unremarkable, except that some niches were packed full of bones, and none were empty. This must have become a favored place to be buried. Good company, maybe? He imagined corpses partying when no one was looking.

The southern tunnel was the same, except it also held several very grand tombs, like marble doors set in the walls, with names carved in them. And that was all. The tunnel ended with more bone-packed niches. Either they held more than one body, or old-style people had owned more than one head apiece. He retraced his steps to the hole in the roof and Lizard's face, crosslit by the lantern.

"What did you see?"

Long ago, when Maddy read bedtime fairytales to him, there had been one about a boy who went into a cave to retrieve a magic lamp for a sorcerer. Brad held up a hand for the rope. "Help me out first."

"No. Tell me what you saw."

"Just some grand tombs."

"What names on them?"

"Um. *Tillman, Conybear,* and, er, looked like *Bonser.*"

"Good boy!" Lizard dropped the rope, and Mule hauled the *boy* up. The hole was quite wide enough for Lizard to have gone down himself, so who was the better *man*?

Lizard questioned him about the cave-in and signs of recent use, of which there were none. Then he asked Mule, "Can you have it ready in two days?"

"Yes, sir. With Horse's help, I can."

"Good. I'm sure Lion will want to go ahead before the moon wanes."

CHAPTER 34

EVERY ALBIURN COUNTY WAS OVERSEEN BY A LORD lieutenant, usually a peer of the realm, who was required to report promptly any unusual occurrences in his area of concern and submit a monthly letter even if nothing whatsoever happened. Much the same was true of mayors of major towns and cities, governors of certain strategic castles, envoys and ambassadors in foreign lands, spies both domestic and foreign, senior naval and military commanders, and heads of government departments. This blizzard of paper settled on the desk of the king's first secretary, Master William Kipping, the best-informed person in the kingdom.

That unassuming man, who bore an unassuming title and lived in an unassuming house in a corner of the palace grounds, was tolerated by the nobility because he knew his place and did not presume to rise above his station. He was admired by everyone else who knew of his existence because he toiled for his bread at least as hard as a slater's apprentice. He was heartily hated by those who had ever tried to bribe him in any way whatsoever, because the results were invariably disastrous. Most important, he had the trust of the king. His Majesty rarely attended meetings of his Privy Council these days, so they were conducted by Master Kipping, who reported to the monarch in person at least once a day.

Such a workload required long hours, but he never took papers home with him. His first action on returning was always to check on Irene, although by spring her health had deteriorated so much and the apothecaries' dosages were so high that she was sleeping away the dregs of her life. Then he would relax over a light supper with his companion, Mindy Wells, whose origin and history he knew better than anyone other than herself. She could play the spinet for him, read poetry, even sing. They entertained rarely and socialized little, but she never complained, was always delighted to see him, and fitted effortlessly into his current mood, whatever it might be. He never discussed affairs of state with her—unless they concerned her. He felt he owed her that.

He owed her a lot already, and more every day as Irene slipped away from him. The domestic staff, originally shocked by the arrival of a concubine, had warmed to Mistress Wells as they discovered that she was a gentlewoman by birth and manner. By spring they had accepted her as acting mistress of the house, who would decide on menus, staff changes, seating plans, flower arrangements, and all the myriad trivia of running a gentleman's household. She had even won over Master Kipping's chief of security, Steven Veal, who wouldn't trust his own mother to stay safely dead.

Kipping himself felt bewitched by her. He never mentioned the word *love* in her presence, and would not do so as long as Irene lived, but he blessed the day he had decided, cynically and in cold blood, to acquire the valuable human package being peddled around Albiurn society. The original suggestion had come from Irene, and at first he had rejected it with shock and disgust. She had been insistent, and their long marriage had taught him to trust her judgment more than anyone else's. So he had looked over the current market and seen that there was only one candidate he could possibly consider. He had made inquiries with his unmatched resources and realized that Maddy Woodbridge might also have advantages to him politically, which made his ethical dilemma even murkier. He had justified his subsequent actions to himself a thousand different ways and believed none of them. But he had done it, and his life had blossomed anew. To the winter of his troubles, she had brought spring.

Only once, so far, had she asked a favor.

"Who would you say was Albi's premier pimp?" she asked one evening.

"The Honorable Tristan Rastel, of course. What of him?" Kipping spoke lightly, for he could guess how distasteful this topic must be to her. He could also guess roughly what was coming, and he admired her for wanting to honor a debt that could not be enforced in law. Rastel was not above sending toughs to collect his dues, but he would not dare threaten Mindy Wells now.

"If I generally perform my duties to Your Lordship's satisfaction, the credit is his. He trained me. He made money off me, yes, probably a lot, but he spent at least as much on me, and I owe him much more than a mere cash—"

"What does the scoundrel want?"

"A withdrawal of charges against some young man caught red-handed pilfering his hostess's jewel box while she was in bed with his father."

"And in the same room!"

Mindy smiled as only she could smile. "Really? He ought to be given an earldom for audacity, whoever he is. The Hon doesn't mention his name in his letter, just says you will know who he means."

"I do. The lout deserves a thorough beating, and his father three or four." Several approaches had been made already to the Privy Council, large sums or favors mentioned. All had been refused. The Hon was probably the family's last resort. He would pick up a thousand suns or more if he could avert the scandal. Then he would make sure that everyone knew, and his reputation as universal fixer would soar even higher.

The incorruptible Master Kipping shrugged and slugged his conscience into submission. The youth in question had undoubtedly learned his lesson, and while there would be some political advantages to embarrassing his father, most of them had already been collected as high society watched his frantic efforts to avoid full disclosure in court.

"You may inform the Hon that the matter will be settled two days from now, but the fairy queen will grant him only two more wishes, and neither any greater than this one."

Her smile hit him like a jolt of triple-distilled brandy, promising wonderful rewards in store. "Thank you, kind sir."

⟡

Maddy, for her part, was happier than she had ever expected to be after the manor house burned. She could cheerfully imagine dedicating the rest of her life to William Kipping's happiness, and if that wasn't love, she could not imagine what was. In return, he did everything he reasonably could to promote her contentment. He held dinner parties for selected men of mature years—officials, merchants, minor nobles—persons who were sure to arrive with much younger consorts, some of them acquired in late marriages, others just arrangements of convenience like his. Maddy hit it off with several of the women, and friendships were blooming.

She did everything she could for Irene, which was almost nothing. Irene had rejected healer priests as useless a long time ago. A wise woman might still help, Maddy insisted.

The invalid smiled. "You think even William could smuggle a wise woman in here without it being known? The Church would destroy him."

That seemed horribly cruel, but Irene insisted. She made Maddy promise to be kind to him after...after? Marriage was one *after* that need not be considered. No gentleman, let alone a privy councilor, could wed a woman with her past.

 ⌒⌒

On the rare occasions Kipping talked business with Maddy, the topic was always the everlasting coiling of the Uptree serpents. The "contretemps" between her and the earl at his dinner party had caused him to pull back from whatever unspecified mischief he had been attempting at that time. But soon he popped up again, trying to persuade the king that a nobleman should chair the Privy Council when His Majesty was absent. Like cockroaches, Kipping said, the Uptrees never gave up and never went away.

The clerical brother, however, won some grudging admiration from the first secretary. "He's a crook, too, but he takes his job seriously. He's Supreme Hierarch Uptree at the moment, and seems to be trying to clean up the Church administration, which reeks of dry rot."

William kept her informed of the mounting pile of evidence he had amassed against both brothers. Outright theft was the least of their sins, and he could send them both to the gallows for that alone. But, as he explained, Earl Uptree was a personal friend of the king, who would block any action against him. Osborn's fall must wait for a new reign. Hierarch Uptree was protected by his holy office, but someday a split would appear in the Hierarchy, as happened every generation or so, and that would be the time to strike at Garrett. Justice was the child of patience.

One spring evening she noted William was more solemn than usual. He said nothing special at supper, but when they settled by the fire for a glass of sweet wine, he broke the news.

"There's been another disaster at Stonebridge. At least a score killed and injured still uncounted." He told her an incredible story of Rafe Dampier bursting into flames in the pulpit and a terrified mob fighting to escape from the church.

"William," Maddy said, sending a silent prayer for forgiveness to the Mother, "I simply cannot mourn Dampier, but I am appalled at what you are telling me. The revenge sounds worse than the crime." She hadn't meant to use that word, *revenge*. It had implications. "Who did it?"

"We don't know." Kipping was watching her very carefully. "It must be revenge for the burning of your family home, but John Hawke is against violence, just as Trull was."

"Who's John Hawke?"

Something changed behind his eyes. "Leader of the Earth Children in this country, calls himself Prelate Albi. If the Children are behind this—and they must be—then Hawke may be losing control. The hotheads may be breaking loose."

"I have had no contact with the Children since before my marriage to Stroud. But vengeance..." This would seem to be the moment to ask that long-suppressed question. "The only member of my family who survived was my brother Rollo. He was a prisoner in Swine Hall at the time. I never heard what happened to him." Even now she hated to ask, because the answer might close the very thin slit of hope that Rollo had survived, somehow, somewhere.

Kipping sighed. "I wish I knew, Mindy. He literally vanished out of Swine Hall right in front of a guard's eyes. Whatever it was that happened, the warden saw it, also, and went insane. The Church accused the Privy Council of treason. The Privy Council suspected the Church. We both suspected the Children's witchcraft, of course. Nobody ever heard of him again. I have my suspicions, but they're only guesswork."

She knew he hated guesswork.

She could not imagine the Rollo she had known just walking away from his mission if he was still alive and in Albi. Perhaps the Children had whisked him out of the country and he was back at Gaudry, training younger recruits. And she could not imagine him setting even the vile Rafe Dampier on fire, or overlooking the panic that must result. Rollo was neither so brutal nor so stupid.

"I am not sorry about Dampier," she repeated.

Kipping smiled, faintly. "No one is. Even the Church, I suspect. He had talent, obviously, but that doesn't fit their theology, because the Teacher denounced talent as fakery. No one *liked* Dampier."

Two evenings later, Master Kipping came home long after his usual time, and his face was very long indeed. There had been an attack on a royal jail, Umberly Castle, just outside Weypool. Two dozen prisoners had escaped, ten guards were killed, and the warden had committed suicide. The king was furious. The Church would demand that heads roll, probably starting with First Secretary Kipping's.

Again the Children of the Mother were the logical suspects, and again they had demonstrated a ruthless disregard for human life and collateral damage. People were worrying that the Gods' War might start up all over again.

Whether or not Master Kipping's head had been at risk, he survived the crisis, and nothing dramatic seemed to happen for the next couple of weeks. Nothing that he mentioned to Maddy, anyway. The weather was fine, and she went riding in the park every day. She traded visits with some of her new friends. Irene continued to sink.

But one night Master Kipping failed to return at all. Maddy sat up, waiting for him, dozing a little. She heard Steven Veal a few times, for he was always the last one to retire for the night. When the bell rang in the small hours, he answered the door, and soon thereafter came to tell Maddy that the master would not be home until tomorrow, possibly not even then.

He had a paper in his hand.

"Bad news, then?"

"He doesn't say, miss."

Only one problem could be so serious that Master Kipping would keep it from Steven Veal.

CHAPTER 35

THE NEXT DAY, LIFE CONTINUED AS USUAL. DELIVERYMEN and nonresident servants turned up as usual; none brought any dread news. Maddy asked the kitchen staff to keep the fires up all day and have hot water on hand in case the master wanted to bathe when he returned. She canceled a social call, pleading indisposition. The morning dragged on. Right at noon, Master Kipping did return, looking as if he had not slept in a week.

He had his own chief clerk with him, Master Walter Carey, a colorless, threadbare sort of man, who always seemed weary and now looked even more exhausted than his boss. And the first thing Master Kipping wanted was not a bath; it was a word with Maddy herself. Sorely puzzled and discarding her guess that the king's health must be the problem, she followed the two men into the withdrawing room and closed the door. No one sat or was invited to sit.

Kipping wasted no words. "His Majesty has had a stroke. He collapsed yesterday morning, while he was dressing. He is still in a coma, and the situation is very grave. The priests have been wailing prayers over him all night and half the day, achieving nothing. I need you to do something."

"Anything at all," she said, meaning it literally.

"Very secret."

"Of course."

"The day of the Umberly breakout, we took…never mind. Master Carey will explain. He'll take you there, but you're to do the negotiating, understand? Not him. Thank you, Mindy. I can't begin to explain how important this is. Bring them back here if you can, and we'll try to smuggle him in after dark." And with those cryptic and unhelpful hints, he hurried past her and ran up the stairs with his valet right behind.

Maddy went out to the hall. Nan, her wardrobe maid, was there, waiting for instructions.

"A cloak, hat, and shoes, please. Any of them. Fast as you can." She turned to Carey, now behind her. "We are driving, aren't we?" Carey was not dressed for riding.

"Yes, miss."

That was all right, then. "Sometimes I think he keeps secrets from himself," she prompted, hoping for some information. At the best of times Walter Carey had no sense of humor whatsoever, and in his present condition he just stared at her blankly.

Nan came running down again.

⌒⌒

It was an unmarked coach, Maddy noted, large enough for six. She settled on the rear bench, facing her escort. The moment the door was closed, she said, "And where are we headed, Master Carey?"

"Caverleigh House. Just a few minutes."

Red-eyed, haggard, the man could be said to be out on his feet, except he was sitting. He wasn't going to catch up on his dreams anytime soon, though, for the postilion was whipping the horses, making the coach bounce and rattle.

Maddy tried again, speaking over the racket. "And with whom am I to be negotiating?"

Carey blinked a couple of times and eventually recalled, or deduced, that Master Kipping had not told her any names. "Master John Hawke, miss. The man who claims to lead the heretics."

She would have had to guess a long time to come up with that name.

"Why me?"

More blinks. "He thought you knew him."

Well, for once *he* had thought wrong. This was turning into one of those nightmares where everything was urgent and nothing was possible. "And just what am I supposed to negotiate with Master Hawke?" She, who had no experience negotiating, with him she had never met.

Carey looked at her as if she were being incredibly stupid. "Get him to heal the king. He's the best healer they've got. That's why he's their gang leader."

Surely anyone would rush to save the king. Perhaps not if that king had been hunting down and murdering your friends. Maddy herself had been raised to worship the Mother, her family had been foully murdered, and the killer had been praised for his action. King Ethan's hatred for the Children was notorious. John Hawke would certainly laugh in her face.

Bouncing, rattling, squeaking leather, thump of hooves, angry roars from other traffic...

They were still in the "best" part of Weypool, near the palace, full of rich folks' houses. Master Hawke must be doing well for himself. How much would he charge for treating royalty?

"How will we know we've got the real John Hawke?" she asked.

Again that look of disbelief.

"I was the one who arrested him."

"Something else Master Kipping omitted to mention." That might explain why Carey was not to handle negotiations, but not why she was. She could concede that William was exhausted and grossly overstressed by the sudden emergency, but it would always be dangerous to assume that a Kipping mistake was accidental. "When did that happen?"

"On the day of the Umberly breakout. So Hawke doesn't know about that. Don't mention it."

The coach took a sharp right turn, roared through an archway into a courtyard, and came to an abrupt, shuddering stop before an impressive mansion, complete with turrets, high chimney pots, stables, and other outbuildings. If men dressed as royal fusiliers had not been closing the gate, she'd have said that Master Hawke must be as rich as a duke. Carey claimed to have arrested him, but this surely wasn't Swine Hall.

Maddy had counted ten fusiliers by the time she and Carey reached the grand staircase—heading up, not down to a dungeon. She wondered who owned this mansion, which was finer by far than the Master Kipping's. Probably the king; the crown acquired property in many ways without having to pay for it. Two more men-at-arms stood at the top of the stairs, and a pair armed with crossbows kept watch from a landing higher up. Carey conferred with one of the guards and turned to the right. He went halfway to the end, stopped, and pointed.

"That one. Good luck."

"You'll be here to catch me when he throws me out?"

"Hawke may refuse you, but he won't hurt you. He's not that sort."

With her heart dancing a nervous jig, Maddy walked to the door indicated, going slowly, trying to plan what she would say. *Good afternoon. The first secretary sent me, his doxy...*

Master Kipping had bewildered her before, but never like this. And he had always turned out to know exactly what he was doing. *I admit King Ethan is a tyrant and a religious fanatic, Master Hawke, but at the moment...*

Or perhaps she should confess that she had been brought up in the old faith but could not support it now for political reasons?

It was absurd. She paused with her hand raised to knock and decided not to. Hawke was a prisoner, after all, and she needed all the authority she could find, however counterfeit. She quietly opened the door, and...

She paused, hearing a woman's voice.

> *"I wrestle not with rage,*
> *While fury's flame doth burn;*
> *It is in vain to stop the stream*
> *Until the tide doth turn.*

"But when the flame is out,
And ebbing wrath doth end,
I turn a late-enraged foe
Into a quiet friend."

"Oh, I like that!" a man said. "I could preach for hours on that theme."

That voice!

"You can preach on anything, dear. Especially the evils of my cooking."

By then Maddy was through the door. The room was large and gracious, furnished with silk brocade and glossy oak, tiled floor, portraits on the walls. Vast windows over-looking parkland stood wide to let the spring in: bird song, blossom scent, and misguided bumblebees. This was *not* Swine Hall. The two occupants were sitting by the window. She was holding a book and facing toward the door. He glanced around and rose to his feet, looking puzzled. He was tall, slight, and had a trim fringe of black beard.

"Rollo!"

Enlightenment: *"Maddy! Oh, Maddy!"*

They met halfway in a crashing embrace. How long? Five years! She had been only a child when they parted. He swept her off her feet. They hugged and hugged.

"I thought you were dead," he said. "The house burned."

"I thought you must be dead or exiled. Nobody knew…"

Master Kipping had admitted to having "suspicions," but he had been sure enough to pick up John Hawke's sister as his courtesan when she came on the market. He always walked on many roads, the first secretary. How very convenient when he needed to beg a favor of the enemy that he just happened to have the perfect emissary! Maddy had been deceived, used, and now she was supposed to deliver her brother to the slaughter.

"You were a child," Rollo said, "and now…" He put her back at arm's length to look at her, not letting go. "Now you're…you're a great beauty, Maddy!"

She had dyed her bleached hair back to black, her makeup was no more than *proper* women used, and her clothes were suitable for the wife of a wealthy gentleman. Growing eyebrows was another matter, but many ladies plucked theirs. Yet Rollo was sensing something was not right.

She was never going to try to deceive him—probably couldn't if she tried. "No husband. I'm a kept woman. Not suitable work for the sister of a prelate."

He took it well, with only the merest twitch of his eyes. "The lucky man?"

"Master William Kipping, the king's first secretary."

That did shock him. "Mother bless me! How did…? Never mind. Is this visit pleasure or business?"

"I came here thinking it was business. Now I know who I'm dealing with, it's purely pleasure."

Rollo's gaze flickered to a tapestry picture and back to her. "You mean Master Kipping did not warn you who I was? Was once, I mean."

"No. He said he did not know what had happened to the former you. He could only guess, he said, but he didn't tell me what he was guessing." Lying, cunning, duplicitous Kipping!

"Who brought you here?"

"Mister Walter Carey."

"Ah, that explains much. Master Carey, why don't you join us so we can get the business part out of the way?" Rollo had not raised his voice or even looked again to the tapestry. "But I am remiss. My wife Nell. My sister Madeline, always known as Maddy for obvious reasons."

If there was a great beauty in the room, it wasn't Maddy. With high cheekbones, sensuous lips, and the most lustrous dark eyes Maddy had ever seen, Nell conveyed both strength and sexuality. She moved with the grace of gossamer. Her shabby, shapeless brown dress and ugly bonnet were a scandal; she would be sensational in a ball gown. Nothing would escape her, the sort of woman who would have recognized Rollo's superiority at first sight and claimed him before anyone else had a chance.

The two women embraced.

"This is wonderful," Nell said. Even her voice impressed. "The dead restored to us! I am so happy for both of you. Praise the Mother!"

"Amen to that," Maddy said.

A shape hurtled in through the window, wings beating. Rollo's hand flashed up, and a bird settled on his wrist. A peregrine falcon, fastest of birds. A raptor's talons were its weapons, and any other man who let a falcon perch on his unprotected arm would be pierced to the bone. Maddy had forgotten that he could do that.

"Perry! She's come to welcome you back to the family, Maddy." But the gleam in his eyes carried an unspoken hint that his familiar was approving the visitor, and therefore her mission. Master Carey, if indeed he were listening, would miss that.

Maddy put out a finger to stroke the soft white plumage below the dagger beak. She didn't lose the finger, which was an encouraging sign.

"Good to see you again, Perry. I'd introduce you to my own guide, but he naps in the daytime and might be too tempting as a snack for you."

"Off you go," Rollo said, and launched the bird at the window. "I have the impression that Master Carey does not intend to accept my invitation."

"If he sat down after we arrived, he probably went straight to sleep. None of them slept at all last night." Maddy could almost see that remark fly like an arrow into the bull's-eye of Rollo's mind. *None of them?* Not many things could keep an entire government awake. He exchanged glances with his wife, who was likewise picking up all the hints.

"In that case, maybe we should talk about it after all. Sit here. Nell, here…" He rapidly arranged three chairs in a group facing the tapestry. "Now tell me what you need of me, Sister."

"The king has suffered a stroke."

"When?"

"Yesterday morning. He's been ailing for two or three years, but this is new. He collapsed, hasn't regained consciousness. The priests have been unable to help."

Rollo was frowning. "Of course not. If I had been called right away…so long after a stroke the prognosis is very bad. They seriously want me to try? Who does? The Privy Council? Certainly not the Hierarchy."

"Master Kipping asked me personally and told me almost nothing. I suspect that he's putting his own neck on the line, but I can never tell what he's thinking."

"Oh, this is ridiculous! You and I could sit here for days, Maddy, sharing our adventures and sorrows, but meanwhile one of the Mother's children is dying. Carey! Come in here, or go home and tell them you failed." Rollo folded his arms and crossed his ankles.

Maddy's eyes met Nell's; both looked away without speaking. Tough young lady, that one. Rollo's choice of wife was none of Maddy's business, and most men would envy him his good fortune. But he had been a catch, too. Who had caught whom in that chase? Were Mistress Hawke's talons sharper than Master Tercel's?

A minute passed very slowly; then the door opened. Master Walter Carey entered and closed it, but came no closer.

Rollo rose and bowed. "I gave you my parole in exchange for a safe conduct from Master Kipping, conveyed by you. I will not leave your custody without his permission. You want me to try to heal King Ethan, although you all know he would probably rather die than accept anything at all from someone he regards as a traitor?"

"What's your price?" Carey growled.

"Nothing. I do not charge for medical services. They are available to anyone, whichever god they follow. But this patient is like to die, and I want to know what happens then. Will that be a signal to launch another pogrom? Yet another bloodbath, a holy war against the Children?"

Carey's face was gray; he looked as if he would start swaying at any moment. "I don't know. Wasn't discussed."

"I am familiar with King Ethan's bloody taste in religious matters. I have heard little about Prince Emil."

Before Carey could speak, Maddy said, "Prince Emil has a laugh like a jackass and about as much sense."

Rollo raised his eyebrows at this evidence of his sister's knowledge of the great. "So will the Hierarchy approve his accession, I wonder?"

"They can stop it?" Nell said, shocked.

"According to the *Illuminations* they can. But enough of this! We are wasting time. My terms, Mister Carey, are that I will come with you, but I will not enter the palace until Master Kipping has satisfied me as to what happens if the patient dies. I will not be used as a pretext for mass murder."

The clerk nodded. "Is fair."

"Come, wife," Rollo said. "Your cloak? Let us go and call on Brother Ethan. You too, Sister. I look forward to meeting your friend and giving him a stern lecture on the proper ways to treat a lady." He laughed joyfully, grabbed Maddy, and kissed her.

CHAPTER 36

A GUARD SHUT THE COACH DOOR. OTHERS WERE OPENING the gate. Maddy was sitting beside Carey, across from Rollo.

"I always find mansions *boring*," Rollo said. "A change of scenery will be welcome."

A living, breathing, incredible brother! She just wanted to sit and stare at him, with or without her jaw hanging open, as if he would soon vanish like a mirage. Why had she been kept in ignorance of his existence so long? Granted that Walter Carey was not at his unimpressive best, he was the jailer and Rollo the prisoner, yet just sitting there Rollo outshone him like the sun among stars. He must have lived these past two years in shadow, constantly hunted, in peril of torture and a fearful death, but Maddy could see no scars—none of the nervous twitches or bitterness such a life might produce in a man. If the government had accepted his parole and so confined him under house arrest in Caverleigh House instead of chaining him in a dungeon at Swine Hall, then he must have a prodigious reputation for honor and keeping his word. Now the government was on its knees to him, and he was answering its appeal.

But had that been the government meaning the Privy Council, or had it been Master Kipping on his own? Had His Majesty ever been informed that the chief rebel, the so-called Prelate Albi, was now in custody? Probably not. King Ethan was a chain-'em-up-and-flog-'em type and would not have tolerated the Caverleigh House nonsense. There were many currents in these waters now. Once there had only been two contestants, Church and government against the Children, but she was belatedly coming to realize that there must be factions within both teams. There might even be splits within the Hierarchy, if William's hints about Hierarch Uptree cleaning it up had been based on more than guesswork.

Why had Carey ordered her not to tell "John Hawke" about the Umberly breakout? Clearly she must now do so at the first opportunity.

The coach rattled and rolled out to the street and began to pick up speed as all the splendid horses exerted themselves. There were a million questions she dared not ask Rollo in the presence of Walter Carey—which told her exactly whose side she was on now, as if there could be any doubt.

"I am agog," Rollo said, "to learn how my mousy little sister ever—"

"I never knew you had a mousy little sister. Did I ever meet her?"

"She disappeared many years ago. As I was saying, I am agog to know how you escaped the Dampier massacre, when the rest of our family and so many other innocents were slain by the breath of the dragon."

"By the mercy of the Mother." Maddy told her history briefly and quickly. She described her marriage to Sam

Stroud and her vow of vengeance against the Uptrees. She outlined her subsequent career without dwelling on details any more than she had to.

"I have heard tell of Earl Uptree and his holy brother," Rollo said. "They are the sort who gave corruption a bad name. But where does Master Kipping fit into this sad story?"

"He has the king's trust, and runs the Privy—"

"I know what he did do. I am curious to know what he is doing now. Did he inform the king he had taken me 'into custody,' as Master Carey likes to put it? Does he now presume to ask me to heal the king's ailment without the king's permission, all on his own, or does he have the rest of the Privy Council behind him? I suspect King Ethan himself would sooner die that be beholden in any way to the Mother he denies. So who does Master Kipping serve now? Just Master Kipping? Or some other faction?"

"I don't know the answers to any of those questions," Maddy said.

"It might be wise to find out."

Yes, it might.

Nell spoke up for the first time. "And is there a Mistress Kipping?"

Dear sister-in-law!

"There is. She is an invalid and cannot last much longer now."

Maybe. Everything was changing so fast. Maddy herself was bringing the finest healer the Children had to the Kipping residence. How did she feel about that? Kipping had deceived her, used her, so did she still love him? Was he trying to save the king or hoping to save his wife?

"Master Carey," Nell said, "have you seen His Majesty today? Any observations would help my husband diagnose the problem. His face, for example? Any distortion of the mouth?"

"No, mistress. I have not been admitted to his sickroom."

"Goodness!" She glanced at Rollo. "I do hope Master Kipping will be able to give you more information, dear."

A warning that they only had Kipping's word for the king's condition. He might be already dead or as healthy as he had been two days ago. Rollo nodded with a smile of approval, hinting that he had already thought of that, but encouraging her to continue.

Which she did. "Master Carey, my husband and I are puzzled about procedures. It is two weeks since we were arrested, but we have not been charged with any crime. We were ordered to remain in Caverleigh House and given a half promise that Master Kipping would call on us shortly, but—"

Carey yawned loudly. "I do beg your pardon, Mistress Hawke! I am sadly short of sleep. I think I did explain to you that you were in protective custody, being sheltered from the Church Police."

"Mm? Is that legal?"

"Probably not. Are you worried about compounding a felony? Would you prefer to be handed over?"

Point to Carey. Even Nell had no answer to that.

Maddy took the next serve. "The day you were, um, taken into custody, was the day of the Umberly Castle breakout, and I expect that caused some disruption in plans. I know that Master Kipping has been extremely busy since then."

Carey grunted, a sort of angry growling noise, but did not speak.

Nell returned the ball. "We haven't heard about that, Sister. Isn't Umberly a prison?"

"Here we are," Carey said. "Master Kipping's residence. I hope you will not take offence if we smuggle you in through the kitchen door."

"I won't take offence," Rollo said, "but I would call it a foolish move if you are trying to deceive either external watchers or internal spies. Coaches do not draw up at kitchen doors. You will merely draw attention to our arrival." And who knew more about clandestinity than Prelate Albi?

⤜⤛

The coach did drop its passengers at the kitchen door. As if viewing her present home through Rollo's eyes, Maddy found it poky and shabby after Caverleigh House, unworthy of the king's first secretary. The deliberate insult of the rear entrance did nothing to improve her angry, confused mood. Whose idea had that been, Carey's own, or Master Kipping's?

The visitors were greeted in the hallway by the security chief and supposed almoner, the hulking Steven Veal. He addressed the newcomers as Master and Mistress Hawke, politely enough, but it seemed that he had not been allowed into the secret behind the emergency. "We have persuaded Master Kipping to rest for a couple of hours. It will not be dark for a long time yet, so if you do not—"

"Dark may be too late," Rollo said. "Every minute counts in a case like this."

"I have never seen him so exhausted."

"I think you should waken him," Maddy said. "At least tell him that Brother Hawke is here and regards immediate access to the patient as most urgent."

The big man twitched at hearing the word *patient*. He thought for a moment, then nodded. "Very well. Miss Wells will show you into the withdrawing room, if you will excuse me." He hurried upstairs. Carey had disappeared, so Maddy was now hostess.

"If you will—"

Rollo said, "Do you wish to have me look at Mistress Kipping?"

About an hour ago Maddy might have hesitated, might have quoted Irene's own stated wish not to imperil her husband's career and perhaps even his life, by admitting a "heretic" healer to the house. But now the deed was done, and the chief heretic was already present. And now, Maddy decided, she was not even tempted. She had lost her illusions about the sly and crafty Master Kipping. She saw him now to be a shameless hypocrite, who had used her and deceived her. He had lost his place in her dreams. They could have no future together.

"If you would be so kind," she said, and led the way upstairs.

Irene was asleep, and the nurse seated by her bed was nodding, half asleep herself on a warm afternoon. The unexpected invasion startled her, but she obeyed Maddy's request that she wait outside. Nell closed the door on her. Rollo went to the bed and laid a hand on the patient's forehead. He stood like that for several minutes, then put his fingers to her throat, as if to count her pulse or breathing.

He was still in that pose when the door flew open and Master Kipping appeared, hatless, hair awry, and doublet unlaced. He frowned at the tableau but gave Maddy no time to start introductions.

"Master Hawke?" He offered a modest bow, not adding anything about him or his house being honored, as he normally did when greeting visitors. Small hypocrisy was beneath him.

Rollo bowed to about the same angle. "First Secretary... Mistress Hawke."

Pause for bow and curtsy.

"I did not summon you for...for this."

"No matter," Rollo said. "I have completed my examination. Let us speak outside."

"Downstairs, if you don't mind. I shall be with you in a moment."

Kipping was as good as his word, arriving at the withdrawing room properly attired almost before the visitors had sat down.

Rollo promptly stood up again. "I cannot halt or even slow your wife's decline, Master Kipping. I have managed to ease her pain, I think, so she should not need as much of the apothecaries' foul potions. But the tumors are too widespread now for my skill to treat. I wish I could give you better news."

"How long?"

"A month? Two at the most."

Kipping nodded as if he had expected about that. "I am told you regard the other case as urgent."

"Very much so. Had you called me yesterday, I might have been able to undo some of the damage. Now…I can but try."

"And your terms?"

"Only that there will be no retaliation if the patient dies—against me or anyone else."

Kipping somehow managed to shrug without moving his shoulders. "You have my word on it for as long as my word means anything. If he dies, then I may fall also, and then my guarantees are worthless."

Rollo looked to Maddy. She nodded before she realized what she was telling him.

He said, "Then, sir, let us go at once and see what I can do."

The first secretary half turned and then paused. "Was your name once Woodbridge, Master Hawke?"

"It was."

"I wasn't sure." He went to open the door without looking at Maddy.

No one said Maddy could not go with them, so she did. It wasn't every day that a girl had a brother brought back from the dead, her lover exposed as a worthless toad, and then got to see behind the scenes in the royal palace, which she had visited only once, on the evening of the debutantes' ball. The drive to a side entrance took only a few minutes, during which nobody spoke a word. Kipping might have realized Maddy's anger, or he might be just brooding over his own danger. By taking a notorious, hunted traitor into the palace, he must be treading very close to the edge of treason, possibly on the wrong side.

No one questioned his authority, though. Sentries saluted him and his guests. Footmen eager to assist accepted dismissal without argument, and the first secretary led the way up a back staircase much grander than the stairs in his own house. Then along a corridor of many doors.

"If you would wait in here, please," he said. "I must make arrangements."

The room was large, and furnished with three worktables and two ironing boards, but no chairs. The big fireplace was set but not lit, and fitted with metal racks for the heating of irons. Closets lining the walls showed that this must be the royal wardrobe. An air of desolation haunted a place that normally must bustle with the activity of many men serving one man and the numerous changes of clothing he might require in a single day. Now that man was stricken, so all was silent and unneeded.

"The lavender is blooming early this year," Nell said, sniffing. She opened one of the closets. "Oh, do see this one, dear. You'd look splendid in scarlet and ermine."

"Don't pry," Rollo said resignedly. "We don't want to be accused of stealing the crown jewels. Maddy, what happened at Umberly Castle that Master Carey didn't want you to discuss?"

"I'm not sure of the details. William...the first secretary has been closemouthed about it, but some of my friends have heard stories. Seems it happened two or three days after that ghastly affair at Stonebridge. You did hear about that?"

"Dampier's burning? Yes I did, and I am appalled. I have warned and warned about the retaliation that sort of atrocity will provoke, but some people won't listen. Go on."

"Two young men turned up at Umberly and asked to visit with one of the prisoners. Visitation isn't allowed at Umberly, but they didn't know that or pretended not to. They were jailed and tested with gold, and one of them showed very high talent. Then there was some sort of fight. The prisoners all escaped and half the garrison died, either killed by the other half or caught in the fire. The castle burned down. The...the one they are calling the witch seems to have had the same fire-throwing power as whoever killed Dampier. May be the same person, even."

"Oh, Mother!" Rollo covered his face with his hands.

"Did anyone describe these boys?" Nell asked.

Why did she call them boys? She couldn't be much older than Maddy herself. Did she know the culprits, or at least have a fair idea who they might be?

"I heard that one was dark and one was fair."

"Sizer!" Rollo snapped. "The fair one was young Sizer, wasn't he?"

"Could be," his wife said. "Could very well be. I wonder where they went next?"

Rollo clenched his fists. "If Sizer Senior's got hold of the Armstrong brat, then it's going to rain dung."

The door opened and Master Kipping looked in. "Come this way, please."

They crossed the corridor and entered the king's bedroom, coming face to face with two young men in court dress, one a flashy red and white, the other a more discreet white and blue. Each bore a broad smile and a rapier. Maddy recognized them as indefatigable dancers she had met at balls. The red one had tried to enlist her for some private entertainment.

"May I present," Master Kipping said, "Master and Mistress Hawke...the Honorable Darren Darley, winner of the palace fencing tournament for two years in a row, and the deadliest swordsman in Albi."

Red-and-white bowed. "*Potentially* deadliest, if you please, First Secretary. I have not yet had an opportunity to put theory into practice."

"We hope you continue to be disappointed. And, secondly, Sir Simon Hogarth, runner-up in the fencing."

"Second deadliest," Sir Simon said, "and next year's winner."

"Over my dead body," his friend countered.

"If you insist."

"I quake," Rollo said with a matching smile. "But I understand the need for your presence." He turned and headed for the bed with Darley and Hogarth close behind.

The king's chamber was large, of course, dominated by a great four-poster whose drapes hung open. The rest of the room was sparingly furnished, just a few chairs and a couple of tables to hold the bottles and implements His Majesty's valets would need to shave and groom him. Maddy was most impressed by a full-length wall mirror, the largest mirror she had ever seen, apparently flawless. Now *that* was a treasure!

The royal patient reclined against a heap of pillows on the great bed, close to the far side, where attendants could reach him. His eyes were closed. His face, the color of parchment, and well-crumpled parchment at that, did not in the least resemble the handsome man on coins of the realm. Even without presuming to go close, Maddy could see that the right side of his mouth now drooped, the sign that Nell had inquired about. She waited at the foot of the bed with Nell and Master Kipping.

Rollo laid a hand on the patient's forehead, as he had with Irene. Ethan, the terror of traitors, who had relentlessly tortured and executed the Children of the Mother all his reign, was now being tended by one of them in his last sickness. Behind Rollo, left and right, stood Hogarth and Darley with drawn swords. What one could not see, the other should, and either could look across the bed and watch what was happening in the wall mirror. If the heretic witch should try to harm the king, he could be slain instantly.

Time passed. The white and gold brocade drapes were admirable, as were the white marble fireplace with gilded carvings, the thick rugs on the floor, and the frescoes on the thirty-foot ceilings. But how did one sleep in such grandeur? How could anyone unwind enough to indulge in the antic rollicking of sex in such overpowering surroundings?

Rollo moved his hand to the king's neck for a few more minutes, then lifted back the covers to expose the royal nightshirt and laid a hand over his heart. He palpated the abdomen. Satisfied at last, he replaced the covers and backed away into the space that had been occupied by Darley's rapier an instant before. Whether Rollo hadn't known of that or was just testing the swordsman's reflexes, Darley was faster. He downed his sword in time and stepped clear.

Rollo came around to the bottom of the bed. "Can we talk outside, please?"

"No. This is safer," Kipping said.

"I may just be superstitious, but I never discuss a prognosis where the patient can hear—even if the patient seems to be unconscious, as in this case."

"Talk here," the first secretary insisted.

Rollo sighed, annoyed. "Very well. I am sure you know he has an intestinal tumor. I am almost certain it is benign, so even yet I could cure it. But the stroke is mortal. He will never come out of the coma. Death in two or three days at the most—if I do nothing."

"What can you do?"

"I could keep him alive for longer, say a month, maybe even two. But he will not change, will never open his eyes or speak again. Is that what you want of me?"

All eyes were on Master William Kipping. His king's life was in his hands. Maddy could almost feel sorry for him.

"That decision cannot be mine to make," he muttered.

The mirror slid aside, and a man stepped out through the gap. Kipping, Hogarth, and Darley bowed low; Maddy dropped in a curtsy; and the Hawkes quickly followed their leads.

"By blood and rank that choice is mine," the newcomer said. "But it is an easy one. If you can extend my father's life without causing him pain, Prelate Hawke, then the law, common humanity, and I all require that you do so." He was a young man, neither ugly nor notably handsome, well dressed but in somber shades, as befitted a mourning son. He had protuberant eyes, sandy hair, and a reddish beard. He hadn't brayed yet.

He had granted Rollo his title.

Rollo bowed. "Your words gladden me, Your Highness, for that is also my duty as both a healer and a loyal subject."

Crown Prince Emil nodded to Kipping, "Well done, First Secretary," then, "and you, Darren...Simon..." then, "Mistress Hawke." Finally he came to Maddy and shot a puzzled glance at Kipping before saying, "Have you changed you views on the purpose of life since we last spoke, Miss Wells?"

Aware that her face must be turning redder than holly berries, Maddy curtsied again. "Not in the slightest, Your Highness." She wondered what Rollo made of this royal recognition.

"Miss Wells is also Prelate Hawke's sister, sir," Master Kipping said.

"Ah! Then doubly welcome. How long will the treatment require, Prelate?"

"A few minutes, sir. Some charlatans would want to repeat it every day, of course, but I charge no fees and so need not make work for myself."

"Then we shall leave you to it, with our trusty swordsmen keeping you company in case any evil-minded person ever asks what you got up to. Join us next door when he is done, Darren." He beckoned for the others to follow him.

The room beyond the mirror was a gentleman's study, a place of bookshelves, leather chairs, a writing table, and secretarial clutter. A bed in one corner seemed grossly out of place but implied that a doctor or perhaps the prince himself had been sleeping here, close to the dying king. Emil bade his guests be seated and played host, personally handing out glasses of wine. He was behaving with grace, with no donkey laughs or stupid remarks. A wise man could play the fool, but a fool could not portray gentility like that. Could a man live a lie all his life and stay sane? He sat down and took a sip of wine to indicate that everyone else could. He offered no toasts, going straight to business.

"First Secretary, if Prelate Hawke can truly gain us a month, then our chances of a smooth transition are much improved. Pray outline your proposal again in the light of this new information."

Master Kipping looked uneasily at the audience.

"If we trust Prelate Hawke, we can trust his wife and sister, especially once they understand the stakes."

"Yes, Your Highness, but time is short. The Privy Council is due to reassemble in…," he glanced at the sunlight, "… less than an hour. I will report that His Majesty's condition remains unchanged and propose that Your Highness be proclaimed regent for the duration of his disability."

"Which the other side won't be expecting and will have made no plans for. How do the odds look now?"

"You can count on five votes, possibly two more if everyone attends. The…the Uptree faction can muster no more than four, at most, and may not even oppose the motion, because they do not expect His Majesty to survive more than a few days. Three members are out of town and cannot influence the result."

"And then you all swear allegiance to the regent?"

Maddy saw now that Emil was not an idiot; he was an actor. He had played the fool all his life, at least in public, and now he was playing monarch. He was rehearsing a new role, with Maddy and Nell as his audience. This was a revelation, and a wild card in Albiurn politics. Was the Uptree faction aware of the transformation? How long had Kipping been aware of the truth?

"There are no precedents for a regency, sir. I can ask for oaths if you wish, but privy councilors are sworn in by a hierarch, and Exalted Uptree might make difficulties. Your father is still king, so the same Privy Council continues. There is no way the Sons can interfere with that."

"Then let us not drag the holy man from his prayers. What next?"

"The Grand Council. Now we have time, I suggest that you summon it for a date at least three weeks away—a month if you dare—to allow the more distant nobles to receive the summons and make the journey. The Church has more support in Weypool and its surroundings than in the countryside. The Uptree faction on the Privy Council will certainly support the delay, because the Hierarchy has been summoned to meet tomorrow, and the holy terrors will hope to have the situation well in hand before the nobles assemble."

He drew breath. "When they do, then I would advise you, as regent, to make a speech waiving some taxes and redressing some grievances, which of course their lordships will accept. In effect, they will be recognizing you as king in waiting."

"Excellent! Brilliant, in fact. And here comes our miracle worker."

CHAPTER 37

MIRACLES WERE NOT AS EASY AS THEY MIGHT SEEM. ROLLO was drained, in need of a rest that he could not have. His task done and an even harder one now looming, he stepped around the mirror with his two warders at his back. He glanced quickly around the room; took a second, envious, look at the book collection; and bowed to the prince. "I have done all I can, Your Highness. He will need careful nursing, but with good care he should survive for several weeks."

Nell unobtrusively rubbed her right eye, which meant that her insight was favorable. Left eye would have been a warning not to trust Emil.

"That is welcome news. First Secretary, you have our leave to attend the Privy Council. Pray see that these ladies are safely returned to your residence, for I wish a private word with Prelate Hawke." Emil chuckled, not brayed, and raised a hand. "All right, Darren, I know you don't trust him not to bewitch me. Prelate, will you object if my friends continue to stand behind you with their swords at your back?"

"Certainly not, sir. I won't be insulted if you wish to blindfold me." Rollo bowed as the women left. Maddy alive! A real miracle, that. And the king-to-be wanting to talk with him as a human being. Two miracles. The murderous old tyrant was alive but could do no more harm. That made three—truly a day to remember.

Sir Simon fetched a stool and thumped it down a long way from the prince's chair. As soon as the prince sat, Rollo did. No one tried to blindfold him. Two rapiers remained inches from his kidneys, but they bothered him less than his weariness did. He had done his best for the king, given much more than he usually would, but his conscience had insisted that his enemies must not be given less than his friends. He was drained, while the young man facing him was a very long way from being the fool Maddy had described. Yet even as a child, she had rarely been mistaken in people. To have carried off such a deception for years would take an exceptional mind and a ton of willpower.

"This conversation never happened, Prelate."

"No, sir. I, too, must worry about what my followers would think."

The prince smiled faintly in acknowledgment. "I want your opinion on politics."

"I know nothing of politics, sir."

"You studied them at Gaudry."

"Oh, *that* sort of politics! Yes, I did."

"Why does King Clovis keep up the absurd pretense that his sister-in-law is rightful ruler of Albi?"

"My understanding, sir, is that he offered to drop the claim if your father stopped persecuting our faith in Albi, but His Majesty refused."

"Understandably so," Emil said. "Kings do not like being coerced. What do you know of the woman?"

"Very little, sir. She was to be married a few days after I left Xennia."

"No. Her betrothed died the day before the wedding— legitimately, it seems. If—and this is a big if—if I were to offer to marry her, then a condition of the marriage treaty would be an end to the persecution, wouldn't it?"

That topped anything that had happened so far. That would lift the suspicion of treason from the Mother's Children in Albi. Rollo could only gasp, "Sire!" After a moment he managed, "Sir, we are not traitors! I meet thousands of people every year, and they are all loyal to the crown. They just don't understand why...why your father persecutes them so. They are good, kind people. I counsel patience and forbearance, not violence, so that the rest of his people will learn we are not monsters. We do not poison wells or eat babies."

The prince was nodding. "I have known that for a long time."

"I have struggled...always I denounce violence, and I do think it is starting to work! I believe that the people of Albi are growing tired of the butchery. Very few of the specta- tors jeered Jake Trull when he was put to death. I'm told such executions used to be much better attended and the condemned was pelted with filth on his way to the gallows."

"I agree with you there, and my witnesses are less biased than yours. I had to attend Rafe Dampier's funeral. It was a state occasion, and yet the church was only a quarter full. Anyone who dared to stay away did so. When the prisoners escaped from Umberly, many spectators cheered them."

"Well, that proves…" Then Rollo saw the trap.

The prince's normally placid face chilled to anger. "Umberly changes things, Master Hawke. An impartial jury, if such a thing could be found, might refuse to convict for Dampier's murder, if the accused could show that he—or she, I suppose—had lost loved ones in the Woodbridge 'miracle.' If Dampier himself could not be brought to justice, then justice must be found elsewhere. That is a very human reaction, if an illegal one. The ensuing disaster as the congregation tried to flee was arguably a horrible accident."

"I see it as criminal stupidity, sir. I don't think I can be as forgiving as Your Highness."

"Few people will be. But Umberly was an assault on a royal castle. Ten men of the Royal Fusiliers were shot dead by their comrades, and others wounded. The warden blew his own brains out later."

The sun of hope was setting already. "I heard no rumors of such an act beforehand, sir, and have been held incommunicado since, so I knew nothing of Umberly until my sister told me an hour ago. Master Kipping had told her no details, and she could only pass on gossip. There are two suspects, she said."

"Two *boys*. One of them wanted to visit with a prisoner, Richard Sizer. We believe that boy was his son. The other we think was a schoolmate of his, one named Bradwell Armstrong, thought to be a nephew of Lady Mary Whatman. Warrants have been issued for the arrest of all three of them."

Rollo must not reveal what he knew of them, at least not yet. Nell had quoted Brother Alfred as saying that the

Armstrong boy had "wagonloads" of talent, although he was very young still. Meanwhile, the prince's intentions were becoming horribly clear, and John Hawke was caught in a vise.

"Youth and talent are a dangerous combination, sir."

"Youth can only be excused so far, Master Hawke. If Stonebridge was gross stupidity, what do you call Umberly?"

"Even worse. Morally right or morally wrong, it is utterly stupid to provoke an enemy much stronger than yourself. But there are some who grow tired of waiting. Sizer, I know. He belongs to a shadowy group that calls itself the Underground. It may well be behind this."

Emil stared at him for a minute or two, probably weighing the first real decision of his reign. "I do want to end the persecution, Hawke. A king should be the guardian of his people, not the tormentor. I am seriously considering offering to marry Duchess Yvette and establish freedom of conscience in Albi. That will engage me in a huge battle with the Church of the Light, and I cannot afford a defeat before I have come into my inheritance. Just talking to you now is a considerable risk for me. To launch a religious revolution while I have Stonebridge and Umberly hanging over me is unthinkable. The Church is already tearing strips off Master Kipping every day for not finding the killers. Whoever was behind them must be punished before we can proceed."

"Yes, sir."

"And it would be a great help if the Children themselves handed over the criminals."

Of course it would. But it might also splinter them into warring factions, and Emil was quite clever enough to know that. Rollo sighed.

"Yes, Your Highness."

"I am willing to amend the terms of your parole. You and your wife must continue to sleep at Caverleigh House. You will be free to come and go during the day, as long as you report each evening to...who is your keeper?"

"Master Walter Carey."

"In return for that, I want you to prove your sincerity about nonviolence. I want the hotheaded leaders of the so-called Underground arrested again, because we had most of them in Umberly. But most of all I want this maniac young lout called Bradwell Armstrong! Light knows what he may get up to next. I want him delivered alive—gagged and blindfolded. Will you do that?"

"Will you guarantee no torture, Your Highness? I know what it is like to hang on a wall for days, and I cannot condemn any human being to such treatment."

The prince scowled at the resistance. He nodded reluctantly. "Very well, no torture. A fast trial in open court and a simple hanging or beheading if proven guilty. Those are the terms. Have I your oath on it?"

"I swear I will do my best, sir."

"Alive, bound, gagged, and blindfolded?"

"Alive, bound, gagged, and blindfolded," Rollo agreed. "If I possibly can."

"Darren, Simon, you are the witnesses. I wish you good hunting, Prelate."

Rollo was delivered back to the Kipping house to rejoin his wife and await a warrant from the prince authorizing his release on parole. He ought to be finding this carriage-set life exhilarating after so many years of poverty, but he was worn out by the day and oppressed by the task he had just accepted and its taint of betrayal. He found his wife and sister in the withdrawing room, drinking sweet wine and gabbling like starlings. About him, no doubt. Maddy was a beautiful woman now, but he still saw Nell as a flame of feminine perfection.

She read his mood instantly, of course, even before he was seated. "Bad news?" She refilled her goblet and passed it to him.

He drained it. "Good and bad. The prince seems sincere in wanting to end the repression, which is the best news in two hundred years, but he is irate about this violence at Umberly Castle. I have promised to find the Armstrong boy and turn him over to the authorities. Then I suppose I will be branded a traitor, lackey, and stool pigeon."

Nell sprang to his defense automatically. "Just by the loonies in the Underground, and they do that already. Your abhorrence of violence is well-known, and that boy is a monster. He's killed dozens of people already."

"Thirty-four, I think."

"Can you find him?" Maddy asked.

"I expect so. I know the main leaders of the Underground, so I can start with them. I have my days free to search, as long as Nell and I sleep at Caverleigh House."

"Well then," Maddy said. "What do you know about him?" Even as a child she had always been practical and down-to-earth.

"Rollo's never met him," Nell said, "but I have. He's very young, about fourteen now, but enormously gifted. Very polite and well spoken, but my insight saw him as a bit creepy—too bitter for one of his years. Has a black dog familiar, named Smut."

Rollo added, "He lives—or did live—at Rose Hall with that hare-brained Whatman beldame breathing poison in his ears all—" Rollo paused and looked at Maddy. "Are you all right?"

Maddy had turned chalky white. She shook her head and had trouble speaking. "How far from Woodbridge to Rose Hall?"

Rollo shrugged and looked to Nell, for she did the route planning.

"Not sure," she said. "I tend to think by counties. Woodbridge is in Angleshire and Rose Hall in Dorsia, but I doubt they're more than a day's walk apart, if that. Why?"

"Because," Maddy said hoarsely, "the last time I saw our brother Brat was two years ago. He was eleven years old and had just been adopted by a jet-black puppy that came out of nowhere. Named Smut. That was the day before Dampier burned the house down. Black hair, brilliant blue eyes?"

Name of the Mother!

Nell whispered, "Oh no!"

"Bram, Brat, Brad?" Rollo said. "A puppy sleeping in his room, demanding to go out in the middle of the night, sounds of a mob approaching—"

Maddy was shaking her head. "No. Not like that. If it had been that way, he would have known that I was married, and he'd have come looking for me at Beaconbeck. The day after the attack, when I went to see the ruins and they were still digging bones out of the ashes...I was told that Brat had disappeared. His pony had come back without him. Father had called off the hunt, so everyone assumed he had been found."

"Or he called it off because Corbin told him that Brat was safe?" Rollo closed his eyes in prayer.

"It's my fault," Nell said. "When I met him he reminded me of you, dear, but I thought it was just the eyes and all the talent. I should have guessed I was seeing more than that."

Too late, too late! He had promised the prince...*Mother, Mother, what have you done?*

CHAPTER 38

GUS TWEMLOW MOSTLY WORKED AT THE DOCKS, BUT he had a sometime night job at the Jones factory. Moonlighting they called it, rightly enough. Once every few weeks he would be called in to do sentry duty on the gate. There were always three sentries, and only rarely did he recognize either of the other two as someone he had met before. That way they couldn't conspire to accept a bribe, and if one slacked off the other two would snitch on him. They were supplied with cudgels, helmets, and breastplates. No firearms, of course. The pay was excellent, but they had to spend two-thirds of the night on their feet, no shirking. The sentry box bench was wide enough for only one, and the other two were out in the weather, no matter how cold or wet their asses got. They had an hourglass to see fair play, and a tower with a bell. If anything suspicious happened, they were to haul on the rope to alert the watch in the army barracks a block away. Nothing suspicious ever did happen, though.

That night was cool but not cold, the moon round and bright. Harry was snoring in the box. In half an hour it

would be Gus's turn to do that. The one who called himself Roy was from up north and spoke funny. There wasn't
much you could talk about with a man you'd never met
before and likely wouldn't again. Roy had heard a rumor
the king was dead. Who cared? They parted and walked in
opposite directions for a change. The moon was brilliant,
the wide street as empty as a beggar's plate. There was a
beardless face right in front of him. Where had he come
from?

"DREAM," Brad said. "YOU HAVEN'T SEEN ME. JUST
STAND THERE AND DREAM OF WHAT YOU LIKE BEST." He
ran to the other man, who was already turning around to
retrace his steps but didn't see Brad until they were nose to
nose and Brad dropped his distraction. He had to waken
the third man to put him back to sleep.

Then the worst part was over already, and he wished
his heart understood that so it would stop trying to leap
out of his chest. The sign above the gate said, *Jones Brothers.*
There was also a royal coat-of-arms, rather faded, and in
smaller letters, *Suppliers to His Majesty.* The wall was about
fifteen feet high, with spikes on top, and the gate itself was
built for wagons and looked so massive that he doubted he
could move it. Fortunately, he wouldn't have to, because
there was a wicket gate inset in it. That was the one with
locks, three of them.

Jiggle...*click...click...click...*

He climbed through, into the yard. Bear and Wolf were
watching from shadowed doorways farther along the street,
and now one of them would be running to summon the
wagon. Brad went back out and ordered the three sentries
inside; there he told them to lie down in the weeds, clear

of the driveway, and not to wake up until he said to. He was a very good burglar, for a beginner.

The Joneses' factory itself was one story high and not nearly as big as one would expect from the amount of ground enclosed by the wall. He ran along the driveway in the moonlight until he came to the loading dock and jumped up on it. No, he should have known that way would be too easy. There were no locks or handles on the outside. So he had to go around to the front door and open more locks. And the next door in was locked, too. He had worried about dogs, because they needed a special sort of mastery he wasn't good at, but there was no dog scent.

The storage area itself smelled very dusty. It was also dark as a tomb, as Matt had told him it would be, and that was because no intruder would ever bring a candle or lantern in there. Any flame near that sort of dust would make the whole building hit the moon and the intruder with it. But a man who could see in the dark had no trouble making his way between the stacks of barrels to unlatch the shutters and let in the moonlight. By the time Brad had done that, Lizard and Horse were in the building and opening the loading door. More men were swinging up the bars on the main gate to let the wagon in.

He could find a place to sit and watch, then. He had done his bit, and those barrels of gunpowder weighed a hundred pounds apiece, almost as much as he did. As long as no one had nails in his boots to strike sparks, everything should go smoothly.

Sit, but not relax. He had proved his value to the Underground, but was he worth keeping? That was their problem, and their answer might, or might not, be his.

Useful didn't necessarily mean trustworthy. He knew his loyalty was shaky, because he kept worrying what Brother Alfred would say. In retrospect, Lady Whatman had always been slightly crazy. He'd been stupid to tell Lion and the rest that he wouldn't kill anyone, because killing people was what they intended. He couldn't be the only talented man in the menagerie, and if any of the other animals had insight, then they knew just how shaky Hagfish's loyalty was. They had been careful not to tell him what were they planning to do with that wagonload of black powder, and if Lion had decided that he wasn't to be trusted, there were miles of catacombs to store bodies in.

He just couldn't see what choice he had.

First man in and last man out. It was Brad who closed the shutters on the looted but still well-stocked storeroom, Brad who locked all the locks. Make it look legitimate, he'd been told, and it might be days before the Joneses' men realized they'd been robbed. Rousing the guards and putting them back in position was the hardest part. He told them not to wake up until first light and not to remember what had happened. That might work, or it might not.

The wagon had gone, too heavily laden to take passengers. Half a dozen Underground men were waiting for him, to escort him back "home." It would be long walk, for the gunpowder works and army barracks were on the outskirts of town. But why six? And why did they cluster around him so? Matt on his left, Lynx on his right; two in front, two behind. He wasn't convinced by all the chatter from Matt and Lynx about what a great job he had done and what a great asset he was to the cause and their not knowing what they would have done without him, gabble, gabble. Did they know what they were going to do *with* him? That was the question. House arrest until after the big bang was the best he could hope for.

Yet his prescience was shining bright, no qualms. That made no sense! People with prescience often went crazy. He should have gone to Gaudry while he had the chance. Often the Mother's gifts had two edges.

The big road divided. They took the left branch, then a turn to the south, a narrower street. The full moon was sinking low as dawn approached. That put the roadway in shadow, so he would have an advantage if he wanted to make a break for it. But then what? If the Underground didn't want him, the government and the Church surely did. The Underground's solution would be quicker and less painful.

As they passed an especially narrow and dark alley, a dog exploded in excited barking. Brad jumped. His companions cursed.

"Pay no attention," Owl said. "It probably does that every time anyone…"

But it was Smut's bark. Smut had come back at last! Brad distracted and stopped walking. The two behind him separated to go by him without registering that he was there. His talent wouldn't hold so many for more than a moment. He dived for the alley.

"Hey!" someone shouted; then more but quieter voices took up the cry. "The boy! The boy! Catch him!"

The alley was covered in places, a tunnel. It had garbage everywhere, and it had branches. And it had Smut, whose tail was wagging so fast it almost hummed. The footsteps behind him were slower, and the voices were cursing. Someone slipped and fell in the muck. Smut raced ahead, then made a sharp right. Brad followed, black dog in black alley. It was a dead end, but there were wooden steps up to a door on the left, and Smut dived underneath them. Brad wriggled in beside him, squeezing himself into the smallest ball possible. He had deliberately worn dark clothing for the break-in, so his face was the lightest part of him. He kept it down, buying his nose in Smut's fur. The familiar dog smell was better than the sick-making stink under the steps.

Light. Someone had a lantern. The steps had no risers, only treads, and Brad could peer out at a pair of boots. Boots, luckily, could not peer in.

"Nope," said Matt's voice.

"I wanted to knife him and leave him there as payment," said the other man, whichever he was. "The reward money would have paid them for the powder."

They strode away, laughing at the joke.

Matt, too?

Now what? He must let Smut guide. That was what he was for. Smut lay and scratched for a while, then seemed to decide that it was safe to squirm out, licking Brad's face when he crawled out after him—dog humor. Back at the main alley, he turned right confidently and led the way out of the maze, tail wagging high. Smut had no problems. He could drink straight town water without being poisoned and find plenty to eat in the gutters. He must know where he was going, but Brad had no clue at all. He was a killer on the run. No friends, no place to hide, no money.

He was shivering, but whether from cold or fright he didn't know.

He walked for hours through the dark streets, following a black dog. He rarely saw anyone, except once in a while a small group of horseman or a rumbling coach. He hoped the anonymous heaps in corners were only sleeping, not dead. Gradually the houses began to grow larger and grander, and he guessed he was approaching the newest parts of the city, where the palace and the temple were. His feet and legs ached. First light brought out more people: servants and apprentices hurrying to work, early delivery-men taking around the fresh milk and bread—which smelled heavenly to a very hungry, footsore, frightened boy, who had recently fancied himself as a man but now didn't.

Once he found a poster offering a reward of five hundred suns for the arrest of a "tall youth of sixteen summers, named Bradwell Armstrong." So not only the Underground and the government would be looking for him. At that price everyone would be looking for him. The description was vague, and he wasn't sixteen. But he was a vagrant at the least, with no address and no friends or family to testify that he was a loyal and law-abiding subject of the king.

The sun came up, and traffic increased, but still Smut kept walking, although even he seemed weary now. People looked at Brad suspiciously now. He was filthy and probably shifty. Five hundred suns was a fortune.

Then Smut lay down alongside an archway set in a high stone wall and closed by a wrought iron gate, wide enough to admit a coach and four. Peering through the bars, Brad could see a mansion with stables and carriage houses. More important, he saw soldiers, men with muskets. He looked in disbelief at his dog.

"You going to turn me in?" he demanded. "They won't pay the reward to a dog, you know."

Smut continued to lick his paws.

Brad couldn't lurk there. He would be taken for a beggar or a would-be burglar, although that might be better than being taken for a mass murderer. Already the soldiers inside had noticed him.

"Come on, mutt," he said, and began trekking back to the corner, because there was an alley there, where he would be less conspicuous. Perhaps Smut just needed a rest. It would be nice if Smut would come with him to stand guard over him while he had some sleep himself, but Smut showed no sign of moving away from the gate.

As Brad reached the corner, an open coach came rattling along the street and stopped at the gate. Smut jumped up, tail wagging. Brad gave a wail of dismay as he guessed what was about to happen. He flogged his flagging legs into action and raced back along the road, but he wasn't fast enough. Men inside opened the gate; coach, horses, and Smut disappeared inside. He arrived just as two fusiliers clanged the gate shut in his face.

"Smut!" Brad screamed. "Smut, come here! Smut!"

"That your dog?" one of the soldiers asked.

An officer was handing a lady down from the coach. Smut leaped at her, barking raucously and spattering mud. She yelled in fury and struck at him with her parasol.

Brad knew her!

"Mad!" he shouted, loud as he could. "Maddy! Mad!"

"Look out!" the soldier called to his friends. "Tha's a mad dog!"

"Shoot it!" the officer bellowed, and his men leveled their muskets.

CHAPTER 39

FOR THE FIRST TIME SINCE SHE HAD MOVED INTO MASTER Kipping's house, Maddy closed her side of the connecting doors. She left her light on, though, and tried to read for a while. Her mind refused to make sense of the words. Rollo returned from the unknown would have been stimulus enough, but that paled beside the discovery that Bram had risen from a fiery grave and was murdering people wholesale. When she heard William in his room, she reached over to snuff out the candles, then decided to wait and see what he would do. She still felt he had deceived her, yet she had come to appreciate that he might have had reasons she didn't know. It would be only fair to let him plead his case, if he dared.

He tapped on the door; she bade him enter. He had stripped down to his shirt and britches, his hair was awry, and his eyes were glazed with exhaustion. He stayed in the doorway.

"My thanks for all you have done today, Mindy. It has been an epic day in the history of Albi, and you helped very much."

"Thank you."

"And my congratulations on your brother's return."

"Thank you."

He hesitated, uncertain in a way she had never seen before.

"Believe me, I truly didn't know. Rollo Woodbridge vanished out of Swine Hall, and no one heard another word about him. He might have fled abroad, died of the abuse, anything. A few months later we learned of a new missionary, young John Hawke, who was held in great respect by your people. But I was never sure. How could I raise your hopes when I wasn't sure? I knew no way of getting in touch with him."

"You sent me to talk with him and never warned me!"

"If I told you and was wrong, I would have made him die twice for you. By not telling you, I might give you a wonderful surprise."

She had no answer to that. He had so many troubles just now, and she did not want to add to them. "Does your promise of Earl Uptree's head on a plate still hold?"

His smile was a mockery of what a smile should be. "Not literally, but yes."

She threw back the cover. "Come here, then."

"Not tonight, dear. I'm much too tired."

"I was very cross with you. Please kiss and make up."

He went over to the bed. Her gift of inspiration was not restricted to generating passion. It could bring peace, too. He stayed all night. She found his presence comforting, and suddenly it was morning, with sunlight beyond the drapes.

William always rose early. Maddy was not usually a morning person, but that day she was right behind him, jumping out of bed, eager for the day. She dressed carefully—nothing too flashy, but a cut above the dowdy stuff Nell Hawke wore. A girl needed a few high cards when a game was stacked against her. She canceled a couple of appointments. She was going to go hunting with Rollo and Nell, hunting for Brat. Rollo said his peregrine would lead him to the general area Brat was in, if he were still in Weypool. And Nell thought her familiar, whatever it was because she hadn't said, could help them close in on the right house. Failing that, Rollo had a very good finding talent, and many contacts among the Children who would help. They would locate the missing brother.

What happened then could be decided then.

Nosy Steven Veal saw her off, so he could listen to the directions she gave the driver, and no doubt the men were all trained to report back to him if she changed her mind on the way. Maddy didn't care if he knew she was off to Caverleigh House, because she'd told William so. The weather was holding up, so she rode in the landau with the hood down, using a flowered parasol to keep the sun off her complexion.

Going to see Rollo, going to see Rollo... The words pealed in her head like bells. She must never lose Rollo again. And maybe, maybe, even find Brat. Poor Brat! A Brat wrongly orphaned and now in very deep trouble.

In very few minutes the coach halted at the gate to Caverleigh House. Fusiliers ran to open the gate and let it into the yard. When it halted at the door, their captain handed her down with a smile that managed to be both respectful and admiring. A great black dog hurled itself at her, almost knocking her over, leaving muddy paw marks all over her cloak. She cried out angrily and swung at the brute with her parasol, missing by a mile, of course.

Men shouting about rabies. It didn't look rabid. Then more shouting back at the gate, which had apparently opened itself, and an intruder...a gawky youth running toward her with his arms wide...shouting her name, her real name...shouting to the dog...

"Smut?" This monster had been that tiny puppy? That boy, this lanky young man?

Brat, oh, Brat!

They grabbed each other, while the dog barked excitedly. Brat didn't seem to know whether to laugh or cry, and she was doing both. The captain shouted at his men not to shoot.

Everything was, she assured him, perfectly all right. The young man was an old friend. So was his dog.

But the captain, whatever his name, was rapidly becoming suspicious. Prisoner Hawke was the leader of the heretic witches, after all, and this filthy vagrant would well fit the description of the notorious killer whose capture would make a man wealthy overnight.

Things were about to get ugly.

Men!

Maddy smiled and inspired at full strength. The captain's face turned scarlet and his eyes bulged. She saw a sparkle of sweat appear on his forehead. She turned her back on him before he tried to rape her, clasped her brother by the hand, and led him into Caverleigh House.

Brad sniggered. "What did you just do to General Spew?"

"You're too young to understand."

"No, I'm not."

They started up the splendid staircase, out of earshot of the guards.

"Oh, Brat! I want to hug you until you break in half."

"You just try that, little sister." His eyes gleamed several inches above her own. "I'd never have guessed you'd be so small. Oh, I can't believe this!" He was almost as aroused as the captain had been, although in other ways and for different reasons. "I knew something wonderful was about to happen...never guessed...last night...Smut..."

"You're in fearful danger!"

"You know that already? Good. I have worse news than that. Where is this place? You live here?"

"No. I'm on my way to visit John Hawke."

That burst the bubble. *"The prelate?"* He sobered and lost his idiotic grin.

"The prelate. He..." If Master Kipping could play tricks on her, then she could play tricks on her brothers. Mother knew, they'd played enough on her, back in Woodbridge Manor. "He's very displeased with what you have...what you are supposed to have done. Let me present you, and we'll hope he is not too angry."

Now they were heading along the corridor toward the Hawkes' room. Smut was already standing at the correct door, waiting for it to be opened. Reality was starting to break through Brat's ecstatic fog. For the first time he looked worried. "You can help me, Maddy?"

"I hope so. And I think Brother Hawke will try to help you, too, although you've put him in quite a spot. You stand on that side."

Smut promptly backed away from the door and sat down, tongue lolling, tail swishing. Brat's familiar would not be Brat's familiar if it didn't enjoy pranks.

Maddy opened the door a span and peered in. Nell was embroidering, as carefully posed by the window as if a dozen artists were already painting her. Rollo was leaning both hands on the table, studying a map. Both looked up.

"Prelate, I have a gentleman here who wishes to speak with you."

Rollo frowned. Nell, in the background, smiled knowingly.

Maddy opened the door wide. "Master Woodbridge... Master Woodbridge."

Brat was the faster. *"Prelate...Rollo!?"*

"Brat!" Rollo's expression was worth all the wines of Xennia. Maddy stepped aside to avoid the rush as the two flew to embrace each other. Smut leapt around them, barking. Too late, Rollo realized how obscenely filthy the newcomer was.

"Where in the world have you been?"

Brad's blue eyes gleamed with joy and tears. "Hiding under some steps from men trying to kill me."

Rollo said, "Then a little sewage doesn't matter," and hugged him again.

What of his oath? Maddy and Nell exchanged glances. Bound, blindfolded, and gagged?

Brad regarded Nell with an adolescent's lustful appreciation and bowed low. Then he forgot formality and dropped to his knees to give his dog a hug. He kept flipping back and forth between the adorable child Maddy remembered and an engaging youth who couldn't possibly be the deadly killer the regent had called him.

"Smut saved me. He's the best familiar anyone ever had. He led me here, and I saw him mauling a strange lady, and then I saw who she was." He blinked away tears. "You hungry, Smutty?"

"Sounds like someone is," Nell said wryly. She headed for the bell rope.

"You must tell us all your adventures, Brat," Rollo said, "but you do know that there is a warrant out for your arrest on charges of murder, treason, and witchcraft?"

"I have more important news first!" His excitement flickered like summer lightning.

"Wait!" A servant was at the door. Nell told her to bring meals for a starving youth and a large dog. Quickly. Speed before fancy.

"Everybody sit!" Rollo said firmly. Brad shrugged and dumped his filthy self on a silk brocade sofa. Smut jumped up to join him, curling himself with much wagged approval.

"Right, Brother Brat. Do not admit to anything criminal, but tell me if I am wrong. You are accused of burning Rafe Dampier to death and burning down Umberly Castle."

Brad smiled, not denying it. He seemed unaware of the danger he was in. Had he reverted to childhood, as if the worst in store were a scolding from his big brother and sister?

"And since then?" Rollo asked.

"What I am trying to tell you, big brother, is that last night the Underground stole a whole wagonload of gunpowder from the king's factory."

Nell gasped and put a hand to her mouth. Maddy felt a swirl of nausea.

Rollo said some words a prelate shouldn't even know. Then, "What for?"

"They are planning to mine one of the catacombs. I can lead you to the place, but I can't tell you where it is. What's above it, I mean. But we should find it soon, or there won't be anything there to find, 'cept a big hole." He was enjoying the attention, and who wouldn't? After two years of being an orphan, he suddenly had his family back and an audience hanging on every word.

"Brat," Rollo said, "are you absolutely certain of this? If I spread this story and it isn't—"

"Of course I'm certain, I saw…I mean I am very certain. And I know where it's going—underground, I mean."

"Name it!"

"I can't. The mine will be right by the tombs of some men called Conybear, Tillman, and, um…Bouncer? I know how to get there, is all."

"Then we must act. Walter Carey isn't here, or I'd dump it on him. Maddy, can you get in to see William Kipping?"

"I can certainly try. Steven probably can. My coach has gone…" She glanced down at her cloak and gown, already ruined. "Get me a horse."

A footman arrived with a tray, followed by a maid carrying a meaty bone on a plate. Others came with a bowl and pitcher. The meal was unloaded to the table. Brat, displaying a knowledge of gentle manners that clashed with his foul appearance, accepted the chair pulled out for him, then held his hands over the bowl so that water could be poured over them from the pitcher. Again Nell caught Maddy's eyes, but this time they were suppressing laughter. Rollo ordered two horses saddled at once. As soon as the servants had gone, he rallied his team.

"Brat...no, you'd better be Bram Woodbridge again. Remember that, *Bram*. I want you to stay here with Nell and tell her the whole story. Eat and talk. There are things going on just now that you cannot know, and she understands the politics."

Nell also, Maddy strongly suspected, had enough insight to detect lies and true loyalties.

"Maddy and I will be back in an hour, I hope," Rollo said. "Come, Maddy."

"One thing first. Cut the hem at the back of my skirt and rip it up to my seat, or I'll be arrested for exposure as soon as I get on the horse."

Rollo chuckled and did as she asked.

❧

A brisk gallop got them to the Kipping residence, where there were few people around yet to notice the lady's odd attire. They caught Steven Veal just as he prepared to go for his own morning ride in the park. The three of them rode for the palace.

Then progress slowed. Steven was known there, but not accredited to barge in on the first secretary at work. Master Kipping was believed to be in a meeting. Eventually the visitors were escorted upstairs, and everything came to a dead stop. The Privy Council was in session and could not be interrupted. If the lady and gentlemen would care to sit in the antechamber...

The antechamber was depressingly large and contained very many seats, at least a dozen of which were already occupied by petitioners who probably all had priority over the first secretary's almoner, no matter how desperate he was.

The three of them hesitated in the doorway. The chairs looked comfortable enough but wouldn't be if that ton of gunpowder was being packed into a mine directly below them. *Somewhere* was going to go sky-high soon, but no doubt the honorable councilors were discussing arrangements for a royal funeral. Every second these suspicious visitors took to decide whether to sit down or go away just increased the guards' suspicions. Maddy wanted to scream. Rollo was praying under his breath, and the Mother heard.

Along the wide corridor, striding fast, came Prince Regent Emil himself, escorted by his two swordsman friends, Master Darren Darley and Sir Simon Hogarth. It was a fair guess that the Privy Council had summoned him—or had humbly petitioned His Highness to preside over its deliberations.

Instead of curtsying, as protocol required, Maddy screamed, *"Gunpowder!"*

Heads turned. The regent stopped to see who had shouted and saw John Hawke. He spoke a word. Darren Darley hurried over, hand on sword hilt.

"Gunpowder has been stolen," Rollo said. "Yes? And I have a witness who knows where it has gone."

Two minutes later a small office was tightly packed with the regent, the swordsmen, two Woodbridges, and Master William Kipping, dragged out of the Privy Council's emergency session—which had, in fact, been discussing the lost gunpowder. Steven, to his huge disgust, was left outside, perhaps only because of his size. Nobody sat down. There was nowhere to sit, anyway.

Then Rollo had the floor and the most critical speech of his life to make.

"Your Highness, yesterday you charged me to find a certain person and deliver him bound, blindfolded, and gagged. Last night, I learned to my horror that the youth you sought was almost certainly my lost younger brother, Bram Woodbridge. I had no idea that he might have survived the destruction of our family home two years ago." He watched for reactions, but only the swordsmen's faces revealed anything, and they didn't count.

"I hadn't even started to look for him when he came to me this morning, at Caverleigh House. *He* sought *me* out! Or rather, I should say that the Mother sent him to me. He claims he knows who took that powder and where it is being taken. He is eager to help. He will lead your men to the place now, sir."

The prince was skeptical, his eyes cold. "You're telling me he's reformed? He's turned his coat?"

"I haven't heard the whole story yet, sir. The matter seemed too urgent. I believe that he was coerced into helping and managed to escape. I know he had to hide from men who wanted to kill him."

"So I suppose he will now cooperate in return for a royal pardon?"

"He hasn't asked for anything yet, sir. Nothing! He is still very young. All he has told me is that the conspirators plan to mine the catacomb containing the tombs of Conybear and a couple of other famous soldiers, Bonser and..." Rollo looked to Maddy, whose face was shiny with perspiration and fear.

"Tillman," she said.

Emil turned to Master Kipping. "Your counsel, First Secretary?"

Kipping waited a moment, then said, "Send a contingent of your fusiliers to collect the boy, Highness, and go with him to the catacomb he knows. Ask the court archivist where those tombs are located so we can evacuate the area."

The regent nodded while he considered.

Rollo said, "I respectfully remind Your Highness that you promised no torture. Now that he has turned himself in voluntarily—"

Emil cut him off with an impatient gesture. "Proceed, First Secretary. Send the fusiliers. Warn them how dangerous this may be! Tell them to treat the boy well as long as he is a willing witness, but he is to be considered a suspect and detained. Warn them that he is highly dangerous, to be shot if he tries to escape. Miss Wells, go with them to reassure the lad. Hawke, you come with me."

CHAPTER 40

WHEN BRAM, AS HE MUST REMEMBER TO BE AGAIN, HAD met Mistress Hawke last summer, he'd guessed she had insight. Probably she'd recognized the same talent in him, for their talk had been guarded. He hadn't realized back then quite what an eyeful she was. Lucky Rollo! Now she found him some of Rollo's spare clothes, which were at least clean—loose on him and very inferior quality, but not too long. He'd eaten and changed—while she turned her back—and never stopped talking, answering her questions freely. He could rely on Rollo to get him out of the mess he was in. Prelate Rollo! Smut had gnawed the bone clean and was snoring, flat on his side on the rug.

They heard voices before the door opened. In walked an officer in grandiose livery, with a pistol at his belt and Maddy on his arm. He had gingery muttonchop whiskers and shoulders as wide as a horse's. He ran an appreciative glance over Nell before cooling it down to stare at Bram.

Bram stared back.

"Master Woodbridge? I'm Captain Kenrick, Royal Fusiliers. The Privy Council sent us. Where do you want to lead us?"

Oh, that was flattering! Bram decided he liked Captain Kenrick.

"Bram," Maddy said quickly, "remember what Rollo told you. Be careful what you say. You're not of age, and can ask to have your guardian present."

The look in Captain Kenrick's eye indicated that he found that suggestion to be on the shaky side of hypothetical. So did Bram.

"Don't know street names, sir. Big one with statues?"

"Parade Way?"

"Sounds right. A tavern called the Blue Boar."

"Come along, then. Can you sit a horse?"

"Like a horsefly." Bram strutted out ahead of the captain.

Maddy shouted good luck behind him. He would need it if the Underground decided to blow themselves up rather than be taken alive. Smut raised his head briefly, then went back to sleep.

Down in the yard a dozen mounted horses clumped hooves and jangled harness. Their riders carried muskets. House grooms were holding two mounts, but he was disgusted to see that the spare they'd brought for him, the one with its stirrups tied up out of the way, was a mare, and a smallish mare at that.

Captain Kenrick swung into the saddle. "Any of you degenerates know the Blue Boar, on Parade Way?"

"Green beer downstairs, old women upstairs," said the lieutenant and several voices agreed.

"How many doors?"

Silence, until the lieutenant said, "Just one, I think."

"Three," Bram said. "Front door and two in the cellar—one at the rear for barrels, another down to the catacombs."

By that time Bram was mounted and had adjusted his stirrup leathers. Kenrick swung into the saddle and motioned for him to ride alongside. And off they went, wheeling out into the road at a canter. Pedestrians jumped clear and other traffic swerved aside as the king's men claimed right of way. Fun!

Bram wasn't as skilled as the king's men were at riding a military horse in crowded streets, and the mare was having trouble reading his signals. The captain kept throwing questions at him, not all of which he could answer. But he knew enough that Kenrick could snap out orders when they reached the alley. One man at the back of the troop stayed mounted to close it off and corral the horses. Kenrick tried the tavern door, but it was locked. He stepped aside, and the two largest of his men hit it together. Then it was open.

He roared, "In the king's name!" and marched in with Bram at his heels. There was no one in sight. The beer and smoke odors were still there, and some dirty mugs on the tables. The lieutenant ran through and up the stairs, with three men at his back.

"Cellar?" Kenrick demanded.

"Under that barrel," Bram said. "That's good. That they've tried to hide it, I mean. Means there won't be anyone down there to blow it up before we get to it."

The two biggest fusiliers were already jostling the barrel out of the way.

Kenrick moved to the trap and reached in to haul the ladder up straighter. "Or the fuse is already burning."

That was true. Since he could see in the dark, Bram really ought to go first, but they wouldn't trust him if he suggested it, so he didn't. But he did reach the ladder right after Kenrick. The cellar was emptier than he remembered. The poles had gone, and he still wondered what they had been for. So had the barrels, so they must have held more gunpowder, not beer. The rest of the dusty old junk looked much as he remembered. Kenrick had found the way to the tunnel and was lighting a lantern.

Bram slid past him and set off down the slope. He could see where the dirt had been compacted along the middle of the passage by rolling barrels. Somewhere ahead of him was more than a ton of gunpowder. It might just be sitting there, as harmless as it had been in the warehouse, or it might blow at any moment. Then either the blast would come at him like a ball through a cannon, or the roof would fall on him.

"Wait!" Kenrick shouted behind him, so Bram stopped and waited. Lanterns approached, four of them.

"You stay where I can see you, boy, or I'll give you a hot lead enema."

"Yes, sir."

"How far?"

"About ten minutes, sir. But don't bring any more men, please. The gunpowder will be at the end of a long, straight tunnel, and if there's any shooting, that'll set it off for sure."

"Just you and me, huh?" Kenrick scowled, and Bram realized that the man was terrified. That was scary if even an officer in the fusiliers was scared, but perhaps he was one of those people who didn't like enclosed places. They hadn't even reached the creepy corpses yet.

"Well, maybe bring two down to the split. There's another way out. They could block that."

Kenrick told two to follow him and went after Bram. They passed the latrine stink and reached the divide.

"That's the other way out, sir. That one over there is a dead end."

"How can you see so well?"

"I have very good night sight."

The sloping tunnel that Bram had helped to dig was dark. Good. Any light ahead would mean danger, lots of danger. At least it would be quick if it happened. How had the Underground men manhandled the barrels down the slope? They couldn't have let them run free, because some of them would have been sure to hit someone, or crash into a wall and split open. They must have walked ahead of them, digging in their heels to keep them slow.

The passage had changed, though. Where Mule had broken through to the target catacomb, it had been dug down lower, so now the junction was smooth—steep for a heavy barrel, but a slope, not the long drop where Mule had lowered Bram on a rope.

"We turn right here, sir. Then left. At the end it turns left again, and that's where they were going to put the powder. I think that's right, sir."

"Go ahead, then," Kenrick growled. His face was shiny with fear. "Slowly, and walk softly. There's loose powder on the floor. We mustn't kick up dust or make sparks."

They reached the first of the burial niches, and Bram almost rammed his forehead into a pole. He ducked under it with a word of warning. A couple of niches farther along, there was another. And more. He had reached the first corner before he worked it out. Men had pushed the barrels along the flat corridor, but they were heading for a dead end. Going back for another, they could chin up on those crossbars—maybe tucking their feet out of the way in a lower niche—and the man bringing the next barrel could push it through underneath them. Clever! Dangerously clever, to have thought of that ahead of time.

Bram reached the final corridor and paused with a hand raised in warning. He could see his own shadow ahead, cast by the captain's lantern behind. The Underground might not be planning to detonate their mine right away. If the barrels were just sitting there, harmless, and there was anyone down there guarding them, then Master Woodbridge was going to stop a musket ball. For the first time he felt really, truly scared, not just excited.

"What're you waiting for?" Kenrick muttered.

"This is it. If they have a guard on it, he may be armed."

"If I were guarding gunpowder, I'd do it from a lot farther away."

"Um, yes, sir." Bram stepped around the corner. Nobody shot at him, but in the darkness ahead he saw a very faint star of light. He yelled in horror and ran forward, remembering just in time to crouch so he wouldn't crack his head on any poles. When he drew close, he made out a sputtering glow at the end of a long string, a slow fuse suspended over more of the overhead poles. He grabbed the cord behind the burning end and pulled. It came free easily.

"Don't put it down!" Kenrick yelled.

Bram had very nearly made exactly that mistake. He'd been going to stamp on it to put it out. He'd have blown himself into a shower of red rain. "Thanks, sir!"

The barrels were stacked three high, blocking the way to the grand tombs of Conybear and his friends, whoever they had been. Trembling at his narrow escape, Bram carried the burning end of the fuse carefully, holding his free hand underneath it in case it dropped sparks and trailing the rest of it behind him. When he reached the captain, Kenrick crushed the flame out between the butt of his pistol and the wall of the tunnel. He released a long sigh.

"Well done, lad! Very well done!"

"Thank you, sir," Bram said politely, realizing how wet his shirt was. Fucking well done, he'd have said. For a moment he wished he could go back to Rose Hall and tell the gang what he'd done. But the gang was broken up now, and there was no going back, ever.

"Let's get out of here before I drop my lantern," the captain said. "It would be a pity to spoil it now."

ॐ

They collected the two ashen-faced men guarding the other exit and retraced the rest of their steps to the Blue Boar. There they found more drama. The fusiliers had seven prisoners in the front room, five men standing against the wall and hands tied behind their backs, and two women sitting on a bench.

"Found 'em upstairs, sir," the lieutenant reported. "Not quite red-handed, but black-handed, you might say. Were washing off the evidence."

"You know any of these people, Woodbridge?" Kenrick asked.

The first and largest prisoner was Lion himself, stripped to a hairy waist and still bearing sweaty streaks of catacomb dust. If looks could kill, Bram would have burned to ash on the spot.

You either don't rat at all or you rat the whole rat. He'd warned them he wouldn't kill more people. They'd used him and planned to murder him. He was on Rollo and Maddy's side now.

"That one's their leader, sir. Calls himself Lion, but his real name is Elphick. Has a house on Saddler Street."

On to the next.

"He calls himself Lizard; led the digging team."

Bram looked sadly at the next one, the one he'd thought was a friend. Even his insight had said so, but he had laughed when a companion suggested knifing Bram. "And that's Matt Hewson, called Bear."

"You named yourself well, Hagfish," Matt said. "You slimy little—" A fusilier backhanded him across the face.

"His mother runs a used clothing store, sir, but she doesn't know what he's been up to, I'm sure. And this one was on the raid last night, but I don't know his name. So was this one; he calls himself Wolf."

Neither of the two women were properly dressed. The younger one, not really young, seemed to be naked except for a sheet she had wrapped around herself—rather artfully, showing interesting glimpses. Her face bore traces of paint, and Bram was quite old enough to know how she must earn her living. The older one was muffled in a man's cloak, with bare feet and legs showing below it. Her hair hung in wet rattails, and her wrinkles were black with gunpowder dust. She was Lady Whatman. *Oh shit...*

"Don't know either of those two."

"We'll take them in anyway," said the captain.

"Oh you will, will you?" Lady Whatman screamed in a voice quite unlike her normal tones. "And what's going to happen to my business with a door that you smashed open, eh? Tell me that! All I did was rent my cellar to a fine honest gentleman, and you charge in and wreck it, and now you're going to drag me off to jail leaving free beer for all the gutter trash, and when I come back the place will be sacked and full of squatters."

"I'm going to leave men on guard until the magistrates see the evidence."

"Then it'll be full of drunken soldiers—even worse. You won't have any shortage of volunteers, I'm thinking. Well, my brother's a magistrate, and you just wait until he hears how I've been treated."

Bram knew that Lady Whatman had no brother, and he doubted very much that she owned the Blue Boar, or had perhaps ever been in it before today, but he couldn't say that now. She had been kind to him. Two years...

Kenrick hesitated, out of his depth. He was paid to look decorative around the palace, mostly, not to raid nests of traitors. He had just pulled off a stupendous coup and must be anxious to get back and report. There was a promotion in this. Someone else could take responsibility for a ton of stolen gunpowder and the sooner the better.

"All right. You can stay here, but you're not to leave. Corporal, take two men and guard these premises until the magistrates arrive. Nobody in or out, except you can find a boy and give him a couple of stars to fetch a carpenter to fix that door. Lieutenant, tie each of these men behind a horse, and we'll trot them back to the barracks for now."

As Bram went out, he noticed the corporal gloating over the harlot. He just hoped he wouldn't turn into such an idiot about women as most men did around his age.

⁤⁤⁤⁤⁤⁤⁤⁤⁤⁤⁤⁤⁤⁤⁤⁤⁤⁤⁤

As soon as the sound of hooves had gone, the corporal sent his two loutish helpers outside and advanced on the girl with the obvious intention of conducting a strip search. Without a word, she dropped her sheet and lay down on the table. Lady Whatman mumbled something about getting dressed and went into the back room. The ladder was still in place, and they'd left a lantern lit. Truly the Mother blessed her servants!

She scampered down the ladder, bare feet and all. Clutching the robe about her with her free hand, she hurried off along the tunnel. All the years she'd worked for this day; she wasn't going to let it be snatched away from her at the last minute. Oh, that treacherous little Woodbridge slug! Renegade! Turncoat! He gotten his own revenge by burning Rafe Dampier, and now he'd jumped ship to save his own rotten hide. Cheat her out of her justice, would he? Dampier had been nothing when her son had died. He hadn't even been born when her husband died. Dampier had never mattered much to her. It was the others, the whole evil institution, that she'd sworn to destroy.

All the money she'd poured into helping that idiot Elphick! It had seemed like a good investment when she had to flee from Rose Hall, thanks to young Brad's murderous attack on Dampier. She'd fled in her coach with hardly a rag on her back, but confident that there was a refuge waiting for her in Weypool. Well, there had been, but she certainly hadn't expected it to be so grand. He'd done very well for himself with her money, had Master Lion Elphick. He would swing now, serve him right. And very likely the king would call it treason and give him the full disembowelment treatment while the crowds jeered and laid bets on how long he'd take to die. Same with all of them. And very likely Baby Rat Woodbridge, too. The others would squeal on him and tell how he'd magicked their way into the Jones factory. With luck he would get burned for witchcraft, as Mark had burned. She hoped he'd have a long time in a dark cell to look forward to that.

Not her. She was going to return to the Mother very soon. It would be instantaneous and painless, and she would be made welcome, a daughter who had kept the faith.

The gritty dust was abrading her feet, but she ignored that. The pain would stop soon. She was close now, ducking under the poles. She had brought no fuse, but she didn't need a fuse. The lamp flame alone would do.

CHAPTER 41

"YOUR HIGHNESS! THIS IS INDEED A GREAT HONOR!" THE chief archivist was a tiny husk of a man with a wispy mop and beard of white curls. He bowed to the regent as low as he could, disappearing from view behind the counter and giving the impression that he would grovel if he could just get down to the floor unaided.

The archive hall was very long, with many tables lined up under the windows along the right-hand side. Rollo could not tell how wide it was, because the opposite side displayed only the ends of ceiling-high bookshelves that extended out of sight. The tables were mostly stacked with books, papers, and scrolls, but four or five of them were in use, and the stoop-shouldered men working at them had turned to stare in amazement at the sight of the royal visitor. Rollo assumed that King Ethan had not been seen there often.

Having reappeared from below the counter, the old man was babbling to the prince. "It is about the extra shelving, of course, Your Highness, and we are all greatly honored to see that you have realized the urgency and importance of the national records so early in your reign, er, rule, and if Your Highness would care to come this way...er, no?"

"No!" Prince Emil started over. "I come on very urgent business, Chief Archivist, literally a matter of life and death. Conybear and Tillman, famous generals."

"Indeed, yes, Your Highness. Victors in many great—"

"Where are they buried?"

"What?"

A middle-aged man arose from the nearest table and wandered closer. He wore eyeglasses and the sort of smock scriveners used to protect their clothes from ink stains and dust. He was obviously listening to the conversation. Emil recognized the situation and began addressing him, while not quite ignoring the ancient mummy officially in charge.

Meanwhile, a couple of book-laden apprentices had emerged from the stacks to gape. Rollo recognized the closer one as a follower of the Mother, having led the bonding circle where he had been initiated a few months ago. The lad naturally knew Prelate Hawke and was astounded to see him in the company of the regent. That was tricky, but news of their association was certain to get out sooner or later, and then both churches would start wondering who was selling out to whom. But all problems were merely challenges, and perhaps some good might come of this one. Rollo beckoned the lad with a twitch of his head and walked around the end of the counter. He smiled as the lad hurried to meet him halfway, both arms full of books.

"Obviously you know me, but I would prefer it that you do not mention my name here. I'm ashamed to admit that I can't recall yours."

"Paul Peabody, Your, er, sir."

"Paul, it is extremely urgent that His Highness and I discover where certain ancient warriors were buried. I don't have time to explain. Do you have any maps of the old Weypool catacombs?"

He knew he was trying a very long shot. Apprentices, especially junior apprentices, did drudge work, so books to Paul might be just heavy objects to be filed on shelves. The journeymen archivists were much more likely to know what was in them.

But long shots also hit marks, if not always the one expected. Paul Peabody dropped his entire load, and all of the heaviest volumes seemed to aim for Rollo's feet. He knelt to help the boy gather them up. The lad's hands were shaking, and his face had turned as white as milk, so pale that childhood freckles had emerged faintly, as if through an adolescent mist. Apprentices could certainly get beaten, and archivists' apprentices might be fired for the crime of dropping books, but his terror suggested worse horrors than that.

"Paul," Rollo whispered, "I won't tell anyone and you won't be punished if I can help it, but for the Mother's sake tell me who got them!"

Mouth quavering, Peabody whispered back. "He said it was for the M-m-mother's sake. They were s-s-sacred and the Children should have them."

"Who said that?"

"Brother Gower."

"When?"

"Just after I…about a year ago."

They stood up at the same moment, and Rollo carefully balanced his heap of books on top of those the boy held. "Thank you, Paul. That helps me."

But not much. Gower was one of the leaders of the Underground, and such a notorious tightwad that Rollo doubted the boy would have even been paid for his treachery. He walked back to the group at the counter, which had now been joined by three other archivists and First Secretary Kipping. Had the archives office ever been honored by such illustrious visitors before, or offered such effusive service?

The prince was growing testy. "No, I do not want to sit down! I want information! *Why* can't you find them right now?"

"Because of lack of space, Your Highness," said one of them, with the air of someone repeating words said before. "We have baskets and boxes piled high back there, and it can take weeks to find such ancient material."

Master Kipping inserted himself into the discussion with a diplomatic cough. "Conybear's career ended during the reign of Queen Ingrid III, as I recall. His burial would likely have taken place outside the old city, but Weypool has spread out enormously since those days. Our information is that other notable warriors were interred near him, so that the site may have become a sort of dedicated military cemetery. Are there any descriptions of state funerals that—"

Two archivists said, "Aha!" simultaneously. Both wheeled around and took off at a shuffling run, shouting for help from juniors who had stayed out of the conference. They all vanished into the stacks.

"Perchance we are getting somewhere!" the prince said, drumming fingers on the counter. Time was going by, and a ton of stolen dynamite...

The prince glanced suspiciously at Rollo. "You know that boy?"

Rollo discarded an impulse to lie, although he knew that the truth might mean trouble for Paul Peabody. Emil was quite capable of guessing how and why Rollo knew the boy, and the palace would not knowingly employ heretics. "I recognized him, sir, but I have never spoken to him before. In my experience, the most junior apprentice may know things that the shop master has forgotten. In this case, he didn't."

"Mmf." That was a royal *mmf,* and ominous.

One of the archivists came running into view again, followed by his minions and waving a slim book. He laid it on the counter, while everyone else gathered around.

"A life of the great Marshall Bonser, Your Highness."

"He was mentioned, yes."

"An account of his funeral..." The archivist pawed at the ancient pages.

More time passed. The archivist was visibly sweating as he hunted for an account of Bonser's funeral. There was no sign of the second expedition returning with whatever it had been seeking. A ton of gunpowder...

Somehow Rollo became aware that he was being bombarded with silent psychic messages, although that was not a recognized gift of the Mother. He glanced up and saw young Paul Peabody hovering in the background, clutching a roll of vellum and staring appealing at the great Prelate Hawke.

"You found something, boy?" Rollo asked loudly.

Paul gulped and edged closer. "A map of the old city, sir. It shows the sacred...I mean, the heretical woods where the ungodly worshiped and that were destroyed by the true—"

"Yes! Yes!" Everyone was looking and listening.

"One of them is called Conybear Grove, sir..."

Of course the Children would have consecrated a sacred grove above an especially honored catacomb! Bram had mentioned that the individual graves near Conybear's looked as if many bodies had been crammed into them.

In a flash the map was spread on the counter with Kipping and the prince peering at it and everyone else trying to squeeze in. Paul had already vanished back into obscurity. The ink was faded, the writing cramped and antiquated. A babble of voices tried to be helpful: "Here it is!" "Junction of the North Highway Way and..." "Looks like 'Sailor' maybe?" "Skinners. Skinners Road." "This part of the North Highway was widened and renamed Parade Way when the Coronet Temple was built." "Skinners Road stops at the temple now..." "So the catacomb under the old Conybear Grove is under the temple now?" "Which building of the temple?" "On the north—"

"The Meeting Hall!" Emil roared, banging his fist on the counter. "They're right underneath the Meeting Hall!"

"And the Hierarchy is meeting today!" Kipping said.

Regent and first secretary shot out the door together, leaving the assembled archivists openmouthed. On the point of following, Rollo paused long enough to prod a finger at the middle-aged man who seemed to be the effective leader.

"That's a very smart apprentice you have there. See that he is well rewarded!" Then he, too, dashed away. He had no authority to issue orders in the royal palace, but all the archivists knew about him was that he was a friend of the regent. That would be enough, as long as Paul had the sense not to name him.

By then Emil and Kipping had already disappeared. They could run without being challenged, but Rollo had no credentials and was humbly dressed. If he drew attention to himself like that, he would be stopped and questioned. Fortunately, his finding talent, although not as strong as Wisdom Edith's, was quite capable of locating a ruler in his own palace. He headed that way without hesitation.

He located his quarry already out in the stable yard, waiting impatiently while four fine grays were being harnessed to a coach. More stable hands were rushing about in the background, and frantic fusiliers were even saddling their own mounts so they would not be left behind. Everyone was carefully not noticing that the regent and the first secretary were arguing furiously.

"Guards are not the problem!" the first secretary said. "Guards cannot stop a mine blowing up. I am expendable, sir, and you are not."

"You are far from expendable. And you will never be admitted."

"I will go with Master Kipping," Rollo said. They both turned to him in shock.

"You?"

"I escaped from Swine Hall. I can get Master Kipping into the hierarchs' Meeting Hall."

Emil shook his head in disbelief. His eyes seemed to be bulging even more than usual. "You know what they will do to you if they catch you! You cannot take that risk."

"I cannot take the risk of the lunatics blowing up the Hierarchy, Your Highness. That will provoke a pogrom. All the Mother's Children will burn then."

Emil shrugged in surrender. He pulled off the ring he wore, which had been his father's until the previous day, and gave it to Kipping. "Take this, then. Go in the Light, both of you."

The postilion cracked his whip, horseshoes clattered on cobbles, and the coach rumbled forward to the waiting dignitaries. A white-faced lieutenant in the fusiliers arrived also, leading his mount.

"The captain has ordered me to lead the first squad, sir."

"The temple Meeting Hall, at the junction of Parade Way and Skinners Road," Kipping told him. "As fast as you possibly can!"

Orders were barked, bugles blown, passengers embarked. In moments Rollo and Kipping were clinging to straps and bouncing as the cumbersome vehicle gathered speed along the driveway. Their escort raced ahead and behind in no sort of order.

"If I were a mistrustful sort of person, Prelate, I might suspect that this gunpowder plot was a scam intended to let you pose as a hero." Kipping had a surprisingly attractive smile. It was probably rarely used, but it helped explain Maddy's obvious love for him.

Kipping himself was probably one of the most mistrustful persons in the kingdom. That would be a major requirement for his great office.

"Sir, I would be flattered to be thought capable of organizing it under the circumstances. Pardon my saying that many persons will assume the Privy Council organized it."

"What on earth for?"

"To incriminate the Children? To stage a dramatic rescue of the hierarchs and so win their approval? Both?"

The coach rocked violently as it hurtled through the great gates and cornered on two wheels. Bugles ahead shrilled, warning everyone else to clear the way.

"We may be overly alarmed," Kipping said, more seriously. "The powder was stolen only last night. If we are right in believing that the Meeting Hall is the plotters' objective, they could not have foreseen an opportunity to destroy the Hierarchy arising so soon. They may not even have moved their loot into place. Supreme Uptree called this meeting late yesterday, after learning that the council had appointed a regent. I'm sure he had not foreseen that. He can't have a full session at such short notice, maybe six or seven of the ten."

"If the people I suspect are behind this diabolical plot, I advise you never to underestimate them, First Secretary."

"And whom do you suspect?"

"They call themselves the Underground," Rollo said, avoiding naming names. The hardest problem ahead now was to save his young brother from torture and a traitor's frightful death. "Bradwell Armstrong knows. He is willing to turn king's evidence. He probably helped them steal the powder but was coerced into doing so. He escaped and came to me to confess."

"And just how did he know where to find you, Prelate?"

"Much the same way I located you and the prince just now."

Kipping pulled a face and said, "Oh."

The talents the Mother gave some of her Children frightened the Sons of the Sun, who preferred to deny their existence, and that merely made them more effective. While Rollo had been held in Caverleigh, supposedly incommunicado, he had received three offers of rescue. He had refused them because he had given Master Carey his parole. It would not be tactful to mention them now. Kipping and he were momentary allies, but their cooperation was fragile and might be very brief.

A dead fish hit the window and bounced away. Still the bugles wailed their warnings, wheels clattered, and hooves drummed, but the racket included yells of outrage and a few screams as the royal cavalcade thundered along Parade Way, overturning barrows and people alike. As long as there were no enormous explosions, all was still well.

"How are my patients this morning, First Secretary?"

"Ah...in the turmoil I have forgotten to thank you. My wife is much improved. She is still weak, of course, but conscious. She was asking for...for your sister! Mindy has been very good to her."

"And His Majesty? No change?"

Kipping shook his head. He was undoubtedly troubled by the risk he had taken in seeking Rollo's help for the royal invalid. That move could destroy him if the Church of the Light learned of it, although Rollo was now fairly sure that Prince Emil had initiated the move. It might destroy him, too.

How was Brat faring, leading his guards to the mine itself? If the king's men caught the thieves red-handed, the fanatics would resist arrest. One musket shot into the gunpowder would answer Rollo's question the bad way, and Brat would be a dead hero. Which might be better than being judged a living traitor.

The noise outside changed; the coach slowed.

It had barely stopped before Kipping scrambled out, and Rollo was right behind him. They were at the junction they had sought, with the Meeting Hall looming over them, although it was one of the least imposing buildings in the temple complex. The lieutenant slid from his saddle almost at their feet.

"We believe the mine is directly below this building," Kipping said, "but it could be off target. And it could blow at any minute."

The lieutenant nodded and licked his lips. He glanced back along Parade Way, no doubt wondering when his captain would arrive with reinforcements. It could not be too soon.

"Clear the streets as far back as you can—at least two hundred paces. Then clear the buildings."

"Sir! Sir, on what grounds? Do I tell them about the mine, sir?" He might not be as green as he looked. There was going to be a panic.

Kipping looked to Rollo, who shrugged helplessly. What other excuse could they possibly invent?

The first secretary said, "Just tell them…tell them there's a fire burning in an old catacomb under here and the ground may collapse. Stay out of the plaza. I will deal with that. Come!" he told Rollo.

They ran for the nearest arch, for all temple buildings faced inward. A trio of Church Police were standing there, having heard the commotion and come to defend the holy precincts. All three wore gold and blue livery and had cudgels hanging at their sides. The largest was a beefy, coarse-faced man in his twenties, and was obviously the senior because his chest displayed the grandest sunburst.

"Deacon, I am the king's first secretary and am sent by the regent on a most urgent matter."

"May the Lord bless your labors, William."

"Is the Hierarchy meeting now?"

The big man waited a beat or two before saying, "Of course, I am not at liberty to answer that question. I think you know that."

"His Highness has ordered the streets and buildings around here cleared because there is grave danger of the ground collapsing."

"You know that the government's writ does not run within the temple, William."

"Even to warn the hierarchs that a group of mad heretics is planning to blow them up and may do so at any moment?"

That made the deacon hesitate. His eyes flicked to Rollo without any signs of recognition, then back to Kipping.

"How do I know that you are who you say you are?"

"This is the king's signet, given to me by the regent to show that I speak for him. Now, will you start to understand?"

"You will have to speak to someone with more authority than I, William. Beadle, escort Master Kipping to the—"

"DEACON! JUST STANDING HERE, YOU ARE IN DANGER OF DYING AT ANY MOMENT. YOU MUST DO EXACTLY WHAT THE FIRST SECRETARY SAYS."

Blink.

Kipping said, "First we must empty this building. Quickly!"

The deacon spun around. "Come this way, Master Kipping."

All five hurried around to the front of the building. The great plaza seemed almost deserted, and yet there were at least a hundred of people there. Most of them were heading in this direction, having heard the commotion in the streets outside the colonnade. The entrance to the Meeting Hall was guarded by a squad of no less than eight, under the command of an archdeacon, who was armed with a flintlock pistol and looked no more cooperative than his subordinate. Obviously, the Hierarchy must be in session. Did the Underground know that?

The conversation followed much the same lines as before, and it was obvious that Kipping was not going anywhere by himself. But Rollo got his chance when the officer demanded to know who he was.

He dared not attempt mastery on so many, although it occurred to him that Brat might be able to. He stepped closer and gave his commands in a whisper, ending with, "AND SALUTE ME."

The archdeacon did. "Sir!" His followers would be impressed at their commander so honoring a layman.

"Get everyone out of this building and at least two hundred paces away," Kipping said. "And take us to the exalted hierarchs."

The archdeacon barked orders, then led the way inside and upstairs at a run. Two of his men followed. The first two stories were apartments for hierarchs visiting from out of town, he said, and known to be empty "at present." The stairs ended at the third level and two doors. One was secured with heavy bolts, and to this the archdeacon directed his men. "Move everyone back to the next building and keep them there."

There must be a walkway along the top of the colonnade, and Rollo had not known that. The other door led out into a small anteroom, which was obviously empty. If the hierarchs were in this building, they must be behind the door on the far side of that. The archdeacon stopped and shot a worried look at Rollo, who was his current master, although he could not be truly aware of that.

"You have the key?" Kipping demanded.

"No." The reply was directed to Rollo. "The junior hierarch locks up when the meeting ends. At the moment, it is bolted on the inside and will not be opened for anyone."

"Try! Knock! Louder, man! Kick it. Beat on it with your pistol." The first secretary was obviously feeling the strain.

So was Rollo. Beads of cold sweat crept down his ribs. This was the lions' den. Inside there were his mortal foes, men who would never let him walk out a free man if they could stop him. Men who would kill him.

If his friends did not kill him first.

CHAPTER 42

SUPREME HIERARCH GARRETT UPTREE SAT UNEASY ON HIS throne. It had been a long time since anyone had outwitted him, and he was not yet ready to admit that what had happened yesterday was anything more than a lucky fluke. Even the greatest fool will do the right thing once in a while.

He might have been hasty in calling this assembly, but it would give the other hierarchs a chance to react if they wanted to. Excessive zeal always looked better than being caught napping. Now if the regency turned out badly for the Church, he could not be blamed for inattention.

The supreme had an automatic seat on the Privy Council, but Garrett rarely bothered to attend in person. Lately he had been sending Exalted Ledbury in his place. Ledbury's prayers for the sick were granted more often than most clerics' were—heretics would say he had accepted a gift from their demon goddess, but the penalties for such slanders were severe. So Ledbury had been one of those treating the king's illness, and he had been able to report on his progress to the Privy Council. There had been no progress—until yesterday. Last night Ledbury had hurried back to the temple to inform Garrett that His Majesty, while not exactly improved, did seem to be resting more easily and naturally. The old tyrant might last a little longer than expected, possibly even a week.

He had also reported that the Privy Council had dared to appoint Prince Emil regent. The Hierarchy had not anticipated a regency, and Ledbury's objections had been overruled. Garrett had summoned this emergency meeting.

Only seven had turned up, including himself and old Wyatt Ostler, who had to be given a special welcome and a smatter of applause just for dragging his creaking carcass out of bed. Also present was James Ingram, Garrett's nominee to replace the unlamented Exalted Wybrow. Ingram was a smart youngster, who had been a protégé of his for many years, a reliable aide and henchman. His approval had been unanimous, as usual, but some of the exalted had cast their votes with a show of hesitation, which was their way of indicating disapproval. With the king a-dying, this was not a good time for the hierarchs to be less than rigidly supportive of their leader.

"The question, Your Excellencies," Garrett explained, "is whether we allow this alleged regency to pass without challenge. If we have the right to approve or disapprove the normal succession, we must have the right to approve or disapprove a temporary kingship, which is what a regency is."

"Well, no," he had to admit a moment later, in answer to a question. "It may indeed matter, because now it seems that the old...that His Majesty will linger longer than we expected. Exalted Ledbury?"

Ledbury explained, carefully qualifying his answer and covering his assumptions.

"Furthermore," Garrett continued, "the Grand Council has been summoned to meet three weeks from now. The rustic nobles will have time to arrive, and their views tend to be old-fashioned." That meant *heretical* in temple talk. "If we are to overturn this regency nonsense, Your Excellencies, we had better do it quickly."

Listening to the predictable grumbles that a country needed a ruler, even only for a week or two, Garrett was amazed that no one else seemed to share his suspicions of conspiracy. Should he press the point or just confess that he had been hasty in calling the meeting? To admit mistakes was worse than making them. Mistakes could be denied; confessions could not.

Then Abel Eastwell raised a hand.

What did he want? Garrett hated surprises. "Exalted?"

Abel rose. He had an odd look in his eye. "Your Holiness, Exalted Hierarchs…a couple of weeks ago, we received information that the notorious John Hawke, leader of the heretics, was hiding out in—"

Garrett thumped the floor with the Teacher's staff. "Exalted, your supervision of the Powers of Darkness portfolio is a very important responsibility, but at the moment we are discussing court politics."

He expected the youngster to collapse back on his chair, mumbling apologies about still learning the rules of procedure. That did not happen.

"What I have to say is relevant, Your Holiness—extremely relevant."

The chairman nodded crossly, hiding his misgivings.

"By fortunate chance, this sighting came right after the murder of Exalted Rafe Dampier, and quite close by, so we had forces in the area. Our men reacted with commend-able promptitude. But they were too late. The hawk had flown." If that was a joke, it was in very bad taste. Young Ingram tried a grin and hurriedly buried it when he saw the scowls.

"Come to the point, please." Garrett was already won-dering if his choice of Eastwell to succeed Dampier had been wise. There had been a notable lack of news coming out of the Powers of Darkness Department since Eastwell had been put in charge. That might just be a new chief tightening up procedures, but it could have more sinister explanations.

"The point is, Your Holiness, that we have good reason to believe that the Church Police were forestalled. Less than an hour before they arrived, John Hawke and his wife were taken away by Walter Carey, a lackey of Master William Kip—"

Uproar, very loud.

Garrett needed an unprecedented three bangs of the staff to restore order.

"Why were we not informed of this?"

More important, why had *he* not been informed?

"Because the heretic has not been charged, has not appeared in court, and the palace has made no announce-ment. We are certain that he was deliberately spirited away to safety before we could arrest him. If so, then heresy has penetrated the government to the highest levels." He paused, but the room was silent now. "It seems very likely that the heretics also have spies within the Church itself. I ordered all information withheld until I could identify the traitor or traitors."

"Am I a suspect?" Garrett accompanied the words with his frostiest glare.

Eastwell did not flinch. "Of course not, Holiness, but you employ an extensive staff, and your office, as the very heart of the Church, would be the best place to put a spy. I am happy to assure you that our investigations there have so far gone unrewarded. The Privy Council has provided better hunting. We kept watch on Master Carey and so learned that Hawke was being held under house arrest in a royal mansion not far from the palace."

Garrett had underestimated Abel Eastwell. This speech would be the making of him. From now on he would be a man to watch in the Hierarchy. He would certainly win election to supreme many years before the normal age.

It was hard to find ability not coupled with ambition, or ambition not tinged with ruthlessness. Had he been underestimating Abel Eastwell all these years?

"So we knew where Hawke was being held," he continued, "but he was under armed guard, and we were hesitant to storm a royal property to arrest him. We also wanted to see who came to see him—and the answer was nobody except Carey. Until yesterday. Yesterday Carey brought a woman with him. She is the first secretary's mistress, going by the name of Mindy Wells. Legally she is the wife of a former quarry worker named Stroud. Her maiden name was Madeline Woodbridge, and she was the sister of Rollo Woodbridge, better known to you as John Hawke."

Oh, wonderful! Oh, praise the Lord! There was all the evidence needed to destroy the inquisitive Master Kipping utterly.

But clearly there was more to come. No one moved as much as an eyelash.

"Carey then took Hawke, his wife, and his sister back to Kipping's residence. Kipping was waiting for them there. Exalted Ledbury, you remarked on the change in the king's appearance? Yesterday afternoon, for above an hour, all His Majesty's attendants were removed, while Kipping took John Hawke into the sickroom to apply his diabolical witchcraft…"

Only a sixth thump of the staff restored order.

"You can prove this?"

"I have a reliable witness, Your Holiness."

Eastwell was holding something back, though, perhaps just the names of his spies in the royal palace. Garrett made a mental note to demand a list of them.

"Then I think the Congregation of Conformity should invite Master Kipping in for a little chat. Or even a long interrogation?"

Smiles exposed teeth all around the hall. Garrett was not the only one with a grudge against the first secretary.

One man started to laugh, which was not the same thing at all.

Exalted Wyatt Ostler was a former supreme and a life-long friend of King Ethan, who had appointed him to his Privy Council decades ago. He was so infirm and unsteady now that he had almost given up attending meetings of either body, but he had bestirred himself more often of late, as the king's health failed. Garrett planned to boot him from the Hierarchy as soon as possible.

The old relic did not attempt to rise. "Think you're aiming at the wrong game, Uptree. Knew him as a boy, you know. Smart nipper, he was."

It took Garrett a moment to unravel that tangle. He couldn't possibly be referring to Kipping, who was the son of an obscure attorney.

"The prince?"

"O' course! Emil. I was there yesterday, at the meeting, when he was 'asked if he would serve'! Fine joke, that! You not notice, Ledbury?"

"Notice what?" Ledbury's voice rasped.

"Different man altogether. Quick he was, as a nipper. Changed a lot 'bout the time his whiskers grew in. Now changed back. Fooled you all, did he?"

Garrett drew a deep breath. There might still be time to save this situation.

"Then we thank you for these observations. Exalteds, we return to my initial question: Do we allow this regency to stand? If His Majesty lasts a week or two…and if Hawke has been allowed to employ his foul witchcraft on our king, then only the Lord himself knows how long his sufferings may be extended. By the time the Grand Council assembles…"

He did not need to finish. *It will be too late.* By the time the Grand Council assembled, Emil would be firmly entrenched as his father's successor, and if Emil was indeed the puppet master—pulling Kipping's strings, flirting with the arch-witch Hawke himself—that would be a disaster.

At that moment someone started to hammer on the door.

That had never happened before.

And it did not stop.

Ingram, as junior hierarch, rose without asking for permission or waiting for instructions. No doubt he intended just to peek out and see what emergency could possibly have provoked such an intrusion, but the moment he slid the bolt, the door was flung open, sending him staggering back.

Thereupon entered an officer of the Church Police, First Secretary William Kipping, and another man. It was Kipping who spoke, or rather shouted.

"Your Excellencies! More than a ton of gunpowder was stolen last night from the Jones factory. We have reliable information that it is being used to plant a mine directly under this building. You are in very grave danger."

Uncharacteristically, Garrett found himself at a complete loss for words. Such an outrage could not possibly be real. A hoax? A brainstorm? But who...?

The first person to move was Exalted Eastwell. Calling, "Swann, help me!" he rushed to Ostler. He and Exalted Swann hoisted the old man, chair and all, and carried him toward the door. If Ledbury thought the heretics were capable of such an obscenity, one might be wise to take the warning seriously. All the others were heading for the exit anyway, so Garrett decided that discretion was the better part of dignity. He ran after them, thumping the Teacher's staff to increase his speed.

CHAPTER 43

THE QUICKEST WAY TO LEAVE THE MEETING HALL WAS through the door to the private path. The archdeacon was first out, turning west, and everyone else followed, heading toward the library and the Temple Palace. Garrett made sure he was the last, though, and forced himself to proceed at a dignified walk.

The so-called path along the top of the colonnade was wide enough to take a coach and four, had there been any way to get one up there. Its privacy came from its flanking marble parapets, which were high enough to hide even tall men from spectators at ground level. Garrett could see through its latticed panels, which provided views of both the plaza and the street outside, that there was indeed a general evacuation underway, with scores of royal troopers herding the crowds back with the aid of riding crops. Inside the temple the Church Police were doing the same thing, but on foot. They had fewer people to deal with.

The plague spot at the center of this mass migration was certainly the Meeting Hall. Kipping must be very sure of his information. Unless it was all an elaborate hoax, he had displayed great courage in bringing the warning in person. That would be annoying, but it would not save him. This would be his swan song. His fate was sealed, his goose cooked, his fat fried. Exalted Eastwell's charges were serious enough that the first secretary should not even be allowed to leave the temple precincts. He could be arrested right here and now. That show of authority ought to bring the so-called regent to heel also.

As he progressed around the curve, Supreme Garrett came in sight of his former companions standing outside the library, in the company of four officers of the Church Police and half a dozen nosy acolytes and junior clerics. Wyatt Ostler was still seated on his chair, clutching his cane and leering toothlessly as if this was the most fun he'd had in years. Everyone was watching Garrett's approach, or perhaps they were waiting for the Meeting Hall behind him to explode. He suspected they might wait long enough for that.

Gunpowder, yes. Of course. Of course, searchers would produce barrels of powder they had found in some ancient catacomb under the temple, but who had put them there, mm? That would be the unsolved mystery, a mystery Garrett had just solved to his own satisfaction—Kipping's own men, who else? What better way to disrupt the Hierarchy, make a political point, and distract people's attention from Emil's illegal seizure of power? Tomorrow, without doubt, Kipping's men would search the catacombs and discover the missing powder. If that scheming fool had thought this scam up on his own, he was not as good as schemer as he thought he was.

Garrett reached the men at the library door, stopped, and leaned on the staff, his attention on the junior busybodies at the back of the group. They flinched, as well they might.

"If you do not have work to do, go and ask your superiors to give you some."

They fled. So much for them.

"No, Archdeacon. We did not mean you. You and your men must stay. We may have work for you in a moment."

Now Kipping. Who ought to kneel in the presence of the supreme hierarch. What a trivial, insignificant man he was to presume to head a government! "The Lord must love ordinary men, because he made so many of them," Verse 384. To which the humorists responded, *And he made a few like us to lead them.*

"Your explanation of this outrageous intrusion, William?"

"Just what I said, Your Holiness. Heretic terrorists raided the Weypool gunpowder works last night and stole a wagonload of it. They moved their loot to the Conybear catacomb, which underlies your Meeting Hall. Fortunately, we had an agent among them, who alerted us in time...we hope in time. Even now he is leading the king's men to the site. Once we have the powder secured, then you will be notified that it is safe to resume your meeting. The culprits will be rounded up and brought to justice."

"We hope you will have more success at keeping them... this...time..." Garrett had just noticed the other man standing in Kipping's shadow. He was young, slim, dressed like a clerk. But he wasn't groveling as a clerk should in the presence of the primate of all Albi.

Had Garrett not being wearing his skullcap, his hair might have stood on end. Suddenly he was quite positive that he knew who that arrogant youngster was, staring at him with icy-cold blue eyes.

"Present your companion, William."

"He is not important at—"

"I am Rollo Woodbridge, rightful owner of the Stonebridge Mill."

Two of the watching hierarchs twitched in alarm, confirming Garrett's long-held suspicions. Even better! The notorious John Hawke had walked right into the lions' den. He would not escape so easily this time. And he must not be allowed to issue threats about Stonebridge.

"But you are better known by another name?"

"Sometimes. You ought to fire your miller, Uptree. When my father owned the mill, he charged the lowest rates in the county, and it was always busy. The oaf you have running it now is too greedy, so it stands idle two-thirds of the time. I don't suppose you care much, since it didn't cost you anything."

"Archdeacon, arrest that blasphemer."

"Don't!" Kipping snapped. He held up a glittering jewel. "This is the monarch's ring, given to me by the regent as a token that my companion and I come here in his name."

"The king's writ does not run within the temple."

"The king's peace is the king's business everywhere. Would you rather we had left you and your companions in there to die, Your Holiness? Treason is certainly the king's business. Lay a hand on either of us, Archdeacon, and you will be hanged for it."

Not bad, for so unimpressive a little man. He did not bluster. But he did not convince, either.

"Archdeacon, arrest them both and put them in separate cells. Bring me that ring when you have done so."

"ARCHDEACON, PAY NO ATTENTION TO HIM," said the heretic. "If there are going to be arrests, Father Uptree, then we should begin with you, a thief and forger."

Two or three hierarchs tried to protest at the same time, while Garrett silently cursed greedy Osborn. He banged the Teacher's staff on the marble paving, but it made no significant sound.

"If I recall correctly, a mill at Stonebridge was bequeathed to the Church in the will of the previous owner. If my name appears in the affair at all, it must be because I signed the acceptance as the Church's attorney at that time."

"Not so," Kipping said. "The title deeds show you as the personal owner, but they are clumsy forgeries."

"He also," Hawke said, "conspired to murder my parents."

"Your parents were smitten by the hand of the Lord."

"As was Rafe Dampier himself, two years later?"

"I will not stand for this!" Garrett said and crashed hard into Hierarch Ingram. They took Exalted Ledbury down with them as they fell, and only then did the terrible noise register. Paving rocked and cracked. The parapets on the plaza side collapsed, dropping jagged slabs of rock on human flesh. Men screamed like hurt children, and one of them was Garrett himself. The pain in his leg was worse than anything he had ever imagined. There was darkness, and people were choking and coughing in the dust, but all that mattered was the pain.

Rollo was saved by the hierarchs standing between him and the blast. He was thrown down by one of them, collided with a policeman, and they all three fell in a heap. The noise was what he was to remember most vividly. His ears rang for hours afterward. That and the choking dust, the reek of sulfur, the screams of the wounded. Later he discovered that a flying fragment had sliced off the lobe of his left ear. The gash had bled copiously, of course, but at the time he did not even feel it.

His first concern was Kipping, who lay beside him with shocked eyes staring out of a dusty mask. He had a bleeding wound on his forehead. Rollo touched it gently, stopped the bleeding, and found no sign of fracturing.

"All right, sir?"

"I think so. You?"

"Probably." Rollo struggled free. "You should go home and lie down for a day or so." The hierarch who had hit him was clearly dead, with the back of his head smashed in. Several others were lying where they fell, but most were getting up. The police officer was white with shock and clutching a bleeding shoulder.

"Let me help," Rollo said, and laid a hand on the wound. He sensed extreme pain and soothed it; he stanched the blood. "You'll need to have that arm set." In other circumstances, the man's astonishment at the improvement would have been funny.

One of the priests began chanting, and another joined in. They were crouching in the rubble above a man who was gasping in pain.

"Hawke!" Kipping said. "Supreme Garrett is hurt."

"So he is!" Rollo tried to get close, and more hierarchs jostled him out of the way. They picked up the wailing prayer. Rollo stood it as long as he could and then dragged the smallest priest aside. "STOP THAT RACKET, ALL OF YOU! I can't think when you're making that noise." In the shocked silence, he squatted to take a closer look. Garrett's thigh was pumping out blood.

"You are going to bleed out in a few minutes, Holiness. Bleed to death, you understand? You know who I am and what I can do. Do you want me to heal you, or would you rather die?"

The old scoundrel mumbled incoherently, not truly conscious. But one of the others shouted, "Help him!" and other voices joined in. So Rollo laid a hand on the wound and stopped the bleeding. The bone was unbroken, but the flesh had been badly crushed. If the supreme hierarch ever walked on that leg again, it would be with a severe limp. But he would live.

Rollo wiped his bloody hands on his doublet and stood up again. Now he could take a moment to survey the damage. Either the Underground had miscalculated the location of their mine, or the sheer weight of the Meeting Hall had diverted the explosion. The colonnade to the west had taken the worst of it. The next arch from where he stood was still there, although its paving was badly cracked and one parapet had collapsed into the street. Beyond that lay nothing but a crater and heaps of rock and rubble. The near side of the Meeting Hall was gone, exposing fancy bedroom furniture on two levels, and the hall itself above that standing open, revealing all its sumptuous ivory and gold mosaic ornamentation. What would the poor of Weypool say to that extravagance? The Teacher had raised a rebellion against the Church of the Mother because its leaders had become corrupt and decadent. The disease had returned.

"There are some wounded down there," he told Kipping. "I should go down there and—"

He did not finish, because he was seized from behind in a choke hold.

CHAPTER 44

BRAT RODE BACK ALONG PARADE WAY AT THE CAPTAIN'S side. They were returning much more slowly than they had sallied forth, although the prisoners tethered behind some of the horses were almost running. Curious crowds watched their progress, unwilling to jeer or cheer until they knew who the villains were, and why.

He was a hero now! He wondered what the Underground had been trying to blow up and how many lives he'd saved by turning king's evidence. He hoped he had prevented more deaths today than he had caused in the past. The only death he didn't regret, the only person he'd really meant to kill, was Rafe Dampier. He was *really* sorry about the others. Nobody could prove that he'd killed Dampier. He hadn't even been in the church. If he'd killed Dampier, then Dampier had killed Brat's parents. He ought to get a royal pardon, surely!

The captain would be a hero, too. Yet he kept giving Brat suspicious looks.

"So you were one of the gang? Why'd you decide to fink?"

"I wasn't one of them. I was forced to help. I escaped."

The captain looked away with his mustache curled in a sneer of disbelief. No one liked snitches.

They rode through the gates, into the palace park. Lion and his gang were headed for cells and chains. Brat wondered where he was headed: to a cell, like them, or to the throne room to be thanked by His Majesty? Might be wiser not to find out.

He'd escaped from Umberly Castle, so they wouldn't take any chances with him this time. He glanced around and saw clumps of trees, lots of open grassland, but lots of people, too. Men scything the grass. Gentlemen and some ladies out riding. No use trying to make a break for it here. Then came hope, like a ray of sunshine breaking through the clouds in his mind, for in the distance a black dog was trotting along parallel to the road he was on. Smut! Had he asked to be let out of Caverleigh House, and if so, how had he escaped from the grounds? Or was he just being a spirit guide, able to turn up where Brat needed him? Either way, he was a very comforting sight.

Thunder?

A couple of the fusiliers' horses shied. Brat kept control of his mare. Back from where they had come, a dark cloud was billowing up over the city like some obscene giant tree. The prisoners cheered. The captain roared for a fast trot, and had them all pulled off their feet and dragged to make them shut up. By then the cloud was thinning out and drifting away to the east.

When order was restored, the parade resumed. Kenrick scowled furiously at Brat.

"So there were two fuses? You brought me one and left the other!"

"Did not!" Brat yelled. "You'd have seen it burning in the dark."

"Not if it was hidden inside an empty barrel."

Oh, Mother, that was true! And a backup fuse would have been a good idea. *Mother, Mother, Mother!*

"There was only *one* fuse! You should have left guards watching the barrels. You should have left more men at the Blue Boar. And I *warned* you that there was another way in."

They glared at each other for the rest of the ride. They were both in deep trouble now.

What had been blown up? Not the palace, obviously, but perhaps the temple? Not the whole temple. He couldn't remember any of the other buildings that Alan had shown him; certainly none would have provoked the Underground into such an act. How many more dead? Why did death keep following him around like this?

They reached the stable yard, everyone dismounting at the same time. They had to look after the prisoners first before their horses. Brat distracted as hard as he could and led his mare into the darkness of the nearest stable. He stepped in front of a young stableman hurrying out to help—blocking him, making him jump because he hadn't seen the man and horse coming.

"Give me your hat, take my horse, and forget me."

Brat set off across the yard again, with the hat pulled well down, hoping he wouldn't get lice from it. No one shouted at him to stop. Soon he was slouching across the park with his dog trotting at his side. He hadn't been gone long before half a dozen mounted fusiliers came galloping out of the yard and scattered in all directions, obviously hunting for him. His disguise and his distraction held. They saw a boy and his dog, but they failed to *notice* them.

His feet and legs ached. He hadn't slept at all the previous night. It was noon, and he was hungry again— why did he *always* have to be hungry? And where was Smut leading him this time? Caverleigh House would be a deathtrap now. Everywhere would be a deathtrap now. He was *positive* there hadn't been a second fuse. Some Underground helpers must have stormed the Blue Boar, or come in the other way, or just been hiding somewhere in the catacombs. *Idiot* captain, not to have left men guarding the gunpowder! Brat had *told* him there was another way in.

Terrible questions kept echoing in his head. What had he helped to blow up? How many deaths this time? A man had a right to avenge his parents' deaths, didn't he? If the law wouldn't? A moral right. So why had the Mother heaped all these other deaths on him? He would die only once, but they might see he took a long time doing it.

Smut jostled against his leg, startling him as if he'd been walking in his sleep, which perhaps he had. They were approaching a house, walking up the driveway. It wasn't anything like Rose Hall or Caverleigh, but it was bigger than most of the houses he'd seen in Weypool. With a yelp of alarm, he dived into the flanking shrubbery and huddled down small. And stayed there.

In a moment Smut crept in beside him and whimpered.

"Go away," Brat said. "I'm just going to lie down here and sleep. I'm too tired to go on."

Smut whined louder, took hold of his sleeve, and tugged.

Brat smacked him away. He couldn't get up if he wanted to. So many troubles weighed him down, so tired…

His eyelids began to droop. He looked around for a flat space without rocks or roots. Smut howled like a wolf. Idiot dog! Where had he gone?

Howwwwl! again, even louder. He was standing on the driveway, in full view of the house. And *howwwwling.* Oh, Mother! Any minute now someone would send a servant to investigate, and Brat would be found.

"Smut! Stop that! You trying to get me killed?"

Howwwwl!

An upstairs window flew open and Maddy peered out. Smut looked up at her and wagged his tail.

Brat emerged from the bushes as she approached. She grabbed him, hugging as if she wanted to crush him to a pulp. "Oh, Brat, Brat, Brat! I thought you'd been blown up. You came back from the dead this morning, and I really thought you'd died again, so soon. You're not hurt? Whatever happened?"

He tried to tell her, but his voice wouldn't work properly. Oh, turds, his eyes…he was starting to cry.

"Whoa!" she said. "Relax. You're safe now. Fairly safe, anyway."

Suddenly he felt much better. "You're inspiring me!"

She smiled beautifully. "It's almost the only talent I've got. Well, come along. You can distract, can't you? You must be able to. So distract while we're going in. I'd rather nobody saw you for a while yet."

Maddy put an arm around him and walked him up to the house like that, as if he might fall down if she let go. Perhaps he would. Where had Smut gone?

"There's a big, gray-haired man called Steven Veal," she said as they reached the front door. "Distract as hard as you can if you see him. He's a hard man to deceive. You look as if you need…of course you do! You didn't get much sleep last night. You can sleep here, for a few hours at least."

He mumbled thanks.

There was a big, gray-haired man standing in the hall. He frowned at Maddy, but did not notice Brat, who was distracting like *mad*.

"Why did you do that, mistress—tearing out to pat a stray dog?"

"I thought it might be hurt."

"For all you knew, the brute might have been rabid."

"It's all right," she said. "I bit it and it ran away."

He watched her suspiciously as she led Brat upstairs. But suspicion was ingrained in his face.

The bedroom was obviously hers. It had the same colors as he remembered from Woodbridge Manor, the same feel, even the same scent. And it had a bed that just screamed to him to come and lie down. They went over to it.

"Just sit for a moment," she said. "Quickly, tell me what happened. I really thought you'd been blown up."

He forced his wits to work. "Went with the soldiers, down underground, found the powder, fuse burning, put it out." Something else? Oh yes. "Went back to the Blue Boar. His men arrested Lion and some of the others. I said who they were. But he didn't leave any guards on the powder!"

"You mean somebody else went back after you left?"

He nodded, eyelids dropping. "Where's Rollo?"

She hesitated, and he opened his eyes again.

"I don't know," she said. "He went off with the regent, and I came back here with Steven. Now you must get some sleep." She knelt to pull off his shoes. "Leave the shutters open. I'll lock that door and leave the key in it, see? So you can get out if you must. And I'll go out the other one and lock it on the far side, so no one can get in. Try not to snore!" She smiled and kissed him. Then she was gone.

Mother, help me to help him! And keep your Children safe. That was her other worry. The Coronet Temple was visible from the upstairs windows, so she knew the explosion had destroyed one of its lesser buildings. Had Rollo and the prince learned where the mine was located? If so, then they would certainly have sent warning, and she worried that Kipping might have taken the word himself. It sounded absurd, but the priests would not easily listen to orders from the palace.

Even if no one had died—if the mine had destroyed an empty building—the whole nation would be outraged. The laws against heresy would be multiplied and enforced; there would be lynchings and burnings. What crazy people had done this? Rollo would be thrown back into Swine Hall, Brat's efforts to help forgotten.

She went back to Irene's room, which was where she had been when Smut howled. Irene was much improved since Rollo treated her. She was leaning back on piled pillows, not quite upright, but not flat. And no longer comatose. She had her wits back.

"Well, my dear?"

Well what? Oh…dog… "It wasn't hurt. It ran off as soon as I appeared." Maddy sat down and took up the book she had been reading. "Where was I?"

"I don't recall, but I can see you're deathly worried about something. I would love to know why you gallop downstairs to comfort stray dogs. Is this a frequent affliction?"

Unwilling to lie, Maddy bit her lip and was silent.

Irene said, "I can't possibly tell anyone except William, and I promise I won't tell him."

"He already knows most of it. My real name is Madeline Woodbridge…" She saw at once that Irene already knew that much. One crack in the dam let out the flood. She told the whole terrible story, except that she did not mention that the pubescent boy wanted for treason, witchcraft, and multiple massacres was now asleep in the room across the hall. Irene reached out a hand to her.

Gratefully, Maddy took it. "This is disaster! You see? The Church will retaliate with a mass witch hunt. Bram and Rollo…two days ago I had no brothers and now I have two, and they will both be tortured and put to death!"

Irene sighed. "I thought I had escaped the cares of the world, all except one, and now it seems not. For years William has lived in hope that Prince Emil would make a more tolerant monarch than his father. Just this morning,

443

before he went off to the palace, he said he thought his faith would be justified. But now..."

"The regent cannot ignore this."

"Not if he wishes to succeed his father, he can't."

When the news got out, the public would riot, march, persecute, demonstrate. The Church would preach holy war again. The Grand Council would pass repressive laws. There would be torture, show trials, blacklisting, public barbarities. The atrocities that had followed the Gods' War would start all over again.

"Even if he knows in his own mind that only a few crazies laid the mine, for public consumption he will have to denounce the Children as a whole. Demonize us all."

"I am afraid so, my dear. And it will affect you, too. William will have to send you away." She sighed. "Just when I thought he'd found someone worthy of him at last."

"That was you, not me," Maddy said automatically. She had been trying not to think of the future, but of course the king's first secretary could not cohabit with the sister of both Chief Heretic Woodbridge and the monster killer, Bram Woodbridge. She might well be arrested, too, guilty by blood. It might be too late already. Kipping himself might be irretrievably tainted, guilty by association. At worst, all four of them could find themselves in Swine Hall by sunset, charged with high treason.

"I don't know what to do." Especially about the boy in her bed. "I must wait and hear what the master wants of me."

"Certainly." Irene's voice was growing husky; she tired very easily now. "But have a word with Steve."

"Steven Veal? He's the last person I should trust, surely?"

"No, dear. He's the first. It's a very long story, and I don't have the energy to tell you now, but Steve is fanatically loyal to William. He won't act without William's orders, but you tell him that you may have to go into hiding and he can start thinking about answers. If anyone can help you, it's Steve."

Her eyelids were drooping. Maddy thanked her, gave her a kiss, and slipped away.

She peeked in at Brat, but he slept as if there were no tomorrow. Maybe, for him, there wasn't. Shivering at her forebodings, she closed the door silently and headed downstairs to find Steven. She found Steven and a fusilier helping the first secretary in through the front door.

CHAPTER 45

EVEN AS A CHILD, WILLIAM KIPPING HAD NEVER FAVORED rough sports, and that day life had dealt him a cruel blow. Physically he had suffered only bruises and a minor flesh wound that John Hawke had treated for him, but the mere shock of violence had left him shaky and confused. He could not rid his mouth of the bitter, gritty dust or his ears of their ringing. His face and clothes were covered with dust and dried blood; his dignity was in tatters. Men like Steven Veal would have bounced up, ready to fight another twenty rounds. He was not such a man, but now he felt ashamed of that as he never had before. And ashamed of being ashamed.

"I can walk," he kept insisting, but they kept a tight grip on him all the way into the house. Maddy was in the hall, face pale and eyes wide. Servants, too, were flocking in to view his shame. *"Let me go!"* he bellowed, and accepted Maddy's embrace. She knew she was keeping him from falling, but hopefully the others did not.

"Go and report to the palace," he told the captain. "Send word to the regent that I will attend him shortly. Yes,

I was there," he told the rest of his audience. "Luckily we were able to carry a warning to the temple, and the target building was evacuated in time. A few people were hurt, but not too many—could have been much worse. Now get back to work, all of you."

They fled. Maddy and Steve remained, understanding that he had not meant to include them in that dismissal, and he let the two of them help him upstairs to his room. Even when Maddy began to strip him, he did not protest.

"Bring hot water," he told Steve. "Just a bowlful. No time for a tub. Have to report to the regent."

That left him alone with Maddy. "We located the graves, right under the Meeting Hall. We went to warn them. We evacuated, but we didn't go far enough away. Some men around us were killed, so I got off lightly." He eased a bruised shoulder out of his shirt. Why was being undressed by a woman exciting sometimes and deathly embarrassing at others, even the same woman? "Hawke was wonderful. He cured my cut...one of his ears was nicked, but he was all right."

"*Rollo went to the temple?* Has he gone mad?"

"He insisted. He saw that his skills might be needed. And he told them who he was, Maddy. He accused Exalted Garrett to his face of stealing your father's estate. Then the mine blew."

"So where is my brother now?" She had knelt to remove his shoes but was looking up at him with a face whiter than chalk.

"He saved the supreme's life, Maddy. The wretch was bleeding to death. Hawke saved him, and others, too."

"*Where—*"

"They arrested him! One of their thugs choked him so he couldn't speak, and another stuffed a rag in his mouth and blindfolded him. They accused him of practicing witchcraft."

She untied his britches and said only, "Stand up."

"I protested as hard as—"

"Stand up!"

He obeyed, leaning on her shoulder. She tugged his britches down. When he was seated again, she removed his stockings, leaving him in only his linens.

"The regent won't tolerate this, Maddy. He'll issue a writ of habeas corpus. I'll serve it myself."

"I can't see that honor impressing the holies very much. Even supposing they pay any attention to the writ, what of the regent? Will Emil honor the guarantees you gave Rollo? Or will he be shipped straight from the temple jail to Swine Hall?"

Fortunately, Kipping was saved from answering by Steve Veal returning with a steaming ewer in one hand, a glass of brandy in the other, and a wad of towels under his arm. He offered the brandy to Kipping, who refused it. He did not want Maddy to see his hands shaking, and he would need a clear head in the near future.

Steve fetched the washing bowl, laid it on the floor beside Maddy, and tipped the water in.

Kipping thanked him. "And bring me the Pestilence file."

Steve departed without a word.

Now for the worst part.

"Maddy…the regent sent cavalry to collect your other brother, Bram, so he could guide them to the gunpowder.

That's all I know. Since the mine was detonated, they clearly didn't get there in time. We must keep hoping, of course."

She did not answer. She must see that there was little hope. There might have been a fight in the caves, or a booby trap. Or they had arrived too late.

Face, hands, a few places where blood had seeped through his clothes—the rest of him was clean enough. She fetched a brush to get the dust out of his hair.

"I don't know how bad this is going to be," he said, thinking what an understatement that was. "But I want to move you to a safe place. When the worst blows over…" Meaning, *When Irene has died*, or *When I am driven from office*, or even, *Provided they haven't chopped my head off*. Kings' secretaries had been thrown to the dogs often enough.

"I won't desert you," she said. "You need me."

"Light knows I do, love, but you can't help now. I may be marched off to jail. And you may be, too, because you are the sister of both John Hawke and the monster sorcerer who blew up the Meeting Hall. The wolves are howling already."

"I won't desert you." She could not have achieved what she had already if she were not a tough young lady, and he knew she could be stubborn.

"You will not be deserting me. I will find you or send for you when the storm blows over. Believe me, I would marry you now if I could, Maddy. I love you! My dearest wish is that one day we can yet become man and wife and raise legitimate children." They had never spoken of such things.

She met his gaze, searching for assurance. "That would be nice."

"You do believe me?"

She forced a thin smile. "Yes, I believe you and trust you. I love you. If I must disappear for a while…I'll wait for you."

"And I for you."

They were not demonstrative people. They both went masked through life. Part of their mutual attraction lay in the joy of exploring those deeper emotions the other hid from the outer world. Maddy washed and dried him without another word. His head was clearing, and he was glad of the chance to think. The next couple of hours were going to be crucial.

Kipping winced as she dabbed his forehead with a hot, damp towel. "Ouch! Maddy, I promised you I would bring the Uptrees to justice. That was our arrangement."

"So?"

"We must rescue Rollo as soon as possible. I have several strings to my bow, there, but if worst comes to worst…" She wrung out the towel over the basin, not meeting his eye. "Will they trade?"

"I'm sure they will gladly trade." He wasn't sure, but she did not throw the lie back in his face. She began washing the rest of his face.

"Supposing you can ransom him that way, what happens next? Swine Hall again?"

"No, no. When he gave Carey his parole, Carey gave him my promise that nothing like that would happen. Nothing but a fair trial in court. I gave my word, Maddy." But what was that worth now?

"Then do it, of course."

"And I will try to send him away with you. Pray, Maddy!"

Soon Steve, judging that they had been given time enough together, returned with a bulky document case, such as lawyers carried. By then Kipping was decently clad and examining himself in the mirror. He decided he looked depressingly harrowed, and a bandage not quite hidden by his bonnet failed to give him panache.

"Steve...need your help. First, I want a couple of stalwart hands to accompany me, to guard that bag while I am in the palace." He saw by the resulting nod that his wishes had been foreseen, at least in part. At times Veal's ability to do that seemed almost magical. "Secondly, to be on the safe side, Miss Wells should leave the country for a while. Soon. She will be probably be accompanied by a Master and Mistress, um, Ford. Can you suggest any friends who might help arrange this?"

The big man looked both relieved that he was needed and happy to be given a task he could perform. "Not friends, no. The man I would appeal to would be the Honorable Tristan Rastel."

"The Hon?" Maddy said. "He's the last man I would trust with anything. I wouldn't trust him to guard the poor box."

"Who said anything about trust, miss? Master Kipping has enough evidence against him to burn him at the stake every day for a month."

"True," Kipping said. "But this must be done quickly. In a day or two he may receive worse threats than I can deliver. Tell Master Carey I want to see him downstairs." He was procrastinating. Parting was going to hurt much more than he wanted to show. "Maddy, dear, I may not return until late tonight, and if Steve proves as efficient as he usually does, you may be gone before then. I shall—" Kipping broke off and looked at Steve. "What's wrong?"

The big man was staring at the door through to Maddy's room. "I wonder why that key is on this side, sir. It isn't usually."

For a moment Kipping's heart fell off the edge of the world. A man in there? He rarely came home during the day. Not Maddy, surely? And if she had a lover in there, why lock him in?

"You dare to pry in my room?" she yelled at Steve, which was as good as an outright admission that the corridor door must be locked. She looked to Kipping, her face whitewashed with guilt. "But of course you may look, dear."

He had wondered why she had not commented when he mentioned the other brother, the young one, Bram. So she had known more than he did. He was hurt that she had not confided in him, but he could hardly fault her family loyalty. The boy was gallows meat already. But if Kipping expected her love, he could not refuse his help now, however that action might increase his own peril.

She continued to stare at him in terror—not fear for herself, but for the other brother, the one he had not met. He smiled and raised his eyebrows, which hurt. "I don't want to know. But I suspect we may need passage for four, Steve, not three."

Maddy rushed into his arms, and they shared a parting kiss. He knew—and knew that she must know—that they might never meet again.

CHAPTER 46

HAVING LOOKED IN ON IRENE AND FOUND HER ASLEEP, Master Kipping proceeded downstairs with care. Steve went with him, carrying the document case and insisting on holding his master's arm. Luckily there was no one else around to see that except Walter Carey, waiting at the foot of the stairs. He wouldn't notice, being too worried and hurt that he had not yet been taken into his employer's confidence and given something to do in the crisis.

It was the work of a moment to reassure him with the news that Steve would need his assistance that afternoon. Single-minded and totally lacking in imagination, Carey could follow instructions like a hound following spoor. Like a hound, when anything went wrong he ran in circles.

"The password," Kipping told them both, "will be *birdcage*." He left them, then, and went outside by himself, carrying the document case. He wondered why he had chosen "birdcage." The image of releasing John Hawke, perhaps. That was the most urgent task, for Hawke was far too dangerous to leave in the hands of the Church. What he could reveal could shatter Emil's chances of succeeding his father.

The coach was already waiting for him, with Tom and Larry in livery standing by the door. A couple of Steve's recruits, they looked smart and trim, as long as Larry kept his battered knuckles out of sight and Tom didn't smile to reveal the straight-through view of his tonsils. They were excellent horse trainers and had pretty much learned to behave themselves as a gentleman's servants, although once in a while one or both would snap and go rushing off to brawl somewhere, preferably against odds of four or five to one.

Kipping gave them the password and their instructions, confident that he could rely on them to safeguard his precious document case. Continuing the canine metaphor, they were human mastiffs. Postilion Larry mounted the left lead horse, and Tom sprang up to cling on the back of the coach. First Secretary Kipping was driven off to the palace and an ominous future.

The explosion at the temple had changed the world already. There was a new air of vigilance and suspicion in the palace courtyard; four armed men watched Kipping step down from his coach. For years he had wandered the palace unnoticed; now he was escorted to the regent's presence and there were guards outside the door.

Emil had taken over his father's room in the bureaucratic wing of the palace. As ruler, he needed its facilities: books, files, and bellpulls that could summon a whole gamut of persons in seconds. He was in conference with three clerks when Kipping was announced, but he dismissed them instantly, refused to let his visitor kneel, told him to be seated at the big table, and then came and took the next chair.

"You look like an overripe corpse. How are you? Thankful it wasn't worse. You should be in bed. Have some wine."

Kipping feared what wine would do to his aching head, but one did not refuse royal hospitality. He accepted the glass. Emil turned his chair to face him. He inquired again about the first secretary's well-being. Nevertheless, his manner was dour. There was trouble ahead.

For three years, as the king's health failed, prince and secretary had planned the coming succession. Both had seen a need to rein in a grasping and tyrannical Church. Both had hoped to ease the oppressive burdens laid on Mother worshipers. This morning a soldier on a steaming horse had brought word of the stolen gunpowder, and their hopes had dimmed. The destruction of the Meeting Hall crushed them utterly. Kipping could see that and would be much surprised if Emil did not.

"I understand that you arrived in time to give the warning and have the Meeting Hall evacuated?"

Kipping completed the story as far as he knew it: the gathering outside the library building, John Hawke's folly in revealing his identity, the explosion, Hawke's care for the wounded, then his capture and imprisonment, over Kipping's futile protests.

"I suspect they would have arrested me also, had I not wielded...um, this." He dug the royal ring from his purse and returned it to its rightful wearer.

"So Hawke is now in the temple jail?"

"I assume so, sir."

"And Supreme Uptree?"

"He was dying, as I said. Hawke stemmed the blood flow." Kipping always found it wise to provide the simplest possible answers to simple questions. In government, very few questions were simple.

"So he accepted healing from one of the people he terms witches? Can we use that against him?"

Kipping sighed. "I doubt it very much, sir. What I saw will be contradicted by the unimpeachable testimony of a half a dozen hierarchs, and any lesser witnesses will have been dispersed to parishes unknown. It didn't happen."

The regent leaned back and scowled in frustration. "You heard about the boy? The witch?"

"I have heard nothing, sir."

"He's disappeared. He led Captain, whatsis, Kenrick to the powder and extinguished the fuse. Or *a* fuse. He identified some men found in the Blue Boar as conspirators. But while they were returning to the palace, the mine blew up anyway. By the time they dismounted, the boy just wasn't there, although no one saw him leave. His horse was back in its stall. Kenrick claims that he was playing on both teams, that he must have know about a second fuse. But Kenrick did not leave a guard on the powder itself, only on the surface entrance, and Light knows how many ways in and out of those catacombs there are."

One did not question royalty. One prompted—gently, and ever ready to back off if one detected resistance. "I must say the captain's excuse sounds rather thin."

"It's hog swill. Only a total maniac would do what the captain is suggesting the boy did. Kenrick is now confined to quarters, pending an inquiry. No, stay where you are," the regent snapped, springing up and starting to pace. That had been an annoying habit of his when he was merely the heir. If he continued to do that as king, all Privy Council meetings would have to be held standing. "So now we have culprits in custody, and we've lost our key witness."

He strode the length of the room and back twice, hands behind his back, teeth bared. "How can they be so stupid? What can they hope to achieve by murdering people at random? Terror? Atrocities don't cow people; they make them mad. You can't just swing a sneak punch and expect the fight to end there! The only way to end a fight is to smash your opponent so totally that he can't fight anymore. Wars don't end until one side has lost all its young men in battle, its crops are ruined, its cities destroyed, its women raped, and its children starving. Only then will it admit that it is beaten and give up."

All very true, but much the same argument cut both ways in Albi. The Children had been treated unfairly for a very long time. The Emil who had wanted to introduce tolerance would now have to do the exact opposite. The Children themselves had forced this on him. Had he accepted that stark truth yet?

Evidently he was thinking along the same lines, for he sighed. "It is evil that blocks us from doing good." He growled a few more times and halted his marching. "Your advice, First Secretary?"

"I doubt that the dissident Mother worshipers present a real hazard, sir. If you were already crowned, I would advise that your major concern must be to avoid any panic among the people, suppress any tendency to—"

"But I'm not. So?" Emil was clever and young and impatient. The difference between advising him and his aged father would require some adjustment.

"Then, sir, I must advise you that the Church of the Light presents a greater danger to Your Highness than the Children of the Mother."

This was rank heresy, of course. Emil just nodded irritably, as if any fool could see that. *"What do you recommend I do?"*

"First, I propose that you send me to call on Supreme Exalted Uptree, to convey Your Highness's concern and best wishes for his speedy recovery."

Emil dropped back on his chair, leaning forward, forearms on knees. "Political cow fart! Why not send a herald?"

"To request, or demand if necessary, that the Church hand over Rollo Woodbridge, known as John Hawke."

"And if Uptree refuses?"

"Claim that Hawke has been a spy all along, that he was released from Swine Hall when he promised to act as our agent and betray any seeds of disloyalty or treason among the Children. That will shift the onus of treason on to the priests themselves."

Emil smiled a young man's smile, and then lost it again.

"They're probably already racking Hawke to make him testify that I called him in to use witchcraft against my father."

"There is a certain urgency," Kipping admitted. "But Hawke withstood torture before. He will resist, and he knows that you must try to recover him."

"So does Uptree! He will refuse."

"Uptree will not refuse me, sir. I can send him and his brother to the gallows for theft, forgery, conspiracy, and Light alone knows what else."

Emil had the grace to look impressed. "Such blackmail is utterly unthinkable behavior for an officer of the crown." He chuckled. "You're sure it will work? Most people tolerate a bit of corruption."

"Not like this. The charge sheet is disgusting, a league long. Sir, I know your motives in summoning Woodbridge to the palace yesterday were truly honorable and even courageous, but I honestly believe that Your Highness's accession will be in danger if the incident becomes public knowledge."

So, obviously, did His Highness. "But what do we do with him when we've got him? The Church and the Grand Council will both insist that he be forced to testify—meaning forced to testify the way they want him to testify. He did not strike me as a man to perjure himself."

"I am sending his sister overseas as soon as it can be arranged, sir. I think Hawke and his wife should accompany her." *Birdcage.*

Emil leaped up and began to pace again. "But this would be the second time Woodbridge was 'allowed' to escape. How do you explain that?"

Here it was, the edge of the cliff.

"You dismiss me, Your Highness. You announce that the culprits are already in custody and will be put on trial as soon as they have been thoroughly interrogated. You proclaim a fresh start, a clean slate. You turf out all your father's advisors, rebuild the Meeting Hall at government expense, send the Blue Boar suspects to the gallows, and propose oppressive new laws against the heretics."

The regent stopped just behind his chair and stared hard at Kipping. "If I am driven to that course, then you may need to leave the country also, First Secretary. You will be blamed for everything."

"There I must beg for mercy, sir. My wife is dying. I ask only that I be allowed to stay on in my present residence until…then. A month or two at the most. After that…" He shrugged. In a month or two he would be very lucky indeed to be still at liberty. The Church would be triumphant. Rampant intolerance would bestride the land. The bright dreams were ashes.

"That much, of course," the regent said, "and we shall hold off the dogs as long as we can. Your resignation we shall take under advisement. What do you need for your visit to Supreme Garrett?"

"A personal note from you, sir. I have my coach. A couple of soldiers to take the prisoner into custody. We shall convey him back to Caverleigh House for the time being."

Emil stared at him for a moment, thinking it over. Then he nodded and headed for the bell ropes. "This is a bitter cup. May the Light go with you, Master Kipping."

The sun was nearing the rooftops, and Kipping was wearier than he could ever remember as, for the second time that day, he was driven to the Coronet Temple. The second trip took much longer than the first, because troops had cordoned off the site of the blast. Half the population of

Weypool had arrived to look at it, and the roads were in chaos. Just peering out the windows, he could sense the boiling rage of the crowd. Someone must be made to pay for this! As Emil had said, you don't surrender to a sucker punch.

Kipping's coach and escort were forced to ride almost all around the outside of the complex to reach the Supremes' Palace. There he disembarked, carrying his document case this time and leaving Tom and Larry to guard the coach.

Two fusiliers accompanied him inside.

Of course, he was refused access to Supreme Uptree. His Holiness was resting, and the prince's letter would be conveyed to him as soon as he was well enough to read it.

Kipping had not risen to the highest rank a commoner could achieve without learning how to deal with that sort of nonsense. He wheedled, threatened, persuaded, and cajoled his way up the ranks. He submitted to the usual humiliations imposed by church flunkies: kneeling, kissing hands, fawning to people, addressing them by their absurdly grandiose titles. A lifelong courtier, he had learned long ago to regard these trappings of power as admissions that their wearers were vulnerable if one could find the chinks in their armor.

After an hour or so, he reached the second-highest level, which nobody else would have achieved that night. He was ushered into a shadowy audience chamber, dim because it was illuminated by a mere three candelabra that had been hurriedly lit in his honor. There he was permitted to advance to the base of the steps, where he could kneel and gaze up at the throne on which sat one of the hierarchs.

The hall would look very splendid in daylight, with its columns and pilasters; its frescoes, mosaics, and gilt; its arches and stained glass. To think that the Teacher had denounced the cult of the Mother because its priesthood had grown corrupt! Two centuries of power had certainly blunted his followers' interest in humility. There were other people present, standing in the darkness: priests, no doubt, and officers of the Church Police, and his own two fusiliers, but the only one who mattered was the man on the throne, Exalted Eastwell.

Abel Eastwell was a longtime Garrett crony and a recent recruit to the Hierarchy. The Privy Council staff had long foreseen that he would be promoted to the inner circle as soon as Garrett had a vacancy to fill. It had opened a file on him years ago. Granted that the man was brilliant, ruthless, and obsessively attentive to details, the records also identified the clever Eastwell's vulnerable spot—he was extremely ambitious. He could not be bribed by any normal means. That did not mean he could not be bribed.

Kipping knew that he would progress no higher in the Hierarchy that evening, but Eastwell might suit his purpose just as well as Supreme Garrett Uptree would. Even better, perhaps, if he played his hand correctly.

The cleric regarded his visitor with an intense, unwavering stare. "What is so extremely urgent, William, that it cannot be put off until tomorrow?"

Kipping waited a moment before replying. "A matter of personal concern to the supreme himself."

"He is indisposed and resting. He put me in charge of affairs tonight. I am fully qualified to accept the regent's note and see that it is passed on as soon as possible."

Eastwell's smug little smile left no doubt that he enjoyed blocking the prince's emissary. He had curiously dead eyes that never seemed to blink, but they had noticed the document case.

"It is more than just a note that brings me here tonight, Your Excellency. The matter is very confidential." Kipping glanced around the hall to indicate the silent watchers.

The corpse eyes glanced at the dispatch case again. "Again I must ask what is so urgent that you seek to waken an elderly man recovering from a serious injury."

"Urgent enough to waken the dead, if such were in my power."

"And what is in the bag? Ransom, perhaps?" Eastwell was clever to a fault.

This time Kipping smiled. "Papers...let me show Your Excellency—in strictest confidence, of course." He pulled the document case around in front of him and unbuckled the straps. In the coach he had located the paper he might need first and left it on top. He took it out and passed it up.

Eastwell was not the sort of man to allow his emotions to show on his face. He studied the transfer of ownership of the Stonebridge watermill to "Garrett Uptree, cleric."

"This looks like the original title deed, First Secretary." That was the first time he had given Kipping his title and thus an invitation to continue dealing. "A forgery, I am sure."

"Both original and forgery, Excellency. In a better light you could see the places where the original names have been scraped off the parchment with pumice stone and false names added." There was room in that dispatch case for a hundred other documents like it. Eastwell lowered his voice.

"You came here to blackmail the supreme hierarch?"

"Oh no, Your Excellency! A blackmailer threatens to reveal secrets unless he is paid, and paid often. I came to offer a straight trade."

Eastwell hesitated and was lost. Ambition is acid.

"Rise, William. Come with me."

He led the way to a small conference room off to the side. A scramble of flunkies provided lights and left, closing the door. The hierarch sat on one side of the table and gestured his visitor to the other. Kipping set to work, passing over wills, deeds, affidavits, bills of sale, titles, transfers, and more. He explained as they went. The Stonebridge mill was a minor detail in the Uptrees' litany of larceny and corruption. Properties in Dorsia and Franget counties, warehouses, numerous buildings right there in Weypool, even a couple of brothels, which paid enormous rent. The supreme owned the Church's only supplier of incense and silk fabric, for which it charged extortionate prices. He regarded his oath of celibacy as applying only to women, not small boys. If a fraction of the evidence was revealed, he would be not merely ruined but in grave danger of a date with the hangman. And so would his brother.

"That's all that I know of," the first secretary concluded. "I expect further investigation would uncover more such."

There was life in Eastwell's eyes now—they glittered. Ambition is irresistible.

"And what were you going to demand in return for this sack of filth?"

"Rollo Woodbridge."

"He escaped from a crown jail. He is a fugitive from justice, a heretic, and a witch. We shall keep him securely locked up, as the Privy Council clearly cannot."

"You have a strange way of demonstrating gratitude."

"Gratitude? Gratitude for what?"

"For saving the supreme's life this morning."

"You were confused at the time. No such event occurred."

"But John Hawke is a crown agent. He has been working for us ever since we organized his escape from Swine Hall. His injuries proved his valor to his friends, so they trusted him. Furthermore, he has continually preached against violence! It was he who came in person to the palace this morning to warn us of the mine being installed below the temple. You owe your life to him, Your Excellency, and so do your colleagues. I want him released at once."

"You swear to the truth of that?"

"Certainly," Kipping said. The last few sentences were true.

"If His Holiness had refused to meet your price, what then?"

"Then I would have turned this material over to the Grand Council and let their Lordships deal with it."

For what seemed an age, Eastwell sat and stared at Kipping. Kipping stared right back, bridling his fury at being forced into this shoddy collusion. Eastwell was undoubtedly weighing his own best advantage here. He could tell Kipping to take his evidence and do with it as he liked; then the chances were high that Supreme Garrett Uptree would fall and Abel Eastwell might climb over the wreckage. Or he could agree to the trade and be the reformer hero laying the facts before the Hierarchy himself, thus gaining the credit. He would make enemies, also, of course. That route was not without its dangers. He might even be suspected of being Kipping's cat's-paw.

He decided. In silence he rose and went to open the door. He beckoned for a priest. "Have the prisoner Hawke, also known as Woodbridge, brought here at once."

Rollo was asleep when they came for him. They had chained his hands behind his back and shackled one ankle to the wall. His damaged ear throbbed under its bandage, he was infested with fleas from the straw he lay on, and yet he was asleep. Nell often marveled at his ability to sleep; he always told her it was a sign of a clear conscience, but in this case it was probably a result of emotional exhaustion. There were guards watching him beyond the bars of his cell, who did not muffle their talk as they played, shouting in glee or booing at every good roll of the dice. He did have a bag over his head, which kept the light away.

But the sound of keys in locks penetrated, so perhaps he had not been as soundly asleep as usual. He braced for the kick. It came. It could have been harder.

"Up, witch! You're wanted."

Was this the start of the interrogation? A few days of sleep deprivation would jangle any man's wits. If the sadists only knew how effective such treatment was, they would use that instead of torture. His ankle was unchained; a rough hand reached in under the bag to stuff a cloth in his mouth. He was dragged to his feet and marched out, directed by powerful hands gripping his arms.

Up stairs. Up more stairs. The pervasive stench of the dungeons gave way to faint hints of incense, detectable even through the stink of the bag. He was being taken to meet someone important, which was encouraging. He wondered what the time was. He could not have slept long.

The march ended. A quiet voice gave an order. Chains, bag, and gag were removed. He blinked against the brightness; saw First Secretary Kipping and one of the hierarchs— name unknown, but one of the younger ones—presently engaged in stacking documents into a leather case.

Rollo bowed to Kipping and ignored the other. He could begin to hope that he had just been ransomed. Kipping was looking carefully at him, inspecting him for damage. He managed to smile.

Kipping said, "This concludes our business, Your Excellency. I bid you a good evening."

"May the Light go with you, William."

Rollo did not offer a blessing. They walked out, across a hall. Hours of terror began to fall away like leaves off an autumn tree. Two fusiliers followed them downstairs, then out to a yard, where they mounted their waiting horses. A temple hostler opened the door of the waiting coach.

"I must warn you, First Secretary, that I bring half the fleas of Weypool with me."

"I expect the Church will bill us for them. Get in— quickly before he changes his mind!"

Only when the coach was rattling along the darkening streets could Rollo truly believe that he was free again. Or was he merely exchanging one captor for another?

"I am most grateful for this release, First Secretary. May I inquire what arm you twisted?"

The coach was dark, but Kipping's tone clearly suggested disgust. "For years I have been collecting evidence against the Uptree brothers, a horrible reeking heap of it. When I…when I first spoke with your sister, I promised her that she could help me destroy them. She would, in fact, be one of the few surviving witnesses against them, for those unfortunates have a tendency to move beyond the reach of His Majesty's subpoenas."

Indeed? So had Kipping's interest in Maddy been prompted by a need to preserve an essential witness, or had he bribed her with offers of vengeance? They obviously shared a mutual affection, but Rollo had not watched them in each other's company for long enough to know how deep those feelings were.

"Tonight," Kipping said, "I took that evidence to the temple to ransom you from Supreme Hierarch Garret Uptree."

"Yuck!" Rollo said. "You mean the price of my freedom is letting those two rogues escape justice?"

Kipping chuckled softly in the darkness. "It looked for a while as if that might be the case, but I was refused admittance to the supreme's sickroom—possibly because he was entertaining someone there, I don't know. Instead, I turned it over to Exalted Eastwell, who is most excessively ambitious. He made the trade."

"Ah! So you expect Supreme Uptree to resign his office fairly soon?"

"Very soon, I should think. For reasons of health. He was wounded in the explosion, remember. And he will undoubtedly make generous donations to the Church."

"And his brother?"

"He doesn't have the king's protection now. The Hierarchy would love to embarrass the Privy Council by exposing one its members."

"Then I think I approve of the transaction," Rollo said sincerely. Which was immaterial. "But now that you have purchased me, sir, what do you intend to do with me?"

"I'm about to return you to Caverleigh House, where your wife no doubt anxiously awaits your return. Arrangements are being made to ship both of you across to Xennia, out of harm's way."

That was what Rollo had been afraid he would say.

"First Secretary, grateful as I am, I have obligations here in Albi. There are trying times ahead. I cannot abandon my flock."

"Yes, I fear there is great trouble ahead, but you cannot help them now. They will not trust you now. I assured Eastwell you had been our spy among the Children ever since we 'let' you escape from Swine Hall. Yes, I lied, but you were already tainted. You were seen with the prince in the palace. You arrived at the temple with me. You are branded a government agent, Prelate Hawke."

Now that was a low blow. "I admit that I will not be popular with the Underground, or whatever remains of it, but the others will understand." Even as he spoke, the words turned to dust in his mouth.

"They will knife you and hide your body in the catacombs. And just because Eastwell let you go tonight, don't imagine the Sons will stop hunting for you. That ear of yours makes you easily recognizable. And describable: 'Wanted, John Hawke…' And so on."

"The Mother has laid a duty on me, and I will not lay down that burden until she tells me to do so."

"You're a fool, then. How will your wife feel?"

William Kipping would not have risen as high as he had if he had not possessed an instinct for political gutter fighting. Rollo wondered why he was so likable in spite of it.

"My wife knew the dangers when she married me."

"That is a coward's answer. But if having both Churches pursuing you is not enough, consider the government."

"You mean," Rollo asked, seeing a chance to get in a jab of his own, "that I could testify how Prince Emil called me in to practice witchcraft on his father?"

"That would be another method of committing suicide, yes. But you gave His Highness your solemn oath that you would find the baby devil responsible for the death of Rafe Dampier and the destruction of Umberly Castle; you swore to deliver him alive, bound, and gagged. You haven't done that, Master Woodbridge."

"I don't know where he is."

"I do. Want me to tell you?"

"No," Rollo admitted. Oh, Brat! He had caused all this trouble. He was a walking disaster, a human powder keg. "What will happen to him?"

"He will go with you and your sister, to Xennia."

The coach had stopped. A squeal of hinges announced that the gates of Caverleigh House were being opened.

And what of Brat? He had been betrayed by those he trusted: Brother Alfred, probably too senile to realize what the chick was growing into, and Lady Whatman, too eager to exploit him for her own gruesome ends. Brat was a child playing with loaded muskets. He must be rushed to Gaudry for proper counseling and training before he was put to death for the public good. And who else but Rollo could get him there safely or plead his case when he arrived? Was that true responsibility talking, or was he just using his brother to justify his own abandonment of duty?

"Maddy, too?"

"I can no longer defend her," Kipping said. "My own life may be forfeit before all this is over." His words rang strangely true.

"Why not come with us?"

"I will not leave Irene. But I want you to look after Maddy for me. I will seek her out, as soon as I am free to do so."

The coach had lurched forward to a halt at the steps. A fusilier opened the door. Kipping was not asking for an oath that Rollo would not return to Albi to pick up his mission later.

Rollo offered a hand. "I accept your fine offer, First Secretary, and I am very grateful for what you have done for me."

"Look after Maddy!"

"I will, sir. And I will see that my brother is declawed." He scrambled down from the coach.

CHAPTER 47

As soon as the master left, Steven Veal sent Walter Carey back to Caverleigh House with orders to make sure that Mistress Hawke was still there and to keep her there. Then he went upstairs to Maddy. He had a score to settle.

She was in the master's bedroom, sorting clothes. He gestured to the connecting door.

"Asleep," she said. "Hasn't slept for two days."

"How did you get him in here without my knowing?"

Her smile was enough to start shivers in his belly. "We both have talent. You may find it useful before this is over."

"You can make yourselves invisible?"

"Not exactly, but we can become hard to notice."

Witchcraft! How could he be encouraging witchcraft? How much had she bewitched the master?

"I want you to be seen here," he said. "The house is under observation. Take a ride in the park. I will go and call on the Hon."

"I won't send him my love. He might take it seriously." She smiled that smile again.

Steven left before he was bewitched, too.

For Maddy, the day dragged slower than a dead horse. She rode in the Royal Park, as instructed. Later she slipped into the kitchen, distracting attention while she loaded a tray with pork pie, cheese, a thick slice of roast goose, bread, butter, onions, and two flagons of small beer. This she took to her room and left on her dressing table.

Brat had rolled over on his stomach, but only his breathing showed that he was still alive. She stared at him for a while, wondering how she could love him still, when his hands were so bloody.

She went to check on Irene, who asked the right questions but had trouble understanding the answers and was unable to stay awake very long at a time. When she dozed off, Maddy went downstairs and forced herself to play the spinet to give her mind something better to do than worry.

Near to sunset, she again looked in on Brat. He was sitting on her dressing stool, eating with zest, although two-thirds of the food had gone already.

"Best meal...had in weeks," he said with his mouth full.

"May be the last for some time," she said, perching on an oaken chest. "Master Kipping is making arrangements for you to be smuggled out to Xennia."

He nodded as if such consideration were his right.

"It won't be easy, and we shan't be safe until we're at sea. I'll be coming with you."

He smiled but continued to chew. Nothing much worried him now, she decided. He was the ultimate witch, able to do anything. He might benefit from a taste of reality.

"I haven't heard the details yet," she said, "but I suspect we'll leave here and go to stay a while with the Honorable Tristan Rastel. He's the man who trained me."

"Trained you to do what?" Brat took a mouthful of pork pie and a quaff of ale, more or less simultaneously.

"Trained me to be a courtesan."

"A what?"

"A harlot."

Choke.

"You need your back thumped? No? Good. So listen. He usually has several trainees around, and they're all eager to practice. So while we're there, you will almost certainly be propositioned."

Brat looked alarmed.

"The Hon Tristan himself may set his sights on you. Or any of his catamites."

Brat did not ask what those were, but he guessed and his face flamed red. "I'll burn their, um, ears off!"

"You're probably too young to interest the girls, but I suggest you uninspire them as much as you can. You could catch clap from them, or crabs, or even the pox." Those were unlikely, for the Hon had strict standards, but the warning impressed Bram Woodbridge. How long he would manage to resist temptation in the Hon's den was open to serious question. "I'll let you know the plans as soon as I can. Meanwhile, you'd better stay in here."

Dusk was turning into night when Steven Veal returned, feeling thoroughly soiled and disgusted. He located Maddy

Woodbridge in the withdrawing room, playing the spinet. He dropped onto a chair hard enough to make it creak in protest. She took her hands off the keys and turned to face him.

"Every time I see that man, I want to choke him!"

She nodded agreement, unsurprised.

"But he was even less pleased to see me, which was something. And he was scared! Tristan Rastel, scared!? This temple thing has everyone jumpy as fleas. They all seem to expect the ground to rise up under their feet. Or the Church Police to come calling, which might be worse."

"Did he guess who your travelers were?"

"He didn't ask; I didn't tell. Even so, I had to lean very hard on him before he agreed to help. Then we had to wait for a couple of his 'assistants.' It was the middle of the afternoon and they had to be dragged out of bed, dressed, and fed!"

"What names? I may know them."

"He called them Bunny and Boobie." Very aptly, in Veal's opinion.

"After my time, then. Please go on."

"He took me off to the docks, to meet with a man who imports cattle, name of Gudge. And he agreed that he had a ship deadheading to Xennia and could take four, if they didn't mind the smell."

"And the fare?" she inquired, looking absurdly innocent. He was certain she had already guessed.

"Bunny and Boobie. The Hon promised to pick them up tomorrow. Gudge says his crew is ashore right now, but they are required to sleep on board the night before sailing, so he wants you lot loaded as soon as possible. Said you're to take old blankets or rugs with you, 'cos the deck's none too clean to sit on. We have to leave right away."

"I haven't even packed yet!"

"No packing. We'll have no room in the coach, and I won't allow luggage on the roof. This brother of yours, is he awake yet?"

"Not only awake, Master Veal, but I confess that he was so bored he came down here to listen to my playing and I let him stay. Come out, Brat."

The lanky youth sitting on the green chair was smirking at Steven. He hadn't been there a moment ago. He rose and bowed.

Furious, Steven ignored the bow. "Not polite to sneak up on people!" If other damned witches could spy like this, then nowhere was safe.

"I'm Bram Woodbridge," the boy said, sitting down again. "And for the last two weeks, Master Veal, I have been hunted by the government, the Church, and even the Children of the Mother, all of them wanting to put me to death in more or less horrible ways. Do you wonder that I have become wary of strangers?"

"Suppose not."

"And if you really have arranged means for me to escape from Albi, sir, then I shall be eternally grateful to you, and will remember you in my prayers, whether you credit them or not." He seemed quite earnest, not mocking. Hard to tell at that age.

But suddenly some of the looming problems seemed to dissolve like mist.

"Can the other two do this invisibility thing?"

"Rollo can," Maddy said.

"Nell, too," the boy added.

"Very good!" Steven rose. "That will help. I told Quinn to change the team and bring the coach around to the front door. I will embark alone, for the benefit of watchers. You two will accompany me unseen. We'll stop at Caverleigh House, and I will go in. The other two will join us the same way. It'll be a squash with five, but we should manage. We'll unload you at the docks the same way."

"Sounds fun," the boy said, jumping up.

ᘓᘓ

Brat was feeling much better now. He hoped he'd have a chance to meet Bunny and Boobie. He hoped he would be lucky enough to get squeezed up against Nell on the way to the ship.

Veal disembarked at Caverleigh and was away a nerve-rackingly long time. Brat concentrated on distraction, and Maddy was doing the same, so he often forgot she was on the seat opposite him. His luck was in, because when the luscious Nell climbed aboard, she didn't notice him and sat in his lap. He wrapped his arms around her tight, of course, and was tempted to grab a feel of her breast, but Rollo was right there and Rollo had blindsight. It was a brief little tussle, but life was starting to be fun again.

The coach was an impossible squash for five people and two rolls of blankets, so the baby had to stand between all the legs and feet and hang on to the hat rack. There was no need to distract while they were rolling along almost deserted streets by moonlight. Rollo was wearing a bandage. With his free hand, Brat removed Rollo's hat. Then he jiggled the knot so the bandage fell off. He cupped Rollo's ear gently.

"You can do this, too?" Rollo said.

"Some. All I ever got to practice on were sore throats and scraped knees and Brother Alfred's rheumatics. Why is your hair wet?"

"Because I was in a bathtub."

"Oh." Brat managed not to snigger. "Am I making this better?"

"You certainly are. Is there anything you can't do?"

"Can't judge talents, like Brother Alfred did. Got no sagacity."

"Obviously. We *must* get you to Gaudry!"

"Shouldn't be hard once we reach Xennia, should it?"

"Don't count your chickens, youngster," Veal said. "Your voyage will take anywhere from two days to three weeks, depending on the wind, and if a spring storm blows in, you'll be shipwrecked and drowned."

Old sourpuss! Three weeks, maybe, but not drowning. Brat had a clear prescience of being rowed ashore in a dinghy and Smut waiting for him on the beach, wagging his tail off. He wouldn't tell the others until they were alone. He wondered where Smut was. Maybe he wasn't anywhere when he wasn't being Brat's dog.

Somewhat later, after Rollo had declared his ear healed and donned his hat again, he said, "I hope your postilion knows where we're going, Master Veal."

Brat had been wondering the same. Almost nothing was visible outside. The streets seemed narrower and meaner, and also darker, so the buildings must be higher. There was a sour smell in the air, and sometimes sounds of drunken singing.

"Trust Quinn," Veal said. "He could find anywhere blindfolded. He was shown the way this afternoon. We're to meet a man at the Crab."

A few minutes later, the coach duly rumbled into an alley barely wide enough for it. A few pedestrians staggered aside, shouting insults, and it came to a halt alongside the only light in sight, a lantern illuminating a painting of a spider armed with scissors.

"Just remember," Veal warned, "Quinn's only seen me getting in here, so he mustn't see all of you piling out."

A bystander attempted to open the door and pull down the steps, no doubt hoping for a tip. The side of the building was so close that there was barely room to do either, and Quinn didn't help much by shouting at him, waving his whip, and shoving him away. Veal hastily disembarked. While he was settling what threatened to become a free-for-all, the other passengers scrambled after him, carrying the rolls of blanket and apparently unnoticed, although they made the coach rock mysteriously. They had to give up distracting after that, because more people were crowding in to see what was going on, and threatening to crush them. Coaches so grand rarely came to slums so muddy and stinky.

After Steven Veal had told Quinn to return in half an hour and watched him drive away, the spectators lost interest. It was too dark for them to see and make fun of the new arrivals' fancy clothes. Brat joined the rest of the family on the far side of the alley, next to Maddy, who was beside Nell, with Rollo at the other end of the line. A woman sidled up to Rollo and started a conversation, but when he murmured two words she suddenly lost interest and went away—very nice mastery! Veal had already ducked into the Crab in search of his contact, leaving the door open to reveal a dim and smoky interior packed almost solid with men and a few women, standing, drinking, and shouting. Brat would not have been tempted to join them, even if he had any money, which he didn't. He preferred standing outside in a chilly spring drizzle.

For a while he watched in fascination as a young man leaning against the wall opposite gradually folded at the knees, sliding steadily lower until he was sitting in the mud, still clutching his bottle. People came and went. The Crab did good business.

"I suppose that smell is the river?" Maddy said.

Nell said it was.

A passerby neatly removed the drunkard's bottle and continued on his way, unnoticed by its owner.

At last Veal surfaced, plowing bodily out from the crush inside the Crab. After him came an anonymous sort of man with a rolling walk that suggested badly bowed legs.

Rollo said, "Follow!" and the expedition moved off after them.

They turned a corner. Brat wondered how Veal and his companion could see where they were going, for Maddy was holding his arm, and Nell was clutching Rollo's. They turned another corner and emerged from the crush of houses onto a road along the riverbank. Moonlight gleamed on water and anchored ships. More ships and boats were tied up at jetties and piers, opposite a row of warehouses. The smell of the river was much stronger.

Veal and his guide turned off down a ramp to a ramshackle jetty that had a strong slant to one side, as if it would collapse at any minute. The smell thereabouts said cattle and grew stronger as they approached the solitary vessel moored at the end. A man strolled forward to meet them. Brat didn't hear what was said, because at that moment an owl swooped low over his head.

Oh, Mother! That might have been Barney!

"Take this!" he told Maddy, thrusting his roll of blankets at her. Then he spun around and raced back the way he had come, his boots beating a hollow tattoo on the greasy planks.

"Bram!" Rollo roared behind him. "Come back here!"

But Brat wasn't going to desert a friend. Barney wouldn't have summoned him if he wasn't needed, and when he charged up the ramp to the road, Barney swooped silently by again, to indicate which way to turn. Four or five warehouses along came another swoop, so Brat turned into an alley barely wide enough for a wheelbarrow, let alone a coach or a cart. And not far along there he found Alan, all hunched up on a muddy doorstep.

Brat dropped to his knees. *"What's wrong?"*

A pale face turned in his direction. "Brad? Brad! That you?"

"Who else? What's the matter with you?"

"Tired. Hungry. Sore feet. Been walking hours and hours."

"Come along, then, you're nearly there, but we'd better hurry." Brat wrestled him upright and put one of Alan's arms across his own shoulders. "Lean on me. Oh, man, you are all-in, aren't you!"

Alan was barely able to walk. They staggered along the narrow alley, frequently bouncing off the walls. "How'd you find me?"

"Barney fetched me. What happened to you?"

"They got Dad. He was downstairs with some friends, celebrating the explosion. Someone kicked the door in." A noise very much like a sob. "I hid in a laundry basket."

"And then you started walking, and sagacity brought you to me!"

"S'pose so."

"Well, we're going to Xennia, and we'll take you with us," Brat announced as they emerged on the river road. Of course, the Gudge man had agreed to transport only four. Brat removed his hat and put it on Alan to hide his blond hair. "Don't talk when we get there. I'll make sure they don't notice me till after we've sailed."

"This is good of you, Brad." Alan sounded close to tears. "They'll hang Dad, won't they?"

If he was lucky they would *just* hang him. "Don't think about it. You're coming with us."

And Smut would be waiting on the beach.

ACKNOWLEDGMENT

I WAS INSPIRED TO WRITE THIS STORY BY READING *GOD'S SECRET Agents: Queen Elizabeth's Forbidden Priests and the Hatching of the Gunpowder Plot,* by Alice Hogge.

ABOUT THE AUTHOR

DAVE DUNCAN IS A PROLIFIC WRITER OF FANTASY AND SCIENCE fiction, best known for his fantasy series, particularly *The Seventh Sword*, *A Man of His Word*, and *The King's Blades*. He and his wife Janet, his in-house editor and partner for over fifty years, live in Victoria, British Columbia. They have three children and four grandchildren.